Books by H.S.J. Williams

FAIREST SON

H.S.J. Williams creates a fantastical world of darkness and light, hope and despair, with relatable characters in a vivid world setting. Definitely recommend for fantasy fans!

-Morgan L. Busse, award-winning author of *THE RAVENWOOD SAGA*

MOONSCRIPT is an enjoyable adventure with engaging character dynamics and an encouraging message of hope in the face of suffering.

-Laura Hollingsworth, creator of the webcomic, *THE SILVER EYE*

This is a wondrously beautiful book, raw with pain and rich with hope. H.S.J. Williams's deft imagination breathes life into a vivid world of elves and humans (and other stranger fantastical creatures), lower and higher realms, and the Darkness that seeks to claim it all. Upon this epic tapestry, delightful characters provide a bright contrast and serve as a living embodiment of hope in the face of despair. You'll find yourself alternating between tears, laughter, and smiles in turn.

- Gillian Bronte Adams, author of *THE SONGKEEPER CHRONICLES*

MOONSCRIPT

H. S. J. WILLIAMS

TRILLIUM PRESS

Cover art by Salome Totladze
Map art by Noverantale
Interior illustrations by Hannah S. J. Williams
Part I, II, III art by Hannah Rogers

To the One who gave me this story
and the power to complete it

Also, to Grammie—your appreciation
of Errance is duly noted

ASELVIA

The Celestial Cleft

Shadowshade Forest

☆ DENJI

DORMANDY

ORIM

KORINCE

The Niar O

The North

TERTOREM

OOLUM

PROLOGUE

oOo

The shadow of death swept over the moon.

However brief, the dimming of the celestial light caught the young elf's attention, and he paused on the steps of the inn to look up at the sky. He fingered the necklace upon his chest, a medallion reflecting the crescent moon above. "Did you see that, Miss Daisha?"

The creature draped across his shoulders gave a small yawn, her pink tongue curling. She flapped her wings, throwing him a little off balance, then settled down again, her grey fur rubbing against his neck. "See what?" she asked sleepily.

"The shadow…"

"Errance?"

The voice of his ever alert guardian brought the prince's attention back to earth, and he smiled into the concerned face of the elder elf standing on the steps below him. "Never mind, Reyin, I just thought I saw something."

Reyin, a warrior through and through from the muscles carving his body to the one beating in his chest, spun and stared back into the wood from where they'd come.

The tall pines swayed in a slight wind, the tips of their needles winking in the silver glow. In the shadows below, the ferns whispered a sleepy reply to the breeze.

The prince brushed away the brief unease with a light laugh and rested a hand on the elf man's shoulder. "Easy, General. I'm sure it was nothing more than an owl. Our good ambassador has assured this place is as safe as any in

Orim."

"The only safe place for you, my prince," Reyin muttered, reluctantly releasing the grip on his sword hilt, "is back home." He huffed. "I still can't believe you chose this over reading the Moonscript."

"I can read it when I get back home," Errance said with a shrug. "It's not like the Higher World is going anywhere."

"It's not like the rest of Orim is going anywhere either."

"But...humans do change and die so quickly, yes?"

Reyin's mouth twitched. "Well, you're not wrong."

The inn door opened just then, and a warm light washed out over the company. "Ambassador Ireth, at last, do come in." The man ushering them in had a refined accent unlike any the elf prince had ever heard, and the boy craned his neck to look around his ambassador and see his first human. He heard they grew hair around their mouth, and he couldn't imagine anything odder. Seeing it in illustrations was one thing, but real life was another matter. However, his heart flopped a little to see that their host was clean-shaven. To be sure, he did have a blocky structure and weathered skin, but that wasn't as interesting.

Most of the elves remained outside to stand watch over their horses and the surroundings, but the company of five who entered were enough to make the small inn room seem smaller still. They were a strange contrast to the rustic wooden walls and the simple furniture. Even the amber light of the candles casting myriads of shadows could not detract from how their souls shone with a wild, young life like spring streams and evergreen trees. Handsome and vibrant they were—the ambassador poised with confidence, the fire-gold general strong and intimidating, the autumn colored twins on his either side elegant and sharp-eyed.

And then the prince.

While the others possessed an ageless quality, the prince was truly young, a boy on the cusp of manhood, no more than twenty years. He was beautiful even for his kind, with dark umber hair to contrast his fair skin and the brilliant blue-green of his eyes.

He was even more fantastical with the company of the winged mammalian upon his shoulders, a gracile creature with far too much intelligence in her eyes to be any common beast.

Ambassador Ireth gave a polite bow to their welcoming host. "Prince Errance of Aselvia, I would like you to meet Ambassador Carlson of Dormandy."

"Sir," Prince Errance said with his own courtly bow, "I am honored to meet the man who has shown such faithful alliance to my people."

"The honor is all mine, Your Highness," the man said, dipping low. "I look forward to presenting you to my city. But for tonight, may I present you to the town of Denji and the owners of this fine inn, my cousins."

Two other humans, a man and a woman, emerged from the shadows where they'd hidden in awe of their visitors, and they bent, saluted, and curtsied in an uncertain and excited display.

This man did have a beard, and the prince burst into a grin. Surely, it was so messy to have hair around one's mouth. Did they have to wash and comb after every meal? General Reyin subtly poked him in the back, and recovering his manners, Errance bowed to the couple as well. "Thank you for receiving us at this late hour. We are forever grateful."

This earned quite a puff of pride from the man and a giggle from the woman.

But before a word could be moved beyond introductions, the door burst open again and one of the elf sentries rushed in. "General," he hissed. "You must hear this."

Reyin leapt to the door, Errance pressing in curiously from behind, and they both listened to the silent night outside. Except it was not so silent as one first thought. There was a distant clatter, like small rocks tumbling down a mountain slope, only the sound didn't fade…it grew sharper and nearer.

"Shards," Reyin breathed. He whirled around and glared at the bewildered human ambassador. "Who else did you tell of our coming?"

"I—no one, I swear."

Reyin snarled something elvish, but there was no point in finding out who else, if anyone, had known that the prince had left the safety of his home. There was no point, because it was known. By shadow. By death. And who could have guessed that Darkness would have watched and waited so carefully for its revenge.

"What is it?" Prince Errance asked, and his fair face, as yet unburdened by years and wisdom, bore no fear, only a hope for adventure.

"Retreat to the forest," Reyin ordered the elf sentry. "We race to Aselvia, they cannot reach us there."

"But the village—" Ireth began.

"—will be safer without us," Reyin snapped. "They are here for the prince." As he spoke, he grabbed Errance by the arm and hurried down the steps, bent low. The winged creature launched from Errance's back and headed towards the forest, her wings quickly giving her the lead.

Ambassador Carlson followed behind, confused and stammering. "I am sorry, I don't know what went wrong; we've always been safe h—"

Something hissed through the air, and his voice broke off in a horrible cry. Errance turned to see the human ambassador slumping against the doorframe, a stone bolt buried in his chest. The inn owners cried out and stumbled backwards, the woman reaching for her husband's hand. Ireth took one distressed step towards them.

"MOVE!" Reyin barked, all concern for stealth cast aside. He sprinted for the forest, dragging Errance behind him as the elves flanked them in a circle, bows facing outwards, looking for any sign of their attackers. Not a moment after they had reached the first trees, the air was shattered by the shriek of stone bolts seeking life.

Errance tried to turn, tried to see who had made it with them into the woods, but his general kept pulling him on, hissing out commands to the elves around him. The warriors were safest in the trees and the tall bracken; they had commanded their horses to lie down and hide themselves. Their bows sang in answer to the attack, but the shadows in the forest and village were deep and they still had no sight of their enemy, only the sound, the terrible sound, now crying like scratches against stone.

"What are they?" Errance demanded again, but before he could be answered, an elf near them fell with a gargled cry, another of the stone bolts through him. The prince stared, the sight of death beginning to stain his heart, just as the blood stained the elvish livery. His father had warned him of terrible things in the world beyond, but how little he had listened…how little had he understood.

Reyin threw them both to the ground, under the cover of the tall ferns. "You are going to take your horse and flee back to Aselvia. We will hold them off."

Errance pulled his gaze from the dead body and looked to his general, the meaning of those words clarifying. He shook his head, pushing down the heave of his stomach and swallowing past the cold knot in his throat. "You trained me to be a warrior, Reyin. I will not leave you or my men."

The lord's eyes glinted in a glare. "I am your father's appointed guardian; you will not question me." He whirled back to the elves and ordered, "Cover us!"

The elves rose as one and released a volley into the forest that roused shrieks of steel on stone. In that moment, Reyin whistled sharply to one of the horses and pulled Errance into a crouched run through the ferns, retreating farther into the forest. The summoned horse came alongside them, dancing in fear.

"Take him, Starsilver," the general told the horse as the prince vaulted into the saddle. "Do not stop."

Errance leaned down and caught Reyin's arm. "You still have not answered me! Who attacks us?"

Even in the darkness, he could see Reyin sag as a man might when afraid or in despair, but the general could surely be neither of these things. He reached up to grasp the boy's arm in a gentle squeeze. "Go."

An unknown dread wrapped around Errance's heart. "Reyin…" Panic seeped into his voice. "You *will* meet me in Aselvia?"

"*GO!*" The lord whispered with the force of a shout and slapped the horse's rump. Starsilver leapt forward, surging into the forest. The wind rattled the branches like bones after them.

And the general was left standing alone, shuddering in the gathering cold. Hoping that he and his warriors could keep the attention of the monsters and whatever else was with them. That it was not too late for his prince. For the harsh cries and stone bolts meant the shards of the north, and where shards gathered, Darkness was not far behind.

Through the forest Starsilver fled, without stumble or hesitation. Cold tears ran down Errance's cheeks, and he bitterly cursed the horse's swift flight from the companions whom he should have been fighting alongside. He hadn't even been given a chance to find Miss Daisha again, though she would surely be safe, even if she was too young to fly great distances. But Starsilver had been trained by Lord Reyin and would not be easily swayed.

Their flight brought them into a clearing strewn with shale sharp as knives. The moon shone in the open sky above, peering down like a squinted eye and for the first time in his life, Errance found its beauty mocking. His horse plunged back into the forest, hiding him from the moon's gaze, but branches tore at his skin and hair. Scratches stung his cheeks, though he lay low at his horse's neck, dodging between the trees. Nothing but the pounding of hooves and the pounding of his heart pierced the eerie silence.

He felt a sharp tug against his throat, and before he had time to realize what was happening, the necklace strand snapped and the moon medallion spun away into the consuming shadows.

He twisted in the saddle, reaching out in a useless attempt to catch it. "Stop, I can't lose that!"

Impotent anger rushed through him as the horse galloped on, and he pulled back on the reins with all of his strength. "Stop!"

Neighing, Starsilver reared and skidded to a halt. Errance flung himself from the saddle and staggered back to where the necklace had broken. He trembled at his rashness, but he was far more concerned about returning home without his father's precious heirloom. He searched the forest floor hastily. It would only take a moment. The medallion shone with its own light, so surely it would be easy to find. The wind swirled ever tighter around him, flinging his hair before his eyes, and the night descended into deeper darkness as even the moon hid her face away.

There! Amongst the needles and leaves, the moon medallion glimmered bright and true. Dropping to his knees, Errance caught it up, but the strand was snagged.

Under a booted foot.

The prince stilled, unable to tear his gaze from the sight, unable to understand why he had not heard or sensed another life approach. Slowly, he raised his eyes, hand reaching for his sword.

"Hello, Errance," said the Voice.

And Darkness fell.

SEVENTY YEARS LATER

1

oOo

The forest faded, melting into the darkness of Tellie's slowly waking consciousness. Her jaw ached with pressure, and she slowly uncurled her fists to pull the pillow off her head. The screams still echoed in her mind as she rubbed her eyes and released a shaky breath.

Just a dream. Just a dream, like always.

And as always, she couldn't stop it. She could only watch, helpless, as the elven prince ran straight into death. In waking hours, she knew the tragic legend well enough, but she didn't know why her imagination had decided to conjure up such a vivid depiction of it to dream about over and over again.

Swallowing, she blinked away the remnant horror and nestled deeper into her cot's thin mattress in a hope to reclaim night's peace.

Her door burst open, banging against the wall with a sharp crack. She startled upright, squinting into the unexpected candlelight. Few faces could be welcomed after such a greeting, but the face of Missus Norne, shadowed and glaring, sent her heart pounding all over again.

"Get up, you useless girl! Are you deaf?" The innkeeper's wife reached down and yanked her out of bed. "What good are you if you can't even fetch the door?"

Tellie tottered to her feet, senses reeling. She hadn't been thinking of sound at all before now, but she remembered falling asleep despite the thunder of a spring storm trying to break through the attic roof. The storm had apparently not ceased, for she could still hear the violent pelting of rain on the shingles, the dripping of leaks, and the wuthering wind.

She tried to process Missus Norne's words, something about a door and visitors having come in from the storm. Good heavens. A knock at the door this late of an hour could only be a bad omen. It was a miracle the innkeeper's wife had heard the knock at all, since she and her husband usually went to bed drunk. Whatever strangers had come must have been very insistent indeed.

The Missus stumped back downstairs, and after hurrying into a simple frock, Tellie followed a few moments later. The wood stairs creaked under her wavering footsteps, the sound an eerie echo of the forest through which the elf prince had fled. If she was lucky, this would only be another bad dream.

There were strange stories about The Only Inn in the small town of Denji, stories of sinister shadows and spooks. But in three years of serving food and cleaning rooms, Tellie had never encountered such a feeling of dread. It wasn't because of anything so thrilling as a ghost or a shard, but when she saw the three men waiting in the inn foyer, a shiver went down her spine, chilling her right down to her bare toes. What sort of men traveled in the middle of the night, in such a wild storm? Runaway criminals, bandits, bounty hunters? Whatever the case, they practically screamed 'villain,' from their dark hooded cloaks to their spurred leather boots.

At Missus Norne's barked command, Tellie hurried forward. "I can take your cloaks and hang them to dry," she managed, dipping into a curtsy. The men only huddled deeper into their cloaks, eyes glittering from the depths of their hoods. Another shiver shook her body. She lowered her hands and looked down at the floor. Rainwater was puddling under the men's boots, but the floor was in a terrible state anyway, so what did a few more soggy stains matter?

The hair on the back of her neck prickled and she looked up again, straight into the hard, grey eyes of the leader. His gaze locked on hers, colder than ice. She froze, heartbeat filling her ears, and her breath caught in her throat. Finally he looked away, stepping past and moving toward the dull fireplace.

The hard hand of the Missus dragged her from her stupor and into the kitchen as their unexpected guests headed to the dining room. "Bad enough they show up in these unholy hours and now they want supper, is that it?" the innkeeper complained. "I'll heat up the soup—you'd probably burn it—and you can serve it. After that, you had better finish washing these dishes. A woman can't get any decent help nowadays!"

The woman's unfair complaints stung a little, but Tellie was too tired to respond, even in the privacy of her mind.

She'd never asked to come here to this depilated little inn, ruined by the reputation of its ill-tempered owners and haunting history. But the Nornes, in some cruel twist of fate, were related to her. Second cousins or something like that. In the Dormandy Orphanage she'd thought herself quite alone in the world and had been delighted to learn she had relatives. She'd dreamed of calling them Aunt and Uncle, but soon after she arrived it became painfully clear that she was wanted for work and not for company. With their claim as family, they hadn't even needed to pay to adopt her, and so she was entirely free labor. As the bitterness set in, she'd come to stop thinking of them as family at all, only the Mister and Missus, and so her previous longing for family, a real, loving family, returned.

The Mister she avoided at all costs, for although he was often burdened down by his strong drink, he was also sometimes surprisingly agile and with that, angry. In her kindest moments, Tellie supposed having a husband like that made things very hard for Missus Norne, but the woman did not seem to possess a heart large enough to spare her innocent young relative any measure of love or care.

"Get them bowls over here, the soup's hot enough."

"Yes, Missus Norne." She snatched the wooden bowls from the cupboard in a clumsy stack and hurried over to the pot, ladling a serving into each one.

The innkeeper's task was done and she headed back up the stairs with more groaning and swearing, without a glance to the young maid left behind.

Tellie balanced the bowls on a tray and carefully pushed open the doors with her shoulder as she headed for the dining room. Only one lantern was lit in the far corner, and the three men huddled like vultures about the table, their shadows rising in ominous specters behind them.

One of them was grumbling aloud. "Capture the elf king, indeed! Curse the warden and anyone else who wants this job done!"

They noticed her approach and fell deathly silent. She tried not to tremble as she laid out their bowls and mugs, hoping that exhaustion dulled any exterior interest that had sparked within her at the man's strange words.

Once she hurried away, she paused just on the other side of the door, her ear pressed to the wall. Who knew what they'd do if she was caught eavesdropping, but the temptation was too great. The best stories she heard came from her friend, Kelm Thrander, a young merchant's apprentice who traveled much of Orim and heard all sorts of dazzling tales—from the unscaled cliffs that ended the northwest reach of Orim to the exotic bazaars in Oolum. These strange, shadowed men might be part of a tale even Kelm would be impressed by. She imagined him now, face wrinkled in disgust if she didn't even try to find out more about them. And they'd mentioned elves. That alone was worth the risk.

"You speak boldly as if you were safe and far away. Do not forget that His Darkness is always present," one of the strangers said.

Tellie's skin crawled at the sound of his voice. Surely he was the leader, the one that had met her eyes so coldly.

"He's right, though," said another, words smacking together as he slurped down his food. "The warden gave us an impossible mission. It's his fault that he's waited so long to put a plan into action. And this is the most idiotic plan I've heard. Like we could ever get near the elven king. You know protections surround his realm. If the elf king could be captured, he would have been captured already. I say he's as impossible to reach as the Higher World itself. Don't you think?"

"I'm thinking," said the leader slowly. "I'm thinking what would happen if we succeed."

In the silence that followed, one of the men coughed as if he'd choked on his soup.

"Gore!" the man swore. "Daran, you don't mean it."

"I do," the one called Daran replied. "I do indeed."

"But that's rot. How are we to succeed?"

"I convinced the warden to give me a little leverage." There was a swish of cloth, then sharp intakes of breath.

"By the Darkness himself," a man whispered.

Tellie sucked in a frustrated breath. What were they showing? Luckily, The Only Inn was not a quality establishment and much of the wood was rotting, so she found a perfect knothole through which to peer into the room beyond without showing herself. She squinted, glad that the strangers had moved away from their leader, giving her a chance to see what he presented. A necklace dangled from the man's upraised hand. Upon the necklace strand hung a disc like the full moon, soft grey and paper thin.

"By the Darkness," one of the men repeated, voice quavering. "What are you doing with that cursed thing?"

Daran swung the necklace casually. "You act as if the mere sight is going to burn you, cowards. The Warden told me that the elves might bargain with us for it."

"Aye, if they don't shoot us down and take it," said the other in disgust.

Throwing him a withering glare, Daran growled, "Don't you know anything about elves? They're compassionate, plagues take them. All we have to do is play the poor, unhappy travelers whose only thing of worth is this medallion. Do not worry, I have a story of how we came by it. The elves will see what we want in exchange, so we will ask to speak with their king, and the king comes and..."

"And we grab him and whisk him away before the elves strike us dead. Right." Sarcasm dripped off the words.

"Well," Daran said, sounding uncertain for the first time. "I haven't figured it all out yet." His confidence returned, and he jabbed a finger in the air. "But the moon medallion is the key. Just you wait." Taking another swig of ale, he tucked the medallion into a pocket of his cloak.

But there must have been a hole in the ragged cloak for Tellie watched the moon medallion fall lightly to the floor under the table, making no more sound than a feather.

She backed away from the knothole, her face crumbled. This was more unsettling than she'd hoped for. Everyone in the town of Denji knew the morbid legend of the elven prince who had come to their town—this very same inn— and left death in his wake. It had happened seventy years ago, or so she heard, but that had been the last encounter with elves Denji ever had. There were still reports of them visiting the city of Dormandy now and then, but they were a reclusive folk, and any information about them abounded in rumor. But these men—whoever they were—seemed to think they could find the elves and even harm them.

She tried to take a deep breath. The orphanage matron always scolded her for jumping to fantastic conclusions before she had all the details. So maybe she was misinterpreting something. Maybe they were part of a drama troupe practicing for a play. *That* seemed far-fetched, but one never knew. And it wasn't like she could do anything. The Nornes would never believe her and wouldn't be of any help even if they did.

She would just have to let these strangers pass through the inn and go on with their business. It wouldn't do to get involved.

After all, matters with elves had already ruined her family once before.

Tellie spent a while scrubbing the kitchen while she waited for the men to finish their late supper and turn in for the night. Chores past the midnight hour were not exactly her cup of tea, but she had to do something to stay awake. When at last the guests trooped upstairs to their quarters, she ventured back to the dining room.

The ale mugs and plates were scattered, food strewn across the wood and tableware. Wrinkling her nose in distaste, she began stacking them up. *Last dishes to be washed,* she told herself. *Last—*

In her weariness, she bent too far over, and a cup towering on top of the others fell to the floor. Setting the rest of the ware back on the table, she bent down to pick up the stray mug.

A glimmer caught her eye.

There on the floor lay a small circle of moonlight itself. The necklace she had seen fall out of the leader's cloak. He'd not noticed it missing from his pocket?

Shaking her head, she reached over and picked it up. Her breath skipped a beat as she held it. It was so light that the cord felt no heavier than spider's silk. As for the medallion, she could not feel its weight at all. And it was brighter...far brighter than she recalled. No longer grey, it shone like starlight itself. It was not a perfect circle, now that she saw it up close. Part of it seemed shaved off, like a waxing moon.

Her heart began to thud as she considered what this sort of necklace might be worth. Surely it had to be rare, for Kelm had never told her of anything crafted like this. Where it came from and who it belonged to, she did not know. But everything about those strangers spelled some kind of danger.

What was she to do? She couldn't give it back to them if they'd stolen it, yet she had to because there was no proof otherwise, and they would miss it—miss it and become angry. She'd have to give it back straightaway come morning. But if anyone else came looking for it, she'd point them in the right direction.

Tucking the necklace in her pocket, Tellie grabbed the dishes. She'd worry about it at dawn.

"So. She has found it."

"Yes."

"Then it shall begin at last."

oOo

The rain poured down through the forest, the droplets gathering on branches and needles only to fall in greater splashes to the ground. A small party huddled under the trees, tents hastily set up, horses standing irritably in the downpour. A lone figure hurried across the soggy grass back to the tents, huddling into his waxed cloak, raindrops slipping down his furrowed brow.

Of all times for a storm to blow in. If the night had remained fair, they could have reached the memorial. But no, there had to be a delay, another reason to stay longer in this terrible forest. As an earth elf, forests were usually a balm to his soul compared to a city, but not this one. He avoided Shadowshade on any of his ventures forth from his homeland, considering the fate of the ambassador before him.

And this time, the king was with them. Outside of Aselvia.

King Rendar had taken it into his mind to visit the memorial of his son and soldiers now. *Now* when the people were already fearing for his waning health. *Now*, seventy whole years later.

The elven ambassador tucked away his agitation as he entered the royal tent. He slipped off the wet cloak with relief, handing it with a soft thanks to an accommodating guard and stepped to where the king sat. A lantern hung from the center of the tent and a few more sat along the sides, filling the small room with a gentle glow and thin, intricate shadows from the lanterns' laced sides. The king sat upon another waxed cloak so he did not soak up the wet ground, but he could not have looked more regal than if he'd sat on his throne. He shone, the light glittering off his silver hair, his robes bright and unsullied. His back was straight, but his head was slightly bent, his eyes closed in sleep. Yet something marred his magnificence. Long shadows of troubled years hung under his eyes and hollowed his cheeks.

The ambassador hated to wake him, but he hadn't left his own comfortable tent and gone into the rain to rummage in the saddlebags for nothing. The healer Damarik had sent with them some herbs that would help fight whatever malady afflicted their king, and he was determined that he wouldn't miss a night of it just because the herbs had been momentarily forgotten in the hurry to set up the tent.

He laid a gentle hand upon the king's shoulder. "Your Majesty..."

The king's eyes fluttered open, their silver color flashing in the lantern light.

"Leoren," he said.

"Yes, it's me." Leoren undid the flask from his hip, poured some of the herbs inside, and folded the king's hands around it. "Let this steep for a while before you drink. Damarik said it would soothe you."

The king's lips twitched in a sideways smile, and his gaze flickered over to the ambassador. "I think it might be you who needs soothing."

Well, he wasn't wrong about that. Leoren's anxiety about this whole affair was getting worse. Their king…their long-reigning, ever-shining king was not well. Even worse, Rendar not only acknowledged he wasn't well, but continually hinted at something more terrible.

It was an awful reminder that even though an elf had not died from age in the thousand years of the earth's existence, they were not altogether safe from the grim reaper of death. Sickness or wound could take them, snuffing their fair life without a thought.

Only Rendar was not like the rest of them. He was not an earth elf but a celestial…the only one here upon the Lower World. White-haired and possessed with a powerful light within to heal and restore. Their savior king. To them, he had always been like a star in the heavens. And who had ever heard of a star burning out?

"Poor Leoren," Rendar said, patting his arm. "Always troubled about so many things."

Leoren stared. Well…well…how could he help it? They were out in the middle of the forest where the last ambassador and royal had died!

Rendar sighed. "You are stronger than you know. Casara and you have done so much to help me these past years, and I will need your help more than ever. A new age is coming. A new king. Until then, I know you and Casara will be good stewards. Aselvia needs you both, and so will the heir."

Leoren took a deep breath to steady himself. There it was again. These strange hints, these dreadful words he didn't wish to hear. Part of him hoped that Rendar, who had always possessed an air of mystery but was lately getting worse, was only a tiny bit mad. It was possible, what with the grief scored across his life. And if it was just madness, then surely they could help him return to sanity. For now, they simply had to visit the resting place of the prince and then slip back behind the Aselvian mountains.

No words came to mind at that moment, so he squeezed the king's shoulder wearily and stood to return to his own tent where his wife waited.

"It has been seven decades," Rendar said, tilting his head.

Leoren paused, heart aching. "My king?"

"There are some..." Rendar closed his eyes again, the same sad smile still haunting his lips. "There are some who say that seven is the number of completion."

oOo

Far, far away from where the rain poured, from small inns, from forests, from anything green or good was a grey land that had not seen the light of sun for vanishing years. All who saw it recognized it as the manifestation of despair on earth, and some abhorred it, but others mistook despair for glory.

The unfortunates who toiled there were bound by chains that could not be seen but held stronger than iron. They were pathetic beings, all zest of life wrung out of them like water from a rag. Most of these worked in mines, carving deep into the heart of the grey mountains surrounding the land. What they mined for, they did not know nor did they ask. They understood it was simply one of the tasks which was thrust on them to further break their spirits. Nearly all were crippled creatures, for few passed through those rock passages without mangling themselves on the sharp rocks that rose like knives, or discovering a sudden drop into utter blackness. And always overseers, armed with whips and rods, watched over the prisoners, ready to lash out their anger and broken dreams upon them for any mistake. Never was there a more savage realm devoid of life or love.

But there were yet those few whose spirits were not broken.

An old miner chipped away at a stone wall, his back bent in a permanent arc from bending over. In years he was only middle-aged, but the horror of this imprisonment had cracked his face and greyed his hair. But there gleamed the faintest spark in his eye that revealed he had not given up hope. Not quite.

The chisel he held, worn to a narrow rod, suddenly broke in his hand. He snatched up both ends, hoping one might still serve, but both were too short. He could pretend to keep working; perhaps no one would notice.

But he'd already hesitated too long. One of the overseers saw that he no longer labored. "You," he shouted. "Back to work!"

Hastily, the old miner positioned his hammer into place and swung at the invisible chisel. He might have done this for days without anyone noticing. But the overseer's eye stayed on him and noticed.

"Worthless scum, you lost your tool, did you? It's worth more than you!" He stalked towards him, whip drawing back. It cracked through the air, slapped on skin, but the body it wrapped around was not the miner's.

In his place stood the Prisoner.

The Prisoner, seemingly unaware of the whip's embrace, took one step forward and caught the overseer by the throat, driving him into the wall. "Overseer Normen," he said softly. "I've been looking for you."

Every ring and thud of hammer and stone silenced as each slave turned and stared.

For this Prisoner stood peerless of all the rest. His corded strength defied his malnourished body, the grime and blood could not hide his eerie beauty, and ever his eyes shone with a spirit hotter than the purest flame. There was no greater mystery in this prison, for though he worked in the mines every other week, none of the captives could remember a time when he had not been in the mines, and yet he did not seem to age, and he did not keep his scars, though there were always new ones to replace the old. Thus he had become something of a hero.

The overseer sputtered and struggled, but he could not break free from his captor's hand. "Scum," he coughed. "We'll flay off your skin."

"Beating is as natural to me as breathing," the Prisoner said coolly. "I hardly feel threatened." His eyes narrowed, and he pressed his thumb into the man's jugular vein. "How about you?"

"If you kill me," the overseer gasped, wheezing from the effort to breathe. "The overseers will kill the other slaves. Their blood on your head."

"Such a pity you'll be too dead to see it," the Prisoner said, smile starved. "And then the other overseers. And on and on our bloody exchange shall go." He cocked his head, lips tightening in pensive thought. "Will there ever come the day when the Darkness runs out of masters and miners to send down to me?" Face hardening, he threw the overseer away.

The man caught himself on the rocks and glared at the Prisoner, desire for agonizing vengeance alight in his eyes. "You'll pay," he hissed.

"I will," the Prisoner agreed. "Double for whatever is dealt to me."

The overseer's eyes widened and he slunk away, a coward to the core, or perhaps simply a man who didn't relish the idea of being killed in the middle of the night.

The old miner sat as still as the stone around him. He hoped—tried even—to catch the gaze of the Prisoner as he strode back into the dark tunnels, but the young man never looked his way. Not once.

2

oOo

The storm passed on during the night, and Tellie woke to early sunlight peeking through her shutter windows. The Nornes must have been very drunk last night if they hadn't woken her by now. While she appreciated the extra sleep, it also meant that her masters would be in a fouler mood. She would simply have to avoid them as best she could.

She laid back for a moment to gather her bearings and heaved a sigh. If last night had been any foretelling of her future, things looked grim. This was her last day of being fourteen. Three years ago she'd come to this inn with so many hopes and dreams. Day by day, reality had carved them away. She wasn't wanted, not in a way that mattered. And she was trapped. For some reason, she'd entertained the idea that another family member, a long lost brother perhaps, would arrive in a blaze of glory and take her away. Or that maybe even the Nornes would tire of her and send her back to the orphanage. But it was no use. In just another day, she'd be too old. Her next hope of escape was through marriage, but that was too many years away to be of any comfort. Assuming she'd even have prospects.

Coming to Denji wasn't all bad, of course. For one, it was in the country, a soaring improvement to the cold, stone walls and streets of the mother city. The smell of bright fir, the fiery sunsets, the taste of clear stream water...it was almost enough to make up for the sour treatment and back-aching work.

Then the town of Denji itself was charming—quaint and small, with little houses of wood and plaster. There were such stories surrounding the village, but none half as interesting as the chilling tale of mystery, monsters, and murder that hung in a shroud over The Only Inn. Tellie did not think she believed in ghosts but the tales certainly had taken root in her imagination and dreams.

And last night, a living and breathing tale had come into the inn. In the growing morning sunlight, it was hard to believe that the men last night were real, that the necklace was anything more than a figment of her imagination. But when she rolled over and opened her drawer, the medallion winked right back at her. She stared at it for a long perplexed moment. Surely it was just something wrong with her memory, but it seemed rounder somehow.

She scowled at it. "What am I going to do with you?"

Perhaps Kelm would know who made it. The craftsmanship was so unique that maybe it could be identified to a certain master. Her heart quickly rose. Kelm and his master had returned to town only the night before, on the brink of the storm.

There was no telling when Missus Norne would pound on her door and demand she start work, so Tellie determined to bask in the fragile peace while she had it. She threw open the shutters, and the morning rays whisked into the room, sanctifying the floating dust with a golden glow. The trees and grass outside sparkled from the rain as if strung with diamonds. Inhaling deep, she closed her eyes. It was hard to fear much in the sunshine. Already, she was beginning to wonder if the men were quite as terrifying as they'd seemed last night.

"Good morning," she whispered.

She could not say who she spoke to, but it seemed that a beautiful morning deserved recognition. Back in the orphanage, the matron had caught her saying it to the day and asked her if she was speaking to God. The idea of someone overhearing rather horrified her young mind, making her gasp, "Is he listening?" The matron had looked confused at that and didn't answer. But as Tellie grew, the fear of the notion changed to a wistful desire. It was nice to imagine someone might be interested in her life, as unlikely as that seemed.

Setting the necklace on her shelf, she quickly changed out of her nightgown into a simple homespun frock and pinafore. She ran a brush through her hair, catching the rebellious brown curls with a ribbon. A day as lovely as this deserved a bright ribbon but all she had was a dull blue. Still. Not even the freckles sprayed across her nose and round cheeks could mar her opinion of herself, not since the orphanage matron had called them fetching.

Of course, all her looks had fetched her so far was work in a rundown inn in an isolated country town called Denji. *It could be worse*, she reflected. *I suppose I could be working in some sooty factory.*

A croak of a bird interrupted her morose thoughts.

She turned to see a magpie perched on the rim of her window, its long tail bobbing. "Why hello," she exclaimed. Mornings, trees, birds, she talked to them all. Whether it came from her imagination or lonely need for company, she could never decide.

Magpies were often seen in Shadowshade Forest which lay just beyond the inn, but one had never come so close to her before. It was a handsome bird, brilliant black, blue, and white feathers shining in the light. Cocking its head, it fixed an intelligent dark eye on her as it hopped down onto her table.

"What are you doing?" Tellie continued, stepping towards him. She knew it wasn't wise to let any company wander in uninvited, no matter how handsome. Magpies were notorious thieves, but that was nothing in her room that should attract him except for—

With a gasp, she lunged, but she was too late.

Quick as lightning, the bird darted forward and caught up the precious necklace in its beak.

"No!" She reached wildly for it as it swept out of her room with a flash of its dazzling wings. Horrified, she leaned out the window and watched it soar to a tree where it perched on a branch, necklace still hanging from its large beak.

Panic coursed through her body. The men would wonder where the necklace had gone and they were sure to think she was the thief. Gasping, she flew out of the attic room and pounded down the two flights of stairs to the bottom floor, ignoring the slurred shout of Missus Norne. As she burst out of the main door, she collided with someone coming up the steps.

They both began to fall, but the other gained his balance and steadied her. "I say, Tellie!" he cried. "Watch it!"

Tellie shoved off him and staggered backwards. "Kelm!" she exclaimed, a flush spreading over her cheeks. "What are you doing here?"

"Dropping by to see those charming innkeepers, of course," the boy replied, straightening his vest. When she stared at him incredulously, he rolled his eyes. "I came by to see you, Tellie."

"Oh, there's no time," she said, voice shrill. "You've got to help me catch that dratted bird!"

"Dratted bird?" Kelm's eyebrows rose to his crop of wavy gold hair. "Those are two words that I never expected to hear you say together."

Without bothering to explain, Tellie grabbed her friend's arm and dragged him after her. They ran to the base of the tree where the magpie preened. As soon as they neared, the bird soared over towards the trees that bordered the beginning of Shadowshade Forest.

"After it!" she shouted, practically hysterical. "We mustn't let it get away!"

"Tellie!" he huffed. "What in Orim is going on?"

"That bird! It took the necklace. We've got to catch it!"

Not caring if he followed her or not, she tore off after the magpie as it flew into the wood.

Shadowshade Forest rose on the edge of town, the firs standing like columns of an impregnable wall. The villagers had warned Tellie not to venture far into its depths, saying that the deeper you went, the darker and sadder the wood became. For all her fears, a haunted wood enticed rather than drove away, and she pursued the magpie now with little fear. Despite its name, the wood had never seemed shadowy to her for it was always bright with green fern and vine maple. When taking a stroll, the thick foliage looked beautiful and enchanting, but now it tangled her feet as she plunged headlong through it.

The magpie seemed to be waiting for her, the insolent thing. It perched atop a straggly hemlock, cocking its head, the necklace hanging from its beak.

Tellie halted underneath and stared up. The tree shrub was too tall for her to reach and too flimsy to climb. She was almost in a foul enough mood to try to hit the bird with a stone—but not quite.

Puffing, Kelm ran up alongside her. "Drat it, Tellie! What is going on with the stupid bird? It's not moving now, so you have to tell me."

"That necklace doesn't belong to me," she whimpered, willing the magpie to stay still. "Worse, it doesn't belong to those horrible men in the inn, but they say it's theirs and they'll know I was the last one with it. You know I can't lie to save my life; I wish I could, because I think those men are dangerous, and what am I going to do?"

Kelm made her explain everything in more detail, and once she had, he studied her with a furrowed face. "Golly, Tellie. You sure know how to make a mess of things."

"Me?" she yelped. "How is this my fault? Why, I'll have you know that—" She gasped and pointed as the magpie took flight and soared into the trees beyond. "Oh, why won't he just drop it?"

"If he brings it to his nest, I'll climb the tree for you," he offered as they raced after the thief.

She threw him a grateful smile. If the magpie indeed left the medallion where she could not reach it, she didn't know what she would have done. She hated heights.

The magpie vanished into the dense forest.

"No!" she wailed, stumbling to a stop. "No, I'm done for; they're going to kill me!" Tears began to burn behind her eyes.

"Now, Tellie," Kelm said. "Don't be hasty. I'm sure those fellows aren't nearly as awful as you say nor the medallion as valuable."

She glared at him. Easy for him to say, he hadn't seen either of them.

"But let's just be still here for a moment," he continued. "Magpies are noisy birds. We'll know where he is in a second." They fell silent and listened.

A bird croaked in the distance. "There's one," Kelm said.

"It's in the wrong direction and it's too far away."

He shrugged, striding towards it anyway. "You never know. I'll check it out; you stay here and follow anything else." He disappeared into the forest beyond, leaving her amongst the rustling bracken.

She crossed her arms with a huff and bent her head to listen for any call. A squirrel chittered a distant protest, a stream's song tinkled like silver bells, and the wind in the trees whispered with distant voices.

Distant voices.

Tellie froze. That wasn't just the trees, those were voices. She pulled in a breath to call for Kelm, but then held it. Those strangers would hear her too. Perhaps they'd heard her already. So she should go after her friend for safety, yes, that was the smart thing to do.

But curiosity bloomed in her heart, rose to her head, and tingled to the very tips of her toes. Hardly anyone came this far into Shadowshade. Were they from the village or perhaps more travelers?

Casting a quick glance over her shoulder to make sure Kelm wasn't returning, she crept towards the undulating voices. The nearer she approached, the clearer the voices rang, but no less soft and sibilant. Her skin prickled as she realized they were speaking in another language. Bird, medallion, and dark strangers almost forgotten in the thrill of mystery, she knelt in the fern and crawled on.

At last, she caught her first glimpse of them from between her concealing fronds of sword fern, and her breath was stolen away.

An entire company of folk gathered in the glade, dismounted from their grazing horses. They dressed in clothes unlike any she'd seen, not even travelers from elegant Korince. Tunics swept around their slender bodies and fell halfway to their thighs, layering over leggings and knee-high leather boots. Cloaks draped down their backs, one end clasped to the shoulder, the other to their hip. The color of their attire was muted and soft, like the fog of morning hills or river mist, except for their cloaks which were dark forest green and seemed to flicker with leaf-scattered sunlight.

Three gathered in the center of the glade, while the others silently patrolled the borders.

The dark strangers at the inn had spoken the truth…

…elves had come to Shadowshade Forest.

Their race was undeniable, even without the confirmation of slender, pointed ears peeking from their long hair. It was something about their vibrant eyes, something about the way they moved. They existed in an aura of agelessness and beauty that no one could deny.

Tellie swallowed, mouth dry. How had the strangers known the elves would be coming? Perhaps they came here often in secret, and the whole of Denji didn't know.

One of the three in the center of the glade stood apart from the rest. He seemed strangely old, bent over as if under a great weight, and his hair shone silvery white. As she watched, he drew a slim sword from amongst his draping robes and drove it into the ground. Around it he hung a shredded, dark blue cloak, and around the hilt he dropped a silver circlet that gleamed in the light. One of the other figures beside him murmured quiet words that she did not understand. It struck her that these strangers shared a solemn, sad moment, and that she was rude to be spying, yet she could not look away.

The magpie's call broke the mournful quiet, and to Tellie's astonishment, it flew through the air and alighted upon the bent shoulder of the silver-haired elf. Gently, he held up a hand, and it dropped the moon necklace onto his fingers.

Tellie's gasp was drowned out by the gasps and cries of the surrounding folk. Expressions of disbelief flickered across their fair faces, and they drew close to the necklace as if they expected it to vanish before their eyes.

Only the white-haired one did not seem surprised. Indeed, he seemed calm. Very calm as he looked up and stared right into Tellie's eyes.

Drawing in a sharp breath, she crawled backwards into the fern—right into awaiting hands.

With a shriek, she lunged away, but she jerked to an abrupt halt at the end of her captor's arm. She twisted to find one of the patrolling strangers, a scarf concealing his lower face so that only his eyes, dark and intense, peered back at her. His other hand came forward, spun her back around, and clasped her other shoulder. Quite casually, he lifted her off the ground, hands grasping her arms, and carried her the last few steps out of the brush into the clearing.

A circle of gleaming blades met her eyes, each elf tensed for battle. She choked out another cry as her feet touched the ground, but the elf did not release his grip. The ring of warriors relaxed, their tension easing into something nigh to exasperation. One of the three central figures, a tall elf with a golden circlet around his flaxen hair, stepped forward and spoke a few foreign words to Tellie's captor.

"Let me go!" Tellie shouted, struggling against the steady hold. "I'm not a thief or spy...or...anything bad!"

"Of course not," the one with the circlet said soothingly. "Forgive us, our guards are ordered to keep us safe, and while you are but a child, we weren't expecting anyone out here. Let her go, Valryd. She is no threat."

The one holding Tellie let go, but she could still feel his tension hovering behind her as he obviously hadn't dismissed her as a threat.

Now free, she drew in a deep breath and straightened her dress. She glanced around at the surrounding folk with undisguised curiosity. The fact that they could speak the common tongue brushed a load of fears off her chest.

The man who ordered her release looked at her in growing unease. It was the sort of face adults made when they've been discussing something too mature and serious for a child's ear and fear they might have been understood. "You can go," he said. "We won't detain you."

"But you're elves," she blurted. "I've heard about you!"

His eyebrows drew together. "I'm sure you have. Now run along before your parents miss you. And say nothing of this."

"Leoren," a soft voice said.

Tellie started and turned to see that the third of the central party was a woman with dark brown hair and violet eyes.

"Leoren," the woman said again. "Gently." She smiled with genuine warmth that the girl found rare from adults. "I'm sorry if we seem rude, child, but we were in the middle of a memorial. Is there something you wanted?"

Shocked to be addressed so courteously, Tellie's mouth hung open without an answer. Elves. What would Kelm think? She could barely wait to tell him when she got back to the inn—

The inn. Her skin went cold. The strangers at the inn. The necklace.

"I'm sorry," she said, voice very small. "But your bird stole my necklace."

Several of the elves exclaimed and murmured to each other in their own language. Tellie blushed and stepped backward. She stumbled against the elf who had caught her and jerked away, fear pressing back in from all sides. Had she ever heard stories about what actually happened to travelers who encountered elves?

The man and the woman drew back behind the bodies of their guards, and she could hear the whisper of their swift and soft conversations with the hidden silver-haired man. Tellie began to stand on her tiptoes to see and hear better, but the guards blocking her view were staring back at her with chilly, dangerous eyes, and she quickly pretended not to be so interested by the secret conference.

The woman remerged, eyes curiously intent, but still gentle. "I am Casara. What is your name?"

"Um. Tellie," she said, heart calming a little.

"Why do you say it is your necklace?"

"I—I guess it's not, but it belonged to some men staying at the inn I work at, and they will be angry if I don't return it to them."

The elf called Leoren stepped forward, his hand unconsciously dropping to the hilt of a sword that hung at his side. "What did these men look like?"

Tellie saw the movement and stepped back. "I don't know, just strangers!" Suddenly, the necklace seemed unimportant and her life worth keeping. What would they do if she made a run for it? "Look, I'm sorry I interrupted. I won't say a thing about you if you don't want me to. I didn't mean to pry, I was just trying to—"

"Leoren," Casara said, casting him a reproving look. "You frightened her."

She turned back to Tellie and held up a hand. "We aren't angry at you, Tellie. Forgive us if we seem tense, but that necklace is very special to us and we have not seen it in a very long time."

"So it belongs to you?" Her eyes widened as she struggled to collect her scattered thoughts. It made sense. After all, she had never really believed that the necklace belonged to the men, and she recalled that they had intended to use it in their plot to...to...

She lifted her chin, trying to contain her anxiety behind her tangled fingers. "Excuse me if this seems bold, but I think your king might be in danger."

The breaths around her drew in sharply, and all the tension in the air returned.

Leoren stared at her for a long moment. "Explain," he said at last.

So she haltingly accounted how the strangers had come in the middle of the night and what she had overheard. "It all seemed so strange," she finished. "But they were planning to use this necklace as bait, I think."

"Thank you, Tellie," Casara said softly. "This information is invaluable."

She shifted from one foot to another. "Excuse me again if this is too bold...but..." Her eyes flickered to the sword stuck in the ground and the finery upon it. "Does this...does this have anything to do with the dead prince?"

It was immensely uncomfortable how everything she said affected the elves in such a strong manner. She could feel every breath inhaled, could see every jaw clench.

"What do you know of him?" Leoren said, tight-toned.

"I'm sorry." She'd definitely said the wrong thing. But the legend could not be ignored. "Everybody at Denji knows the story. The attack was quite...the traumatic event for the town." And she couldn't say what that night had changed for her personally, not here, not to them.

"I suppose it was." Leoren gave a regretful sigh. "The effect of such evil always spreads wide. I can say only that there is a connection, but it is better if you do not kn—"

"I can explain." The voice was quiet and low, rich and burnished as fine silver.

The elves looked behind them, and she followed their gaze. The shrouded guards drifted apart, and she saw again the white-haired man with the magpie upon his shoulder.

He was indeed a very old elf, perhaps as old as the world. While not wrinkled, his face was etched with hundreds of years filled with many trials and many tears. Yet his eyes, an astonishing silver ringed in black, held a light that revealed triumph over all his troubles. He held a tall white staff in his hand, but he no longer leaned on it for support.

And he smiled at her. It was subtle, almost imperceptible. But there was warmth and kindness there that filled her heart with wonder and…and there was familiarity. A patient smile that suggested he'd been waiting to see her again for a long time.

What a ridiculous idea, Tellie thought, startled. He'd never seen her before, and she'd certainly never seen him. But nonetheless, he looked as if he knew her.

"The necklace is the heirloom of my people, Tellie," he said. "It belonged to our prince."

It was the necklace she kept seeing in her dreams of the event. She didn't know why she hadn't made the connection before, except that she swore the moon had been a crescent.

He stepped away from the guards, the moon medallion resting in his hand. Leaning his staff against his arm, he reached up and undid a locket brooch at his collar.

Shyly, she took the brooch when it was offered and opened it. Inside was a painting of a handsome young man. Though small, the painting was so detailed and exquisite, Tellie could see it as clearly as if it stood life-size in front of her. The young man, no more than twenty, held a sword against his chest and looked straight at the viewer. His dark brown hair swept back behind his shoulders, and his brilliant eyes could not decide if they were green or blue. At first he seemed serious, but then she saw a slight tilt to his lips and a sparkle in his eyes like he was trying hard not to smile. She very nearly smiled back at him. Around his neck hung the moon medallion.

It was him. The prince in her dream.

3

oOo

"I am sorry for your loss," she murmured, closing the brooch and handing it back. Nervous prickles ran across her arms as she wondered how her imagination had captured the likeness of the real prince so exactly. She was sure there hadn't been a painting of him anywhere in Dormandy. After all, no one had really seen him before his untimely end. Shoving her unease down, she glanced beyond the elves to the sword and the circlet. "You've come to honor him then? I didn't mean to be such an interruption."

"On the contrary, you have done us a great service by bringing this treasure back."

"I think your bird did that."

The magpie croaked, and the silver-haired elf's lips lifted in a faint smile as he reached up to tickle its feathered breast. "True, but you were the one to recover it from our enemies in the first place. They have had it for far too long."

"They said they were going to use it to try and trick your king. Who are they and why are they doing this?" It occurred to her they might not think she deserved such an explanation, but no legend or dream had ever explained why the prince was attacked. In the dream it was the monstrous shards come down from the North, but now it was men. Something bigger was behind all this, and she wanted to know why. Besides political grumbles, she hadn't heard of any real ill will towards the elves.

But the silver haired man did not seem bothered by the forward question. He looked at her thoughtfully for a moment and then smiled. "It is a long story. But I believe we have time for it."

"My liege?" Leoren said anxiously. "If these men wish to threaten you, should we not go and defeat them at once?"

"After a storm last night, I'm sure they had plenty of ale," the elf said smoothly. "They do not think we know, so they will not act in haste."

He was right about the ale for both the strangers and her masters, and she was certainly in no hurry to go back, but still—

Wait. Threaten him? Liege? Her jaw went slack and she stumbled backwards.

"Oh no...oh no! Don't tell me you're the king!" But of course, she should have seen all the signs! Had she been rude to him? Thistles, she was being rude to him even at this moment! She dipped into a deep curtsy. "Your Majesty! I am so sorry!"

A trace of amusement, faded by the ever-present sorrow, flickered across the king's features. "You need not worry, Tellie. If I had been offended, would I not have let you known by now? Yes, I am King Rendar of Aselvia. And you are Tellie Carlson of Denji. Now, please sit and I will answer the questions you had. It is important you know the story."

Sitting in the presence of a king certainly did not seem proper, but denying him was out of the question. Light-headed, she sank to the ground. He'd said her full name, how could he have known...

With a grave face, the king sat in the grass across from her, laying his staff across his knees.

"You know the tale of creation?" he asked.

"Of course," she said. Anybody knew that. Even poor orphan children were expected to have a basic understanding of Ayeshune and the world's beginning lest they be considered absolute heathens.

He raised his hand and the edges of his skin began to glow. Her eyes widened as the light drifted from his fingers and gathered in a shining sphere

before him. Magic? But of course—he was not an earth elf, but a celestial, or so the legends said.

The light separated into several shapes that refined in detail as he spoke, delicate figures moving inside a garden of splendor.

"Once in the beginning of time, the world was without flaw—no fear, no pain, no wrong. Elves, men, and all other races lived in harmony with the Creator, Ayeshune. Each flourished in their way, the lands springing up in beauty under the touch of the earth elves, the humans building up cities and crafts, the chemas carving the stone into beauty, the aliths bending the wind to their will, the daishas claiming the sky as their own. As for the celestial elves, they studied the stars and the heavens, and they became renowned for beautiful artifacts crafted from the light surrounding and inside them.

"But long ago before this creation there were spirits who had been formed to serve the One and yet they rejected their Creator. The greatest among them sought anything other than his Lord and there he found only empty Darkness. This Darkness he wore as a mantle, and the more he saw of Ayeshune's great love and the contentment of His people, the greater his hate grew. At last he crept forth from his exile and walked amongst the people, disguised in a fair form. He planted seeds of discontent in their hearts and whispered to them of greater power. Yes, he even told them that if they followed him they would become gods."

The beautiful figures of light began to shred and writhe, curling into twisted shapes.

"So great was his influence and so cunning his lies, that when he rose up and bade them come to receive his power, all did, forsaking their God. All...but the celestial elves. For in their work they looked to the light, and when faced with Darkness, they sought the stars. They alone refused to listen to the Darkness's honeyed words, and they stood firm when all else fell.

"Those who fell for the trick found only horror and agony and hate. It consumed every one of them, spreading war, slavery, and blood. Yet Ayeshune loved those who had betrayed Him, and He redeemed those who sought Him to rise up and halt the Darkness's ever spreading evil.

"But the damage was done, and the Darkness would never leave the land again until he would be defeated at the end of time. The people who had followed him were soiled, and the world would never be able to commune with their God as they once had. Not unless the Creator Himself stepped down to restore them.

"Only the celestial elves remained pure and holy, and as reward for their faithfulness, they were separated from the sullied world that otherwise would have harmed them. The land upon which they lived was lifted high above all else and was covered with protection so that no evil would penetrate it. And so the worlds were two, one Higher, one Lower. And so should it remain as long as the celestial elves never strayed to Darkness themselves."

Tellie bent to look at the light which had soared upwards to drift like stars above them. He'd gone and told her the creation story again anyway, but it was true she hadn't heard it this way before. Humans only seemed to bear slight knowledge of the celestial elves, mainly remembered for the unsurmountable cliffs that bordered the far northwest of Orim. But...

"I know most of this," she said hesitantly. "What does it have to do with the prince?"

He only smiled at her and continued. "When I said the celestial elves did not fall, I meant all but one. One saw the Darkness and lost sight of the stars. He doubted his Lord's power and turned to his own strength, and by that strength he fell and was taken by enemies.

"In the end, after many struggles, the elf bore witness to the great sacrifice of his Creator—the act in which the people's sin was paid for and their souls were given the chance to be one with their God again. The elf's soul was saved for a new eternity, but his body and mind were still stained by the darkness of the world and he knew he could not return to the land of his people. But two gifts from his people were granted him; first, this necklace, the moon medallion, to remind him of the light."

He paused and a shadow swept across his face, the sorrow intensifying his silver eyes. "Second was a great book called the Moonscript. In it were written letters of counsel and stories of encouragement from the very pens of the celestial elves themselves, dwelling in the Higher World. Only those with celestial light could read its writing and write in return. Precious indeed were these gifts to this elf."

With a slight shake of his head, the shadow passed and he continued. "He took part in freeing the earth elves from slavery, and when he wedded their princess, he was made king of the elves of that realm, Aselvia. For many years, they lived in joy, but children were not given to them. Decades, they prayed for one, and at last their prayer was answered. But the child was born in his absence, and the birth proved too difficult for both, so the mother gave her life for her child. The king named him Errance and poured all love and care into him. To him, he gave the moon medallion, but not the Moonscript, for that would be saved till he was older."

The ancient elf paused, and his voice suddenly lost the cadence of a storyteller and instead bore the weight of one who had seen the story with his very own eyes.

"Like most young men, Errance became restless as he grew and he wished to wander the outside world. But his father was concerned for him, knowing the awaiting danger. But at last he had to let his son go, as all fathers must." He looked down, his fingers restlessly intertwining. "He was of twenty years when he began his first journey. As you know, their party was attacked here. The king had stayed back at Aselvia and the elves did not know anything had gone amiss until the prince's horse returned alone. A company was sent out to search for them and they found the prince's retinue slain in this forest. The decimation of the scene was the work of shards. The shards are not known for intelligence, driven instead by greater forces. There is little doubt that the attack came at behest of the Darkness—he and the king were old enemies, after all. It was a form of revenge. For nothing could be found of the prince. I shall spare you the description of the gruesome scene, but all that was discernible were his clothes and circlet. As for the moon medallion, which he always wore...it was never found until this day."

"So it really does go back to the beginning," Tellie whispered. "The Darkness so hated the celestial king….you….that he killed the prince."

An expression she did not understand briefly flashed across the elf's face. "That is what the people of Aselvia believe, yes."

"I'm glad you have the medallion back," she said. "Again, I'm so sorry." More than ever. He had lost so much already and then his precious son. It wasn't fair.

He bent his head in acceptance of her sympathies, and when he looked up again, a new sharpness lit his silver eyes. "Now then…Lord Leoren. Take three guards and when you return Tellie to the inn, make sure those men are expelled from this region."

Leoren saluted, crossing one arm over his chest. He turned to Tellie. "Once these men realize their plot has been foiled, they shall either return to their master or continue in pursuit of us. Your village should suffer no harm. Are you assured of your safety?"

"Will they recognize me as leading them to you?" she asked timidly.

"If you go in by a back way and remain out of sight while we send them off, they should see no association."

She took a deep breath, feeling some of the tension fade. What an unexpected and strange form of deliverance! Kelm would never believe it!

Curtsying again to the king, she said, "Thank you for the story. And thank you for explaining everything to a servant girl. I know it really didn't matter if I knew or not."

King Rendar looked up at her, a small smile curving his lips. "Do you think so?"

An uncertain laugh escaped her. The way he spoke and the way the elves straightened at the sound made her feel as if she should be important. "Should I think otherwise?" she asked nervously.

"You think this all a coincidence," he said, his intense gaze never wavering. "You think it was a random event that Daran and his men came to your inn, dropped the necklace, so that you might pick it up and bring it to where the magpie could take it and lead you to us. No, Tellie. There are no coincidences in the craft of this world."

She did not know what to say. Perhaps a thank-you was in order. It was all very well if it wasn't a coincidence, but then, what was the point if it was destiny?

"I'm dying, Tellie," the elf king said.

The only sound left in the forest was that of the stirring ferns and the creaking branches.

After a few seconds, she realized she wasn't breathing. She managed to untangle the knot in her throat before gasping, "What do you mean?"

He sighed and rubbed his hand across his knee. "My life is sustained by the light within me and it has waned under shadows of sorrow and pain. I am not long for this world. After my death, my adviser and ambassador, Lord Leoren, will become steward of Aselvia." He fixed Tellie with his gaze. "And I have chosen you, Tellie Carlson, to give the moon medallion to the next king of Aselvia."

"What?" Tellie said.

"What?" Leoren and Casara said.

Calmly ignoring the fact that he'd shocked his entire retinue, the king held out the necklace.

Tellie stared. She couldn't speak. Finally, she squeaked, "You can't be serious!"

Rendar ducked his head to hide a smile, before returning with a perfectly serious expression. "Tellie," he said. "I did not come to Shadowshade Forest just to honor my son, but to find you."

Judging by the nervous whispers of the elves who made no effort to conceal their surprise, she guessed they hadn't been aware of this either. The king sent a brief look their way, and they quieted.

When Tellie still didn't take the necklace, Rendar gently took her hand and slipped the medallion between her fingers. "Do not doubt, child," he whispered in a voice that only she could hear. "There is much you will not understand. But you've been called to this for a reason. Know that I speak the truth by this—the medallion waxes and wanes with the moon itself. Even when your path seems to lose all light, know that darkness cannot endure forever."

Uncertain, Tellie stared back at him, then down at the necklace resting in her palm. It glowed softly with a light that seemed to become more pure with every passing moment in the king's presence. "How will I know who the next king of Aselvia is?" she asked, feeling another wave of panic surface. "I know next to nothing about elves! I know very little of kings! Where will I meet him? Is he going to pass through my inn? What will he look li—"

"Tellie." The king placed a hand on her shoulder and met her eye for eye. "You'll know."

Argument stolen away by that powerful gaze, she nodded and stumbled a few steps back.

"I'd better get back to the inn," she mumbled at last, her mind in a vague daze. "The Nornes will be looking for me." At least that was assured reality. She wasn't altogether sure that this wasn't the strangest dream she'd ever had. If it was a dream, she could at least act less like a distracted hummingbird and show some courtesy. Spreading her skirts out, she sank into another elegant curtsy and said, "Thank you, King Rendar."

After backing up a few paces, she turned and began wading through the ferns again, forcing each step. She heard Lord Leoren address some elves, and when she looked behind her, she saw Leoren, Casara, and three of the elven guards following her. They had an uncanny way of walking through the brush without tripping, and they were alongside her in seconds. Determined to not be overawed by their presence, she focused on not stumbling over the trailing berry vines.

They paused at the edge of the forest and looked across the patch to where the Norne's inn resided, slouched to one side. A few horses poked their heads out of the small stable to consider the approaching strangers. The smoke spiraling from the chimney told Tellie the Nornes were aroused from their drunken slumber.

"Daran and his men should be inside," Tellie whispered. "I'll head in the back and lock the door behind me. Do you think you should go around to the front? That's where they're likely to be."

Leoren nodded, his eyes narrowing.

So far she had only seen Leoren as a sage, worried sort of elf who might study books all day. King's advisor and future steward seemed the appropriate position for such a man. But the keenness that now glinted in his green eyes revealed him as a warrior to reckon with, and it made her skin prickle.

She glanced back over her shoulder at Casara to see if a similar transformation had occurred. But while resolution set her face, the lady looked as gentle as before, and when she caught Tellie staring at her, she offered an encouraging smile.

Tellie's throat seized. That smile…it was a mother's smile. She'd seen mothers wear them, and she'd seen her own mother give it to her, but so long ago.

Before she did anything embarrassing, like burst into tears, she rose to her feet and ran across to the back door of the inn. Closing the door behind her, she threw down the latch and stood with her back against it, heart thudding wildly. The familiar musk of worn wood, dried mud, and pipe smoke drifted around her. The back room was small, with nothing but a hatch leading down into the cellar. A door opened to her left where she would enter the kitchen. She'd gone through the back room a hundred times as she threw out dishwater or shook out sheets. But now she'd met elves, spoken with their king, and was helping them drive out enemies. She never dreamed anything like this would happen to her—did such things really happen outside of stories?

Taking a deep breath, Tellie retied a ribbon around her tangled hair, straightened her pinafore, and pushed open the door into the kitchen, fully expecting the brunt of Missus Norne's wrath.

But the kitchen was empty save for several spiraling flies.

In the hall between the kitchen and the dining room, where guests were first admitted, she heard a thud and then a shriek. *That sounded like Missus Norne.* She hurried to the door, and cracking it open ever so slightly, peered down the hall to the admittance desk.

Mister Norne, his ale-slag face now taut with fear, was held against the desk by a man whose back was turned to Tellie. But she didn't need face or voice to know that the man was Daran. Behind Daran, closer to where she peeked out, stood his other three men, their fists clenching and opening at turns. Missus Norne had shrunk back against the side of the hall, her hand pressed to her heart in shock.

"Let me describe it to you a bit better," Daran snarled. "It's somewhat circular, grey, and worth a fortune. You expect me to believe you didn't accidently pick it up?"

"Never seen it!" Mister Norne rasped, his face grotesquely pale. "Perhaps one of the other visitors took it?"

Daran's voice tightened. "What about that servant girl? She was waiting on us last night. Where is she?"

Biting back a gasp, Tellie pulled away from the door's crack.

"Aven't see the rat all mornin'!" the innkeeper wheezed. "Let me go an' I'll find her for ya!"

"That won't be necessary."

She gasped again at the sound of Leoren's voice and looked through the opening.

The front door beyond the desk had flung open, and the light pouring through it shone so bright that at first the figure standing there was no more than a silhouette. The contrast in light balanced, and the elf was clearly seen.

"Looking for us, Daran of His Darkness?" Leoren said.

oOo

The old miner crept along the floor like a bat, feeling his way along the ruptured rock with one hand while the other cradled a stone cup to his chest. His breath thundered in his ears, threatening to betray him at any moment.

Guards were not the only threat to him—fellow prisoners would betray his wandering if they hoped to curry favor. No saint could be found in these bowels of the earth, and many of the prisoners would soon become guards themselves if they proved cruel enough. The old miner knew he was a rarity, surviving on as he did and yet refusing to join the depravity around him.

Not a sound stirred from the guards' chamber. As he entered, he could see the prostrate forms of the guards. They'd sunk almost to a level of unconsciousness from their drinking. No doubt they had to drink to drown the shame of their actions. The miner inched around them with little fear. It would be an easy thing to slip a knife into them, but doing so would only bring down retribution. There was no place to run or hide. The prisoners existed in hopeless certainty that nothing could be done to improve their fate except to join their very abusers. Even the Prisoner did not often rebel.

The miner flinched as he finally found who he sought. The Prisoner lay in the corner of the room, sprawled on the rocks like a broken doll. His arms were tied tight behind him, though the miner doubted they could truly restrain him.

It was at times like this that the miner's fragile heart fell hardest. If their bravest and best despaired, what hope could be kept for the rest of them?

He took a deep breath to steady himself. He couldn't think like that.

Some thought the Prisoner as a sort of god, for no matter how he was tortured, his body always recovered in days. Seeing him rise again, seeing the cruel guards flinch away from him, seeing him stride down the tunnels like a king...it was easy to idolize him. But the miner knew he couldn't. This man, however unusual, brave, and strong, was just a man. His despair did not signify the fall of cosmos, but the weariness of his own heart. He needed help as greatly as he gave it to others.

The guards had been exchanged again, this time for veterans who'd dealt with the Prisoner before and knew his games and threats. For this reason the miner sought the Prisoner out, knowing that the guards would celebrate their return with savage brutality.

Shadows coiled across the Prisoner's body, veils concealing and revealing at turns. The miner carefully knelt and reached for his shoulder. A ribbon of light danced over the Prisoner's face and caught in his open eyes. The miner froze like a mouse before a snake. He'd assumed the man would be unconscious but those piercing eyes were disconcertingly alert.

The Prisoner made no attempt to hide the hostility in his face, and the miner knew it was well-deserved. For as many prisoners that held his beauty in reverence, others held it in contempt and would harm him if they saw a chance. Too many times the miner had seen the Prisoner betrayed by the very slaves he saved.

"My lord," he said. "I brought ye water." Some time ago, the miner fashioned himself a cup from stone with hammer and chisel, and he'd risked much by sneaking to the guard's storehouses to fill it.

The Prisoner blinked slowly, not even looking at the proffered cup.

"My lord…"

"Do not call me that."

The words, no matter how cutting and cold, pulled a gasp of relief from the miner. The Prisoner hardly ever spoke to his fellows. He might converse and banter with the guards, but he avoided speaking with any of the slaves. It protected him from their betrayal and worse, from their friendship. He'd been here long before any of them had come and would remain here long after they died. He couldn't afford attachments, though the guards used the slave's lives as leverage against him anyway.

"I've nothin' more fitting to call ye, my lord," the miner replied. He reached forward to help the man up, but the Prisoner twisted away from him. "I don't recall the last time I've seen ye drink or eat. Please, won't ye take it?"

There was nothing he could swear by to convince the Prisoner that the water was untouched. It would be his choice whether to risk poison. The Prisoner swallowed involuntarily, his muscles tightening in desperation. In some attempt to keep control, the guards deprived him of almost everything. The miner knew it was something more than a miracle giving him life, but the life was no less miserable. After a pause, the Prisoner gathered himself together and sat up. Careful not to touch him again, the miner lifted the cup to his mouth and let him drink it dry. The last few drops trailed down his lips, glistening like jewels.

The Prisoner's gaze, hooded under his furrowed brows, flicked sideways to the miner. For a moment, it appeared he might express gratitude, might lower his walls just a little.

The moment left.

"Leave me," he said.

The miner crept back to his own dark world.

4

oOo

Daran swore and threw both Mister Norne and the desk away with a thrust of his arms, and then he lunged towards the elf lord, a naked knife gleaming in hand.

Leoren took one step inside, and the three elven guards shot in, passing by Daran with blurring swiftness to engage the three men just beyond.

For one moment, Daran's attention wavered between the elf at hand and the elves behind, but he continued in his leap towards the lord with a snarl. In the final breath before the strike, Leoren turned to the side, allowing the knife to slice through empty air. He swept behind Daran, catching the man's wrist and wrenching it back so that Daran held the knife to his own throat. In the same moment, he caught the man's other arm and folded it neatly behind his back.

Daran's swearing was fit to wake the dead, but no matter how he kicked and struggled, the elf bent and swayed with each wrench, and his hold did not loosen. When the knife pressed in harder against his throat, Daran froze.

Tellie tore her gawking stare from both of them to see that the other elves had likewise caught their adversaries in various manners.

"So," Leoren said. "You wanted to talk with us, didn't you? Negotiate, yes? How would you like to negotiate for your own lives?"

"Demon! Deviant!" Daran cursed, his voice horrible in helpless rage.

"Interesting names to call me considering whom you serve," Leoren replied. Despite holding a man's life in his hands, the elf lord did not look at all cruel or cunning. Instead he looked resigned, even a touch irritable.

"Devil!" Daran shouted again. "I won't speak with you, not unless I'm looking you in the face, you coward!"

"Then you may speak with my lady," the lord said.

At his words, Casara stepped in, the very meaning of cool and imperious. The drab walls of the inn seemed to retreat around her as if ashamed of their state in the presence of such a beautiful creature. She cast a glance beyond her husband's prisoner to where the other elves held the rest of the men hostage, then over to the stupefied innkeepers, then further back where she met eyes with Tellie.

Serenely, her gaze returned to Daran, and even he had the good sense to flinch. "Servant of the Darkness," she said. "For what purpose do you seek out the king of Aselvia?"

Daran writhed in Leoren's hold, eyes rolling and skin greasy with sweat. "I won't tell you anything, witch!" he rasped.

"You hold no advantage," Casara said. "The moon medallion is in its rightful place once more, and you have no hope of reclaiming it. How did it come to you?"

He paused, his mouth curling in a sneer. "So you were the thieves, eh? I should have known. I won't tell you anything."

She shook her head, her eyes almost pitying the crazed man before her. "You would tell us," she said, voice grave. "But there is nothing we really need to know. The medallion is ours once again, you have no hope of deceiving our king, and whoever sent you on this foolish mission will be quite disappointed in you." She stepped back, nodding to Leoren.

Firmly, the elf lord marched the man out the door and threw him down the stairs. The other elves followed suit, and the men tumbled across the dusty ground. "Leave this place at once," Leoren commanded. "We'll have archers making sure you're well on your way."

For a moment, the dark men hunkered in place, as if considering attacking once again. Their eyes glittered in the shadows of their faces, but then they turned and slunk away, hurrying out of the village.

"The three of you follow them," Leoren said softly to his elves as he watched the fleeing figures vanish into the wood. "Be sure they do not stop or turn back until they are well away."

He swung back to the inn and looked upon the Nornes huddled in the hall, arguing with each other in low, angry voices. His eyes swept past them to where Tellie still lingered by the door.

At the encouraging smile offered by the elves, Tellie slipped out of her hiding and hurried over. "Thank you," she whispered. "You were very brave."

"We had no reason to fear. Your courage was greater by far," Casara said. "Do you feel safe now?"

"As safe as I can," Tellie replied, heart swelling at the compliment.

"Then I trust we will see you again, little one," Leoren said, bowing low. His brow creased only slightly as he added, "Upon the day you bring our king to us."

She flushed, a tangle of confusion and disappointment stealing her voice. They spoke it like they had no doubt, though she wondered if they believed it any more than she did. Then the full meaning of his words struck her. "You're leaving *now?*"

They looked at her in surprise. "It would not be wise for us to linger. If any word of our stay traveled, the men who endangered you might become suspicious."

Sudden tears began to well up in her throat. In the little time she'd spent with them, she'd felt more valuable than ever before her life. They couldn't just go and take that with them—she couldn't allow it. "But—but how am I supposed to choose the next king of Aselvia here? What if he's not here? What if he's back at Aselvia? What if I—" The enormity of her words astonished her, frightened her...thrilled her. "What if I am meant to find him in the elf kingdom?"

Casara and Leoren exchanged glances. "It could be true," the elf lord mused.

"That would mean I should come with you, right?" Her heart raced so fast, she felt like it would jump out of her chest.

"Tellie," Casara said. "We could not take you from your parents."

For a moment, Tellie's mouth hung open in surprise. Then she laughed—more of a squawk. "M-my parents? The Nornes aren't my parents! They're my masters. Well, they are related, but distant cousins of some sort. They adopted me only for work. Or bought me, depending on your point of view. I take the latter."

"Bought you?" Leoren frowned, then looked to where the Nornes had disappeared, too frightened by the strange intruders to fetch Tellie away from them. "Slavery's not allowed in this part of Orim."

"Oh," Tellie said, arms shaking from excitement. She tried to make her voice calm and experienced. "It's not, but adopting a child for free labor is cheaper than hiring."

"That shouldn't be allowed either." His frown carved deeper.

"All they do is make me work; they don't care about me at all. All I ever wanted was a loving family, but I haven't been loved in such a long time, and you—" she broke off, terrified of saying something humiliating. "Isn't there something you might do?"

Casara's warm hand cupped her cheek and lifted her face up. "We cannot promise anything," she said softly. "But we'll return to our king and hear his thoughts on the matter. If you must remain here, know that it is God's will for you."

A terrible will that would be, Tellie almost snapped, but she held it back just in time.

"Tel-lie!"

Missus Norne's owl-like screech startled them all. The disagreeable woman peered around the corner of the room, having mustered the courage to retrieve her servant from the strangers. "Don't ya' be fraternizing' with them demons. Get away. And you two! Get you and yer soldiers outta' here, ya hear? This here is peaceful territory and we don't need no military in these parts!"

Ignoring the woman, Casara leaned down and whispered, "Trust Ayeshune." Then her hand slipped away, and like the sun setting behind the hills at the descent of night, she and Leoren left the inn and hurried back to Shadowshade Forest.

Forlornly, Tellie leaned against the door post, hugging it as her only consolation.

"Haven't had such going-on's for ages," Missus Norne continued to grumble. "Strangers, threats, swords, and who knows what hullabaloo." Her strained nerves quivered with a need for release and she pounced upon the sight of Tellie. "You! I spelt some soup when those heathens attacked us. You go fetch some water and clean it up!"

Without a word, Tellie ran past her, making for the back rooms where the buckets were stored. She grabbed a handle and reached for the door, all her mind swept away in dizzying possibilities of the future. Any moment now a shriek of delight would burst from her chest, and she threw herself out the door before it could escape.

"OOF!"

Her body collided hard against another person, and she fell back on her rump.

"Ow! Are we going to start making a habit of this?" a boy's voice complained.

"Kelm?" Unhappily, she reeled her mind back into acknowledgement of the here and now. She stared at the boy in front of her. She knew boys could be filthy, but he surpassed them all. Dirt smudged his cheeks, his shirt was torn, sticks were tangled in his hair, and his hands were grubby with sap. "What on earth have you been doing?" she said with a frown.

He stared at her in disbelief. "What have I been *doing?*" His face turned bright red. "Blast it, Tellie! We were out in the forest searching for the magpie, remember? I chased the stupid bird through the forest, climbed to the top of a tree to look in its nest, and fell out of it climbing back down. What were you doing? Brushing your hair?"

An apology had begun on her lips, but that last bit sent annoyance skittering across her skin like ants. "You needn't get so grouchy," she snapped. "As a matter of fact, I was doing huge things, *important* things!" She shoved past him, bucket firmly clasped against her chest.

But she had not gone far in her march to the town well when he came hurrying after her.

"What things? What did you do?" he demanded.

Tellie hesitated. Kelm was about the only friend she had. Could she dare share her hope with him? Well, maybe not that yet, as it would probably come to nothing after all. "I met elves," she announced as she might have spoken of any ordinary meeting.

He halted behind her. "What?"

She spun, clutching the bucket to her chest, and her flushed face proved her sincerity. "It was the most incredible thing, Kelm; you wouldn't believe it! The magpie belonged to elves, and I met them in the forest!"

"Elves?" Kelm paled, and his eyes widened to saucers. "What are you talking about, Tellie? How'd you know they're elves?"

"Give me a little credit on judgment! They're hardly human, Kelm. I don't know how to describe it; you just have to be there and…feel it. They'd come for a memorial out in Shadowshade. Oh, if only you'd seen them!" The earnestness in her eyes rang so true that Kelm's doubt gave way.

"If only I had!" He kicked a piece of bark out of his way with frustration. "Darn it, Tellie! Why didn't you find me before speaking to them?"

"It's a long story," she said, grabbing the wheel at the well and starting to turn it.

Kelm's hand caught her elbow and pulled her aside. He grasped the wheel. "I'll get the water," he said firmly. "You talk."

As night descended upon the village and candle-lit windows were dimmed, Tellie made her weary way up the creaking steps to her attic room. In a form of revenge for the unexpected events of the day, the Nornes had been especially unpleasant, barking at her every time they saw her face.

If only you knew, she thought. *I could leave you forever.*

She hadn't told Kelm she still had the moon medallion. She'd left off saying that she'd given it to the king, and he had provided warriors to drive Daran and his men away. Kelm had been so excited by the story that he hadn't questioned the hesitating pauses in her tale.

Throughout the day, the moon medallion remained in her pinafore pocket, tightly buttoned. Now as she latched the attic door behind her, she took it out and laid it reverently on the crooked table by her cot. The light and beauty of it seemed to richen the grey-boarded floor and walls, the sagging mattress, and the desk with the cracked washbowl and cloth.

Kneeling, she opened the bottom drawer of her cabinet.

There was only one other wonderful thing she had in this room, lent to her by a sympathetic and kindly old woman of the village. It was a leather-bound book studying the ancient races of Orim. Much of it was simply writing which she couldn't read, but some precious pages were covered in faded paintings of creatures and people.

She pulled it from the drawer and spread it open on her cot. She flipped through the pages, stopping a moment at each one. She had memorized each name of the creatures as they were told to her. There was a painting of a girl in grey, half blending into the stone behind her. *Chema*, those who dwelt in cold mountains of stone, vanishing into its shadows at will. On the opposite page was a great winged beast covered in fur, soaring through the sky. *Daisha*, such fantastic creatures as were only spoken of in the rarest of fairytales. She continued on, passing the illustration of a handsome young man with dark skin and white hair, wielding a sword as the wind whipped around him. *Alith.*

At last she came to the final pages, to a picture that took up both sides. Through a forest at night, the moon glowing overhead, walked a tall and fair people. Her finger rested on their name. *Elf.*

They weren't a fairytale. They weren't a far-away legend that she would never see. They had come to her inn, and she had seen them.

Hugging the book to her chest, she stepped to the window and stared out into the night, listening as the branches rattled against the panes. There was such a wonderful world out there, one she barely knew. If it was possible for her to meet elves even here in her hidden corner of the world, what else might wait for her out yonder?

Just you wait, Tellie, Kelm had promised her once. *When we're older, I'll take you to see Orim, anywhere you want!*

Alright, she'd said, never minding how improper it was to even speak about wandering the world with a young man.

Taking a deep breath, she reached to the desk and picked up the necklace. Its glow brightened in the palm of her hand and she walked back over to her attic window to let it drink in fresh moonlight. Was it her imagination or was the moon medallion fuller?

After staring at it for long while, she tucked both it and her book away into her drawer. It was her nightly habit to kneel and recite the catechism taught to her by the orphanage, and it always served as a steady, if unconscious, comfort to her. Tonight, she stood still. Had Rendar meant it? Was there some divine plan for her life after all?

"Well?" she whispered. "Are you there?"

No one answered.

She hadn't really expected anything anyway.

Outside, the wind whispered through the trees, urging all the villagers to forget their cares and slip into sleep. But there was one that the wind's song did not enchant, one who clung in the branches of the great oak outside Tellie's window. He was a creature grey as stone, lank and wiry, and as still as the boughs themselves. All during the day he had remained high in the tree above the inn, blending into the shadowy branches with ease. He had seen all that had happened, of Tellie's going and returning, of the elves sending Daran and his men away, and of the conversation the elves had had with the girl.

At long last, with the fall of darkness, the grey creature slid down the tree and vanished into the night.

Shadows of lavender and blue cast over and through the forest as twilight fell, the trees shivering in the chill wind. The elves stood as sentinels in a circle amongst the groaning trees, their sharp weapons gleaming with the last of the light. In the center, the horses and other elves rested and partook in light fare. They did not speak, but kept glancing around the wood in unease despite the vigilant guards. No matter the beauty of the wood, this was the site of a terrible slaughter and no restful place to spend the night.

Rendar sat apart, looking upon the memorial of his son without ceasing, while Flyfar preened on his shoulder. He knew the silence around him was more than just unease; he'd rattled them all with his declaration to the mortal girl. And they were afraid for him.

Since the girl had left, the momentary surge of life had left him like a candle bereft of its flame and hardened into cold wax. Every breath he took hurt. And he was so cold.

A slight rustle drew his attention and he glanced over to see Leoren kneeling beside him with worried eyes and holding a loaf of bread.

"Please eat something, Your Majesty," he coaxed.

Instead Rendar reached out a frail hand and patted his arm. "I know I astonished you with choosing that child for a matter of such importance. I'm sorry I hadn't told you earlier. There is so much I wish I could have told you, but you must understand, some burdens are too heavy to pass to another, and you already burden yourself too much already…"

Leoren only looked more alarmed. "Don't trouble yourself, my king. I'm sure you had a good reason."

"Still." He reached into the folds of his tunic and drew out a sealed letter. "This will explain some of it. But…perhaps do not open it now? Soon."

"All right," Leoren said, taking the letter and tucking it into the inside pocket of his cloak.

Rendar sighed, words fluttering from his reach. It was hard to even think straight anymore. "I know you have always struggled to value your place in this world. The girl is the same. So take care of her. And…" He exhaled and bent his chin to his chest, unable to say more.

A cloak nestled around his shoulders, and then Leoren drifted away again to leave him to his rest.

The king closed his eyes and inhaled the scent of the trees, ferns, and mossy turf. He listened to the whisperings of the wind and all it knew, the forlorn cries of birds of the night, and the flittering of eager little bats. Even here in a site of such sorrow, there was beauty, life, and beginning again.

It had been a long and difficult road to this point. But it was here now at last.

When he opened his eyes again, it was to a world much brighter than the one he had left, and the memorial before him was haloed with a soft, warm radiance. The surrounding wood sparkled with thousands of lights as if stars beaded the very branches, and the air thrummed with music as hidden and vital as blood. He inhaled again, his chest rising and falling with the strength of his prime. He rose in one fluid motion, turned, and then knelt in highest respect.

"I have told her your words," he said. "But I fear she will not understand what follows." His silver eyes, gleaming gold in the light, were deeply troubled. "She is so young, so small. Are you sure she is ready for this?"

"I have chosen whom I have chosen. The time is right," the Other replied. "Do no fear for her, Rendar. I am with her, even as I am with you."

Rendar stood and took a step forward, but he suddenly felt the life of his body sag under terrible weight, and his spirit strained at the pull. As he wavered in the flash of pain, a hand slipped under his arm and held with the strength that supported nations.

"It is done," Rendar said with a gasp, when he could speak again. "She is found, and her journey is now set before her. Let me no longer be bound to this waning shell, it is of no more use to me. Call me home, I beg you."

The hand moved from his arm to his cheek, and he leaned into its warmth like a child. And then he heard the words, just a whisper, at last set loose the bindings that had frayed for so long.

"Come home, my son."

A sharp tug at his ear stirred Leoren from light sleep and he opened his eyes to see the magpie staring down its beak at him. "Flyfar," he murmured. "What is it?" He rose, the bird fluttering from his shoulder, and looked to where the king still slumped before the sword. With a heavy sigh, he slipped out from under his wife's arm and walked softly over. "Come and rest in your tent, my king, please," he whispered, taking the king's hand.

Rendar's fingers were cold as ice, absent of all life's warmth.

Time, thought, and heartbeat froze in that single moment, and for many breaths, Leoren neither spoke nor moved. A guard sensed the strangeness of his silence and drew near.

"Wake the company," Leoren said quietly. "His Majesty has passed beyond."

5

oOo

Daran stared into the first flames licking around the logs in his campfire. The morning was cold and wet, and the sun had not yet risen to drive away its gloom.

He'd built so many castles of grandeur on this expedition, and now they were crumbling to dust before him. With the elves on defense, he had little chance of succeeding. What would the warden say when he returned without the moon medallion and without the king? Even more dreadful, what would the Voice say? The Voice, whose return was drawing so near.

They thought him a fool. A failure. Everyone always had. But if Daran had anything to say about it, they would not think that way for much longer. The elves simply saw him as a grunt of a greater evil, but they considered him no real threat.

An approaching shadow darkened the corner of Daran's vision, and he turned in a swift wheel, hand on his knife.

A grey, gangly creature stared back at him before dropping into a hunched crouch before the fire. Light gleamed in its black eyes and white pupils, steaming breath curling from its serrated jaw. No matter how many times Daran saw the monster, a shudder ran down his spine. Perhaps because it hadn't always been this way. Perhaps because the creature had once been different, something close to a friend.

"Where were you, Kilkus?" Daran growled. "It took you blasted long enough."

A harsh, guttural series of clicks and grunts rattled out of the shard's throat, and Daran stiffened at its words.

"What?" the man hissed. "You mean you were in the trees watching all along? What did you see? What did you hear?"

As he listened to the shard's report, disbelief, then savage delight marred Daran's features. "So," he murmured aloud. "The girl was involved. The elves are fond of her, are they? Thinking of taking her with them?" He chuckled. "We'll just see about that."

The elves might be a match for him, even he had to admit that. But if they didn't know about Kilkus, then the odds might have very well turned in his favor.

The king of Aselvia had died during the night.

The morning was gentle, soft, peaceful—it did not seem possible that someone reigning so long on the earth could pass away without nature itself bowing in respect. Dewdrops sparkled on every leaf and blade of grass, veils of morning sunlight streaming down through the trees to wrap the world in a warm amber glow.

Perhaps, Lord Leoren reflected as he leaned against a tree, the beauty of the day was not indifference to the king's death, but an exultation of his life.

He'd warned them this was coming, but how unwilling they had been to believe it. And now here they were, the fate of the throne still uncertain.

One thing was certain, and it hit him with a small stab of pain to the chest. The link to the Higher World and their celestial kin had been severed. The Moonscript had never been for them personally, but knowing their king spoke to their holy brethren was somehow comforting. But never again. The Moonscript would remain locked in a room no one could open, unread and unwritten. A tragic reminder of all that had been lost.

The guards still stood at attention around the king's covered body, waiting for the command to depart. Looking away with a sigh, Leoren turned to his wife as she stepped to his side. Her eyes were misty and tired. He swallowed his own misery enough to reach out and enfold her slender, ivory hand in his. She'd lost far too much in her life already, always bearing it with silent strength.

"It will be alight, Leoren," she said at length. "He seemed at peace. We must be glad he is reunited with Cerene and Errance."

"I only wish he'd prepared us more," Leoren said, then winced in remembrance of the multiple hints. "He hadn't mentioned a new heir until now. And an unknown mortal girl to select him? It is so strange, so cryptic."

"So like him," Casara said, raising a droll brow.

Leoren laughed weakly, then winced. "I suppose that's true. But what shall we do for the girl? This is rather an uncomfortable situation for her too, isn't it?"

Casara sighed, folding her arms. "Well, she did seem eager to escape her current circumstances, and she was the one who suggested coming back with us. It does make sense. After all, it's not like there are elves just wandering this world."

"Well, there's our son..." Leoren said reluctantly.

Her eyes widened. "No, it couldn't be him. He would be miserable tied down to the throne. Anyway, I have no idea how Tellie would meet him, since even we don't know where in Orim he is now."

"Rendar was telling me something about taking care of her," Leoren went on. "So it seems like he was suggesting she return with us..."

For the first time that morning, a little bit of light returned to Casara's eyes. "I think it would be for the best. She seems sweet, and I would hate for her to wither under a harsh hand. But...she is still young. If the innkeepers could be persuaded, we would need to become her guardians. Her family."

You have always struggled to value your place in this world. The girl is the same.

Leoren took a deep breath. No one in Aselvia had ever adopted outside their own people before. But this was an unusual circumstance. It was clearly Rendar's will, or even that of someone higher, that her story be entwined with theirs.

Casara's voice was hushed, barely above a whisper. "And…" Her eyes shone wistfully. "I have always wished for a daughter."

Well then. He squeezed her hand. "Then let us go and speak to the innkeepers."

After a miserable hour of cleaning out chamber pots behind the inn, Tellie staggered back inside, trying to calm her tossing stomach. It did not matter that she'd been cleaning them since she arrived at the Nornes, it never failed to disgust her. Sighing, she picked up two of the nearest buckets and headed inside. As she started through the back rooms, a familiar voice pinned her to the floor. Was that…Leoren speaking?

Quietly, she set the buckets down and hurried to the stairway where she leaned against the wall and listened through the boards.

"Balderdash!" Mister Norne snarled. "What sort of folks do ye take us for?"

"I take you for a businessman, Master Norne, nothing more," Lord Leoren returned. "You seem to have no interest in Tellie's welfare, but in how she benefits you."

"How dare ye talk to us about that brat? Why, if it wasn't for us, she'd be back at the orphanage—"

"What would you sell her for?" Leoren asked abruptly.

Tellie choked on her surprise and clamped her hands to her mouth, trying to keep in the coughs that convulsed her shoulders.

Dead silence hung in the room. Then Mister Norne spoke, trembling with eagerness and disbelief. "What sort of price would you be offering? Mind you, the girl's a good worker, and I wouldn't part with her for nothing less than—"

Tellie's mind stilled. Of course. Of course, she'd known they'd never really cared about her, but it was one thing to know it and another to hear it. She thought she'd stopped caring about their opinion of her, but apparently not, because it sliced across her heart like the fine edge of paper.

"I have no interest in buying Tellie like a mere trinket," the elf interrupted. "I was simply of the opinion that you would be willing to sell her on the first good offer you received. I see now I was right."

Sputtering issued from the innkeeper, but he had no time to speak before a new voice spoke, this time Casara. "We will not buy Tellie. But we will buy her freedom from you."

Her stomach twisting at the incredible words, Tellie wrapped her arms around herself and closed her eyes. She barely had the courage to listen more.

There was a snort. "Where will she go?" Mister Norne snarled. "My wife and I, we're all she's got. She'd live on the streets."

Stung by the truth of the words, the girl waited in breathless suspense.

"We will offer her a home with us," Leoren answered.

It was all Tellie could do to keep from screaming out loud.

"And if she don't want to? Eh? What about that?"

After a moment, Casara called, "Tellie, come out from behind that wall."

Tellie stiffened in disbelief. She hadn't made any noise, had she? How had they known…? Embarrassed, she crept around the corner, staring at the floor, hands folded behind her.

"If you would like to remain here, Tellie," Casara said. "We shall compensate Master Norne for treating you well and will check on you regularly to make sure of it." Taking a deep breath, she continued, "But if you would like…Leoren and I wish to offer our home to you. To take you back with us to Aselvia."

Home. Their home. Did they mean…like family?

"What in tarnation fer?" Mister Norne thundered. "What has she got for ye? Why don't ye traipse around takin' in all the little street rats?"

"Perhaps we will," Leoren said saltily, casting an irritated glance his way. "But we've been led specifically to Tellie."

"What do you say, Tellie?" Casara asked. "If you need time to think, we can return in two weeks or less, after our king has been honored properly."

Stunned, Tellie stepped back, bracing herself against the wall. They wanted her with them? It was a dream come true. She'd always dreamed of someone coming to steal her away, she'd just never pictured them as elves. Tears welling up in her eyes, she gasped, "I don't need to think! I want to come with you now!"

Leoren turned his gaze back to the innkeeper. "If there is any paper that signifies your custody over Tellie, assign them over to her in exchange for this." He reached into his belt and pulled out a small pouch.

Its content wasn't hard to guess from Mister Norne's reaction. Reeling as if drunk, he staggered back to a room and came out with a few crumbled papers. Taking a pen, he slashed ink across the bottom of the page and handed it to Tellie.

She was half afraid that her trembling hands would tear the paper in two as she took it and smoothed it out on a nearby table. Taking the pen, she scrawled out on the bottom line, under Mister Norne's blot, the only words she knew how to write.

Tellie Carlson.

After she was finished, Leoren took the page and inspected it. "It seems official." He handed it back to Tellie with a smile. "There. You belong to no one but yourself."

The statement was unbelievable, thrilling, but sadness suddenly stung her heart. *But I want to belong,* she thought. *I want to belong to someone. A family.* "Do I just come with you now?" she asked.

Casara's face softened. "Fetch your things."

No more encouragement needed, Tellie whirled and bolted up the stairs, the rickety steps screeching under her excited bounds. Her door crashed against the wall as she burst through it.

The little room seemed almost prim, as if it wanted to look its best at parting. Unexpected pain darted through her heart, taking her breath away. She sat down beside the cabinet, her hands hovering at the drawer. The room had become dear without her knowledge, always serving as a refuge from her troubles.

Here she stood at the threshold of a future greater than she ever imagined, and now she felt afraid. *This is ridiculous*, she growled. *Stop it.* But what would happen when she walked out that door, down those steps? What would happen now that the paper to her freedom was in her hand?

This was not the first time she'd found herself before an unknown beginning. She remembered the terror as a child being placed in an orphanage. And then later learning she was to move to a new home in Denji. Each time, terror. Each time fear of the unknown.

But this…this would make everything better. Of course it would. Repeating this over and over in her mind, she stuffed a few extra changes of clothes into a sack and laid her book on top of them.

She descended the stairs much slower, still trying to ignore the growing fear. *You know what to expect here and can live with it,* one voice muttered in her head. *But they were willing to* sell *me. My life could be so much more than this,* her heart argued back.

When she saw the elves waiting by the door and ignoring Mister Norne— who ignored them less skillfully—some of the fear retreated again. "King Rendar does not mind?" she said hesitantly.

Exchanging a look with her husband, Casara answered. "Tellie, there is something you need to know. King Rendar died last night."

Tellie's mouth dropped open. The man had looked old, weary, and ill, but dead? So soon? "But…but I wanted to talk with him more," she whispered.

"More?" Mister Norne exclaimed. "Blimey, ye mean ye met these devils 'afore? Ye're a curse, and I'm glad to be rid of ya." He stumped out of the room, muttering.

Leoren glared after him, and if looks could kill, then the innkeeper just barely escaped with his life.

The elves guided Tellie out onto the porch. She stood quite still, papers clutched to chest. Not until the crisp morning wind kissed her stinging eyes did she realize how close she was to crying.

The rest of the elves stood upon the grass waiting for them, the horses prancing by their sides. One of the horses carried a long, blanket-wrapped bundle upon it. Tellie stared, her gut guessing what it was before her mind caught up.

Casara followed her gaze, eyes saddening. "I wish there was a more honorable way we could carry him," she said.

"Elves really do die," Tellie whispered.

A sad laugh turned into a sigh. "They do."

"Well, yes, you told me, but he didn't look ready to die. Is this how it usually happens?"

"I do not believe any of the earth elves, the natives of Aselvia, have yet died of old age, so I cannot say for certain," Leoren admitted. "Rendar's celestial light caused him to be nigh immortal throughout life for it healed any harm. We can only guess that the more this light is taxed, the quicker it is used up. He spent much of his younger life in turmoil. And he has ever been waning since the loss of his son." His voice nearly broke at the end, and he took a deep breath.

She stared up into his eyes, appalled that something so foreign as an elf could show such familiar grief.

"We must go now, Tellie," he said. "Our people must know. You will ride with Casara."

With a slow nod, she took one step down the porch and towards the horse that would carry her away into a future more uncertain and more wondrous than any she had dreamed. And it was then that her destiny was interrupted by sudden realization.

"Kelm!" she gasped.

"Who?" Casara asked.

"A friend." She whirled towards the woman, eyes wide in desperation. "Please, is there enough time for me to say good-bye to him? He must know where I'm going!"

Sympathy welled up in the lady's eyes and she nodded. "Go then. We can wait."

Shoving her bag into Casara's arms without a second thought, Tellie tore down the street. A few of the villagers called to her, asking about the strangers by the inn, but she paid them no heed. For all she knew, Kelm might have left already. No doubt the broken wheel had been fixed, so they could have already left at dawn. And if he was gone, then he could be gone forever. She gathered up her skirts and ran faster.

There! There they were, just outside of the house belonging to the merchant's aunt. Kelm was climbing into the wagon's seat while the merchant said good-bye to his aunt.

"Wait! Stop!"

Kelm twisted around in surprise. "Tellie?"

"You didn't say good-bye!" she cried, panting as she drew even with the driver's seat.

"Shame on ye, lad, you'll break your girl's heart," the merchant chuckled, slapping Kelm on the shoulder.

Flushing fiercely, Tellie decided to otherwise ignore the comment. "I had something to say," she said. Uneasily, she glanced at the merchant and his portly aunt. She really didn't want to tell her story in front of them; already she could hear demands for long explanations. "Please, could I talk to Kelm a moment?"

"We really must be going," the merchant said.

"Oh, let them talk," the aunt said with a laugh. "They get to see each other so little, the darlings."

Blushing at that, Kelm jumped down from the wagon and followed Tellie as she turned and ran past the houses into the forest. "This better be good," he grumbled. "You know I'm going to be teased about this the entire day."

Tellie continued to trot through the forest until she was sure no one from the village would wander by and overhear. Smiling from ear to ear, she faced him. "I've been adopted," she announced.

"What?" He backed up so fast he nearly tripped over a log.

"Well, I suppose it's not official yet," she admitted, twisting her fingers together. "But I think they're really serious, you know. And I don't belong to the Nornes anymore. That's why I had to talk to you. We need a plan to see each other again. Maybe they will let me come to Dormandy now and then? Or maybe your master could come there?"

"Wait! Hold it, back up!" Kelm exclaimed, waving his hands in a frantic effort to stop her words. "Where are you going?"

"Well, they're taking me with them."

"Who? Where?"

"The elves, of course," Tellie said impatiently.

"The *what?*" Kelm's mouth dropped open and he grabbed her by the arms. "You don't mean to say you're going with them?"

"Yes, and why not?" she answered, irritation creeping up the back of her neck. He was acting excited in all the wrong ways. As if she hadn't enough voices of doubt in her own mind.

"You don't know a thing about them!"

She stiffened. "I do too," she said, hating how he echoed her own questions. "Lord Leoren is the steward of Aselvia. He and his wife are going to be watching over their kingdom until a new king is found. Because, you see, the elf king I told you about…he…he died."

"Did you see him dead?" he asked suspiciously.

"Bother it, Kelm, what galls you?" Tellie cried in frustration, stepping back. "They are the nicest people I've ever met. They paid the Nornes to set me free!"

"They paid?" Kelm's eyes widened, and he looked around as if something was going to leap down on them. "Briars and brights, Tellie, you're being cheated! Why on earth would they pay unless they wanted something from you?"

They want me to choose their next king, so there, Tellie wanted to shout, but it sounded so ludicrous, she did not dare. Fear that he spoke truth clawed up her throat. Really, why were they bothering to help her?

"Why indeed?"

They both gasped at the words growled behind them. A dark and menacing man stepped out from behind a tree, and worse, she knew him.

Daran.

"What are you doing here?" Tellie gasped. "Leoren told you to leave."

Kelm gripped her arm and pulled her back as the man approached.

"And we did, just like obedient little mortals," he said with a sneer. "But

I'm afraid our Kilkus just doesn't give elves enough respect."

At his words, another figure slipped forth from the shadows of brambles and stones. Tellie's blood ran cold at the sight of it. A shard. It had to be. No other creature of legend could match the horror of its existence. Its skin might have been carved from stone, and the flame of a candlewick flickered in its dark eyes. Dark as midnight and terror.

"Tellie, *RUN!*"

Kelm's shout tore through her paralysis, and she found herself yanked off her feet as the boy dragged her through the fern. She took control of her own flight and sprinted to keep up with him, struggling to regain her breath.

"Leoren!" she shouted. "Leoren, Casara!"

Her foot hooked on a fallen branch. She barely had time for dismay as her hand slipped out of Kelm's, and she face-planted into the ground. Thorns and sticks dug into her palms as she scrambled to stand up. A shadow cast over her and she looked back just in time to see one of Daran's men reach down and grab her by the shoulders. She screamed, trying to wrench from the hold. The other hand of her captor clamped over her mouth, cutting any cry off short, and she was swung up to a standing position. As she struggled, she caught sight of Kelm running back, his face pale but resolute.

The next instant, another of Daran's company leapt up from the ferns and caught the boy by the neck, pinning his arms and covering his mouth as well.

The more Tellie struggled, the more the grip tightened, and her skin began to numb from the pressure. Trembling, she let herself go limp, but her eyes rolled wildly for any sign of the elves.

"What about the boy?" Kelm's captor asked, shaking the youth roughly. "He wasn't with them."

"Not that Kilkus saw anyway. He might be," Daran said. "Either way, he's a child. The elves are soft-hearted for such things." He stood looking at both children, hands on hips. "The elf king dead!" he snarled. "If that's true, the entire plan's off!"

A rattle of noise startled them all, and they turned to see another of the dark men come crashing through the brush towards them. "They're coming!" he hissed. "The elves heard the shout!"

His face contorted into a murderous scowl, Daran started undoing a packet on his belt. "Shoot on sight," he ordered.

Tellie twisted, just able to see the village through the trees. Any moment the elves would burst through the forest, arrows flying, and save her.

Her attention jerked back to Daran as he pulled a smooth, black marble from his packet. Not a gleam or line marred its depth.

The men drew back at the sight. "By the Darkness," one of them muttered. "You aren't actually using that thing?"

"Do you want to die here?" Daran growled, his grim face shuddering with the slightest fear. "He started it all, didn't he? He can help us a bit now." Drawing his knife, Daran slid the blade across his knuckles, letting the blood drip upon the surface of the sphere.

A dark mist rose from the orb, curling into a wisp that swirled around Daran's hands. The men muttered in fear, but everyone stood their ground. As Tellie watched, the dark wisp suddenly grew into a thick coil that whipped around Daran's figure and then spread out to all the rest. Terrified, she thrust back against her captor, the gravity of the danger descending with the darkness. She screamed and clawed against the restricting hand, and in the next moment, she broke free, tumbling to the ground.

"Tellie!"

She looked up through tangled hair to see the elves dashing through the trees towards her. She could see nothing of their faces in her blurred vision, but she could hear the terror and anger in their voices, and light glanced off their blades with blinding brightness.

But before she could jump to her feet, before she could race to them, she realized there wasn't any ground beneath her. Horrified, she swept her arms out, trying to feel something, anything! But there was only wind, consuming, ravaging wind. It had to be a dream, or else it wouldn't be so dark. Where had the daylight and the elves gone?

But then the darkness began to recede. Not because it retreated but because she was being pulled above it, the void dropping further and further away beneath her. A glow began to shimmer around her, so pure and bright that all else withdrew, even from memory...

Leaves shimmered like jewels under the sunlight's kiss, trembling with the breath of a breeze. Tellie stared up at the trees, wondering why she could not feel or hear the wind. She stood upon a small walled path, everything beyond it blurred. I'm dreaming, she realized. At least it seemed to be a pleasant dream. She couldn't be sure, but it seemed there had been something unpleasant happening in reality.

In the absolute stillness, she heard a distant door open, and a man walked forth onto a balcony further down the path. It was then that she noticed the small boy sitting upon the nearby wall, and he leapt up and ran towards the man, who swept him up into his arms. She stepped closer, not wishing to startle them, but curious to know who they were.

Rendar.

His face shone far more carefree than before. She studied the child, and when she saw the moon medallion resting on his breast, she realized she looked upon Errance.

"I missed you, Daava," the small boy said, disapproval in every word.

With a laugh, Rendar kissed his son's cheek. "I was gone only for an hour. Surely you could not have missed me so terribly."

"I did," he insisted. "I want to go in there too!"

Smiling, Rendar set him on the wall and swung his arms back and forth. "Someday," he said.

"When?" the little Errance demanded. "When can I read the Moonscript?"

"When you're king," Rendar promised. Then he looked up and straight at Tellie.

She stepped back and found herself falling, unable to scream, unable to catch herself. And as she fell back into darkness, the memories of the dream slipped away like the rays of light themselves...

And then there was nothing.

Nothing at all.

6

oOo

It is said Darkness is empty and that is why it always hungers. A consuming void, unable to be satisfied by that it devours. Whatever vanishes into its depths is lost forever. I know this better than anyone. For I have suffered here in the shadows, and there are none who might find me.

In the northeastern corner of Orim, there hunkered a range of mountains in peaks of serrated teeth and shrouded in shadow. Few neared those fell mountains upon their own free will, and none had ever scaled those heights. For a truth was whispered—though none could say from where this truth came—that the mountains hid a secret too terrifying to reveal. A scar on the world uglier than death.

There were those who had been taken beyond that mountain wall by mysterious ways and never returned to speak of what horrors lurked inside. Only those pledged to the evil within ever ventured out again.

If one could have looked over the high peaks, they would have seen that on the other side, formed from the very rocks of the mountains, there rose a fortress, towers as sharp as spears and the walls as riddled as decaying flesh. None would have noticed the clumsy buildings of wood scattered around the foundation or the mines delving into the mountain sides or even the dramatic proportions of the edifice. When one saw the fortress of Tertorem, one could only look at a single thing.

Between the highest two towers suspended a colossal, black sphere, hovering in mockery of the sun, spreading darkness and fear instead of light and courage. Such was the Nyght, where dwelt the Darkness. The Nyght, his throne—Tertorem, his kingdom. Here he clung, a leech sucking the blood from its prey.

And out in the world where brightness and beauty could yet be found, rumors spread as common folk whispered and imagined what horrors might lie in such a place.

But it was far, far worse than they could have ever dreamed. For where Darkness and soul meet...hell is born.

oOo

Yador, the current warden of Tertorem, sank onto his throne and troubled over the news just brought in along with two young humans. The new prisoners did not concern him—he cared little about fellow mortals, especially ones as dull as these children. But according to Master Daran, the girl was acquainted with the Aselvian elves and had spoken a rather startling declaration.

The king of Aselvia was dead.

Yador flung his head back in disgust and clasped his long-nailed hands under his chin. If this was true, then his excellent plan had died with the king's last breath. He rose with an angry pant and paced from one corner of the small room to the other. There was little to interrupt his pacing for the room was bare save for a table and chair. Other wardens had treated themselves to frivolities, but Yador was conscious of the fact that His Darkness did not like his servants to become too comfortable with wealth. And anyway, how could he, perched in such a precarious position, afford to take liberties?

He knew that he was the first mortal to be given charge of Tertorem, an honor that he could still barely comprehend. When offered the position by the Voice, he'd eagerly accepted, thinking to further himself in His Darkness's favor. At the time he'd held a reputation as a cunning, cruel man, and he had not been intimidated by the mantle all other wardens left behind—charge of the Prisoner. He'd studied methods used on the Prisoner and which ones he reacted to the most before going down to try his own schemes.

But the Prisoner had broken free. It took three men to hammer him unconscious before his fingers could be pried from Yador's throat.

In the reflection of those beautiful cyan eyes, Yador had seen his own death. In that moment, he realized he wasn't ready to die. He was terrified of dying. As those eyes continued to haunt him, he'd felt his will and potential fraying till by the end of the ten year span, he was the broken man and the Prisoner yet unbroken.

Once more, Yador glared at the report he was writing concerning the death of the king. If only…but it was too late now. His ten years were up. He'd failed. His skin bubbled with fear as he contemplated the consequences of failure. How much longer until *he* showed up? How much longer did he have to come up with a convincing argument?

"Curse that Prisoner," he muttered. "If only he had given in years ago."

"If only he had given in, My Darkness would even now be enthroned in the Higher World."

Yador blanched at the sound of the Voice. There could be no doubt to the identity for no other voice was so smooth as silk, strong as iron, and cold as the heart of evil. Dreading what he knew he would see, Yador slowly lifted his gaze to the yawning hallway before him.

Gliding down the passage came a figure not quite a man, for no man could carry such a presence of power and depravity in such a beautiful form. Dark iron twisted into ghoulish hands and arms that wrapped around his body, and his cloak whorled in his wake as a consuming void.

The demons of His Darkness walked here and there in the shadows of the world, but none were so feared and so reverenced as the Voice, for he had been chosen to represent and speak the Darkness's command.

The Voice did not glance Yador's way as he walked to the table and picked up the report. "But the Prisoner has not given in, and the Higher World remains untouched." His eyes lifted, and he looked over the top of the paper, darker shades of grey swirling around his piercing pupils. "Perhaps you would like to explain why he has not given in?"

Yador's mouth went dry. Why not? Why not for the past several decades, when he'd been under the hands of evil far more powerful? But some sense of self-preservation kept him silent.

"Where is the Prisoner now?" the Voice asked, glancing around as if he expected to see him there in the very room.

"Working in the mines," Yador rasped. "I've sent for him. He should be returning soon."

The Voice nodded, continuing to sift through the papers on the desk. "Perhaps," he said, "you would like to show me what strategy you employed, and perhaps I shall be able to see where you went wrong." His swift gaze bit with the sting of a wasp. "Physical torture in the Mormare Chambers, yes?"

"Yes," Yador gasped. "And every other week, he was sent to the mines." He was fairly sure he heard the Voice mutter, "*completely unoriginal*," and he trembled.

"Well then," the Voice said setting the papers down with a brisk slap. "Let us go to Mormare and see what you devised, shall we?" His face split in a fearfully brilliant smile as he reached out and took Yador by the elbow.

The man flinched, but to his surprise, he felt a hand, without warmth, but with firm flesh and solid bone. He was not comforted. He knew what ran through the Voice's veins.

The Voice turned to a door on the left wall, a door that should have opened to a stairway leading down into bottomless depths. But instead, the pale wisps of Mormare slipped through the entry way and curled around their feet.

Yador had heard that that the demons were given the power to change Tertorem at will, but he had never seen it done. His pupils dilated as they passed into the chamber.

In years past, the warden had been a man to shiver with delight as the spectral fog breathed through his bones, to look with pride upon the hideous instruments and machines contorted in gleams of drifting lights. But now the fog seemed to wrap around him like snakes and the acid of its touch burned his skin, eyes, and lungs. Every step he took, he feared the spurting little fires to burst under his feet. And on every terrible torment, he fancied he read his very name.

The Voice stood amongst the mist and sparks like a king in his hall, and he breathed deep the venomous fumes. "So," he said, thin and soft. "Do tell? Mormare is only as marvelous as its wielder. Tell me…"

What had been expected of him; to create more than what was given? He'd been ruthless yes, but he'd never been an inspired inventor! Yador's mind desperately spiraled in search for the tortures he had ordered. His wavering vision fixed on the furnishings of the chamber, and his memory slowly returned. He stumbled through a loose explanation of his plan, but through it all he watched the demon's face turn steadily colder, and at last his voice faltered and snuffed out like a candle.

One long hiss slipped out from between the Voice's lips, and his eyes narrowed. "You gave him a *routine?*" he growled, and the quiet tone was far worse than any shout. "You gave him a routine?" He snarled, his face twisting into that of a monster. "A body—*especially* an elven body—can get used to almost anything! And you give him a routine!" The Voice was shouting now, anger held by the thinnest of threads. "Don't give him something he can get used to! Switch ideas every day, pull him out in the middle of the night, *invent* new ways to hurt him, rob him of his sleep as he lives in terror wondering what you dream up next!"

The warden stood still as the dead. One wrong move could be his last.

And then the Voice smiled. "Well done," he said.

Yador blinked. The words were wrong. Or if true, they'd surely be followed by death. Neither proved true. "My…my lord?" Swallowing hard, he managed, "I don't understand."

"Of course you don't, you darling fool. Which is what makes you so perfect. No doubt the Prisoner thinks we are tiring of him, that we are becoming inept. He's had time to draw up his strength again, if he has any left. It's very important to be sure you have all your enemy's reserves in the forefront when you strike the devastating blow, always remember that."

With a brisk clap of his hands, he said, "I shall be taking over management of the Prisoner now. Obedience can be taken in ways other than brute force or seduction. From what I have seen, you blundering idiots have only accomplished convincing him of his own self-righteousness and courage."

He turned and walked out of the chamber back to the small study, Yador timidly creeping behind.

"The king of Aselvia is dead," the Voice said, carelessly throwing aside the table to sit in the chair. "Well, he shall be missed. As missed as a thorn in the foot. Chances with him failed anyway, so it's not as if we're now at a disadvantage. I always knew my one chance would be with this Prisoner, and I have planned and plotted far too long to fail. When the Moonscript is mine, My Darkness shall assault the Higher World and bring those pandered celestials into corruption as he should have done from the beginning. The time is right for the endgame."

"How?" Yador whispered, flinching at how his voice shook. "How will you accomplish it, sire?"

The Voice remained silent for another few moments before speaking. "The two children brought in today…"

"Yes, sire?"

The Voice paused, considering. Children. Rarely were they brought to Tertorem, and rarely did the Voice include them in his plans. Though such simple things, they proved a mystery to him, a pawn he could not predict. So full of curiosity they were, so quick to run to the safety of bright places and warm arms. They were not yet set in stubborn pride, and when confronted with fear and pain, they sought comfort and healing. And in that simple seeking, they drew dreadfully near the truth. The Voice dared not keep them among the other prisoners lest they lead the elders after them.

But in this case, he admitted with begrudging, children would serve his purpose well.

"Send in the girl to me, the one whom the elves fancied. And when the Prisoner arrives, send him to the cells next to the children in the Dormen level."

"Sire?" The Dormen level was by far the tamest and most comfortable of quarters to be found in Tertorem.

"Why of course," the Voice said, his face wide with mock offense. "Where'd you think I send them, the Well? No, no, that is no place to become acquainted. It's not always about blood, after all. Often it's about love. At best, love and blood."

oOo

Fear rose to greater heights than Tellie ever dreamt possible. Every time she thought she couldn't possibly feel worse, worse happened. Fear took predominance over everything else—thought, speech, movement. She was no more capable than a corpse as the guards pushed her along, bound and gagged. Nothing existed beyond her fear. It took a long while for her to realize that everything was silent and still, that she'd stopped moving some time ago. It took even longer for her to realize that her hands were no longer bound.

A breath puffed out of her lips, and she became aware of her cold, aching body. Hesitantly, she reached up and pushed the cloth off her eyes. She stood in a simple stone room, quite narrow and small, lit with an eerie twilight. For a moment, she thought she was all alone. The next, she saw the man seated on a throne. Except it wasn't a man. It couldn't be. For no man could embody such evil, could so clearly reveal the ravishment of cruelty in his eyes, could look so horrible and so alluring at the same time.

She hadn't known until she saw him that there was something worse than mere fear.

She hardly dared breathe, frozen like a mouse in sight of a hawk. He wasn't looking at her yet, as his fascination seemed fixed by the wall, but he would look at her, and he would destroy her with his gaze.

Then he did look, and she was not destroyed.

"So you're the little mortal Rendar took an interest in. How charitable of him; I'd expect nothing less," the Voice said.

No one so dreadful should be able to speak so casually and personally, as if Rendar was an old friend. But the impossibility of it seemed to break a chain inside Tellie, giving her a chance for the impossible as well. Her mind's voice, so faint and thin as to be unrecognizable, flitted across her mind. *Tell him nothing of Rendar. The king must be kept safe.* Then she remembered with both a relieving and devastating blow that Rendar was dead, and so in a way, already safe.

The Voice rose, robes swelling like thunder clouds, and swept towards her. She only came to his waist, and he had to pause a few steps away and bend to really look at her.

"Won't you say hello?" he said, brows arching.

She stared up into his eyes. There was no difference between the pupil and iris, and the whites were dark gray, unable to mask the Darkness beneath.

Shaking his head with a tisk, he tried again. "Do you know why you're here?"

This time she managed to whisper, "No."

His teeth were the only white in the room, bright and gleaming. One of his fingers reached out, and though she longed to recoil, she could only stand there as his nails dipped under her collar, then remerged, dragging the necklace's string with them.

The moon medallion lay translucent upon the palm of his hand, perhaps trying to hide. He rubbed his thumb across its surface several times as if he could rub it out. Then he let it drop back onto her chest.

His smile flashed in front of her eyes again, the white-washed walls of a tomb. "We'll speak again later, yes, Tellie? In the meantime, enjoy your quarters."

Footsteps thudded behind her, hands grabbed her shoulders again, and her vision eddied as she fell into darkness once more.

Ever since she could remember, Tellie had been afraid of the dark. Whether in a warm bed or caught outside, a cloud-covered night sent shivers through her bones. But never, never had there been darkness like this. Here, light had never existed. The very blackness was thick and suffocating. It was in and of itself terrifying. She did not fear anything it might hide lurking in the void beyond, for nothing would dare enter this horrible place. It was so silent. She couldn't even hear her own breath.

She was alone, oh, so alone! Alone, alone, alone—

"Tellie?"

She shrieked.

"Oh, bother it, Tellie! I'm right here, don't startle so." Kelm heaved a grumpy sigh and then mumbled something that shouldn't have been heard except in that silence: "Girls."

Her breath returned in hiccupping gasps. She could hear Kelm shifting on the floor nearby. She could feel cold iron clasps around her wrists and stone beneath and behind her. Oh thank heaven, she was not alone and she was somewhere.

"Kelm!" she gasped. "Oh, Kelm!" If she hadn't been in shackles she would have flung herself in his direction and covered him in kisses. She blinked. Where had that thought come from?

"Yeah, yeah, I'm here," the boy grumbled. "I can't believe this is actually happening."

"You could have spoken up sooner! I've been dying of fright!" she snapped, everything inside blazing up in anger. "Where are we and why did they take us?"

"Don't ask me," Kelm snapped. "You were the one meddling with elves, and magpies, and magic necklaces!" At her dead silence, he softened and said, "It was some sort of dark magic. I've heard the merchant talk about such things, but...but well, I guess I never expected to experience it."

"But where are we?" she whispered. "Do you think they took us very far?"

"They used some kind of portal, I guess." He hesitated for a dreadful moment before admitting, "And we are far from home, Tell. I don't know how far, but…far. You were in a faint when they took us down here, but we're a long ways below ground."

Tellie absorbed the news slowly, fearing that any swift processing would send her into a panic. She shifted, the shackles clacking together sharply.

"They locked us in individual cells down here," Kelm continued. "I'm not sure why they bothered to chain us. I thought I might be able to pull out of the cuffs, but they're just too small. What about you?"

Gladly seizing the welcome distraction, she wiggled and strained her wrists till the edge cut into her skin. But the chains had clearly been designed for someone larger, and with a raw scrape, she slid free. "I'm out! I can't believe that worked!"

"Is the cell locked?"

Lifting herself on unsteady legs, she stumbled up and explored her cell. A stone wall bordered the back, and the other two walls were built by metal bars. Kelm's cell was to her left. The door of her cell was also barred. She found the lock, but after fiddling with it for several minutes, she gave up with a sigh. "No good," she moaned. She wrapped her arms around her knees and rubbed her chaffed wrists.

The silence was too hideous, so she whispered, "What are we going to do?"

But any answer was interrupted by the distant clang of an opening and closing gate. Several footsteps tramped towards them, and the light of a torch bounced across the walls of a stone passage.

She almost let out a yelp of joy at the sight of that light. But around a corner came four figures, and all her fear returned. One walked in front, carrying the torch, and two others followed, holding the fourth figure between them. She expected them to turn into one of the many cells they were passing, but to her shock, they came right to the cell next to her. She shrank back against the wall, hoping they wouldn't notice that she was out of her chains.

Grumbling something, one of the guards unlocked the door and swung it open. The other two marched in, pushed their prisoner roughly to the ground and chained him to the wall. Snapping some curse at him, they withdrew, locked the cell shut, and went away.

The metal door slammed in the distance, and the prison plunged once more into heavy darkness. She didn't dare try to speak to the prisoner. After all, he might actually be deserving of cells and chains. A madman, a murderer, you just couldn't tell…

Kelm had no such fear. "Hey," he called. "Who are you?"

The prisoner gave a startled cry, followed by an indistinguishable curse as if he was angry the cry escaped.

"Neighbors," the stranger said, voice harsh and cutting. "Just my luck."

Yes, Tellie thought, scooting to the far side. *Sounds like the mad, murdering type.*

"Sorry," Kelm said. "We didn't mean to intrude, but we were just brought in…er…well, do you know what this place is?"

There was a long pause. Then—

"Tertorem."

It was then that Tellie was struck by the sound of the stranger's voice. It was a clear voice—clear and strong, not the sort one would expect to hear in a prison. Strange, it was almost familiar, but not familiar enough for her to place it.

"Well, that's a fittingly awful name," her friend said with an unsteady laugh. "I'm Kelm. And you are?"

Another interminable silence hung in the air. And then the answer came.

"Errance."

7

These games never end. Every time I think they have run out of new cruelties, another begins. It is the way of it, the way of death.

A name was only a name. There could have been dozens of men named Errance. But she knew of only one, and in that moment she recognized why the stranger's voice sounded so familiar—it was like Rendar's, only younger and full of hate.

No. The possibility was too much to consider. It was far too overwhelming. He couldn't...couldn't be...

A hush held the cells captive since the stranger had spoken his name, but now the man spoke again, and the bitterness in his voice whipped like a lash. "You're here to win my trust, aren't you? In a gesture of *good will*, I'll let you know now that you'd best kill yourselves the first chance you get before they decide to doom you to eternal torment in reward for your failure."

Stunned, Tellie sagged back against the wall and raised trembling hands to her head. She'd barely heard his words, barely noticed the cruelty of them.

"You think me morbid," the man said at last in a tone that indicated he really didn't care what they thought at all.

Kelm's voice sputtered back into life. "Um. Uh. I...I don't think we are who you think we are, and we're not working for anyone if that's what you're saying. We don't have a notion who you are."

Tellie's tangled senses knotted and unknotted before bursting out into four words. "*Prince* Errance? Of *Aselvia?*"

There was a moment's pause.

"Don't have a clue who I am, hmm?" the prisoner said, sarcasm as sharp as a sword. "So there's two of you, is there? Very well."

It was him. It had to be! It was impossible, but there was no other explanation.

She crawled over to the side of the cell and gripped the iron bars till her fingers ached. "Errance!" she said, struggling to keep her voice steady. "I know who you are. You are the prince of Aselvia. But...but how are you alive? They all think you've been dead for seventy years. I met the elves! They're so kind, and I learned all about you, and you died, but you didn't, and now I'm here, and you're here, and it's so unbelievable, but it's true! How can you possibly be alive? There was your picture and everything, and the stories say you died. What happened, Errance?"

She ran out of breath and waited for a response, panting. Kelm had gone dead silent, most likely too bewildered to compose a word. She peered into the solid blackness where the prisoner sat, straining to see any sign of him.

Then he spoke.

"Very clever."

He didn't believe her. Of course he didn't. If he'd been in this dark place since his assumed death, then he had no reason to trust her declaration. And yet disappointment dropped heavily onto her shoulders, and she crept back over to the side near Kelm and drew her knees up to her chest, wrapping her arms around her legs.

Chains jangled. "Tellie," Kelm whispered, "How do you know this man?"

Tellie bit her lip, fearing his doubt as well. "You remember the story of the elf prince who died in Shadowshade Forest?" she said in a voice barely above a sigh. "The elves I met were there to honor him...Prince Errance was his name." Her voice rose higher as her emotions began to knot in her throat. "Kelm, I just know this man is the same Errance, but he thinks we're evil, and I have no idea where we are, but wherever we are, he's here, and that's a miracle! But he doesn't trust us, so what's the point? Errance isn't dead, he's alive. Oh, Kelm, this would mean so much to Leoren and Casara. What am I saying—this means so much to me! I was told to find the next king of Aselvia, and I have! It's him—I've found the prince!" And then, unable to express herself further in words, she buried her face in her knees and burst into tears.

"What in Orim are you babbling about?" Kelm demanded. "Did you say you were supposed to find the next king? That doesn't make any sense! Tellie! What didn't you tell me?"

The only answer she could give him was a stormy sob.

He sighed. "Honestly."

She was unable to stop crying for quite a while, but at last her sobs faded into sniffles before dying away altogether. Kelm did not press her at once for any answer, and the captive next cell had not volunteered a sound since. How long the silence continued could not be certain. In that deep dungeon, hours or days might have passed without recognition. It was long enough that Tellie startled when Kelm spoke again.

"So can you explain any better now?"

Rubbing a hand across her eyes, she managed, "Well, um—"

The door far down the passage slammed open.

Torchlight flickered across the corner wall, followed by one man broad enough to be two. After hooking the torch in a wall bracket, he paused in front of the Errrance's cell, fumbled for the keys, and unlocked it. Since the light did not reach into the shadows of the cell, Tellie listened to the guard unlock eight chains on the captive. When the guard shoved the prisoner out into the hall ahead of him, she noted that the captive was the taller of the two. Not as tall as Rendar, but still his silhouette struck her as so elvish that any last doubts about his identity fled.

"Didn't I just get back?" Errance asked dryly.

The guard snorted. "The Voice has come," he said, roughly pulling the elf's arms behind his back and drawing a cord tight around the wrists.

At the mention of that name, Tellie remembered the terrible man she'd met just before coming to this cell. His grinning teeth flashed in her mind's eye, and she flinched.

Then the guard left the elf standing alone and turned to her cell. Her hands flew over her mouth to stifle a cry of dismay as the huge man opened the door and stomped inside. She shrank back and tried to slip her hands back into the shackles, but it was too late. The guard reached for the chains and started in surprise.

"Clever little wretch," he growled. Grabbing her by the arm, he thrust her out into the hall next to the elf and headed to Kelm's cell.

Her heart ramming against her throat, Tellie turned to the elf.

There in flesh and blood stood Prince Errance.

Three things struck her at once. First, the orphanage matron had once told her it was improper to stare at a man with no shirt. Second, it was surely more improper if that man was an elf. Third, no one had ever told her what to do if the man looked like this.

Scars and shadows rippled in jagged streaks across his body—burns, lashes, piercings. Red, white, dark, and light. Fresh and bloody, old and deep. Mottled bruises. Scars as thick and webbed as lace. Muscles stood out on his gaunt frame, but they didn't seem quite right, as if they were forced to exist even while skin stretched over jutting bones. Though his face was still as handsome as in the painting, all the fair features were now hard with pain and loathing. Three thin black scars ran through his right brow and into the cheek, and his dark hair fell in heavy strands to his skeletal waist. The light of the torch reflected in his eyes as it might have reflected on shattered glass.

Tellie stared, horror chilling her being, and she could not tear her eyes away.

Errance stared back, and something like surprise flitted over his face. "You are but children," he murmured.

"Actually, I'm fourteen," Kelm said as he was pushed up alongside them by the guard.

"No talking 'mongst the captives," the guard snarled. He turned towards them, his ugly face stuck in a permanent leer, and peered into each of their faces. He looked at Tellie last. There he paused, squinting.

Tellie looked back at him, watching the torch shadows flicker on his meaty face. A chill prickled up along the back of her neck. All at once she had no idea what to do or how to get him to stop staring at her. Her gaze darted down to the floor.

"Well," the man snarled. "A pretty girl down 'ere. What's yor name, 'ittle princess?" He made a grab for her chin, and she stumbled back with a gasping cry.

A shadow stepped between them, a tall and solid shadow. "Guard," Errance said. "Leave the girl alone."

The guard took a pace back and considered him. Then he gave a throaty chuckle and wagged his head. "I've heard you have some spice. I'll fix that." He drew back his arm and struck Errance across the face. The elf's head snapped to the side, and the grunt of the guard's laughter rumbled down the hall.

Aghast, Tellie shrank against Kelm, who moved protectively in front of her, though his whole body trembled.

For a moment, Errance remained still, looking only at the wall. His eyes turned back to the guard first. Then his head slowly pivoted around to face him. He breathed in deep, his chest rising and falling. "You're new, aren't you?" he said, strangely quiet.

The guard sneered.

"You must be," the elf continued softly, his gaze dropping to the floor. "Otherwise you would know that people have done that so many times, I don't even feel it anymore."

Without warning, he dipped into a low crouch and twisted, swinging his elbow up and into the man's jaw. He whirled back, driving his opposite knee up into the man's stomach, and as the guard doubled over with a gasp, he took a few steps back, spun and swung his leg like a sword, smashing the heel into the guard's temple.

With an awful groan, the man dropped to the ground in a heap.

Errance tossed his head back, flicking long brown hair behind his shoulder. "What about you? Could you feel that?"

The guard gave an inarticulate moan.

"I'll take that as a yes." Errance took a step forward and bent slightly at the waist towards him. "Listen, *human*, I might be a plaything for demons, but I will not be toyed with by mere mortal scraps." He straightened and glared down at him. "Now get up and lead us on. I, for one, am never late."

Slowly the man stumbled to his feet and took up the torch. He held the side of his head, blood from a broken tooth or bitten tongue sliding down his jaw, and gave Errance a wide berth as he slunk forward. He motioned them on, the torch's flames fluttering.

Errance turned to the two children.

Tellie and Kelm gasped and backed away, their eyes as round as saucers. Who was in charge of whom here? This elf, beaten and bound, had proven the master of the cringing guard.

The prince looked the two up and down, his face shadowed with the departing light of the torch. "Keep close," he said, at last. "And keep quiet."

He turned and walked forward into the devouring darkness.

With scarcely a glance, the Voice had turned the warden's small study into a wider hall of dark glass and destroyed the warden's old desk and chair in a spiral of fire. Whether or not Yador recognized that sign of future reckoning could not be said. It could be certain that the mortal was a pale shadow of his former self, cringing at the side of the Voice's great throne.

The Voice drummed his fingers impatiently atop the chair arm. Errance would come in time, guard or no guard. He would have no choice, and the manner of his arrival would answer many things.

At long last the door on the left side of the room—the very one that led to the torture chambers minutes before—opened and the guard stepped through. The Voice looked past him in an attempt to see his Prisoner, but his gleaming eyes caught sight of the blood upon the man's mouth.

"Oh," he said, amused. "Did you trip and fall down the stairs?"

The man's face wrinkled in confusion. "The Prisoner hit me," he blurted, his eyes widening in fear

"Of course he did," the Voice said, teeth baring in a hungry grin. "Now step aside, idiot, and let him in."

Tellie had begun to fear that the stairs would never end. Now that they'd reached the top, she wished the steps would rise on forever rather than meet whatever waited for them. But when Errance stepped through the door, she followed. Some part of her recognized the room as the same she had stood in hours before. But it was not the same. The floors and walls cast back reflections twisted and cut into horrific images, and beyond that glass writhed visions darker still, threatening to shatter through.

Trembling, she tore her gaze from the walls and floors and focused on the flower print of her dress. But even the pretty little flowers seemed to take different shapes that concealed leering faces. A suffocating terror rose in her throat, choking away the breath to scream.

Then she saw Errance.

Like a banner in a battlefield, like a pillar upholding a roof, he stood proud and defiant. He did not deign to look at anything in the room, but his mere stance defied it all. No matter how wasted or broken, he stood straight, and for a moment, that was all that mattered.

Tellie's shaking stilled. So the Voice did not hold sway over everything here. The knowledge swelled inside her like fresh air, and though she still hunkered in the shadows with Kelm, her mind rang clear. Kelm's hand squeezed her own, and she knew he'd recovered too. She risked a glance at the Voice, fearing that if he turned his smile towards her, all gained ground would wash out from under her feet.

She needn't have worried.

The Voice had eyes only for his Prisoner. He leaned back into his throne, hand resting under his smiling mouth and leg crossed over knee like a dandy king. For several moments he remained exactly like that. Staring. Smiling.

And then he rose. The very movement might have sent armies into retreat, but the prisoner prince did not flinch even as his captor walked to within inches of him.

"Always, always," the Voice said, "you surprise me. I admit, I had hoped you'd recovered since the last few times we met, but this…." He took a step back, waving an appraising arm, and chuckled deep in his throat. "You've outdone yourself really. It seems each time you are torn down, you rise greater than before. I can only attribute it to your celestial light. Such a marvel it is to sustain and strengthen you."

He swung away and spread out his arms as if he addressed a great audience, though no one stood in front of him save the cringing warden in the corner. "My Darkness, is he not magnificent? Is he not the brightest star in this Lower World?" He wheeled back, cloak wafting like wings. "All hail the new king of Aselvia!"

Dead silence followed his declaration.

For a moment, Tellie did not even understand the significance of it.

Until Errance, so still and so strong, suddenly swayed like a tree in a storm. The pillar shuddered as if struck at the foundation. The banner torn from its place. And she watched as he started to keel and fall.

He's fainting. Someone should catch him. Not me. I'm not strong enough. The thought vaguely flitted into her mind, but before she could call out any appeal, The Voice stepped forward, hand outstretched.

Errance recoiled and stumbled back a few steps. Then he straightened and stood tall again, and his face became more like stone than ever.

"What? No questions? No tears?" The Voice shook his head, eyes wide. "My, you are heartless. Don't even want to know the details of your father's death. Afraid I'll tell a lie? You believed me quick enough just now. Very well, we'll ask the witness. No one could doubt the innocence of her face!"

Tellie did not realize he meant her till she felt the heat of his gaze begin to wither her skin. Gasping in terror, she looked at him, then to Errance, and then back to the floor. *I should have told him before! He should not have had to know like this,* she thought desperately. But there had been no time, no time, and this certainly was not the time. "I...I..."

"See here, mister." Kelm's voice broke the condemning hush. "From what I understand, she wasn't even there for the elf king's death. Personally, I still have my doubts—"

"Silence, whelp!" The Voice's teeth snapped, the bars of a cage slamming shut.

He dismissed the children in the same moment his gaze left their faces and returned to Errance. "Perhaps you have no questions, no doubts, because you know. You know better than anyone." Fingers lashed out and caught Errance by the chin. The Voice bent down, close. "He's gone...gone to a place you cannot ever follow." The whisper curled into steam, ghostly and fading. The demon's pale fingers curled against the prince's cheek, as gentle and kind as a father's caress. "Poor boy...." the Voice whispered. "All alone."

Then his arm whipped back and struck the elf as if to shatter bone.

Tellie yelped and clung tighter to Kelm as the prince staggered and collapsed to one knee under the blow. She willed him to remain as unscathed as from the guard's fist, but even he had called himself a plaything for the demons, and he remained on his knees, head bowed. And yet—her heart leapt in eager hope—and yet even from here she could see his eyes glittering with the same defiance, the same strength.

Circling behind, the Voice caught his hair at the scalp and pulled back till his chin nearly pointed to the ceiling. "Just as well, though," he said, lip curling. "I wonder if your father would even recognize you now. Such a sweet thing you were when we first met, but so pathetic. Pale and bruised, blood and tears streaming down your cheeks. Such fear. And now...now...I do believe that is hatred in your beautiful blue eyes." He looked horrifically pleased, like a little boy who just mutilated a creature and was very proud of it.

Errance had met his tormenter's stare without waver, no matter the strain of his neck, but now his eyes fluttered shut, his throat collapsed in a labored swallow, and his shoulders shuddered.

For just that one flitting second, Tellie saw that frightened young prince long ago, saw the same blood now trailing from his mouth. And she snapped.

"LEAVE HIM ALONE!" she shouted.

Both their heads lashed towards her, stunned.

Tellie paled, and her breath left her as the Voice's eyes narrowed. For the first time he looked at her. Not as a pawn, not as a joke. But at her. His consideration chilled her core.

Errance looked from the Voice to Tellie and back again. Then he spat out a stream of words, strange and beautiful, but spoken with such viciousness that Tellie flinched.

The Voice looked again to the elf, the surprise on his face increasing. "Well, then," he scoffed. "Who knew you could still speak your native tongue? And what a nasty thing to say with such an exquisite language. Precious little prince, you aren't so pure and perfect anymore, are you?"

Kelm grabbed Tellie's wrist, and she gave in to his tug without a struggle for her knees trembled like jelly. She knew that whatever Errance had said, he'd said only to remove the Voice's attention from her. She was terribly grateful to him and terribly furious at herself.

"An obvious diversion, of course, but lucky for her," the Voice continued, somehow giving Tellie a pointed look without turning his gaze from Errance, "it worked." He raised his hand, the prince's hair still caught fast, and pulled him to his feet.

"Now then, Your Highness," the Voice said softly, slipping an arm around his shoulders and pulling him towards the far wall. "Shall we go and celebrate your rise to rule? We must have a coronation ceremony later, of course, you can hardly be called a king without one. For now, shall we mourn the death of your father? I have memories to share I'll warrant you've never heard."

Don't let him go in there, Tellie's mind whispered. *Do something. Don't just let him be taken there.* But she remained as still as the stone upon which she stood.

The wall opened as they approached. And for a moment, a dark red smoke spilled forth....and then it was not smoke, but the gentle mist of a spring morning. And beyond the door rolled a green land of forest and glades, all sunlit and sparkling with fresh rain. If there was any land that looked as paradise imagined....

Tellie's mouth dropped open, and despite the warning screaming within, her feet stumbled forward. She forced herself to stop when she saw Errance halt.

The Voice looked back at Errance, brow raised in mock curiosity. "What now, Prince? Surely it's a sight for sore eyes." He laughed and jerked him from his defiant stance like one jerked a balking horse. "Come along."

"What about them?" the warden suddenly said.

Pausing at the very threshold, the Voice of His Darkness sent the man a look that would have withered an entire world. "What about whom?"

"The children," the man said, pointing a trembling finger.

Tellie and Kelm shrank together, willing their very bodies to become as small as dust on the air.

"The children," the Voice repeated. Then he shrugged. "What are they to me?" And without another glance, he thrust Errance ahead, and the walls closed shut behind them.

8

As the wall closes, the vibration of its force courses through my body. That is why my heart shudders; it is not because of fear. Fear, ha, that is a weakness, and pain has purged such things from me. Yet as I look into my captor's dark eyes, another shudder runs through me, this one without reason, curse it. This is the seventh time we have met since that night long ago. He had always come to pawn me off to the next Master. He has never taken the role of Master himself.

Not until the cage door clanged shut behind her did Tellie realize she'd been taken back to the cell. The guard snapped the lock into place with fumbling fingers, took the torch, and left the dungeon to the darkness.

After a dazed moment she huddled down into the corner, noticing that the guard had been in too frightened a state to chain her.

"Kelm, are you there?"

"Yes," the boy replied miserably. "Golly, this is a mess."

"They took him. And I did nothing. What are they doing to him?"

"Better not to know," he said with a shudder. "But...but...he can take it, I think. He is an elf, after all." The fear in his voice changed to admiration. "The first elf I've ever met! Did you see how he stood up to that villain? Barely flinched."

"Yeah," she said, a bit more dreamily than intended. "I saw…"

"Well," Kelm said after a moment's pause. "You needn't say it quite that way."

"What way?"

"Like you're smitten."

"Kelm!" she squeaked. "I am not! He's just…just very impressive." But she blushed scarlet and thanked the fates he couldn't see her. "Anyway," she continued, uncomfortable and subdued. "We shouldn't be talking like this when they're h-hurting him."

She rubbed a hand down her stiff neck with a sigh, and her fingers brushed across the thin thread against her skin.

The moon medallion. It had quite left her mind in all the excitement. She clawed for the delicate strand and pulled it out. There it shone in front of her bleary eyes, almost a perfect circle of light.

Kelm stirred. "Do you have a candle?" he asked incredulously.

"It's that necklace I found," she breathed. "The moon medallion." She sank back against the wall, the necklace cradled against her chest. Perhaps it was her imagination, but it almost made her feel warmer. Why hadn't that dark villain taken it from her when he had the chance? Why had it come to her at all?

"Kelm," she said very softly, very uncertainly. "What do you think about God?"

The boy coughed. "Pardon?"

"I mean, I've sort of believed in him. I was always taught to pray to him. But the elves actually seemed to believe in his existence as a guiding force in the world. And they have a name for him and everything. I mean, I've heard that name, but they use it so personally. And since we seem to be caught on the wrong side of spiritual things, well…" Her throat thickened as she talked as if the shadows wanted to suffocate her. She swallowed, relieved to discover she could still breathe. "What do you think?"

Kelm gave it lengthy consideration. "Well, I've always respected him, but like you said, it's just sort of an engrained behavior. It's the popular religion of West Orim, but you find many other beliefs and gods in the east, north, and south. Still, there is something special about the stories told of Ayeshune. There's a lot of hope to it, a promise of redemption from darkness."

"The elves believe in him," she said again. "And they are still alive from the beginning of the world. They would know better than anyone who the real God is, right?"

"I'd think so," he said. "It's a pity then that the elves have hidden away so long that many people have dismissed them as myths as well."

Tellie did not reply, and the dark closed back between them with malicious swiftness. The medallion fell forgotten from her grasp, and she sank into the swallowing void with little thought. After all, she was so tired, and slipping into sleep would free her from this endless...

The prison door hammered against the wall. She jumped at the sound, and immediately tucked the moon medallion into her apron pocket. Again, the light of a torch came flickering down the passage, but only three figures followed this time, and the man in the middle hung upright only by the mercy of his captors. The guards brought the prisoner to Errance's cell and locked him back in shackles, then retreated without a word. The light faded away and the door banged again, the crash echoing through the passages with despairing doom.

"Errance!" She scrambled to the bars, trying to see some difference in the black curtain before her vision. "Are you hurt very much?"

No answer came. But the silence was now shattered by a faint and rasping sound, like a crusty piece of paper torn again and again. She listened to it, puzzled, for several minutes before at last understanding the source. She should have recognized it at once, but then, it had been so long since she'd heard the final breaths of the dying.

No, no, she could not have found him now just for him to die. Pain tearing through her heart, she clung to the bars and anxiously waited for each hoarse swell.

Then she became aware of the smell. This too was both horrid and familiar.

Her memory flew back to the time when while at the orphanage, she had been sent by the Madame on an errand to the butcher's shop. She had not been able to find the butcher and had gone in the back of his shed to search for him and—*oh!* Carcasses of animals hung everywhere, and upon a table, a deer cut in half, red liquid pooling off the table onto the floor, filling the air with the sinister, sordid smell of blood.

Her hands clamping over her mouth, Tellie scrambled back from the cell. Her foot caught on her skirt and she fell flat on her back. The momentary pain distracted her from her churning stomach, and the bile that had been threatening to spew out sank back down. She shuddered and tried not to breathe in the aroma. Blood. She hated the smell of it, she hated the sight of it. The boys and even some of the girls at the orphanage had accused her of being weak, but no amount of teasing ever convinced her to get over the horror of blood.

"Kelm," she whispered and reached through the bars in desperation for her friend. Her heart leaped as his fingers twined through hers, and then his breath was warm upon her cheek. She did not need to speak her fear for the shuddering breath filled the silence around.

"Kelm," she said again, voice very small. "I don't want to die. My life seems so very empty."

The boy shifted beside her, his hand gripping hers a little tighter. "Why...why, that's a silly thing to say, Tellie! True, you've had a rough go of it at times, but there's been plenty of brightness."

"Like what?" she said. "I haven't done anything worthwhile." This darkness consumed all knowledge of beauty and peace.

"Well, well," Kelm said, clearly struggling. "Well, you met me! I made you spill your bucket of water, but I filled another for you. You had some blue flowers in your hair. And there was the time I helped you get the bee nest from the forest. We ate the comb on the miller's roof."

Tellie did remember then, and many other moments of sunshine and happiness besides. But that felt so long ago now, and so pointless if only to end in this dungeon. Just for a few moments of her life, she had felt true purpose in the elf king's commission. Now that chance drained away like sand through an hourglass. And as hours of their lives passed, they listened together to the elf's breath fade, sputter, and then finally perish.

"He's dead," Tellie said with a hiccupping sob. "Oh, they killed him!"

Errance laughed.

The harsh sound broke on a cry of pain, followed by a hiss of anger. "A happy thought," he growled. "Sadly, no."

Both the girl and boy yelped in a mix of terror and delight.

"But you stopped breathing!" Tellie protested.

He coughed, a thick and wet cough. "I started breathing quietly. Now hush. I need time."

If time was what Errance needed, it was the one blessing granted him. Time stretched endlessly in this void. For Tellie and Kelm, the void was a monster, consuming their mortal lives with no promise of anything but death at the end. Sometimes Tellie would touch her hand just to be sure that wrinkles hadn't yet appeared on her skin.

When Errance spoke again, his voice had much changed. It was now controlled, calm, charismatic even. Such a far cry from before that Tellie almost wondered if the body next door had somehow been exchanged.

"So. You have a story, I suspect. I must ask, did they give you the script or did you have to come up with everything from the top of your head?"

Well. For being so wounded, he was remarkably insolent. Before either could answer, the elf spoke again, and now he carefully concealed pain and fear in his manner.

"You saw my father die?"

"No!" Tellie exclaimed. "No, Leoren only told me so. As I said, I met the elves and they told me about you."

"And my father. You spoke to him?"

"Yes."

After a dreadful pause, he asked, "What did he say?"

Tellie took a deep breath, reassured by the squeeze of Kelm's hand on her shoulder. "He said I was to give the moon medallion to the next king of Aselvia." And she held the necklace aloft.

Errance swore.

Tellie's mouth dropped open in shock. Hearing humans swear was annoying enough, but hearing an elf swear was appalling.

Errance lunged against the bars, taut on his chains, and his hand stretched through, grasping wildly. "Give that to me!" he shouted.

She flinched back. "You needn't shout so."

He spoke through his teeth. "*Give it* to me."

But her temper flared to life. "As far as I'm concerned, the next king of Aselvia does *not* swear." Kelm snickered, but she ignored him. "Especially in the presence of a lady."

The elf's hand closed and drew back against the bar. He did not speak for a few minutes, and his haggard breaths gradually died down. "All right," he hissed. "I apologize, *your ladyship*. But that is my necklace and...and..." He paused and took a deep breath. "Could I at least touch it?"

At the sudden pleading in his voice, Tellie's irritation cooled, but she still gripped the necklace strand tightly as she held it out to him.

The instant his fingers brushed the medallion's surface, the light dimmed and the moon turned grey. She stared at the medallion in surprise.

Errance's hand drew back into the darkness. "You are right," he said, subdued and barely audible. "I'm not ready for it."

Then as quickly as flint is struck, his fire snapped back into life, and he snarled, "The necklace was taken the same night as me. How dare you suggest my father had it?"

"Oh, but the dark men did have it," she said in haste. "They showed up in my inn with it, but the magpie stole it away, and then Kelm and I chased after..."

"The magpie. The magpie?" His voice became very terrible, but she could not say if that was frightening or tragic. "What was this magpie's name?"

"Why would a magpie have a name...?" Kelm began, but she was quick to

interrupt him.

"Oh, oh, er…Farflight. No, not that. Fly…Flyfar! Your father called him Flyfar, I think."

This was considered without response, and she held her breath in silent hope for his belief. She had to win his trust, or else how could she ever bring him back? If they ever had a chance to escape this miserable place, anyway.

"What else did my father say?" he whispered.

She searched desperately for something comforting, something kind. "He said…he said darkness could not last forever."

Silence fell with the impact of a stone shutting a tomb. A tomb that could never be opened. A tomb hiding away a body as it decayed. A body once full of life and love. A love meant for him, now torn away for eternity.

She shrank away, and suddenly she sat no longer in a dank dungeon, but within an attic, curled up in the shadows. She was a child again, sobbing herself to sleep, because the undertaker had carried her parent's bodies away. The only people who loved her were dead, and she was alone. *Alone.*

Then Errance spoke, sardonic venom laced through every word. "Your story is well conceived. I'll let the Darkness know you were good little pawns, and perhaps he'll think about using you again."

"I say," Kelm exclaimed, drowning out Tellie's yelp of frustration. "That's not fair at all. We're locked down here, same as you, and we don't want to stay any more than you do."

"And if you don't believe my story," Tellie cried, "for that matter, I can hardly believe you! The elves were certain you died, so explain that!"

"That's simple," he said with a snort. "My clothes drenched in blood and the gore of my comrades should have been convincing enough. No other body was left whole and recognizable so why should have mine been different?"

She pretended she hadn't asked and that he hadn't told her.

"But according to Tellie," Kelm said doubtfully, "that was seventy years ago. Have you been kept here the entire time? What for?"

"You mean they didn't tell you?" he snipped.

Taking a deep breath, Tellie tried to push back the hot anger rising in her chest. "Rendar told me some. The Darkness wanted vengeance against the celestial elves, yes?"

"Fine, I can be fair. You might as well know what you're after. Only those with Celestial light can read the Moonscript, and the Darkness believes that through that book he can reach the Higher World and destroy its people. There. Does that make any more sense?"

"No," said Kelm.

"Yes!" Tellie cried. "That explains everything. You mean this entire time they have tried to bend you to their will, and it hasn't worked? How brave of you!"

She paused and considered her own words for a moment. How on earth did anyone survive seventy years of this kind of life anyway? Holding up the moon medallion, she peered through the bars in an effort to see some glimpse of him. The faintest impressions she saw suggested far too much. "How are you still alive?"

"For knowing so much, you're remarkably uninformed."

"Does it have do with your light? Casara said something about it making a person immortal."

He sighed. Heavily. It sounded too wet and strained. "It heals me. No one else. But I'm only alive because the Darkness wishes for me to be."

"Well, this is all splendid," Kelm said. "But I have a question of my own now. Is this the privy bucket?"

All the glorious thunder and excitement in Tellie's head zipped into oblivion. "*Kelm!* What kind of question is that?"

Errance sighed again. His chains rattled as he shifted, followed by the thunk of wood against stone. "Yes, it appears they gave us some. My. Somebody felt generous."

Tellie opened her mouth to ask what was so generous about that, but then she was gripped with the horror of reality. She'd never considered such a drawback of prison life.

But Kelm wasn't done. "Where do they dump it?"

"I've been in this part of Tertorem no longer than you. These are far tamer cells than I've encountered. But I assume if they bothered with buckets, they empty them into some sewer drain nearby."

"Just how big are the sewer drains?"

"Large? There are many cells here. Must have been for an overabundance of unimportant prisoners."

"Please just get to the point," Tellie begged. "This is disgusting."

"I'm not being disgusting, I'm being smart," Kelm shot back, wounded dignity in every syllable. "Errance, I wonder if it's possible for people to escape this place by traveling through the sewer passages."

Utter silence.

I wonder if it's possible to throw up on an empty stomach, Tellie thought. Her limber imagination conjured up various images at Kelm's words. Her tongue lumped up several times before she gagged, "Kelm, that is the awfulest thing you've ever come up with and that is so…so…so very like a boy!"

"Shut up," Errance said.

Her mouth dropped open, and she wheeled around towards the elf, churning stomach forgotten in her outrage. Shut up? He, an elf, had told her to… Disheartened, she scooted back against the wall.

"No," Errance said after a moment of consideration. "It would not work. The Darkness would have thought to block off such an escape."

"But why would he?" Kelm protested. "He's not physical and doesn't have to worry about such…er…things."

Wonderful tact, Tellie thought in disgust. But an uncomfortable feeling began to steal across her mind, a horrible, prickling voice saying that Kelm might be right.

"You do not understand. You cannot get out. The only way in is by the Darkness that brought you here. Even if you found a way physically possible, his will would bar your escape."

"Oh come," the boy said. "He can't be everywhere at once. And if he isn't paying attention to the sewers, why would that be barred?"

"You are a little fool. But do as you wish, your kind always does."

"About that," Kelm said. "It will be necessary to have the keys, and I'm not, well, I'm not quite certain I could heist them off the guard. I mean, I could have a go, but…" His voice faded away in hopeful suggestion, but he received no reply.

The door far down the passage opened and slammed again. Tellie straightened in alarm. "Just how often do they come down here?"

Errance drew in a long breath. "Either I've been summoned or these guards think themselves bold. Just be quiet. I'll take care of it if they try anything."

Tellie slid over to her corner next to Kelm, and tucked her hand into her pocket, drawing comfort from the smooth, unsullied surface of the medallion.

"What is it this time?" Errance asked when the guard entered his cell. His voice was a sheathed knife just waiting to be drawn.

"Orders of the Voice," was the only thing the man said, but it was enough. Errance gave no protest as the guard unsnapped the shackles and pulled him to his feet.

Tellie shot up. "Leave him be, he's still hurt!" The words echoed back unheeded, sounding silly even in her own ears. She could only watch, sorry and helpless, as the prince was stolen away again. At the sound of the closing door, she sank back to the floor. She wouldn't cry, she told herself. Crying never helped anything, it just gave headaches.

"Kelm," she whispered. "Are you certain the sewers would work?"

His voice sounded small and frightened. "I read a book where it did. It's our best chance, I think."

"How do you know it will lead a way out and not just go forever into the ground? What about the men who built it, why did they not escape?"

"They were probably killed," Kelm said glumly. "I heard of a king who killed all the workers who built his temple just so they couldn't build another like it."

She swallowed hard, leaning back and contemplating the idea of traveling deeper and deeper into the earth, only for there to be no way out but back to this dungeon. Yet worse still was the thought of the elven prince captive here a day longer.

"We must try it then," she said.

oOo

One could hardly believe how swiftly the world fell to pieces.

Leoren ran a hand through his hair, trying to steady his ragged heart with a long breath. His first task upon the king's death, and he'd already failed. They'd lost the girl…she'd vanished before their very eyes, leaving only dark markings upon the ground in her place. And they'd had no idea how to find her. In the end, there was no choice but to return to Aselvia, there to lay Rendar's body to rest and to plan some way to track the poor girl's whereabouts.

Usually, when he came back to Aselvia from the world beyond, the peace of his surroundings would soothe the stress lining his face. The serene birdsongs, the floral scents, the comfort of his own chair. But not this time.

This…Tellie…this orphan girl who needed help. And he had thought that he could help her…give her a chance like others had taken a chance on him—a half-breed. He paused, surprised. It had been a while since his mind had flung that accusation at him, so what brought it up now?

I know you have always struggled to value your place in this world. The girl is the same. So take care of her.

His fingers fisted into his hair. What kind of horrible fate had they lost her to? She was innocent; she'd trusted them, and then this—? He'd seen Darkness in those men's shadows, but he hadn't expected this level of power. They weren't mere thugs—they were directly working for the Darkness himself.

That made these men their only real lead. His best chance was to return to Dormandy and seek knowledge of their identities. Ask for stories of similar occurrences.

Similar occurrences. Ha.

That forest was cursed to steal young, beautiful life.

But he'd find her. He had to.

In the meantime, they would have to bury Rendar without him. That was hard to swallow, but it was the only option. The entire kingdom was reeling in shock of their king's death, but already a grave was being carefully dug next to their fair queen beneath her tree. Every elf would gather there in the Forest of Souls and light a candle in the night to remember and mourn.

A rap at the door startled his misery, and a tall elf woman in armor stepped inside. "I have selected soldiers for the search force, my lord," she said. "We are ready to depart on your command."

"Thank you, Commander Maril," Leoren sighed. He picked up his cloak and a piece of paper fluttered from one of its pockets to the ground. Oh. Rendar's letter. He'd quite forgotten it in the wake of his death and the orphan girl's disappearance.

Hope suddenly tugged in his heart. Rendar had said it would hold a sort of explanation, had he not? Perhaps this would provide some clue to this mess. Rendar was no seer of the future, but he'd always seemed to know more than the rest of them. He broke the seal and tore it open, eyes darting over the words.

The letter dropped from his hands, all strength suddenly gone.

"My lord!" Maril jumped forward, catching his fall and guiding him onto a seat.

He felt as pale as he surely looked. "It can't be," he whispered. "Why would he have waited till now to tell us?"

"What is it, what does it say?" Maril demanded. She was a fierce woman who could not be ignored, so he fluttered a hand toward the paper as a response.

She snatched it up and read aloud. Warrior or not, he was still impressed she could read it with only the slightest shake in her voice.

"My dear Leoren and Casara,

You have always been my greatest support in these troubled years. You share and know my grief, but...I have not been truthful with the full of it. I have held my tongue, because until now there was nothing more that could be done.

So I have kept it as my burden. Until now. The time has come now for a chance. The chance to save his life.

Errance is alive.

The Darkness stole him to Tertorem. He has been lost to shadow we could not penetrate in physical force. But it has been revealed to me that this girl, this Tellie, will find him somehow. It is not for me to know the whole of it, but Ayeshune has promised that he will be given help from her and many more. So you must be prepared.

Forgive me. Forgive me for keeping this from all of you. It is a secret that has driven me to my grave, but I shall not bury it there with me. Help my son. If we miss this chance, there is no saying what doom it could bring."

Maril lowered the letter, the paper crinkling in her white-knuckled grip. "Dear God," she said softly.

"Is it madness?" Leoren asked fearfully. It was the easiest answer. And yet it hadn't been written like a man gone out of his mind. It was too terrible, too wonderful…and if it was true…then everything had changed.

"Tertorem," he rasped. "Our attack on Tertorem after Errance's death…Rendar called it a quest of justice, but do you think it could be that he was trying to get Errance back? All those months, and we never breached those mountains. I can't see Rendar giving up, but—" A chill ran down his spine as he recalled the king's fading health over the years since. Perhaps he hadn't given up, not quite.

"If that's where you think he is and where they took the girl, then what is to be done?" Maril said savagely. "Our efforts to cross those mountains were in vain!"

"I know," Leoren said, his head sinking into his hands. "But. We have to go back. Perhaps something has changed. Rendar seemed to hold a great deal of faith in this girl. Perhaps it will be different this time. If Errance is alive…."

May the Lord have mercy. If their poor boy was alive, he'd be ruined. Even if they got him back, would they really? He'd surely be changed beyond all recall. But it didn't matter.

"We have to save him. We have to save them both."

9

I don't know why I insist on lying to myself. Maybe because I think if I say it enough, it will become true. But there is no use in pretending otherwise. I am afraid.

It could have been hours later when Errance at last returned. His muffled groan at the guard's rough hassling sent a sword through Tellie's heart, but she remained silent until the guard left and all had gone dark again.

"So Errance," Kelm called. "The next time the guard comes, do you think you can knock him out and get the keys? I mean, we've got to try to escape at least, you can't keep living this way!"

It wasn't living, Tellie thought. It was some horrid state of eternal death. As she listened to the prince's torn breaths and smelt the acidic burns, more morbid memories began to pool with the fever and the slaughterhouse—the sound of a mouse's delicate little bones snapping between a cat's jaws, the open carcass of a dog she'd found in an alley. Each terrible sight and sound replayed over and over in her mind, the details reddening and blurring, then reshaping to become the prince instead. She whimpered, cradling her head in her hands.

When Errance did not answer, Kelm glumly retreated into silence, and so they all three remained, in darkness and descending despair.

The prison door banged open. Never mind that this was the third time she'd heard the sound, Tellie jolted upright from sleep with a breathless cry. She blinked hard, wondering briefly why it was so dark.

Tertorem. The Voice. Errance. Each remembrance hit her like a punch to the stomach.

But she had precious little time to process everything, for a guard came into view and hung his torch in the bracket on the wall.

Errance shifted, groaning softy, "How much more....?"

She wasn't sure if he realized he'd spoken aloud or if he'd forgotten he wasn't alone, but the exhaustion of his voice wilted her spirit. That it was then. He would not fight the guard for the keys—he could not. It was foolish to hope he'd help them when he could not even help himself. They would take him away, and if they returned him, he would be closer to death than before.

The guard threw Errance out of the cell, leaving the elf to find his own balance, before turning back to wrench the key from the lock.

Errance's transformation was so silent, so sudden, that she almost didn't see what happened. One moment, he swayed in spent dejection and the next his body was a reaper's shade sweeping in upon its prey. The guard's arms flailed in panic as Errance's hands wrapped around his mouth, and they both staggered back into the darkness, silhouettes swallowed up in the shadows.

All her skin tingled as the silence was broken by a sharp crack. *No...no, DON'T*, she told herself as her mind jumped to the possibilities of the reason for the sound.

Errance stepped back out of the shadows, and she wasn't sure if the twist of her stomach came from the relief of seeing him again or discomfort that the guard did not reappear.

She scrambled to her feet and wrapped her hands around the bars, knowing with sickening certainty that this moment would decide whether he unlocked their cells or left them behind. But yes...yes, he came, and the key turned in the lock with a beautiful metal click. She leapt out before he could change his mind. As she waited for him to release Kelm, she peered into the lurking dark, fearing that the guard would emerge even while knowing he would not.

In the pale light, Kelm looked particularly ghastly, and she didn't want to dwell long on her own appearance. As for Errance, she refused to see what sort of damage had been wreaked, so she kept her head slightly ducked and eyes averted. "How much time do we have before they realize you're not coming?" she asked.

"Not much," Errance muttered grimly.

"I suppose," Kelm said, voice floating in the darkness, "that we could have waited until they brought you back."

Errance rasped a disagreeing chuckle and started down the long hallway opposite the door. The darkness became an unexpected ally, cloaking their flight. But all too quickly it became a bane as they hit the far wall and began to desperately search for any sign of a sewage hatch at the side or the floor.

Tellie's arms shivered as she smoothed her palm across the slick stone. The arch of a handle bumped under her fingers. "Here," she whispered.

Errance knelt alongside, testing the door. "Locked," he hissed. "Someone did not completely overlook its potential."

"Will the keys—" Kelm began, but he was answered by the grating turn of the bolt.

All three let out deep breaths of relief and all three of those breaths were cut short when the door lifted. The most insidious of smells that had ever assaulted Tellie's nose was nothing compared to the reek that billowed out of the hole in the floor. Both children coughed, gagged, and stumbled backwards.

"Is there a way to retract my wonderful idea?" Kelm asked in a squeak.

Errance did not answer, did not cringe away. He hunkered at the pit's mouth, unafraid of the smell or the plunge. He took a deep breath, grabbed the edge, and swung down.

Warnings of 'it might be too far down,' stuck too late in Tellie's throat, and in her silence she could only listen to the gentle sound of his grip slip from the stone and the soft following fall.

A subtle splash.

Then Errance's voice, muted and distant. "Come on."

"You go first," Kelm said, breath rattling between his teeth.

"Golly, thanks," she muttered. She sat and lowered her legs into the hole, but there she froze. The darkness waited below like a predator, and here she was about to drop into its open throat.

"Errance," she called. "Will you catch me?"

"No."

"Oh."

For just that moment, her surprise surpassed her fear, and so she slipped off the brink and plummeted.

Happily, the fall was not nearly as far as she'd feared. No, the landing was much worse.

Her feet sank into water, thick, sticky water. She lost her balance and flailed wildly. For a horrid moment, she thought she was going to fall backwards. Just in time, she caught herself against the wall and stood there shivering. Heaven help her, even the stone was sticky.

The trapdoor above thudded shut, and immediately afterwards came a splash, a squelch, and a yelp from Kelm.

"All right," Errance said. "Go."

Tellie didn't move. "I don't think I can do this..." she breathed.

Water sloshed at the elf's movement. "You will come or you will be caught," he said. "And you will beg for death long before the end."

"What would they do to you?" Kelm asked curiously.

"Nothing they haven't done already," he answered, words cut between a vicious smile.

At that, she stepped forward. For him, if nothing else. She could not slow him down, and she needed to bring him back safely to his home. Home. Her home too perhaps. And those thoughts compelled each step.

After several minutes of listening only to the sound of each slurping step, Kelm spoke up. "How about a marching song? It's not like anyone could hear us down here. And we must keep our spirits up. *Hey ho, to the abbey we go, to confess our sins, and forgo our woe...*"

After the fifth marching song, Tellie began to wonder how a repetitive ditty could lift anyone's spirits. Maybe if progress could be seen, the song would wile away the time, but without any end in sight, the verses just went on and on and on and—

"Kelm," she said faintly. "Maybe we can just have quiet?"

"Oh. Sure."

They continued on down the dank passage. There was no time in that realm devoid of light. Tellie began to understand how Errance had survived seventy years. All of time passed and then vanished into an unreachable vacuum. No step could be taken back, not one could be brought sooner. They simply walked, sometimes at an ascent, sometimes at a descent. It could have been minutes or hours or days, there was nothing to measure it by but the beat of her heart, and that passed a count beyond reckoning.

The first hope that time still existed came with the realization that the water about their feet picked up pace. They were on a slight slope in the passage where the walls began to narrow. Simultaneously, the water became higher till she was waist deep in the sewage. By this time, she had ceased caring. The movement of the water grew ever quicker, till it was starting to pull at her limbs. She slipped and fell completely under.

The muted sound of gurgling water enveloped her skull, the thick liquid coiling around her limbs and dragged her downward. She wanted to scream. She couldn't. Not without getting a mouthful of sewage. So instead she threw out a panicked arm.

A hand grabbed her wrist and pulled her to her feet. She panted, her hair clinging to the skin. The hold remained tight around her wrist, and she recognized the calloused fingers as Kelm's.

"Are you all right?" he asked.

"Yes," she gasped, teeth chattering.

She heard a strange sound, a muffled snorting. "Are you laughing?" she demanded.

"No!"

118

"You are!" She nearly shoved him but stopped at the possibility of sending them both into the slough.

"Enough," Errance hissed, and they obeyed at once.

The tunnel took a sharp turn, and bright white stabbed their eyes. Tellie covered her face with a cry, pressing fingers hard into her temples as if she could somehow suppress the pounding ache. She heard Errance swear softly, but hardly cared.

"Daylight," Kelm gasped. "That's daylight."

Hesitantly, she looked again, and through the squirming spots in her vision, she saw the passage slope in a steep decline to a small door filled nearly to the top with bright water.

She braced her hands on either wall to keep her feet as they descended, for the current was growing stronger. Fifteen steps. Ten. Only when she heard the rushing roar outside did she finally understand that the sewers emptied into a river.

"Errance," she choked. "I can't swim!"

Then the current sucked her off her feet. Her body swept out the exit, bringing her shoulder into sharp contact with a wall. She was in the river, shards of light slashing across her vision. Thrashing her arms and legs against the raging water, she searched for the surface. She should come back up, shouldn't she? She needed air! But all she could see were churning bubbles, and she gasped in panic only to choke on water. The river spun her like a doll, but in that helpless floundering, her hand broke the surface. She fought upwards, but another current sucked her back down to the depths. Needles began to prick behind her eyes, and her head throbbed in terror and desperation for air.

Ayeshune! she silently screamed. *Please! Please!*

Her hair pulled taut and her body jerked back against the current. An arm clamped around her waist, and she felt herself surge to the surface. The moment her head burst free she drew in shrill gasps of air.

Next thing she knew, she was sprawled over something secure and solid, violently choking up water. Some part of her mind recognized that her feet still hung in the strong current, but she was no longer at the mercy of the river, so that hardly mattered. After the silence in the prison, the roar of the water felt deafening, even muffled by the water clogging her ears. Worse still was the brightness shining red through her closed lids. No, she would just stay here and breathe and not think, not until she could move without shaking apart.

"Tellie? Tellie?"

A boy's voice—Kelm's—reached through the thick fog enveloping her mind, forcing her eyes to flicker open in a painful squint.

She was draped over the thick branch of a tree that had fallen into the water, and Errance slumped upon another branch nearby. Kelm's voice drew her gaze upwards to the bank where he stood at the base of the tree, balancing between roots. Dark-soiled banks rose steeply on either side of the river and thickly foliaged boughs arched overhead, slicing the sunlight into perfect rays of gold. She glanced over her shoulder to the side they'd come from and there the bank steepened into a cliff that rose higher than she could see.

Again, she looked to Errance, who still had not moved. Between the glistening dark ribbons of his hair, she could see raw stripes of lacerated flesh.

"Errance?" she croaked. He was the one that had pulled her out of the river, of that she had no doubt. "Are you alive?"

He shifted his arm ever so slightly across the log in response.

"*I'm* alive, if you're interested," Kelm called, tripping across the log and reaching down. She clasped tight hold of his wrist, and with a tense struggle, pulled free of the water's hungry mouth. The tree trunk bobbed in the rapids, and it was a relief to clamber onto steady ground. With a sputtering laugh, she dropped to the earth and rolled over to stare up into the swaying canopy. Kelm plopped beside her, that cheeky grin wrinkling his nose.

"There," he said. "Didn't I tell you it would work?"

"You never actually promised that," she corrected. "But I'm so glad it did. Even if that was—" she gulped down the sick tang coating her throat "—the worst experience of my life."

She faded into silence and studied the leaves stirring above. She had never seen such large and thick leaves or the rope-like vines tangling the wandering boughs. Warm moisture hung in the air, as unlike the cold cells as could be. And there was a deep humming noise, so loud she could hear it even above the water. Thousands of small whirling insect wings and clicking chirps rolled into one thick melody.

"Kelm," she said after a long pause. "Where are we?"

He craned his head this way and that, biting his lip between teeth. "Well," he said very slowly. "I have no idea."

Wonderful. Lost in both world and time. She squinted up at the sky and found the sun hovering directly overhead. Mid-day, then. How long had it been since she'd entered Tertorem? A few days? A week? Forever?

A thought occurred to her and she pulled out the moon medallion. The moon was waning now. So it had turned completely full at some point which meant…they had only been there two nights? Was that all? It had felt like an eternity.

It was then she heard Kelm whisper the exact same swear word Errance had said earlier. She whirled on him, planning to give him every inch of the tongue lashing he deserved.

But when she saw Errance, all words failed her.

He stood upon the bank, swaying, face tilted up to stare at the blue sky and the green leaves. What might have gone through his mind as he stood there free, no one could fully know, but in those few moments all wonder and fear flickered across his face. The dappled light and the glistening water upon his skin and hair adorned him fairer than any king's finest jewels and silks. In many ways, it should have been a beautiful sight.

But all was ruined by the sight of his afflictions.

It did not seem possible that he could be standing. The river had washed away some of the blood staining his skin, but that only revealed every raw bruise, tear, and break. She did not know what could have mangled his body and flesh to such a state, could not dream how such horror might be worked. Burnt black upon his chest were the words *Property Of* and below it was a strange

121

symbol—a black ball clasped by a skeletal hand, a symbol she could only assume represented His Darkness. The words were emblazoned with enflamed flesh, both yellow and red.

Her eyes skipped over the unknown torments of his body and focused on his twisted right arm that he cradled to his chest. An arm that had grabbed either her hair or her waist, saving her life.

Shakily, she leaned against the side of the bank. She was going to faint. She could not look at that dreadful sight and not faint. Turning, she pressed her fists and brow into the earth, measuring each sickly breath. She had an imagination and she knew how to use it. She was…a great and masterful heroine, and she rescued broken men like this every day. Yes, that was it. After a threatening minute, her whirling head balanced and her stomach agreed to stay put.

She turned, trying not to look straight at him. "Do you know where we go from here, Errance?"

He jerked, startled from his entrancement with the golden sunlight. Without a word, without a glance, he started up the steep slope of the bank and headed into the trees the moment he gained level ground.

Exchanging alarmed looks, Tellie and Kelm hurried after him. His limping gait proved surprisingly swift and sure, and they were hard-pressed to keep up.

"Wait!" Tellie cried. "Should you even be moving?" There was an obvious answer to that, and an even more obvious answer as to why it didn't matter. She looked behind and saw that the sight of the river had already been swallowed up by the trees and foliage. They were sure to be lost. More than they already were anyway.

He didn't pause, and so they plunged deeper and deeper into the wild unknown.

As the roar of the river faded, the noise Tellie had heard before increased. It was a sort of music really—the hum of insects, the screech of birds, the harsh squall of a wild animal. Vivid, ravenous life pulsed in the blood of the land, from the tiniest gnat to the unseen predator stalking through the trees. The trees grew taller and the thick undergrowth lessened.

As they traveled, the ground moistened, but not until Kelm's feet sank into mud up to his ankles did they realize that they were about to run into a bog. One could hardly tell by looking as the surface was covered in green and brown growth like the rest of the jungle, but it was a surface that liked to swallow heavy things. Unfazed, Errance turned to the fallen trees and cage-like branches as his new road, and he never once looked back to see how the children managed to walk along the slimy trunks. Tellie kept tight hold to the vines hanging overhead or else Kelm's arm, and together they navigated the treacherous path across the soggy ground.

When the land at last turned firm and they descended back to earth, Errance had advanced far ahead of them. Just as Tellie opened her mouth to call for a moment of rest, he paused. Even from that distance, she saw how he swayed and only just caught himself against a tree.

"Let's take a break," Kelm called. "I think we could all use a breather."

As if he hadn't heard, Errance took another step.

And collapsed.

"Errance!" Tellie and Kelm screamed. They sprinted to his side and dropped to their knees. He lay face down in the turf and, heedless of his wounds, they pushed him over onto his back. His slick skin shone white as marble and shadows hung under every feature.

"Plagues take it, he can't be dead now!" Kelm exclaimed. "He's not dead! Is he?"

Tellie pressed her ear to the elf's chest, knocking her head against his chin in her haste. She couldn't hear a heartbeat, could only feel sticky blood. Fighting nausea, she dropped her cheek to his lips and was rewarded with the barest warm breath exhaling from his mouth and nose. She straightened with a dizzy smile. "He's alive."

Kelm whooped in relief, leaning back onto his heels. But a moment later his triumphant smile faded to concern as he studied the elf's haggard figure. "What do we do?" he muttered. "I mean, how do we even touch him without hurting him? And do we just wait for him to wake up?"

"Don't ask me, I'm no nurse!"

"What if he doesn't wake up?" He became quite shrill with alarm. "I once heard of a man who hit his head and fell into an eternal sleep. Kept breathing, just never woke up."

"That doesn't help at all," she said crossly. "Do you know anything useful?"

His brow wrinkled. "Er. I once heard that a man kissed a dead woman and she came back to life."

"What? No, that's just a fairy tale!"

"I tell you, it's true. He was some sort of doctor, and he knew a type of kiss that could breathe life back into the body."

"Well, I don't know that kind of kiss, and I am most certainly not practicing on Errance!" She felt her face burn hot just thinking about it.

And then out of the jungle, a women's voice called, "Are you hurt? I'm coming!"

oOo

Yador, former warden of Tertorem, lay dead on the ground amidst the shattered ruin of his ambitions and dreams. Whatever deal he had signed with the devil had fallen through, or perhaps it had reached fulfillment if he had only read the fine print.

The Voice lifted his gaze from the ruin of the body to the cowering men beyond and slowly smiled. "Does anyone else believe that the Prisoner has escaped?"

Shuddering, the men murmured dissent.

"Then know that he is not free. No one enters this realm and no one leaves it but by My Darkness's consent. Now go." He swept them out the door with a mere gesture and turned to the throne, skimming his fingers across the smooth stone.

To be certain, he had lifted the binds constraining his Prisoner some time ago, but the former prince had shown no interest in challenging the single guard sent to bring him to torment again and again. It was delicious to see him so resigned to his fate, but still, he needed to stir up some desire for escape in him.

But the sewer passages?

The serenity on the Voice's face morphed to fury. The sewers—a small mortal detail of his demesne that he had never built. No, some other, perhaps even Yador, had ordered the thing constructed. Which one of the prisoners had the insolence to come up with that sort of escape? His pride was wounded to the quick for them to have found a passage out unprepared by his hand. Anger simmered inside him, threatening to erupt.

He was in control, this was his kingdom, and no quivering captive could waltz out on their own whim. Well, no one else would escape *that* way anymore, he'd made sure of it.

Taking a deep breath, he smoothed a hand down his face. He'd always prided himself on seeing the humor in bad situations, especially in bad situations, and now that he reflected, it really was quite funny. After all, he had planned on letting them go by a far more pleasant route. In the end, the result was the same. The Prisoner had flown the nest. Let him spread his wings, let him soar to new heights.

Let his feathers snap.

10

oOo

Sunlight. I think...I think it was real. The faintest of memories tell me so, and it was so different from fire or the false light when....But it's gone again. So why love it if it cannot last.

"There." The young woman finished wrapping the bandage around the child's arm and tied it off with a dainty bow. "And a kiss to make it all better," she concluded with said parting gift.

The little boy looked up at her with a sort of awe as if the airy kiss on his bandaged elbow really had expelled all the pain. "T'anks!" he said, then ran off hollering to find his abandoned playmates.

The young woman hardly finished pushing herself up from the jungle floor before she was hailed again, this time by a mother of four. "Tryss!" the mother called, wiping sweat from her brow. "Could you perhaps keep watch over these hellions as I do the washing?"

"Well I—" Tryss began.

"Actually." A figure stepped in front of her and she could not help but smile at the command with which Master Holivari carried himself no matter how short his stature. "I need Tryss to find me some talith leaves at once. I am afraid you will just need to find someone else."

Tryss dipped in a bow, trying to hide her relieved and excited smile from the disappointed mother. After all, she was willing and able to watch the children of her village, and it was a role expected of her and something she excelled at. But beyond that, she trained in the healing arts under the Master, and he knew that she loved nothing more than a chance to go off into the jungle on her own and just—just breathe.

The buzz of delight hummed in her ears as she darted back to her hut and grabbed her bow and quiver and knife. The jungle was a dangerous place even for her kind and one never could be too careful. And then she was sprinting for the wilds, soon deep within the humid fronds and dangling vines.

The birds and animals were more skittish further out, accustomed to being hunted rather than hunting the village's scraps. But she was silent even as quickly as she moved, leaping from turf to branches with as much ease and elegance as any tree creature. And out of instinct more than thought, she let her appearance melt into the shadow and sunlight spangled background. Her flaxen hair became a bright flicker of gold, her green clothes moss against the trees, her skin translucent as water.

The talith vines grew up in the jungle canopy, and she had gone out some distance before finally choosing a mighty trunk to scale. Her slim hands and feet gripped each knot of the thick wood and she soon climbed to the tree's enormous summit, vanishing into its palace of branches and leaves. As she knew well, it was one of the tallest trees of the jungle, and when her head at last broke from the top she overlooked the entire green canopy as if it was a living carpet. For just a few moments she breathed the fresh air, letting the wind whip the sweaty strands of hair from her face.

And there, to the west, it glittered. The sea. It was something so different from her world. So still, so level, so full of sparkle. The strange smell of salt sometimes drifted even here on the wind. One day, she would ask her many-times-great-grandfather if he would allow her to accompany the peddlers of her village who traded with the city by the sea.

But...until then...she plucked the leaves of the talith vine and stuffed her bag. Until then, she would do her duties well. As eldest of her siblings still at home—ever since her elder brother had abandoned them for the North—she understood responsibility. Already, she was feeling the guilt for taking longer than necessary.

She clambered down, then jumped the rest of the way. She'd just settled the bag of leaves more comfortably against her hip when a strange cry made her pause. Really, there were so many sounds in this jungle, so many that could make intelligent noises that she was surprised she noticed this one at all. But it had sounded...very young. A monkey's infant in distress perhaps. But...no. There was something distinctly human about the sound. She blended even further into jungle colors and silently drew near. Yes, two children talking in the common tongue, so not of her village.

She peered over a fallen log and saw them. A boy and a girl, and they were bent over a body.

"What in Orim..." she breathed. Then louder, she called, "Are you hurt? I'm coming!"

The stranger's words still hung in the air as Tellie lifted fear-stricken eyes to Kelm.

They looked at each other, hoping the other would say that they'd heard nothing. Perhaps it was just their imagination. It was plausible; who could say what the trauma of the last few days had done to their senses?

Tree branches rustled.

Inhaling sharply, they whirled around to look at the forest behind them. The leaves were swaying, but there was no wind. A sudden flicker, like spots in her vision, caught Tellie's eye. For one moment, she could have sworn she saw the bark of the tree move. The same flicker moved down to the bushes below. It was like she was staring through glass at the growth beyond, but the glass was formed like—

A woman materialized out of the air.

Tellie's scream strangled her throat, and she scrambled backwards on her hands and feet.

The woman stalked forward, her body bent and her head tilted, like a wildcat cornering its prey. Even visible she was difficult to see for her lithe body was covered in shades of green that seemed to take on the image of the jungle around her.

Kelm stood, shaking. In both hands, he gripped a stout branch. "Back!" he shouted, with a threatening swing. "Don't take a step closer!"

The woman paused and stared at him. Her eyes, large and brilliant with color, flicked down to Tellie and then rested on Errance. A thousand thoughts swam across her face and then in the same lilting voice, she commanded, "Stay right there. I'll bring help." The next moment, she vanished back into the trees.

"What *was* that?" Tellie cried. An ache stabbed behind her eyes from seeing the impossible.

"A chema?" Kelm suggested. "The stories say they go nearly invisible, you know."

"She looked different than I've heard!"

"Well do you know of anything else that can vanish like that? She might be a scout from Tertorem. Bring help, is it? We'll see about that." Kelm bent over Errance, grabbing his arms. "Come on! We have to get out of here!"

She reached to take Errance's other arm and shoulder, and her fingers sank into open flesh. With a cry, she jerked back.

"Come *on!*" Kelm bawled.

Gritting her teeth, she thought of all the grand stories she'd ever been told, grabbed hold, and pulled.

Errance's body scraped across the ground. He was not as heavy as they expected, and they pulled faster. His broken flesh caught on the roughage below, and he murmured in pain, head turning.

Tellie dropped down beside him, patting his cheeks sharply. "Wake up, Errance!" she pleaded. "Come on, wake up!"

His face remained still and white.

"We'll go faster this way," Kelm gasped, pushing the limp elf up to a sitting position and tucking his own shoulder underneath Errance's arm. He grabbed the arm and flung it around his neck, then wrapped his other arm behind the elf's back. Tellie placed herself in the same position, wincing as she felt fresh blood soak into her dress. Together, they pushed to a stand and staggered forward, taking the opposite direction the woman had gone.

The trees seemed to close in around them, the thick branches and vines barring their way. All sense of direction was stolen from them, and they did not know if they were returning the very way they'd come.

Voices rose in a whirr behind them.

"Quick," Kelm rasped. "Into this bush."

The bush was thick and broad-leafed, the greatest protection that could be found in a short distance. As they staggered in, Tellie's foot caught on a branch. She lost her balance and fell forward, dragging Errance and Kelm down with her. The twigs snapped and crackled underneath them. Such a small noise it was amongst the constant chatter of the jungle, but for them it was resounding cacophony echoing in their ears. They froze.

The murmur of voices came steadily nearer, the voices of several people.

Kelm hissed, and Tellie realized her foot was still sticking out of the shrub. Panicked, she yanked it in and tried to make sure her sadly browned dress was concealed enough. Her movement merited another hiss, so she went still. She curled up with her back facing the jungle, and she could see Kelm crouched near the trunk of the bush, his eyes wide and his hands clenched. The voices were drawing ever closer, and now she could hear them searching through brush.

She buried her face into her arms, cheek resting on Errance's chest. She could feel the flutter of his heartbeat, and for a moment she wondered, even if they did escape this, if he would survive much longer. He did not look like he should be alive. What would happen after this? Where would they go? How could they get him to wake up? The questions slammed in one after another with such force, her breath spun away.

The branches thrust aside.

Tellie screamed, but with a wild roar, Kelm sprang up and threw himself at the man standing above them. The man stepped aside in surprise, but he grabbed the attacking boy in an effort to restrain him.

Tellie shoved to her feet and stumbled forward, clawing at the man, but hands descended on her shoulders. With a cry, she twisted from the grip and raced away into the trees, the strangers shouting in a foreign chatter after her. She dashed through the jungle, tearing through vines and leaves and leaping like a deer over fallen trees and broken ground. When she came to a wide stream, she dove into the reeds and huddled down in them, submerged up to her chin.

Each breath shuddering, she leaned against the bank and listened. The reeds swayed around her like chimes, but all the voices were in the distance, smothered in the jungle purr. In that gentle tranquility, realization of what she'd done collapsed on her with the weight of a mountain.

She'd left Kelm and Errance.

Without a thought for their safety, she had obeyed instinct and dashed off into the wild. She sank into the stream, mouth listlessly dropping open. What sort of weak coward was she?

She had to go back, go back and help them. And if she could not help them, she must stay with them anyway. Or...or maybe it was good that she was free? Maybe she would be able to follow and find a better time to rescue them?

Dismally, she sank deeper into the water, watching the currents swirl around the reeds.

A current of water was moving upstream.

She bolted upright. "Stop it! Stop it right there!"

The same woman as before slowly appeared from the air, an unexpected blush of shame on her cheeks. She did not appear as frightening up close for she was young and lovely, with flaxen hair pulled back into a long braid. Her style of dress was unlike anything Tellie had ever seen and its leafy patterns did not seem fitting to His Darkness. She extended a lithe hand, eyes large and pleading. "Sorry, I didn't mean to scare you," she said. "You mustn't run; you need help."

Yes, she certainly did. But not from strangers slipping in and out of visibility. Tellie jumped up onto the opposite bank, but there she paused. She needed to return to her friends, she'd already decided that. Now that she'd been found, there was no use in running again. So...there was only one thing to do.

Lifting her chin, she marched back the way she'd come, not waiting to see if she was followed or not.

Several men gathered in the glade now, all of them as flaxen-haired and strangely garbed as the woman. Kelm stood firmly secured in the midst of them, wrists caught behind his back in a loose binding. One man kept a hand on his shoulder, but the boy looked defeated. Errance had been pulled out of the bush and was lying on a litter woven from branches and vines. Several men bent over him, murmuring in velvet voices like the color red.

Terror—and anger—filled Tellie's breast and she sprinted forward, shoving her way between the surrounding men and the elf. "Get away from him!" she shouted. "Don't you touch him!"

The men fell back, faces open with surprise. She knelt protectively over the prince and glared back at them. Shrugging, one man stepped forward and picked her up by the shoulders, neatly pulling her away from Errance. With a snarl, she squirmed under his hold. Then to her utter horror, he scooped her up and carried her under one arm like a sack of potatoes. "Put me down!" she cried. "Lemme' go!"

The young woman darted forward and snapped a hummingbird-like chitter at the man holding Tellie.

Whatever was said caused the man to lower her back to the ground. She swung around to face the woman. "Who are you? Are you from Tertorem?"

"Ter...what?" the lady repeated. She took a step back, face clouded. But before she could answer another word, the men around Errance lifted the litter and began walking off into the trees.

Tellie sprang after in pursuit, before coming to an abrupt halt at the end of her captor's arm. To her relief, he also began to walk in the same direction as the litter. She looked around for Kelm and saw him, pale with frustration and fear, led by another man.

There was nothing that could be done. They were captured again, for better or for worse.

"Master Holivari!" Tryss shouted, scattering the various animals and children come to greet her as she pounded into the village ahead of the litter's procession. Her course was set straight for the healer's hut, and the man opened the thatched door just as she arrived.

"What kind of injury?" he inquired calmly.

"They're bringing him here," she panted. "It's a stranger and he's...brutalized. By people." *But by what people?* The question tore through her mind over and over. There were other chema tribes in the forest, but as far as she knew they shared common decency and would never go so far in cruelty as what she'd briefly seen.

"Start the bath," the Master said, heading back in to prepare his medicines. Tryss followed him, heading to the far corner of the healing hut where a square hollow was built into the ground, carefully tiled. She bent low and opened a hatch, letting water pour in from a pipe to fill the bath. The healing hut had been purposefully built near a hot spring to allow easy access to the boiling water.

A commotion at the door said that their patient had arrived. Master Holivari opened wide the door so that the men could carefully bring the stretcher in and lie it upon the thatched floor. The healer knelt by the body, inhaling slowly. It was the first time Tryss had actually seen a flicker of horror cross his face. Always her teacher kept an aura of poise and unflinching steel. From hunting accidents to animal attacks, they'd seen their share of injuries, but these wounds spoke of something else entirely.

"Fill a trough from the hot water, Tryss," the master said. "We will need to clean him." His expert hands began feeling the body for internal damage, and his face only grew more troubled. "Where was he found?"

"I found him," she replied. "By the mountains. There were two children with him."

"Children?" Master Holivari looked up sharply. "Are they injured? Alive?"

"They were very dirty and afraid but seemed otherwise healthy." She struggled to bring the heavy trough over without spilling it. "There's no way he traveled far like this. Do you think he could have come from the mountains themselves? But those cliffs are far too steep to travel down."

"He may not ever wake to give us the answers," the healer said grimly.

Her heart sunk like a stone. "It is…that bad then?"

The healer hesitated. "He has many broken bones besides these outer injuries. Still, none of them seem designed to kill him. They are…carefully chosen. Nevertheless, the amount of them and the blood he must have lost is enough to end most men. Bring a flask of the sillosk bark. He may be unconscious now, but if we can start to deaden the pain, our treatments will be less shocking."

She retrieved it in a blur, heart hammering. When she held it out to her teacher he was already starting to sponge the filth from the body and only nodded at her to proceed. She looked to the face of their patient. Somehow, even unconscious, his features seemed clenched in pain. She set her fingers at his jaw, gently coaxing his mouth open. If she couldn't get him to respond even a little, he'd only choke on the medicine. When his lips twitched, she poured a little inside, then stroked fingers down his throat in an encouragement to swallow. After a few tries, it worked, and little by little she forced enough down.

He grimaced and turned his face away from her hand, his long hair shifting. The tip of a pointed ear peeked out from the oily strands, and she caught her breath. "Master Holivari…?" she began. "Look, is he a…?"

The healer took one look and a sharp sound hissed from between his teeth. "Yes, he's an elf."

"All the way out here?"

The old man shook his head. "Perhaps the children with him will have answers."

Traveling through the jungle with their strange captors was much easier than before. They seemed to follow invisible paths and soon the ground growth diminished, glades grew more frequent, and the canopy thinned in signs of man-made clearings. They entered a village of round huts built of thatched reeds, each cluster of buildings surrounding a central fire pit. More strange folk filled the village, some busy at work, others stopping to stare.

Tellie faltered in her determined pursuit of Errance and gawked at her surroundings—the children at play, the women weaving baskets, the little pigs rooting through the soil. This didn't look anything like Tertorem. So perhaps they were among friends and not foes.

When she looked back, Errance had vanished. "Where'd he go?" she yelled, throwing herself against her captor's unbreakable hold. "What did you do with him?"

A great many of the folk gathered around them, murmuring with perplexed tones and expressions. Then the crowd parted to make way for a small, tottering figure, leaning heavily on a great staff. His skin was so aged it had turned from fair to brown, and it crumbled in thousands of wrinkles. His hair curled out in ghostly wisps from under his green cap and surrounded his head in a gentle halo. Indeed, he was so old he looked half ready to die in front of them. Nevertheless, there was a twinkle and brightness in his clouded eyes.

Slowly, the children relaxed, and when they did so, their captor's grip lessened.

"Where do you come from, children?" the old man said.

"That's none of your business," Kelm fired back. "We ought to know who you are first. Why are we captive?"

The old man blinked. Then he said gently, "For generations we have lived in this jungle. Never have we found strangers in the trees close to the grey mountains. The strangers we find—two children weary to the point of collapsing and a grievously wounded man. My dear boy…we have not captured you, we have rescued you."

Tellie stared about her at the onlooking faces, some young, some old, some fair, some plain, but all curious and none cruel. "Are…are you chemas?" she asked. All the stories of the skin-blenders she'd heard said they lived in cold mountains with equally cold personalities, but the opposite seemed true here.

"We are."

"I thought you all lived up north," Kelm said suspiciously.

"Most do," the old man conceded. "But that is another story. We still need to know where you came from. This jungle is large and for you to show up in its most remote corner...is troubling."

When Kelm did not answer, Tellie drew in a deep breath. "From those mountains. We're escaping the Darkness."

The old man inhaled, murmuring a few words as either a curse or a prayer. Whatever he said, the surrounding people gasped in horror and drew away in fear. "So it is true...the Darkness has taken root behind those mountains."

"For seventy years at least. That's how long our friend—the injured man— has been there."

"Tellie," Kelm growled.

She glared. "If they're our enemies, I'm not telling them anything they don't already know!" Turning back to the man, she demanded. "Now where did you take him? If you're friends, you won't keep him from us!"

For a moment, the old one just stared at her, chewing his lip thoughtfully. Then he turned, joints crackling, and gestured with his staff. "Come then. Our healers are already tending him in the healing hut." He spoke a curt order in the strange language, and the children's captors released their hold.

He led the way to a hut near a bubbling warm stream. "Tryss," he called to the same fair maid who was just stepping back through the door, her arms full of white cloth.

"Wait a moment," she said. "Master Holivari is washing him, the children can't come in."

"How long is that going to take?" Tellie said, tugging at her fingers. She stared at the thatch door, hating for it to hide the poor prince from her, however decently.

Tryss called in query in the other tongue, and a man answered in kind from within. "He is finished for now, but," she cast an anxious look at the two youths, "I don't know that they should watch."

"We absolutely will!" Tellie cried. "And anyway, it's not like we haven't seen him already!"

"We don't know who you really are," Kelm said, "and I insist on being there for whatever you do to him!"

The young woman's eyes softened in some understanding and she looked to her grandfather. "Ancient?"

"Let them go. What they speak is true."

Tryss pulled the thatched door open for the two children. The inside of the hut was dimly lit by a hole in the roof and a few woven lanterns hanging on the wall. A pool bubbled on one side of the chamber and on the other stood a low cot covering in woven blankets. Errance lay upon it, lit with the shaft of light from the roof, and a man knelt beside him, busily tearing cloths into strips.

Tellie paused, head spinning again at the sight of the Aselvian prince.

Butchered. He looked nothing less than butchered. The blood and dirt had been washed from his body, leaving his skin as listless and pale as a corpse. Only his flushed cheeks and the occasional shudder showed any sign of life. A fresh cloth draped over his middle, but no other bandage yet hid the mottled bruising, burn, and gash across the marbled skin.

The room tilted before Tellie's eyes. A hand grabbed her arm, startling her back into focus. The young woman looked at her with concern, gesturing to a seat on the ground nearby. "We shall try to save him," Tryss said. "But be strong, he may scream."

"No," she whispered. "Not him."

The master healer frowned at the sight of the two children and spoke sternly to Tryss, but she chattered back a reply that seemed to convince him however begrudgingly. He handed a mortar and pestle to Tryss, which she began vigorously working, before he turned to bend over the unconscious elf.

Tellie scooted a little closer so she could watch, though she tried to keep her eyes on the healer's inspecting fingers rather than the wounds themselves.

Finishing grinding whatever herbs, Tryss poured the powder into a cup of milk and bent to spoon it into Errance's mouth.

"What is that?" Tellie asked anxiously.

"*Lyofieth*. It will keep him asleep," she answered.

The healer reached for a kettle of steaming hot water and withdrew a knife, then turned the blade towards Errance.

"What are you doing?" Kelm shouted, lunging forward.

The man startled, shoving an arm out to keep the boy away, but Tryss leaned forward to press Kelm back. "Infected wounds are closed, and he must open them if they are to be properly cleaned," she said.

Kelm turned suspicious eyes from the knife to the careless cauterization and stitching slashed across the tortured figure, and at last he drew back. Tellie closed her eyes as the knife descended.

"There's not much blood," Kelm said, surprised.

"No." Tryss's voice was grim, strained. "There is not."

For the next hour the children sat in anxiety as the strangers washed Errance's wounds, spread them with salve, and wrapped him up in bandages till he looked very much like a body to be buried.

Tryss washed her hands in water drawn from the pool and stood with a stretch of her back. "Master Holivari says there is nothing more to be done but to keep water in his body and change the bandages when needed. It is late and you both look tired. Come on, I will show you where you might sleep."

"But—" Tellie glanced at Errance's still form. "But what if he wakes? We must be here if he's frightened."

"He'll not wake for some while yet with as much *lyofieth* as is in him," she replied, holding out an encouraging hand. "He will sleep soundly, and in that, he may recover. Come on."

Tellie looked at Kelm and she saw her own weariness reflected in his eyes, so she accepted the hand and let herself be led out of the room. Evening was falling, she realized, and shadows had cast over the village. She looked back one time to see Errance asleep in the warm, glowing hut before the door closed and hid him from view.

oOo

Among the glow of stars and dancing fireflies of the jungle, the figure stood, bent head cupped in his hand. When the One came alongside him, he lifted his face and smiled through his tears. "He is free."

"Not yet." A gentle, but painful reminder.

"Still, he has escaped in body. I never thought I'd live to see the day." He laughed softly, considering his words. "Well. I don't suppose I have."

"You are more alive than ever," the One said with a chuckle.

"Yes...yes...and seeing him again. He...is much altered." The smile faded from both their faces. "Was there no other way, my Lord?"

"There are many things that might have changed in history if a different choice had been made."

"If only I had taught him better," the first said, his voice catching. "If I'd had the courage to reveal my own past more, I might have spared him so much."

"You gave everything you could to him. His choices are his own, and the Darkness will plague his steps. But do not fear, for I am ever with him."

There was silence. Then the first said, "Is it time for her to aid me?"

"Soon. Very soon."

11

oOo

Pain pulses far away and may it stay that distance. I might be able to stop it if I drew near, but I'll find no victory in fighting this Darkness crushing me. Voices hiss in my ear, but I do not respond or rather I cannot. Something stirs at the edge of my consciousness, a flicker of true thought. Another voice, this one foreign yet somehow familiar, whispers that this pain is not meant for harm. If I could only laugh.

Pain always harms.

Aselvia was still. Not a sound stirred the night, not a bird's cry, an elk's bugle, or a wolf's howl. The lights that flickered in the forest winked out one by one. Only the leaves trembled in an invisible breeze.

The same tremble ran through Casara's hands as she swept a brush through the long hair of the woman seated in front of her. It was her habit to brush her mother's hair at morning and night, a calming ritual, but tonight it brought little comfort.

They had lit their candles at twilight for Rendar's memorial, and then a good half of Aselvia had made their departure, Leoren at their head. Rendar's death had shocked all of them, but the blow had been doubled with the hope that Errance was still alive. And now the kingdom was silent in the wake of their army's departure, doing what Casara was doing now—processing.

Her mother hadn't said a word the entire evening, and Casara wondered just how aware she was of the changes that had so suddenly taken place these last few days. True, she'd tried to keep most of the chaos away because she couldn't stand to let more hurt chase her mother further into whatever world she hid in. Tragedy had marked the woman's life from the beginning of the dark days, reflected in the silver strands that streaked her long dark hair. She'd lost her husband, two children, a grandson, and now her son-in-law, the king. But with this hope of Errance...perhaps the grandson could be a life restored.

Perhaps it wasn't true. Perhaps the rescue would fail. Yet she spoke the hope anyway. "Maava...Errance...he's alive. Leoren has gone to bring him home." She leaned forward, trying to see any glimmer that she'd been heard. But the only flicker in the woman's eyes was that of candlelight. Her face remained the same serene blank it usually was. Some days were better. Tonight was not one of them.

She sighed and leaned back, the brush fumbling from her hand and dropping to the ground with a thud in a dull echo of her heart.

Not a moment later, a knock came at the door, and a bright-eyed young woman peered in. "May I come in?"

"Of course, Dahlya."

The healer's daughter slipped in, her usual cheeriness replaced by a restless anxiety. "Can I talk about...him...in front of her?" She glanced at the quiet queen mother.

"I already tried telling her, but I don't think she's hearing, so there's no harm anyway."

Not needing a second invitation, Dahlya plopped down onto the settee beside them. "He was such a sweet little baby. And he grew up so well. Daava and brother are talking; they're worried about what condition he'll be in when he's brought back, but if anyone can help him, they can. Besides, he has the light from his mother."

"If they can rescue him," Casara said without meaning to. It was a horribly hopeless thing to say, but she'd had her share of disappointments in life. "Rendar seemed to indicate the orphan girl we found would be the key, though heavens know how, and I'm so..." Her voice shook, and she sank her head into her hands.

"Tellie is her name, yes?" Dahlya said hesitantly. "You were bringing her here before she vanished, I heard?"

"I had thought..." Casara said. "I had thought for a few wonderful moments that I would have a daughter of my own. If I couldn't have a second child, this would be my chance. And she *needed* a mother. But instead, we've thrown her into the worst sort of danger by involving her in all this."

"So you were going to adopt her?" Dahlya's head tilted in interest. "Are human children much different from ours?"

"Not from what I've heard. We all have the same Designer, after all. And anyway, she couldn't shock me more than my own son."

Dahlya gave her usual bubble of laughter. "That's true."

"Errance."

The whisper-soft voice startled them both, and they stared at the old queen. Casara threaded her mother's thick hair through her hands and began plaiting. "Yes, Maava, Errance. Do you remember? How Errance would bring you flowers so I could braid them into your hair? How he and the little miss daisha would play at your feet? Do you remember how strong he grew up? How handsome?"

But the old queen said nothing more.

oOo

Soft sunshine brushed gentle fingers across Tellie's face and her eyes fluttered open under its caress. For a moment, she pressed a little deeper into her bed, quite unbothered by the certain scolding from Missus Norne...

She bolted upright with a shrill gasp.

No, she was nowhere near the inn; she was in a strange little hut in the middle of the jungle far from the land she knew! And then there was Errance, and the Voice, and the strange people who had found them. All of it descended in a whirl, and she caught her reeling head between her hands.

"It's all right," a female voice said sweetly. "You've had a long sleep."

Tellie squinted up to see the sunlight had swept in from the open door where Tryss stood. A little of her fear slid away, and she rubbed her eyes. "H-how long have I been sleeping?"

"You fell asleep yesterday afternoon, and it is afternoon now."

"What?" Tellie yelped. "What?"

"You seemed very tired, dear, so it's no surprise. When did you sleep last?"

"I…I don't know." She rubbed her aching neck, feeling the crust of dirt on skin.

"How about a bath?" Tryss said, helping her to her feet. "I won't lie—you need it badly."

"What about Errance?"

"He hasn't woken."

"And Kelm?"

"He's been up twice already, demanding to see you and your elf friend. I think he's finally beginning to trust us, so he's sleeping soundly now." She shifted several folds of cloth under her arm and gestured out the door with a merry flick of her chin.

Tellie stumbled out after her, blinking at the golden green world. The people were about their work as before and as Tellie was led past them, they paused in whatever they were doing and stared at her. She blushed to think of how she looked and what state her poor dress was in, but she stared back just as openly. They wore such different clothes than she'd ever seen, quilted fabric fitting their forms and gathered tunics over that. All of them had hair as bright as the sunlight, and now she noticed their ears were not even slightly human, instead shaped like a fawn's, but small and against the scalp.

"So…you don't live in the North. Where exactly are we then?"

"This is East Orim. And yes, most chemas live up North and are…" Tryss paused, biting her lip in careful consideration, "...different than us. My Grandfather, the Ancient of our tribe, led his people to this land many years ago so they might develop a new culture and life."

"Oh," Tellie said, but she mostly only heard the words East Orim. So far away and across the sea! It was mind-boggling to think about, especially since they had to return to the West, and would they take a ship, or could they make it around the bay—

"Here." Tryss paused, and Tellie looked up to realize they'd come some way from the main village to where several circular enclosures of bound reeds stood among a steamy swamp of warm springs and pools. Tryss opened a gate in one of these and gestured inside. "Afterwards, you may speak with the Ancient," she said. "I know your curiously is only whetted, and well, ours has not even begun to be answered."

A blue-green pool waited in the center of the enclosure, and when she dipped her toe in it, the water felt hot, but not scalding to the touch. Tellie glanced around to make sure she was quite hidden, before slipping out of her dress and wading into the water. It was strange to take a bath in the ground, but the sides of the pool had been inset with smooth stones and the cracks were stuffed with moss. She nestled her head in her arms on the downy earth and sighed deeply, willing all the misery of the last few days to pass away.

She did know how long she let herself drift until Tryss called, "Did you get lost in there?"

Forcing her mouth and eyes open, Tellie called back in a slurred voice, "Nooo..."

"If you're planning on going to sleep, we have a bed that you won't drown in. How about you come on out? Here, I brought you some clothes." A pile of clothes sailed over the top of the fence and landed a few feet from Tellie's nose.

Every muscle in her body protested as she dragged herself out of the pool. After drying off with a towel that had also been thrown over, she dressed in her new clothes. They were the same as the tribe wore, and when she put on the shirt and leggings, she felt like she should have been wearing a good deal more. Only boys wore trousers, after all. The tunic was made of a material she had never seen nor felt. The cloth was smooth and sheer, folding in thousands of little creases. It fell to her knees, and she thought herself decent enough to be seen.

The moon medallion! Where had she put it? She dove for her discarded clothes and riffled through them until her fingers reached in the last pocket and tangled in the strands of a necklace. Sighing in relief, she pulled out the medallion. It shimmered gently under her fingers. She tucked it into the pocket of her new tunic.

Feeling foreign, Tellie stepped hesitantly out.

Tryss was sitting just outside on a log, weaving a braid of grass fibers. Her face lit up and she smiled widely when Tellie appeared. "There you are!" she exclaimed. "You're a proper chema. I can fetch you some normal human clothes if you really want them, but I did want to see you in our attire."

Tellie could barely keep up with what she was saying, the fog in her head was so thick. "Yes," she answered, figuring that would be a safe answer.

Together, they left the mist of the jungle streams and returned to the village where torches and fires were already being lit to drive away night's oncoming shadows and dangers. The old man, the Ancient, sat in front one of these fires.

Tellie headed straight for him. "Errance, how is he?"

"He sleeps," the Ancient replied, not turning his gaze from the beginning sparks of the fire. "If sleep it may be called." He sighed under the weight of a thousand troubles. "So long have I denied the rumors of the Darkness behind those grey mountains, but in the face of this vicious cruelty done to your friend and the brand he bears, I can do so no longer. I have been a fool. My tribe can no longer live here."

"Yes, and you might think of leaving soon, because they'll be searching for us and might find you!"

"Worry not about us, child," the old man said, patting her on the cheek. "We may vanish into the trees if so. But of you and your friends, what is to be done? Who is the elf man the Darkness has taken such fascination in?"

Tellie hesitated, looking about the village and at the faces of both the

Ancient and Tryss as if to make sure one last time that they weren't hiding a dark secret. She slid her hand into her tunic's pocket and wrapped her fingers around the warmth of the moon medallion. "Well...he's the prince of Aselvia."

The old man drew in a sharp, jagged gasp. "Ah! Ah, it is so!"

She started, mouth dropping open. "Wait, what? You mean you already guessed?"

"You said...you said your friend has been a captive for seventy years and the tale of the prince's tragic end was heard that number of years ago. But more than this, his body heals with greater strength and swiftness than even the enduring elves...if he is half celestial, the reason is clear."

"He's healing?" she exclaimed, followed by an exasperated, "How do you know about the celestials?" Did everyone, except her, know about this story?

The old man shifted and raised a hand to Tryss. "Granddaughter, go and see how the elf fares and bring back word."

When she departed, the Ancient turned again to Tellie. "Though I have lived four hundred years—yes, do not look so surprised—I have never met the fair elves of Aselvia. But I listen, I listen and learn what I may, and though my former people told the story of the Dark Days differently than the elves, I sought the stories of the last celestial and the peace he brought to the earth elf kingdom. I know of the Higher World, and how the Darkness longs to conquer it...and if what you say is true..."

"It is."

"...then the grace and power of Ayeshune must be with this prince for him to have endured so long."

For a brief moment, Tellie thought of the anguish and anger on Errance's face, and she wondered if *he* would have called it God's grace and power.

"And what about you, maiden?" the Ancient said, snapping her attention back into focus. "How do you and the boy play into this?"

She shrugged helplessly, all explanations of the elves she had met and the mission she'd been given tangling on her tongue. "We were also captured. We're his friends, and we just want to get him back home."

The old man's brow raised in several wrinkles at that aloof explanation, but he did not press for answers. Instead he rose to his feet with a weary groan and gestured with his hand. "Let us hear what our healers have to say about your friend."

She scrambled to her feet in haste, but his pace was slow so she politely matched it despite her anxiety. As they approached the healing hut, she saw Tryss standing with her teacher just outside, caught in distressed chatter. Tellie's heart lurched to see Tryss's face crumbled near to tears, and she leapt forward in dismay.

"What is it, what's wrong?"

Tryss spun to face her and glanced between the master healer and the Ancient. Then with a choked murmur, she hurried past them and off into the village. The healer began to speak to the Ancient, and Tellie waited in fretful suspense. When the healer finished speaking, he swept back into the hut, leaving the girl and the old man alone.

Tellie stared into the Ancient's sad eyes, her throat knotting. "What did he say?"

He took her hand—the action she'd prayed he would not do. "He still lives. But he has been off the sleeping medicine long enough to wake, and instead…have you ever seen a dead body?"

She swallowed hard. "Yes."

"Master Holivari says that though he breathes and his body is swiftly showing signs of healing, he is…he is like one dead. It as if his spirit has flown or else hidden far away…and he does not know if he will wake or how we can keep him alive if he does not."

Sick tingles ran from her scalp to her fingertips, and she hugged herself in a sudden chill. "But…but it's soon to worry, isn't it? I mean…"

"Yes, yes, child," he assured. "There is hope yet. The village shall pray for him tonight and tomorrow morning. However long it takes until he wakes."

He set a fatherly hand on her shoulder, guiding her back to the village center where folk were gathering around the savory smell of roasted meat. "Now then…how about some supper?"

"I don't know if I can eat," she mumbled.

"Tellie!"

She spun around at the sound of Kelm's cry and gasped in relief and joy to see him running towards her. His fierce hug near took her breath away.

"Oh, ow, you're awake!" she managed to squeak.

"Me? This is my third time awake. You've been sleeping like a log!"

"Thanks for that," she said. "Anyway, have you heard about Errance?"

His merry face sobered, and he nodded. "Tryss just told me. Not much we can do I guess, except hope he pulls through."

She nodded and let herself be led to the sawn logs around the firepits where the evening meal was being served.

But through the meal and above the lively chatter of their hosts and the noises of the night, she only thought, *there must be something I can do.*

Long after most of the village had gone to sleep Tellie lay awake. She had been given a bed in the loft of a hut belonging to a kind, elderly couple, and though the mattress of soft grass wrapped in blankets proved a compelling reason to rest, her mind only circled like a stricken dove.

After all that had happened, it was so very strange to be back in a bed, by all appearances safe. She still couldn't help but wonder now and then if this wasn't just a strange nightmare and she would be shaken awake back in Denji. Yet every time she pulled out the moon medallion, she knew it was no lie.

She wondered if Leoren and Casara searched for her, and what they had thought when she was taken away. If Errance died, would they even still want to give her a home?

Rolling over, she buried her face into the straw and finally slept.

She opened her eyes, certain she'd heard someone call her name. Slowly, she sat up, gazing around the loft. A little hatch had blown up, and she went to close it, not liking any entrance, no matter how small, into her room. As she started to pull it shut, a flash of white caught her eye in the trees beyond. She squinted and saw a magpie bouncing from moonlit branch to branch. Frowning at the sight of the bird that had started this whole ordeal, she wrenched the window shut and turned back.

A man sat on the other side of the room.

Her heart banging to a stop, Tellie opened her mouth to scream.

"Fear not, Tellie," the man said softly. "It is I, Rendar."

12

oOo

How strange it is when endless eternity...alters....

I almost thought I had escaped again, so far cast was my spirit from its form. But then came that change, and I felt my body twist, jerking my spirit back on its cord. The Darkness wraps around closer, binding me as linens bind the dead. It hides from me that which it does not wish me to see. If only it knew how little I care to look.

*I*t was Rendar.

No matter how hard Tellie rubbed her eyes, the celestial king of Aselvia remained sitting on the other side of the room.

Yet he was not the same. He was not the ancient elf she had met in the forest. While his hair still shone silver and his eyes still held the wisdom of millennia, the age of his years seemed to have been wiped away, replaced with...not youth...but timelessness.

"You're dead," she whispered.

"My body deceased, yes," Rendar replied.

It was a dream. Oh! Of course it was. The simple acknowledgement of that fact sent a wave of relief over Tellie. Suddenly, she could breathe again. Still, dreaming about a ghost, how unpleasant! If he hadn't introduced himself, she might have thought he was Errance come to haunt her.

Rendar tilted his head, studying her keenly. "You think me a wraith," he said, with a hint of amusement in his voice.

She couldn't help but shudder. Must she dream about dead people speaking to her? "Naturally."

With a smile, he held out his hand to hers.

Tellie stared at it, uncertain. Did he want her to shake it? Best humor him. It didn't seem wise to offend a ghost, even an elven one. And while he seemed to be in character at the moment, you could never tell where a dream would go next. He could turn into a snarling shard any second.

Timidly, she placed her small hand in his. To her shock, it was warm and solid, as alive as any hand she'd ever felt, if not more so. "Wait, what?" she said. "You're real."

"I am no wraith. A ghost you would have seen within the mortal realm and likely that of a soul mourning their lost chance to change their fate. It is rare for the Saved to pass back there, unless for God's chosen purpose. We are only to come this far. Here in the Unseen, the spirit realm, I am as true and real as I ever was in mortal life."

She stared, a horrible fear running up her spine. "Are you....are you saying I've DIED?" What could have happened—the chemas turned evil? The food disagreed with her stomach?

Rendar laughed gently, shaking his head. "Oh no, no, I am sorry for inferring that. No, you have only been given special sight by Ayeshune for such a purpose as this. Errance needs you."

Her heart sank and tears flooded her eyes. This was swiftly turning into a cruel dream. It was too terrible for Rendar to think she could help Errance when he was beyond even the healer's aid. "I'm sorry, Your Majesty, but...but they say he may die..."

"Errance's spirit is in more peril than his body," Rendar interrupted. "It is smothered by Darkness, and so long as it remains thus, he will not recover." A snarl entered his voice. "The Darkness plays games with visions and chains. We can combat it."

"I'm sorry..." Tellie said politely. "We?"

"I have lived long and seen many things," he said. "The Darkness and I have a history—one that has given him a greater drive to persecute my son—and while I have been given great power, especially in the Unseen, the Darkness would use memories of my past sins and failures against me, distracting me from the purpose at hand. I may combat his attacks, but you...you, Tellie...you have powers that I do not."

By all the stars above, this dream was taking more liberties than she ever had in real life. Imagine! An elf king saying he lacked powers she had!

"What sort of powers?" she asked, curious to see what outrageous answers the dream would give.

"You are akin to who Errance once was, what he has lost, what he needs to remember. You are innocent and kind, and that takes courage. And you have faith in the Lord, even if it is a young faith. If you did not, it would not be safe for you to come here, but as it is your belief seeks strength. If the Darkness attacks with shame and pain—and he will—you will be a bright, contrasting light."

"But I've known pain," she whispered, heart jerking as she remembered the sound of the racking coughs in the cold house...and then later...silence.

"Your pain was born from love, something the Darkness does not understand. You are able for this. Ayeshune has called you. Will you answer?"

Slowly, she nodded and rose to her feet. "Yes. I mean, yes, if it's really going to help Errance."

"It will be frightening," he warned. "But I and the One are with you to keep the Darkness at bay while you fight for Errance's life."

Would she get a sword? Armor? Where exactly was this dream going next? Tellie slipped her hand into the king's, and he turned and strode forward. They passed through the wall as if it wasn't there. Tellie gasped and stammered for words, but she turned silent in the sight of the night. Though the moon was not full, she could see the entire village in soft brilliance from the straws of the roof to the moths fluttering from leaf to leaf. And in the huts, she could see the bright forms of people past the thatched walls.

"Are those the chemas?" she asked.

"Yes, and their spirits are bright in the shade of these mountains. I admit, their aid was most unexpected to me, as were their sincere prayers tonight that have weakened the Darkness. He is frightened now, so intent to keep Errance under shadow…"

As they approached the healing hut, Tellie's steps faltered as a phantom of fear touched cold fingers to her heart. The night darkened here, and only Rendar remained haloed in soft radiance.

"Might I have a light?" she asked.

"You already have one."

The necklace? Yes, it had come into the dream with her, in her pocket exactly as she'd left it. She lifted the medallion before her eyes, letting it spin till it looked whole. Yet so very fragile it seemed, so very easily shrouded.

"Come," the elf king said, and taking her hand, they passed through the hut's wall.

The Darkness enveloped them, as poisonous as hate. Whispers shuddered through it, memories of hopeless ages and fallen lives. Shadows lurked in every corner and so dense were their weight, that very breath was forgotten.

Without thinking, Tellie clung to Rendar, burying her face in his side. Gently, he sank to one knee and, cupping one hand under her chin, looked deep into her eyes.

Tellie looked back, and all darkness fled forgotten as she stood mesmerized by that stunning, silver gaze. She could see a life lived and finished and then beyond in the endless depths of his eyes, and she shivered, not with fear, but wonder.

"What are you afraid of, Tellie?" he asked.

"Well," she said, squirming with embarrassment. "It's…dark."

"Why is that to be feared?"

She hesitated, trying to tell if it was a trick question. "I…can't see anything…and anything could be hiding in it." She blushed at how ridiculous the simple answers sounded.

"Where can darkness not abide?" he continued calmly.

"Um...in light?"

"And what is contrary to hate?"

"Love, I guess."

"What can conquer despair?"

"Hope."

At each answer, the moon medallion shone brighter and brighter till the two of them knelt within a sphere of light.

But the darkness seethed just outside, and Tellie trembled as she fancied she heard voices calling from it. Were those the glowing eyes of devils just in the corner of her vision? Quickly, she forced herself to stare directly at them, and they vanished. Clamping her teeth together to keep them from chattering, she reached for Rendar's arm. To her panic, he stood and took a step back, gazing away from her into the void beyond, one hand resting lightly on the hilt of his sword.

"Your Majesty!" she whispered in a voice far too shrill.

"What are your dreams, Tellie?" he asked.

She sat back on her heels with a frown. What sort of question was that to ask in a place where dreams so obviously died? And her dreams were precious to her. She'd never really discussed them with anyone before. Rubbing the moon medallion between her fingers, she studied its perfect craft. Then she murmured, "I...I'd like to have a family...a real home. My parents died when I was little, and the orphanage and the Nornes really just weren't...loving."

"What about beyond?" Rendar continued as if they were having a pleasant conversation over tea. "When you're grown up?"

Tellie blushed. Here were things she barely had allowed herself to muse over. But the elf's voice was warm and kind, and she could not refuse to share. "I want to be married...in a white dress with flowers...and puffed sleeves!" she blurted. "I...I'd like to have children, I suppose."

"How many?" Rendar said with a chuckle.

"Two," Tellie answered promptly. "Boy first and girl second, so she has a brother she can look up to."

"And of course so she can't flaunt her age over him. Dreadfully annoying," Rendar laughed.

"I never thought of that. But I suppose him flaunting his age could be just as irritating," she shot back.

"Point taken."

A snarl sounded from the darkness, and the steel swish of Rendar's sword being drawn. There was a quiet scuffle with strange sounds, not like metal and flesh, but will against will, power battling power.

Tellie gasped, and in the following silence, she heard distant cries echoing in wraithlike sibilance. Screams. Screams of agony unimaginable, with cruel laughter ringing alongside.

Biting back a scream of her own, Tellie cried, "Rendar, I can't do this! I don't even see Errance? Where is he, anyway? I thought you said we were going to help him!"

"Errance is here."

Her rapid breaths of terror came to a halt. He was in here? Well, of course he was. They had entered the healing hut. But she saw no glowing spirit like Rendar's or the chemas, and she had a dreadful suspicion she wouldn't be able to feel anything if she explored either—nothing she wanted to feel anyway.

She swallowed hard. She couldn't leave Errance here in this devouring darkness, not when he hadn't left her in the prison of Tertorem. "What do I do?"

"Sing," the king of old responded. "Sing with all your heart and with all your soul. All the things of which we just spoke...they are powerful weapons against the Darkness, gifts that Errance needs restored. So sing and pour your very love into the words."

Uncertainly, Tellie began to obey. Her voice quavered like an autumn leaf ready to fall, and the song she sang was simple—a mere child's ditty. More screams and snarls stirred around her, and in a desperate bid to drown them out, she sang louder. The child's song ended, and she picked up an old hymn, *her voice, though not perfect, ringing out unashamed.*

> *"The world is slowly fading;*
> *The paint is turning grey.*
> *As the canvas frays around us,*
> *All we can do is pray.*
>
> *The picture will be repainted*
> *With a paint that does not fade.*
> *The day is soon in coming*
> *When the picture will be remade"*

Words sprang to her mind, and she sang them out, filling each note with memories of blue skies where swallows flew, and green fields where flowers grew. She sang of hope and dreams come true. Of broken bonds, and coming through. And as each word danced off her tongue, the darkness began to turn and run.

Then Tellie fell, her strength flown, and darkness closed around once more.

oOo

"Tellie. Tellie, wake up."

A hand shook her shoulder. Most annoying. There were few things she disliked more than being woken up from a deep sleep. Irritably, she opened her eyes. Sunlight streamed in through the loft window, and she squinted. When her sight focused, she found herself staring at Tryss.

The young woman's smile beamed as bright as the new morning.

Heart fluttering, Tellie sat up, hardly daring to hope. "Errance?" she gasped.

"He will live," Tryss cried, grabbing her by the shoulders and wrapping her up in her arms. "Master Holivari says his spirit has returned, and he is recovering!"

Tears flooding her eyes, Tellie hugged Tryss in return with all her strength. Just for a moment, she remembered the dream and wondered if more than the healer's skill had touched Errance, but she quickly dismissed that fancy.

"Is he awake?"

"No, not yet, that is why I woke you. It would be best if he sees your friendly face first."

They hurried down the ladder, bidding farewell to the kind hostess stirring a pot of morning gruel, and ran through the already lively village to the healing hut. The freshness of the morning air and light swept Tellie's heart up upon wings. As she passed through the doorway, a brief memory of shadows and screams flitted across her mind, but she couldn't see how such things could exist here.

The Ancient and the healer stood inside, speaking in low voices. Errance was now lying on a cot, and she winced to see his mangled body again, even though the bandages covered most of him.

"Ah, Tellie," the Ancient said when they entered. "Good, you are here. Holivari has questions about our elf prince. Is there anything else about him that you think we should know?"

Tellie glanced down at Errance and watched his eyes open.

"Yes," she said. "He's awake."

Errance took one look at the strangers standing around him.

And attacked.

157

13

oOo

The Darkness lifts. And as my strength returns and my eyes open, I see—

Errance lunged for Master Holivari, but fell short as the chema leapt backwards. The elf fell to the floor, clearly not anticipating his arms being bound to his chest. One arm ripped free of the bandages and propelled him to his feet with a powerful thrust. He grabbed the leg of a small table as he went and swung it with all his force at the Ancient.

The Ancient vanished, then reappeared by the door, calling for aid.

Frozen, Tellie watched in horror as Errance turned again to Master Holivari, reaching for his throat. She snapped from her petrified state, and without any thought of her own safety, she dashed across the room and grabbed the elf's arm. "Errance, stop it, STOP IT!"

He swung around to face her, muscle and sinew straining the frame of his gaunt body, wild anger ablaze in his eyes. She paralyzed, unable to move or breathe.

But he made no move to strike. Confusion clouded over the anger, and he staggered backwards.

Then Tellie found herself against the wall, pinned in place by Errance's arm as he stood protectively in front of her, bent and ready to pounce, facing the chema men gathered in the door. She pushed against his arm, but it felt more like a rod of iron than flesh and bone.

"Errance! Errance, these are our friends, for goodness sake!" She squirmed free and darted away before he could pull her back, running to the Ancient's side. Spreading out her arms to shield them, she cried, "They've saved us, see? They saved us!"

For a moment more the wild craze flickered through the elf's eyes. Then he blinked rapidly, and his gaze was clear, though no less hostile. He regarded the chemas with deep suspicion—defensive men, withered Ancient, and dismayed Tryss alike. He hunkered against the wall, rattling breath panting in the shaken silence.

Wheeling around to the Ancient, Tellie whispered, "You and your people better leave for a bit. I can tell him what's happened."

The poor old man's eyes were stretched so wide he looked like an owl. He nodded at her words, but whispered in return, "Someone could stay…"

She knew at once what he meant. A chema could blend into the surroundings and remain with her in case Errance stayed savage. But no. Errance needed someone he could trust. She wouldn't give him false security. "No."

"Tellie…" Tryss whispered, eyes pleading.

"No. I'm fine, Errance and I are friends."

The chemas retreated enough to shut the door, and while Tellie suspected they still hovered outside, the privacy would have to be enough. She looked back to see that Errance had sunk to the ground, knees drawn up his chest as if that could be a wall between him and the rest of the world. His fingers fluttered like broken wings over the wrapped bandages.

"Where are we?" he rasped.

When she stepped towards him, he started like she'd drawn a knife, so she remained where she stood.

"It's all right, Errance," she said, trying to sound both bright and gentle. "You collapsed, but we were found by some natives of the forest. I admit, I was scared of them at first too, but they really are wonderful. They took care of you as best they could, as you can see, but we were still afraid you wouldn't make it. I can't say how glad I am to see you awake."

"They're chemas."

She shivered at the harshness of his voice. "Yes, that's right. They're quite extraordinary. I never heard too many stories about them, so I wasn't—"

"Chemas live in the North."

Even with their linens so tenderly wrapped around his wounds, would he spare them no grace? "They said so too, but apparently this is a different kind of chema—"

"How much have you told them?"

She swallowed hard. *Here it comes.* "Oh, everything," she said cheerfully.

She might as well have drawn a knife and stabbed him for all the shock on his face was worth. "Everything?" he yelped. Quickly slipping a less honest expression over his fear, he hunkered down deeper and growled between his teeth, "Everything."

"They're quite kind, really, especially Tryss, who's been taking such good care of you."

He hissed, lifting red-rimmed eyes. "You are such a child."

Heat flared in her cheeks, but she managed to bite down a retort. "Look, I know you're scared," she said, "but the fact is that we needed help and these people are providing it. You're not in prison anymore. Not everyone is trying to hurt you."

Clearly, he did not believe her. The pain, anger, and fear slowly faded from his face, but it was only replaced by a mask. A fragile wall, and if it fell, Tellie guessed the fire beyond it burned even deadlier than before.

She swallowed hard, touching the door's handle behind her just to make sure she had a way out. "How about…how about you just try meeting them, all right? I promise, they are not so bad."

His eyes followed her hand to the door, and his body tightened. "No. They will not touch me again."

The veiled threat in his words clearly told he was not to be crossed in this matter. "How about some clothes then?" she offered. "It would look better than bandages."

After a long moment of silently staring at the door handle, even though her hand had left it, he said, "Only if they're black."

"Black?" She wrinkled her nose. She wasn't sure the chemas possessed such a color in their wardrobe, and anyway, it was sort of a depressing choice after prison.

He lifted his gaze, cold, challenging, and contemptuous. "My father is dead. What else do you think I should wear?"

Her heart squeezed. How could she have forgotten, so carelessly overlooked the only wound still bleeding? Shutting her eyes, she searched for some way to apologize, to make it right. And why wasn't she more sorry about Rendar's death? She'd looked into his wise face and though she hadn't known him long, it was strange she didn't feel his death more keenly. Why did she feel like was forgetting something, something that she ought to tell Errance? But no words came, so she silently left the hut.

The chemas stood just outside, the men taut with unease and the women wide-eyed with fear.

Wonderful, they probably heard everything, she thought with an inward wince. But she only smiled and said, "See, I told you we're friends."

oOo

Silence hung with perilous balance in the hall of the Voice. For the past several minutes he had neither blinked nor breathed as he stared at the man he'd summoned. Of course, he knew everything about the man before he had stepped through the door, but there was nothing like making a mortal wait.

This man was the sort who'd fought his entire life to make something of himself. Every pinch of respect he'd fought and clawed for, now clinging to it with savage desperation. A man swelling with poisonous pride in a bid to feel of worth around anyone better than him. Lack of love, evil taunts, and ridicule had turned him into this—a monster willing to hurt anything so long as it made him feel stronger. He was a common sort of man. A common sort that the Darkness loved to use.

"So," said the Voice. "What did you say your name was, again?"

The man's throat knotted in a hard swallow. "Daran, Your Greatness."

The demon leaned back, fingers splaying over the edge of the throne arms. "Ah. You are the one who brought in the two children."

"Yes."

"Hmm." He smiled at the mortal until he saw drops of sweat appear, then continued. "Well. Since you've proved yourself able, I have another mission for you. You must have heard by now that the Prisoner has escaped. You see, I'm playing a little game. And part of my game is that you go out and hunt him and—if you can catch him—bring my Prisoner back."

Daran straightened, a glint flickering across his steely eyes. "As you command."

The Voice cocked his head, like a hawk watching a mouse. He'd seen the look, however brief, and how delicious it was. "What's this? Your interest intrigues me. Explain."

Reddening, the man stuttered, "It's just...it's just that he's a legend. All speak of the Unbroken Prisoner, and we...your servants...like to think of ways we'd crush him."

"Oh?" The Voice widened his eyes. It was all he could do not to laugh. These little fantasies of the mortal men always amused him. Like they thought they could do what he had not accomplished. Yet perhaps all they wanted was the chance to be above and better than the elven prince. The only way they could ever delude themselves with that was for his bloody body to be ground under their heel.

"His resilience is remarkable," the Voice continued aloud. "When I think of how he endures and recovers from so much, my desire for the celestial race turns to frenzy. He is only half celestial, you realize; imagine the potential of a true blood turned to my side. Of course, the prince turned to my side would be sweet as well, but he is stubborn. Ah, so very stubborn. It's what I love most about him, truth be told. An individual trait, I believe, as I heard he was stubborn and

somewhat rebellious as a youth. It is what drove him to my clutches after all."
He inhaled deeply as if he smelt some heady fragrance. "There is nothing quite
like the consequences of indiscretion."

His eyes flared open, fixing upon the mortal man. "Go then. Retrieve that
which is lost."

Daran swallowed. "Is there…there a reward for catching him?"

Reward. Oh, but this one was ambitious and all kinds of stupid. Refraining
from rolling his eyes, the Voice leaned back and tapped his finger to chin.
"That's for you to decide. The Unbroken Prisoner…in your hand…well…I only
require you bring him back alive."

The embers of his wicked soul flared to life in Daran's eyes, and with a
sharp bow, he departed.

The Voice stared where the man had stood long after he'd left, chin in hand.
He spoke to the thin air. "It almost makes one weep how thoroughly my
corruption spreads."

And he smiled.

oOo

"Black clothes?" Tryss blinked in surprise at Tellie's question. "Well yes,
we do have some human clothes for traveling when we need to blend in more
than just by color." She searched through the baskets until she found a black
shirt and trousers. They were a little worn and loose, but they would work.

Tellie carried them back and announced her arrival. She couldn't see Errance
through the narrow crack of the door when she brought him the clothes, only his
gaunt hand as he snatched the material inside and then slammed the door shut
again.

She sat on a log outside to wait, Tryss perched beside her.

"I told the cooks to prepare a mild broth," the chema woman said in an effort
to make conversation. "Hopefully, he can keep it down. A starving stomach
doesn't handle food well."

Tellie only half listened as the minutes ticked by. He was certainly taking a while to change. True, he'd be slow with his injuries—he should have had someone to help him—but nevertheless, she wondered if he'd fainted again. Still, from the fear he'd shown earlier, it could be that he was just dragging it out as long as possible.

She hopped down and trotted over to the door. "Errance? Errance, are you all right in there?" There was no answer. "Errance, if you don't answer, I'm coming in."

Tryss raised her brows.

Tellie blushed. "Or...or I'll send some men in or something."

The door flew open.

Errance loomed, glaring with all his terrifying might.

Tellie blinked. For a man who had looked like a corpse not too long ago...he still looked like a corpse. But one living, breathing, and ready to strike. One sleeve hung loose, his broken arm still bound to chest. As far as she could see, he'd been wise enough not to remove many of the bandages.

His gaze lifted above her and—he blanched. He retreated behind the door, pulling it in front like a shield.

The childish gesture pricked her heart. How very well she recalled that feeling, the moment she stepped from the orphanage to go by wagon to her new home. She'd hoped that something better awaited—a whole new world of opportunity and hope. And yet what if it wasn't? What if it was worse and she'd be safer remaining in the cage she knew?

"Hey," she said softly. "It will be all right, Errance." She looked behind to see what had alarmed him so. "Oh, that's Tryss. She's a healer, and she found us."

The Ancient approached them, leaning heavily on his staff. When he'd come quite near, he bowed. "Prince Errance," he said, and the elf stiffened. "You would do my tribe great honor if you would sup with us this morning."

Errance said nothing, and when he continued to say nothing, Tellie stepped forward. "I'm sure that would be very nice! I'm still hungry after a few meals, so

I'm sure Errance is starving."

The old man beckoned and headed for the fire pits where the chemas were gathered. After a tense moment, Errance stepped after him.

The girls followed a safe distance behind. "Don't mind him," Tellie whispered to Tryss. "You're probably the first pretty woman he's seen in a while."

"Yes," Tryss said, rolling her eyes. "You could tell he was utterly charmed."

The chemas sat around their ashen fire pits, laughing and chattering as they awaited the meal, but the largest circle of all belonged to the Ancient and his family, and he led his guests to this one. Some empty seats on the log benches waited near the Ancient's chair.

It might have been proper for the elf heir to sit beside the village chief, but Tellie took one look at Errance's face and sat in the honored seat. No one made objections, and she patted the space beside her. Errance remained standing, staring at the empty seat next to his.

"Errance!" Kelm came bounding in, hair and face still mussed from sleep. "You're finally awake! Oh, you gave us a scare." He stuck out his hand to shake, and never had a glad grin been more honest.

When Errance did not respond, the boy sat with a hearty sigh, and after a few heavy moments, the elf sank slowly down between the two children.

The chemas, who had fallen to silent staring, returned to their gaiety, and many women of the village wove from circle to circle bearing great trays of fruit and meat. As Tellie took her breakfast with a grateful smile, she realized that in all the anxiety of the last few meals, she'd not noticed the food. Three sticks skewered with roasted meat and fruit lay on the wooden tray, along with rolled-up leaves stuffed with a grainy sort of cheese. She pulled off a chunk of meat and popped it her mouth, only to choke in surprise at the spice. She drowned the heat with a cup of milk. But even that tasted strange. It wasn't goat or cow.

"Tryss," she said as the chema girl returned from serving with a tray of her own. "What type of milk is this?"

"Oh, that's from our milthi moth aviaries," she said, pointing away to the jungle.

Kelm choked mid-swallow. "You mean I'm drinking moth-spit?" he said.

Tryss lifted an eyebrow. "I suppose so. Do you avoid bee-spit for the same reason?"

"That's different," he said, wiping his mouth. "That's honey."

Though the idea of moth milk didn't appeal to her either, Tellie didn't want to come across ungrateful, so she took another swallow. It wasn't really a bad taste, just thick and strong.

She glanced at Errance. Not to her surprise, he hadn't touched his bowl of broth. "It's not poisoned," she said with a huff. "Here, let me try it."

He pulled it back from her hands. "Chemas," he said suddenly. "Are well known for their lies."

The mood around the fire changed. The chatter stopped, and every face turned and looked at the elf prince.

"Errance, that's rude," Tellie began.

"Well," Kelm interrupted, looking quite uncomfortable, "He's not exactly wrong, Tellie."

They all looked to the Ancient, waiting to see how he would respond. The old man gave one nod. "It is true," he said at last. "Most chemas you will encounter in this part of Orim are hired as thieves, spies, assassins. Our gift is suited to such shameful acts."

"They have ever lived in the North," Errance continued, "hiding away in their cold mountains and cold halls, writing histories of their false self-glory." He leaned back, eyes narrowed. There was a gleam in them and a lift to his mouth that sent a shiver down Tellie's spine. It was too much like how she'd seen him with the prison guard. The moment right before he'd struck. "Who'd believe they were anything other than liars, thieves, murderers, and monsters whose claws are still scored across my body. So tell me"—his lip curled—"why should I trust anything you do?"

The folk around the fire were murmuring. Scowls flickered in the firelight. There was the creak of shifting in seats.

But the old man only nodded again. "All that you say is true. It is because of these things that we separated from those in the North long ago, rejecting more than their culture, but their beliefs. We are followers of God, not of our own Glorification, and no one here has murdered anyone. As for the scars you speak of, I am sorry, but there is difference to be found between the chema and their fallen kind."

"Oh please!" Errance spat. "Everyone knows that a chema is a stone's throw from a shard!"

The entire tribe erupted. Men shouted, leaping to their feet, and women shook their fists, yelling any manner of protest or insult. Errance bolted to his feet, free arm tense for battle.

Falling back against Kelm in dismay, Tellie looked from face to face, seeing either hatred or confusion in every expression. At first she did not understand why Errance's bitter words ignited such a reaction from their hosts, but as the accusation replayed through her mind, its meaning dawned on her with pale horror. The nightmarish face of Kilkus the shard flashed before her vision, yet it bore no resemblance to the people here. How could Errance say they turned into such monsters?

The Ancient stood, raising his frail hand over his head. "Enough," he said, voice gaining unusual strength. "Enough!"

At his command, the chemas ceased their angry roar, but many of them did not sit or remove their hand from their weapons. They glared at Errance with contempt, and he glared back with equal potency.

The Ancient slowly pivoted, turning solemn eyes on each and every one of his people, before facing Errance again. "Elf prince, you are too young to remember the dealings our kind had with yours, but you were taught the facts well enough." He sat again, heaving a heavy breath. "You have every right to question us. But I cannot prove to you we are not your enemies any more than we have. Did they ever wash you or bandage you or give you food?"

"They're creative," Errance said, which wasn't an exact answer.

Nobody seemed to know what to say next. And then a sudden movement in the tense stillness. Tryss stood up, dipped her spoon into Errance's bowl of broth and took a sip. "It's not poisoned," she said.

He jolted, spilling the broth over his hand, and stared at her.

And then without a word, he turned away and walked out of the gathering. He headed straight for the empty healing hut, the door slamming so hard behind him that the reeds shook.

The supper continued in uneasy silence. But Tellie could not help but notice that Errance had taken the bowl of broth with him.

14

oOo

The air is hot, humid, suffocating, and my stomach churns and threatens to be sick from the food I dared eat. I do not pace, for that would mean I was caged, and I have entered these brittle walls again by my own choice. Better to give yourself breakable bonds than be held captive by others. When night comes, perhaps I shall split the reeds apart and go...go...where..? I don't know where I am. I don't know who these people are. The children believe they are friends, but what do they know of friends, what do they know of lies and betrayal? I know it, and that knowledge is power.

Tryss had never been invited to a Council. She always stayed behind to care for her younger siblings and send them off to bed while her parents and elders conferred in the village center.

But her great-great grandfather, the Ancient, had summoned her, and so for the first time she sat among the village elders upon the logs ringing the largest fire pit under the jungle canopy and the starry sky above. She shifted in the heavy hush as all waited for the Ancient to arrive, hoping that the warm light of the fire did not reveal how nervous she felt. Really, the fluttering of her pulse surprised her for she'd only ever looked forward to sitting among the leaders and listening to their wisdom.

Perhaps it was because this night, true fear held every tongue still, turned every face solemn. Perhaps it was because of the strangers asleep in the nearby huts. Perhaps it was because the darkness of night now felt like devouring Darkness pressing down upon the hearts of all.

The Ancient approached, slow and frail after the long day, leaning upon his staff and the arm of one of his grandsons. He sat at his place in the circle and fixed his star-twinkling eyes upon the tense faces before him. "Quite an unexpected turn of events, yes?" he said, mouth twitching into a smile.

A few unsteady laughs, and everyone exhaled. Their Ancient was good and wise and surely he would lead them to peace as he always had before.

"What is to be done about this elf prince?" asked one of the eldest sons.

Rubbing the stubble on his chin, the old man mused, "Well, he must be seen safely back to Aselvia. As Ayeshune saw it fit to lead them to our care, we cannot send them on their way without help. But who could we send that the elf would accept?"

"Ha," scoffed another. "He will accept no one. His prejudice is clear enough."

"And justified," the Ancient said sternly. "We must send one who is not a threat. A strong male and protector they do not need, Errance is that enough. A guide and a caretaker is what we should provide." He blinked as he gazed around the gathering and then settled on one person. "And I can think of no one more suited than our beloved Tryss."

An empty silence followed, the sort of silence that happens when every thought has spun out of the mind.

Tryss sat blinking in muddled shock, not quite certain she'd actually heard her grandfather utter her name.

Then the circle erupted into protest. Her parents, uncles, aunts, elder cousins, and wise mentors aside shouted their disapproval, but through all their dissent, the Ancient merely sat quiet, his gaze fixed on Tryss. She stared back, pouring her own questions and uncertainties into her large eyes and anxious mouth.

"She is not safe with him! He nearly struck you down!"

"But he didn't," the Ancient said mildly.

"He attacked our healer!"

"He had just woken—cornered and frightened," reminded the old man. "If there's anyone with a gentle hand to soothe fear, it is Tryss."

"Yes," exclaimed Tryss's mother, "which is why she must stay here and care for the children."

"Oh come now, Felisii," the Ancient said. "You have other daughters of age to lend more help in the household."

"You would send our next master healer?"

"With the most wounded man I have seen in all my life? Yes."

"He would harm her!"

"There that is again," the Ancient said. "But no. No, you must but look into his eyes and see he would harm nothing but in self-defense."

"What do *we owe him?*"

The question spewed from the lips of the Ancient's second-born, a sinewy man with flashing eyes. Crimson anger stained his face, the firelight colored his bared teeth. "What do we owe that man? We give him nothing but good-will, and he throws it back in our face with insults. Why should we sacrifice one of our brightest and best to him?"

No one spoke as they considered the question. Tryss hunkered back into the shadows but no one looked her way, so lost were they in their own conflict. And as for her, what was her answer to the question? When she had found the children and the elf in the forest, her heart had overflowed with compassion for them, and when she'd wrapped the wounds of the prince, she'd pitied him with all her soul. But when he'd woken…the harshness of his spirit, the violence of his actions…she'd not expected that. Perhaps she should have, perhaps she should give him grace in light of his torments. Still, he'd reviled them at the feast. It'd hurt her, hurt with a sharpness she hadn't expected.

But still…

"Because it is the right thing to do," she said, standing and striding to the circle's center. "Everyone has given their opinion on whether or not I should go, but no one has asked me. And I am willing. If the Ancient says that I need not fear him, I'll trust that. And there are the children, whom we've hardly mentioned. Are we expecting the prince to take care of them—him, a prisoner for seventy years? Ha! I'll be surprised if he even knows how to take care of himself!"

Wide eyes turned to her, and in their depths, she saw guilt and understanding, but then one firm voice spoke.

"Tryss," said her father. "I will not allow it."

"And where then," the Ancient said, struggling to his feet, "do you suggest we find our new home?"

Confused murmurs winged through the gathering, and Tryss's father frowned. "My elder, what does that have to do with Tryss?"

A certain sadness creased the old man's brow as if he was sorry to speak, to bring it this far, but he said, "The question has arisen of what we owe the prince. *The heir of Aselvia.* If we aided him, the question should be what does he owe us?"

Tryss sat silently back on the bench, mouth falling open in the same graceful movement. It was a fair question, perhaps, but it seemed vastly unjust and selfish when the fugitives' plot was so dire.

"There have not been good dealings between the chemas and the elves since the days of true Glory," the Ancient said, wheezing and clutching his staff with frail fingers. "If we helped the heir to the throne, do none of you see how that could change? The Darkness is on our doorstep. We are now doomed to seek a new home, but where are we to find one? Mid Orim is not the same as it was when I first traveled here, cities of men have arisen and forests are scarce. We would be hard-pressed to find land to welcome us, but in Aselvia there may be room for all."

"You suggest," said one of the lesser chieftains, "that we might live in the sacred valley of the elves?" More than a few breaths inhaled at the thought of that, more than a few lips tightened.

"If not that," the old man amended carefully, "then at least they might show us where we can find sanctuary."

Uncertainty tearing across his face, Tryss's father looked to her. His voice wavered as he said, "And she would be safe? Even if he is no danger, darkness dogs his flight and you cannot deny that."

"Nor can I claim that we are any safer here so near to the heart of Darkness as it spills out in search. She is chema, my son, and may be unseen if she wishes. You taught her the way of the bow and the knife. She is as safe as any we might send."

"Father." Tryss struggled to make sure her voice did not falter. She was not certain of this herself, did not wish to think too closely of what it might mean. But if what her grandfather said was true, what choice did she have? And besides…there was a certain thrill to the thought of seeing a world only gazed upon from the highest trees…and rescuing an elf prince…and the children, of whom she was already fond. "Father, I can do this. For our honor and home, I can."

Deep sadness sank into his lined face, and he exhaled heavily, passing a resentful glance to the Ancient. But when his eyes lifted back to hers, she saw the pride and hope within. "Do so then," he said. "Do so, my daughter."

oOo

As Tellie awoke, one thought cleared her mind with bright morning sun.

Today, they journeyed home.

With a squeak of excitement, she scrambled up from the cot and yanked the blankets back into order. But as suddenly as the thrill came, so did the fear, and her hands stilled. Home. What would that mean exactly? It certainly did not mean the Nornes or the orphanage. No, this was a place brand new, and as she already had the heir with her, it wasn't like she needed to stay at Aselvia in case he showed up. If they didn't want her anymore, what would she do…?

Shaking away such worries, she focused on the present one. First of all, getting home safely was the trick. She'd never seen many maps but East sounded rather far from West, and if there was an entire ocean between them, how long would they have to sail to cross it?

Only their hosts could answer such questions and maybe Kelm, so she hurried to fix the room as she left it, then darted out into the village center.

Errance was easy to spot, tall and dark among the short, pale people, and for all appearances he stood alone and separate in the world, but as Tellie approached she realized that the Ancient stood near him speaking to him and holding a map with trembling hands.

"Oolum is the nearest port city, only two days walk from here," the Ancient said. "The bay is narrower here as well, so a voyage to the west side should only be a few days trip. Now, I feel I should warn you that Oolum will be very different from anything you've experienced. It's a prosperous market city, attracting various people from all over the world, full of revelries and pleasures that entice; but do not be deceived, it would only bring you harm."

"Oh," Errance said through a hard, short smile. "It may not be very different."

After the silence became too awkward, he finally cast aside his aloof posture and turned slightly to eye the scrawling on the goat-skin map. "What about if I went by land?"

The Ancient sighed, his wrinkles multiplying. "See for yourself, Your Highness, the way up around the bay would take you over a week. The possibilities of getting caught increase. So as to insure you reach your destination safely, I will provide you with a guide."

"A guide?" His brow arched, mouth tightening in a subtle sneer. "From what I understand, all you people do is hide in a jungle."

The Ancient straightened his spine and met the elf's intense stare squarely. "We go to trade in Oolum from time to time. We are more knowledgeable about this side of the world than a stranger, let alone one cut off from the land for seventy years."

Tellie paused a few steps away to avoid the crossfire, hiding a little smile. She noticed Kelm already nearby, an interested grin on his face, and he beckoned her over with a toss of his head.

"How long have they been going like this?" she whispered, trotting over.

"Oh, a good while. It took the Ancient forever to even get Errance to talk about the journey." The boy shook his head, half in exasperation, half in admiration. "Save me, but your elf prince is an ornery fellow."

"He's not *my* elf prince," she mumbled, looking back to the debate.

"And there is another thing, Your Highness," the old man continued. "You are not traveling alone. You have Tellie and Kelm to think of."

Surprise, no matter how brief, flitted across Errance's face. "They aren't coming with me."

Tellie gasped, leaping forward. "We most certainly are!"

Right alongside her protest, the Ancient asked, "Then what exactly do you plan to do with them?"

Uncertainty flushed his cheeks, and he looked away to regather defense. But his stray hair and turned head could not hide the trapped expression that stole across his face, the dawning of unexpected responsibility. Even he must have seen he could not foist the children off on the chemas, far from anything they knew.

"Leoren and Casara offered to take me to Aselvia, and I still intend to go there!" Tellie cried.

"And my master only has routes in the West," Kelm said, sounding more than a little alarmed. "Look here, Errance, we escaped together and you can't abandon us now."

"Fine!" Errance said, the force of his voice silencing them. He took a deep breath to compose himself as he addressed the Ancient. "What do the children have to do with a guide?"

"They are children, just like you said," replied the old man. "I don't suppose you've had much experience taking care of children, especially two youths with antagonistic attitudes."

Offended, Tellie opened her mouth to reply, before she saw the Ancient was smiling at her.

Errance ran his fingers across the outlines of the arm still bound against his chest. His gaze was fixed on the ground as if that would help hide his insecurity.

"I…I see your point."

The Ancient plunged ahead. "And then there is cooking, washing, and oh, such other sundry things to do while on a journey."

The elf hesitated, a struggle flickering across his face. It could not be said what made up his mind, but it was clear when a side finally won, and he lifted his eyes, grim and determined. "Very well. I accept your offer."

"Wonderful," the Ancient said happily. "I shall go tell Tryss you've agreed."

"Oh, Tryss is coming?" Tellie exclaimed in delight, but her smile stuttered as Errance stiffened like he'd been whipped.

He took one hard step after the Ancient. "No woman," he hissed, "is accompanying me."

The old man faltered, his wrinkles caving in sudden alarm. He turned sharply and looked deep into Errance's eyes, deeper than the elf preferred if his retreating step back was any indication. But whatever the Ancient saw in those flaming blue depths turned his expression to an overwhelming and profound pity.

When he spoke, his voice was cheerful and kind, "Ah, but my dear boy, you already have a young lady with you."

Errance blinked and he glanced down at Tellie in confusion. "But…" he stammered. "She's just a girl."

Flushing, Tellie straightened and tried to look as grown-up as possible.

"Maidens are married and mothers by her age in some parts of the land," the Ancient reminded.

Tellie blushed even redder, especially at Kelm's snort, not so skillfully turned into a cough. Errance muttered something about "*idiotic.*" She could only hope he was talking about the practice and not her.

"So," the old man concluded, "it is most improper for a young lady to accompany two young men on such a long journey. Oh, I know she has nothing to fear from you both, very nice gentlemen you are no doubt, but the fact is neither of you men know how to cope with a young woman's needs. Tellie most certainly needs another female with her. And Tryss is perfectly adequate to care for you all."

"She will care for the children," Errance bit. "Not me."

"Of course, of course," the Ancient said amiably. "Now is it all settled?"

Tellie did not think herself particularly cunning, but she knew a shrewd mind when she saw one and it seemed to her as if she watched dozens of possibilities and routes and plans and escapes dash through Errance's eyes. But it was all gone in a moment, and there only remained that same cold fear that ever froze the surface.

A shiver ran through his shoulders. But his chin dipped in a firm and decisive nod.

15

oOo

The snakes. They think they can trick me like this, tie a spy to my ankle. Even before I was devoured by Darkness, I knew what chemas were. Sly, deceitful, cunning. But the trap they've set is real—I do not know what to do with these children, and their fates have been given to me, unfortunate as that may be. So I will play the game for now and allow this woman to come if it means care for the girl and boy. But I will be watching her for I know that sometime, eventually, she will make her move...

The warm air was so wet that it felt like you could have scooped up a dollop with a spoon. Tryss was used to such atmosphere, but she could see how it lagged the progress of her companions. There was nothing for it though. Slow or not, she led their path through vine-woven drapes, buggy bogs, and vivid, green gardens.

The curiosity of the children delighted her, and she answered all their questions with a smile. What was the name of the bulbous fungus on the trees? What was that brilliant blue bird that flashed across the way? Almost every extraordinary thing had a personal story attached to it, and her wild tales sent them into fits of laughter.

But through it all, Errance said nothing.

He might have walked and breathed in another world and on another journey for all the distance he set between them. If silence was a virtue, then he was indeed very righteous and rather too good to look their way. Not even the birds or the chimp ducking down from a branch could deter his concentration.

The light dwindled as the day wore on, and the children's energy dwindled long before that. As the shadows began to settle, Tryss called for the end of their march, and both Tellie and Kelm collapsed on fallen logs.

"We must start a fire," Tryss said, dropping her pack from her shoulder, "if we are to keep off the wild beasts of the night."

"What sort of wild beasts?" Kelm asked, voice catching, but he quickly cleared his throat, and added, "Tellie's scared of bears."

"No bears," Tryss said, smiling at Tellie's insulted face. "Wild cats, yes, but there aren't many large ones."

In a matter of moments, she'd built the frame for a strong fire and struck a flame between flint under its shelter. The flame fed on the fresh sap, sparking and crackling as it spread to the rest of the wood.

"Watch the fire, I'll be back." She headed out a short distance into the jungle, found the sort of tree she was looking for and scrambled up into its depths. Soon she came crawling back down, branches of clustered fruit hung over her shoulders.

When she stepped back into the firelight, she found that the children were trying to sponge the sweat off their faces, and Errance was sitting on the opposite side of the fire on the far edge of a log. She handed the fruit off to Kelm and continued observing the elf prince. His gaze had not strayed from a specific spot on the ground nor had his braced posture changed. From a brief appraisal, he seemed to be handling these changes well…but…as she studied him longer, she wondered if he stared at that spot because he couldn't handle anything more. Her study wandered to his hands, almost always an accurate telling of hidden emotion, but she noticed instead the dark, yellow skin spreading from under his bandages.

"Errance, would you let me change the dressing on your wounds?"

"No." If his mouth moved, she missed it, but his response had the force of a door slamming in place.

Taking a deep breath, she searched for another way in. There were always a few patients who feared nursing, but a calm smile and a sure hand could guide them into trust. This was more than that. He reminded her of a feral animal, still at the moment, but ready to lash, claw, and bite at the slightest provocation.

"Please…those wounds will get infected."

"They will heal." He said it with complete certainty.

"That's impressive." She touched her healer's satchel and drifted a few steps closer. "But you needn't heal on your own anymore. I'm here to help."

His eyes snapped from their exiled corner and met hers, ablaze with warning. She stopped in her tracks, resisting the urge to hide the satchel behind her back like a naughty child. Very well then. It wasn't as if she could force him.

"Oh come on, Errance." Tellie piped up from across the fire. "You've got to recover your strength."

"That's right," Tryss said softly. "I'm not going to hurt you. I mean I'll try not to, but I imagine you're in pain already. If you want me to stop, I will. Or you can walk away." As she spoke, she moved forward again and sat down on the log next to him. "May I?"

His focus had returned to his selected prison, and he didn't answer. But neither did he refuse her outright again, so she decided to take the risk. Carefully, she slipped her hand under his arm and guided it out into the open light. A shudder passed through him, but he showed no other resistance. With experienced hands, she began unwrapping the bandages, smearing oil where the cloth met skin to better loosen it. As it pulled free from his ravaged flesh, he let out a sharp breath and yanked his arm back to his side.

"Easy," she soothed. "Let me apply this balm. It's very gentle, and I won't apply it directly on your injuries. It's just going to numb your arm. So I can wash it."

"No," he whispered.

She should have stopped, she *knew* she should have, but she already had the balm on her fingers and was already reaching.

His arm whirred towards her, meeting her wrist with a sharp crack, and he nearly fell off the log in his haste to get away. "I SAID NO!" He scrambled to his feet, whirling around to face her as if he was about to fend off an attack.

She stared, clutching her smarting wrist to her chest. The children stared, frozen in the middle of their meal.

Then Errance closed his eyes, spun on his heel, and vanished into the darkness, snapping aside branches.

They finished eating in troubled silence, Tellie and Kelm casting anxious glances into the darkness where the prince had disappeared.

"You should sleep now," Tryss murmured, wrapping up the rest of the fruit for the morning. "We have a long day tomorrow." She was glad her voice stayed steady and that the shadows hid the trembling of her hands.

When the first light of morning lifted the night's shroud, Tellie groaned to find her clothes soaked with dew. In the jungle, the night barely cooled and so she still felt as hot and sticky as if she'd stepped into a bathhouse. As she stood and rubbed her aching back, she looked across the snoring body of Kelm and saw the figure leaning against a tree in the dim shadows. For a moment, her heart stilled in fear. The next, it leapt in relief, for it was Errance.

He did not look her way, in fact he was pointedly not looking at anyone. Just as pointedly, Tryss was not looking at him, sitting some distance away and peeling fruit for the morning fare.

Tellie gave an inward groan of frustration, but some of it must have slipped out because Tryss's attention jerked to her.

"Ah, was just about to wake you," Tryss said. "Wake Kelm, we can eat on the way. We need to keep up the pace if we want to reach the border by tonight. Walking to Oolum will only be bearable in the morning hours."

When all was made ready, they started out again into the thick wild. The birdsong had not ceased even during the night, different kinds just exchanged shifts, and they all trilled, squawked, and hooted till Tellie's head began to ache. No, more than her head. Every part of her was sore from sleeping on the ground and the long trek yesterday. There was very little time to pause and smell the roses, as it were. There was little time to pause at all. When there was chance of being caught by pursuing villains, one had to simply push on and on and on. Today, adventure was miserable and somebody else could have it!

To make things worse, the whole mood of the company was tense. Tryss led the way as if only she and the children existed, and Errance walked his own path even further from them than before.

Tellie kept casting him sidelong glances, biting her lip in frustration. Here, surrounded by greenery, birdsong, and fresh air, he looked more the prisoner than in the dungeons. What had happened to the man who had defied his captors so fearlessly, who had trod the path to freedom with such determination? He couldn't be this slump-shouldered, heavy-footed creature across from her.

Setting her jaw, she gradually tilted her steps to the side till she walked alongside him. "Did you want your necklace now?" she asked, fishing the medallion out from under her blouse and holding it up.

His eyes startled to hers, like he'd just noticed her, like he hadn't known anyone else still existed. Then the medallion claimed his attention, pulling his gaze left and right with its swing. His eyes shut; he looked back to the ground and shook his head.

Sighing, she let it drop. "Just as well." She noticed he'd unbound his broken arm and that it now swung stiffly by his side. The sleeves rolled halfway up his forearm, and she could see the fading bruises and scars on his wrists and hands.

As they trekked on, there was little else to do beside imagine stories or guess what Aselvia would be like once they reached it. Even now, that thought sent a flutter through her stomach. In her favorite dream, Leoren and Casara swept her into their fold with joy and showered her with every kind of adoring act she could think of.

"Errance," she began hesitantly, "You knew Leoren and Casara, right?"

He gave a short nod.

"Do they have children?" She wasn't against the idea if the siblings were older and also doting, but she rather hoped to be the center of attention no matter how dreadfully selfish that sounded.

"What?" He stopped dead in his tracks and stared at her with a stung expression.

"Um. Do they have children?"

"Are they married?"

"Er. Yes. Didn't you know?"

"No!" he said, and for once, he sounded young and unsure of himself. "He finally asked her? Everyone always encouraged him, but he'd somehow set it in his mind that he wasn't good enough to marry a princess!"

"Princess!" Tellie's heart dropped, then surged up on wings, then dropped again. Oh, why had they not told her! She'd almost been adopted by a princess. The dream just couldn't get any more surreal. "What do you mean she's the princess? She can't be Rendar's sister!"

"My mother's sister."

Tellie mulled this over. If poor Leoren did not think himself of worth to marry a princess, how on earth did she presume she'd be adopted by one? "Well, Leoren's the ambassador and now the steward," she said, unsure of where exactly elves drew the lines for castes. "Isn't that rather good enough?"

He delayed in answer, and when he spoke, the life in his voice had died away. "Ambassador. I see. I suppose…I suppose the position…needed to be filled…"

She remembered then the other elves who had died the night Errance was taken and winced at her lack of sensitivity. She plunged ahead to a better topic, hoping to cheer him, to fill his heart with dreams and longings as beautiful as hers. "What stories can you tell me about Aselvia?"

He did not answer for a moment. "Shall I tell you about the time its rivers ran red with blood and bodies lay hewn upon the white tile?"

"Wait, what?"

"Then do not ask me to discern memory from illusion," he said coldly.

She stopped walking, but he did not and so he was soon far ahead. Instead, Tryss came alongside her, having drawn gradually nearer with graceful subtlety.

"Probably better to leave him alone," she said quietly.

"I was only trying to lift his spirits," Tellie said, voice a little thick with frustration.

"Sweet of you, but he's a dangerous man."

"Well, he might be, but we're friends—"

"From your point of view."

Hurt, Tellie tried to speak again, but Tryss continued. "The fact is, you *don't* know what he's gone through. None of us do. He's under a terrible strain, and it is unwise to bait him." She cast an uneasy look after Errance's distant figure, her mouth drawing in a thin line.

Then she held up her arm. For the first time, Tellie noticed intricate scarring on the underside of her forearm.

"Once," Tryss said, "I had a pet monkey whose side had been torn open by a wildcat. I was only a little girl who thought I could save him. But when I picked him up, he attacked me. It's what animals and people do when they're frightened and in pain—they can't think straight."

"But Errance wouldn't hurt me. Why, he's saved me three times already!"

"He seems to care for you," she said, voice tiptoeing on the edge of doubt. "And that should make you all the more cautious, because in his condition, he is likelier to snap if he feels that someone he cares for is being cruel to him."

"I wasn't—"

"I know you weren't trying to be. But if he wants to leave the past in the past, it is better to let it stay there."

Tellie remained silent a while longer as they struggled through a dense tangle of the jungle, then asked. "What happened to the monkey?"

Tryss sighed. "It ran away. It ran away and died."

After considering that for a few sober moments, Tellie spoke again, her voice soft and sweet. "There used to be this window up in the orphanage attic. It could hardly let in any light because it was so covered in mold and dirt. I was afraid to play up there because it was so dark, so I determined to clean the glass. It took me days and days, but when I did, I discovered that the glass was every color of the rainbow. It showed a design of a mother holding a child. It was the most beautiful thing I had ever seen, and I'd have never known if I hadn't tried so hard to look underneath the grime."

Tryss listened, her mouth pursing in thought. She gave Tellie a fond look, the sort a mother gives when she is proud, but also ready to amend a slight error. "A window is not the best comparison to a man," she said.

"No," Tellie agreed. "But it's a pretty good comparison to a soul, don't you think?"

And Tryss had nothing to say to that, nothing at all.

As hoped, they reached the edge of the jungle by evening, but heavy rain clouds were beginning to gather in the sky, so when Errance showed signs of continuing onward, Tryss convinced him that it was best to spend the night under the lingering trees. Tellie and Kelm were sent to gather kindling for the fire, and when they returned Errance was nowhere in sight. Only Tryss remained, cutting up the remnants of the jungle grouse she'd shot earlier that afternoon and impaling the pieces on sticks to roast over the fire.

"Where's Errance?" Kelm asked.

Tryss brushed a tendril of hair from her eyes and replied, "I don't know. He just left. I don't think he went far."

All three flinched at the sound of an enormous splash in the nearby stream. "Yes," Tryss said. "I'm almost sure of it."

"What is he doing?" Tellie asked with a frown, starting off in the direction of the noise.

"Oh, for goodness sake, Tellie," Tryss gasped. "Give him some privacy. He might be bathing. Just leave him alone."

"Well, he could have told us not to bother him," Tellie retorted. Her frown deepened as there was another splash followed by a heavy thunk. "It sounds like he's waging a war."

"Maybe he's fighting off river sharks," Kelm suggested.

"Yes, Kelm, I'm sure that's exactly what he's doing," Tryss said, rolling her eyes.

The mysterious sounds continued, with fewer splashes but more thunks. With maddening calm, Tryss continued preparing dinner while the youths fidgeted, but after an especially large splash, she sat bolt upright and snapped, "All right, Kelm, go see what he's up to."

The boy crept off, and Tellie paced, forgetting such trivial things as helping Tryss with supper, until he came creeping back.

"Well?"

Kelm's brow was furrowed, and he sat down on a nearby log. "He's just in the middle of the stream building a dam out of the rocks."

"What on earth for?" Tellie yelped.

Instead of answering, Kelm pulled out the small knife given to him by the chemas and began chipping at a block of wood. "Well," he said, after a moment. "Well, I suppose it's just his way of keeping busy. My pa always did say it was good for a man to keep his hands and mind busy with work. And I suppose he's used to labor anyway."

Tryss bent back over the meat. "Leave him to it then. Kelm, could you build a shelter to protect us from the rain?"

"Sure," he said, rubbing the back of his neck. "But I don't know how good it will be at keeping the rain out."

Sighing, she stood. "Tellie, watch the food to be sure nothing steals it." She joined Kelm and they disappeared into the forest, their voices blending into the harmony of insect humming.

Tellie sat with a sigh and began building a miniature hut out of twigs to pass the time. The crash of falling river rocks rattled in her ears. She glanced back into the trees where the others had vanished. Then she quickly covered the meat with broad leaves and dashed off to find Errance.

The stream was not far. She climbed a steep ridge in the trees behind the camp with the help of exposed roots, and when she reached the top, she had a full view of the stream below, winding through a crumble of large rocks and fallen trees. Errance stood knee-deep in a large pool, stacking rocks upon each other, drenched clothes and hair sticking to his skin. He had not noticed her yet so she crept along the trees till she reached a moss-covered boulder and peeked over it, her chin and palms resting on the top.

For a while she did nothing but watch him as he continued to bend, pick up a rock, and place it upon another. Tellie doubted she could wrap her arms around some of the boulders he wrestled into place. He seemed to work tirelessly, but when the wall had become quite large, he finally faltered. He caught himself on a log when he stumbled, and his arm shook with fatigue.

She decided it was time for a distraction. She pulled herself fully up on the rock, crossing her legs beneath her. "Aren't you a little old to be playing in a stream?" she asked with a grin.

He didn't startle; barely glanced at her. But that bare glance was so icy, she felt obliged to say, "I was teasing."

Few things can be more discouraging than a one-sided conversation, but when Errance turned back to his work, she spoke doggedly on. "I mean, I understand." She cleared her throat. "You've got to keep busy some way. All you've been doing for years is work and work, and you can't suddenly stop. If you stop, you might rest, and if you rest, you might think. And if you think…you get scared. And it's hard to wait. Because you'd rather just be home at once and have it all over with. It's something like that, yes?"

Nothing answered her but the back of his rolling shoulders.

She swallowed hard. "I know you're angry with me. I've heard it's a good idea to release your anger in work, so I guess that's what you're doing too." Biting her lip, she looked down at her folded hands. "Anyway, I guess I upset you earlier with my prying. I have been told I ask too many questions. I'm sorry."

At that, he stiffened, and his head flicked to the side so he might see her face. Questions swam in his eyes, questions and confusion as he searched for any mocking in her expression, any hint of a lie. As if he had never heard an apology in years. Which maybe he hadn't. With a jerk, he whirled back to the wall with ferocious vigor.

Clearly, she wasn't going to get any real response. She should go back and guard the food before Tryss returned with a scolding. Anyway, it was beginning to rain.

"I..." His voice brought her whirling back. He was not looking at her, only at the water swirling around his legs. "If we make it back...I don't know...if I'll fit in."

Her lips shaped a perfect O. That was *her* problem, not his. She was the one who hoped for home but had every chance of being turned away because her purpose was fulfilled. But he was the prince, he was the heir, he was the king— why did he have to worry about fitting in?

Yet he did. Because those seventy years had mauled him into a new creature, and what would that mean for his country, for his family and friends? He was no longer the elegant and lovely elf, even she had to admit that. He was savage and feral, and how long would that take to change?

"Well," she said slowly. "This is your chance for a new life."

"Life." A bitter laugh choked in his throat. "What is that?"

The last light of the evening was fast fading, dragging the remnants of Tellie's good humor after it. "Please, Errance. Don't say things like that."

Abandoning his rock wall, he sloshed back onto the bank. "Ever consider life is a harsh sentence?" The words were a tight fit, scraping on the edges.

"Most people find death harsher," she snapped back.

"So I've become accustomed to death."

She hoped the water in her eyes came from the rain dampening her hair and cheeks, but the tightness of her throat suggested otherwise. "But Errance, isn't life—no matter how hard—worth it?" It was better than the alternative. Because when someone died, they always left someone behind...and how was that fair?

He did not answer, so she wrapped her arms tight around herself to keep from shivering. "I hope we'll make it worth it," she whispered.

It was then she noticed the rain was coming down heavier, utterly soaking both of them. She'd always imagined having a dramatic speech in a storm, but it really wasn't so wonderful after all. It was in fact, wet. "Ugh, come on," she said, "Let's see if they've built that shelter yet."

When she reached for his arm, he pulled back like she would hurt him. Like she'd hurt him already.

"Errance! What on earth? I'm not going to harm you, I'm only a kid!"

"Really?" he said, a sardonic lilt to his voice. "I thought you were all grown-up."

He'd just teased her. She was almost sure of it. It might have been rather spitefully spoken, but it was a jest, and that was something. "I'm almost grown-up," she hedged. "How about that? Now can we please get out of this rain?"

Silently, he led the way back to camp, and neither of them noticed the figure of leaves and rain huddled by the bank watching them. It hunkered low to the ground as they came and hurried back ahead of them so that when they arrived, Tryss was sitting by the fire as if she had been there the entire time.

Kelm was making good progress on the shelter under the command of Tryss, stacking dead branches around a tree that bent sideways, then weaving a net in between the branches with sticks and grass, then layering it all with the broad, waxy leaves of the jungle.

Tellie glanced at the meat-sticks trying to warm over the sputtering fire, and she flinched, expecting a scolding for neglecting her job. But the chema only glanced at them both and said, "We should get inside."

A distant rumble of thunder confirmed her suggestion, and Tellie grabbed her meat-stick and crawled into the shelter as Kelm declared it as good as it would get. Both the boy and Tryss followed soon after, each with their own meal, but Errance remained standing outside. "Aren't you coming in?" Tellie asked, poking her head out into the thickening rain.

Errance shook his head, a grey and phantom figure in the failing light and watery veil. "Already wet," he said. He turned to a nearby tree, caught the lowest branch, and swung himself upwards, vanishing from view.

Tellie huffed in exasperation and huddled against Kelm as she began to tear the meat off its skewer, licking her sticky fingers with each bite.

16

oOo

**The chema woman is frightened of me, and some of the knots in my chest
relax. So long as my enemies fear me, I have strength, power, advantage.
But for some reason the girl named Tellie doesn't fear me. She would try to
pet a growling wolf, I think. Was I really ever that innocent? No, stop. No
use thinking of that. But it is strange to see innocence again. She blushes at
everything, quick to action, and quick to shame. The world will not be kind
to her.**

Before dawn promised a fair day after the storm, Tryss woke all the
company and led them the last length of the jungle and out into the
land beyond. As the world colored, Tellie saw a terrain far different
from the jungle—sloping hills covered in stiff dry grass. The further they
traveled, even the ground turned from soil to sand. When she inquired how it
was possible that two such varying lands should be neighbors, Tryss explained
that both hot and cold springs from underground rivers gave the jungle constant
humidity and life. "Also," she said, "the clouds traveling from the sea catch
against those mountains and pile there until they release their watery burden."

Tellie glanced back with a shiver at the mountains, marveling at how high
they did reach, even now vanishing into the clouds. And yet...she smiled
suddenly...the sun could scale it. Again and again, the morning sun would climb
from the east horizon and rise above those dark mountains.

She opened her mouth to voice the thought to Errance, but all fancy fled her mind as they crested a high hill and looked out upon an eternal stretch of shimmering grey that met the horizon. It glimmered and winked in the light, and as is it came towards the shore, crests of white curled the soft, silver plain.

It was the ocean.

She stared, mouth agape and legs weak. "Oh," she breathed. "I never knew it would be so huge. It's so beautiful...have you ever seen the like?"

"I've seen the other side," Kelm promptly informed. "At the city of Korince while I was there with my master. The sea is called Niar Ocean, and this is only a small bit of it that carves into Orim. Nobody has ever crossed the ocean to the south to see if there is any land on the other side."

She glared at him. There were times she wanted to take his vast sum of knowledge and stomp on it.

Tryss laughed and rested her hand on the girl's shoulder. "I've seen it from a distance in the tallest trees of the jungle," she admitted. "But my breath is still stolen at the sight."

"What about you, Errance?" Tellie asked, craning her head around to look at him, hoping to glimpse a little bit of life.

He stared out over the ocean with eyes of stone. "No," he said. "I have never seen it."

Well then, she would simply enjoy its splendor by herself. Each wave stroked her gaze forward, then back, then again, before her eyes skimmed further down to the shore near them and set upon the city of Oolum. For the second time, her breath left her lungs, but now more in dismay than awe.

Oolum sat by the shore like an ornate sandcastle, its thousands of flat and domed buildings clustered within a thick square wall. On one side of the wall, ships upon ships anchored in harbor like swans come for feeding, and on all the other three sides of the city clustered a brilliantly colored garden of tents and wagons. A road along the sea vanished into the south side of the city and reappeared on the north. And traveling upon it—hundreds upon hundreds of people and animals, desperate to reach the city walls before the sun scorched them off the sand.

"Good heavens!" Tellie gasped. "Do we really have to go in that crowd?"

"We could try skirting the city to reach the docks," Tryss said. "But the people there will be lazier and far more likely to notice us. We'll be the most invisible going straight through the activity and bustle."

Just as she said, their approach was unnoticed by the river of folk and so they joined the ragged skirt of the crowd. Despite their best efforts they were soon packed as potatoes in a sack. Never in her life had Tellie been surrounded by so many people, and they were so different than anyone she'd seen in West Orim. Most of them were colored in a variety of dark shades, from golden tan to glistening ebony, and their hair was either short and curly or long and braided. Some wore bright and colorful clothes, others wore hardly anything.

She had lived in Dormandy for a spell, yes, but she'd usually stayed in the orphanage, and the streets were only politely busy. These people chattered in voices thick and thin, words blending together so no language could be told apart. Then there was the smell, not only of sweat and dirt, but of dung from the animals that lumbered along with their masters.

Tellie staggered along with her friends, dizzily wondering why anyone would want to live in such a crowded environment. The pace was slow, and it seemed to take forever till they passed through the wide arched entrance. She craned her head back to look at the mosaic mural faded above the gate, but then the pace became too fast, and she rushed under it without a proper study. Overwhelmed by the close-pressing bodies, she grabbed Errance's arm, mostly for her own assurance and out of a vague idea that he had to be even more uncomfortable than her. Errance jumped and half-spun around before he saw it was her. With a huff, he pulled his arm out of her hand in a blink of an eye.

A shoulder knocked into her, and she stumbled. One horrid moment, she thought she was going to fall, and images of being trampled by a merciless tide of feet flashed across her mind. But a hand gripped her arm, and she looked up to see Tryss.

The chema was paler than usual, features tight. "Don't be embarrassed," she murmured. "I'm not used to all this commotion either."

Nodding, Tellie clung to her hand as the crowd oozed on.

As a matter of fact, the only one who did seem used to it and thoroughly enjoying himself was Kelm, but this came as no surprise he had to be used to busy markets.

As the main road into the city branched off into several streets, the path became a little less cramped, but no less chaotic. They pushed through the bustle, passing brightly colored tents and bargaining buyers. Filthy urchins and mangy dogs darted through the mass, snatching unattended items, while the glorious rich dined on succulent fruits on shaded balconies. Each and every soul lived entirely in and for themselves no matter how often they rubbed shoulders.

Sellers were always shouting, always calling for attention, and Tellie's neck began to ache from turning to see whatever demanded her focus. There were stalls filled with embroidered fabric or jars of spices or dried meat. They passed a large wooden stage where people in chains stood in dejected silence while a man in golden robes shouted eagerly at the audience gathered in front of him. She shivered, suddenly cold even in the oppressive heat.

At one point, shouts turned to alarm and people pressed to the side as a coach flew by, hardly caring if the road was clear or not. The horse's hooves kicked up a cloud of dust that momentarily blinded everyone in a hazy fog.

"Is every merchant city this wild, Kelm?" Tellie coughed, wiping her hair out of her mouth and eyes. He did not reply. She looked for him, then looked again, her heartbeat skipping in fear. "Kelm? Errance, where is Kelm?"

Never in all his travels, which were worthy for a boy his age, had Kelm seen such a market as this one. The intoxicating smells sent his senses swimming, the entrancing sights tugged his eyes back and forth till they burned. Every tasty morsel begged to be sampled, every spice sought to be sniffed, every craft called to be fondled. But he was just a boy, not trusted to touch anything. Still, he eagerly ate up every sight.

When he saw a tent full of wood carvings, he halted mid-stride. The carving of wood was his favorite form of art, a craft he wistfully pursued by keeping a small knife in his pocket to whittle with whenever he found the chance. So he could not deny himself this one chance to take a closer look.

"Hey, hold on a moment, won't you," he called over his shoulder, and then without waiting to see if they had, he darted to the closest wooden figure and admired its sand-smoothed surface. And that one over there—that was surely a work of Luthe Lavral, greatest carver to come from Korince in the past century. Throwing all propriety to the wind, Kelm carefully lifted the piece and looked underneath it for initials, but there was no sign. Perhaps it was only an imitation.

A meaty hand thudded onto his shoulder. He gasped and twisted around to look up into the vendor's face.

"You miserable thief," the man growled. "Get your filthy hands off my wares!"

"But I'm not a thief, I—" Kelm's protest cut off as the man clouted him across the mouth. Jaw stinging, Kelm looked quickly about for his friends. He gasped again and his stomach dropped. Where *were* they?

"Dor, go and fetch the wardens!" his captor shouted to a passer-by. "I finally caught that pesky urchin."

"You've got the wrong person, I wasn't doing anything wrong!" Kelm argued. He was rewarded with another heavy smack on the head. With a quick drop, he tried to twist out of the man's grasp. But the grip only tightened, and he was yanked back to his feet.

"A little rough, doncha' think, darling?" said a woman's voice.

Kelm felt the change in his captor's hold and he wiggled around to see who spoke.

A woman stood a few paces back, one like he had never seen. Her skin, a dark shade of brown with hair matching color, and deep black eyes were common among many of the native people of East Orim, but her eyes were so huge and her smile so large and brilliant that they did not seem able to fit in her round-cheeked face. She wore a sleeveless tunic of royal purple, tied with a beaded sash of orange and her leggings were yellow. Furthermore, she wore several necklaces, bangles, and clasps. There was something unsettling about how she stood there as if she owned the entire world, hands on her hips, eyebrows raised.

The vendor smiled and removed one of his hands from Kelm's collar. "Well, if it isn't Zizain! What interest do you have in this flea-ridden brat?"

She tossed her head. "What interest? Why, you dog, he's my wage-collector, as honest as they come!" Every word she spoke was thickly accented with a sharp 'z' sound, rolling off her tongue as fast as wasp's wings.

Gaping in astonishment, Kelm glanced at his captor to see if he was buying it.

The man narrowed his eyes. "What was he doing poking through my wares?"

"Why, he wants to be a carver of course!" she cried, throwing up her hands. "He's always admired you, poor boy, and you smack him on the head!"

A guilty expression crawled onto the features of the carver. Sheepishly, he released Kelm. "Sorry, lad," he said, giving him a pat on the shoulders that nearly knocked him down. "You can't tell an honest person from a truthful one in this city anymore."

"Isn't that the truth!" agreed the woman. She took Kelm's arm. "Come along, Hari, we have work to do."

For a moment, the idea of breaking free and dashing off flashed across Kelm's mind. But as the woman's strong fingers encircled his arm, he suddenly realized he had no more chance of escaping her than the vendor.

"Now then, boy, my name's Zizain," she whispered as she subtly guided him through the crowds. "Perchance you can tell me what you were doing with his things?"

"I'm a merchant's apprentice, I was just admiring it!" he gasped.

"Where's your master?"

His mind reeled. "Um...he's not here. I'm traveling with friends." A convincing story, if there ever was one, no doubt a true original. He could have slapped himself.

"Well then, you show me your friends and all will be well, yes?" Zizain smiled.

He nodded frantically and led the way through the crowd, seeking the faces of his friends. The woman's grip on his arm was disconcerting at best, unnervingly strong and yet unmistakably feminine. What if he couldn't find them? What would she do? She didn't look particularly cruel or capricious, but—

There they were! Huddled in the shadow of a stall, speaking anxiously to each other. Gasping with relief, Kelm struggled through the last barricade of bodies and waved wildly. "Ho! Here I am!"

Tellie yelped, Tryss exhaled heavily, and Errance...Errance grabbed his arm with the ferocity of a wolf.

"Kelm!" he hissed. "Do *not* wander off like that! You could have been—" His voice trailed off as he realized that Kelm's other arm was occupied.

Zizain fluttered her lashes. "My," she drawled. "If you'd told me your friend was so handsome I would have come much quicker, see?"

A scowl scored deep into Errance's face, and he took a cautious step back. His wary eyes swept up and down her liquid posture and flashy clothing.

The woman did not seem to notice she was being scrutinized and found wanting; she only stuck out a distracted hand to Tellie and Tryss with a cheery, "Hello girls!" while never peeling her fascinated focus from Errance.

"Well, sir," she said, the 'z' sound sharper than ever. "If you are the leader of this unusual party, I must ask your name."

Ever so slightly shaking his head, Errance continued to back away.

Tryss spoke instead, eyes flashing in suspicion and voice cross. "I don't really see what business it is of yours."

Zizain drew her hand to her cheek, looking abashed. "Oh, I'm sorry, dear, you must think I'm very forward and presumptuous. Is this your husband?"

"NO!" Errance said, drowning out Tryss's denial.

With a grin, Zizain said, "My mistake. Is it correct for me to assume that these two children are not yours, then? You look too young for either of them, but I have been wrong before."

"No!" Tryss exclaimed, turning brilliant red. "No, we're not related at all."

"And yet traveling together? So it's not so strange for me to want to unravel the mystery after all, is it?"

Silence answered her, or at least as much silence as could be found in the raucous street. Errance looked trapped, the children both wore the expressions of thinking very hard without any answers, and Tryss was simply stiff.

"Excuse us," the chema said, walking around Zizain, pulling Tellie and Kelm along by the arms.

But as Errance warily stepped by, the strange woman stuck out her foot, caught his ankle, and yanked hard. Reeling forward, Errance caught himself against a crate, but in the brief moment his head was near her level, Zizain reached out and lifted his hair from his ear, revealing its pointed tip.

Errance slapped her hand away, scrambling backwards with a strangled gasp.

Zizain stepped out of range, a knowing smile curving her lush lips. "Well. That explains a lot, does it not?"

With a sharp intake of air, the prince stepped towards her. Tryss stepped after him, hand reaching, though it was apparent she had no idea what he was about to do or how she was supposed to stop him or even if she should.

But in that instant, a loose donkey crashed into a booth behind them, arousing shouts and curses. The commotion distracted them all for one moment, and when they'd turned back, Zizain was nowhere in sight.

"We must get out of the open," Errance said, voice low.

"Yes," Tryss agreed. "Yes, I think that's a very good idea." She grabbed Tellie and Kelm's arms and hurried after Errance who cut through the crowd like a pike through a shoal of fish.

Tellie craned her neck around in hopes of glimpsing the mysterious Zizain. "What did she mean by 'that explains a lot'?"

"It means we've been noticed," Tryss said grimly. "She might be working for the people we're fleeing. Even if she's not, she might spread the word that an elf is around. Which I imagine it is very unusual for an elf to be here."

"But she did help me," Kelm reminded. "I'd been caught for touching something, and she stopped the man from arresting me."

"Saved the little thief, yes, she definitely deserves a medal," Errance bit in return.

They squeezed between shoulders, keeping their heads low. For the moment, any destination seemed unsafe, the wharf, an inn, the other gate. Nothing could promise shelter, so they simply pushed on and on, darting to the gutter when carriages rolled past.

Tellie wiped sweat from her brow, trying to calm her racing pulse. This whole city was a bad dream, no matter its pretty plumage.

Her eyes lit on a group of grey-clad men roughly pushing their way through entertainers and flinched at how similar they were to Daran's men.

So very similar…

She gasped and spun around, snatching at Errance's arm. "Stop, stop," she whispered frantically. "Turn around, go the other way. It's Daran! It's the men who kidnapped me and Kelm!"

One bolt of devastation flashed in Errance's eyes, a jagged streak of lightning. It vanished as quickly as it came, and Tellie found herself staring into the perilous face of the Prisoner. He turned with her tug and dropped to one knee in the shadow of a merchant stall, bending over his boot as if something bothered his foot.

"Something in your shoe?" Kelm teased, as he and Tryss paused alongside them.

Tellie shook her head. "No, it's Daran, Kelm, they're just up the street. I swear it's them!"

"Oh, saints." The boy turned deathly pale and he ducked into the shade with her.

"Who?" Tryss asked.

"The men who captured us."

Tryss breathed in and closed her eyes. "All right. No one panic." She reached out and took Tellie's hand. "We'll simply go another way. It's not like they know we're here." Looping her other arm around Kelm's elbow, she led the way to another street they'd passed a few minutes back. It was narrower than the main road, but still packed with sellers and buyers.

The sedate pace Tryss set maddened Tellie—her heart bounded several strides ahead. But it would do no good to look hunted. No, she must smile and look as if she was enjoying a stroll on the streets with her friends. Pretend there was no possibility they were already being followed. Sharp aches stabbed through her stomach as she recalled the fear in the presence of those evil men. Not that she had ever been paid much attention to. But what did it matter if Daran noticed her or not? She was inexplicably entangled in his purpose, and if he succeeded, all her dreams would unravel. She began to look over her shoulder, but Tryss halted her with a sharp hiss.

"I will look back," the chema said. "They do not know me." She looked, then faintly smiled. "They did not come down the same road."

Tellie exhaled, fear receding. So they had not been spotted, and it was such a very busy city that they surely wouldn't run into each other again. Daran may not have even been here to look for them. After all, how would the Darkness have known where they would go?

Errance stopped. "They are ahead of us."

At a crossway just before them, two of Daran's men lounged against a wall, chatting to each other and smoking on pipes.

Tellie stared in frozen dismay before Tryss nearly jerked her off her feet as the four of them hurried into a narrow alley between two market houses. The damp chill in the brief shade was a welcome relief from the scorching sun and their predator's searching eyes.

But as they came back out onto a bustling road, Tellie's quick eyes spotted Daran and his men again, this time in this new street and much closer. She grabbed Errance's arm and pointed.

He muttered a curse under his breath, ducked his head, and kept striding forward all the way across the street and into another alley on the opposite side.

Every muscle in her body ached to run after him, but as her arm was still severely locked in Tryss's elbow, she had to match the chema's prim pace as she and Kelm were led across the street.

The alley did not lead to another public road, but to the backways of the markets where crates and garbage piled in stacks and heaps between the close fitting buildings. The stench burned the nostrils, fouled every breath, was heard in the buzz of thousands of flies.

They paused, panting and glancing around uncertainly. "We need to reach the docks," Tryss said. "Where…wherever they are."

"At the sea, probably," a familiar voice drawled.

They all whirled around to see Zizain perched atop a barrel not ten paces away, eating an arched, yellow fruit. Her golden-brown eyes danced as she smiled at them. "Are you in some sort of trouble, lovelies?"

Without any kind of acknowledgement, Errance turned and hurried away further down the alleys. Tryss glanced back and forth and then headed after him, tugging the children along despite their curious stares at the mysterious woman.

"If you're looking for the docks, I can show you the way," Zizain called.

"No, thank you," Tryss replied politely.

Sighing, Tellie looked away from the beautiful stranger and back onto the road ahead—just as Daran stepped into the street before them.

She screamed.

She clapped her hands over her mouth, horrified at the sound, horrified at him, horrified at everything.

Daran's head snapped towards them.

17

oOo

**My heart plummets. There the man stands, an emissary of doom, and his
eyes possess the promise of reckoning for my flight. But he is merely a man.
A mortal vessel. And those easily die.**

For one splinter of eternity, Daran stared at them. Or rather he stared at
Errance, the nearest to him, though still an alley's length away.
Disbelief flared in his eyes, and then his brows hunkered low, and his
mouth stretched wide to shout.

But Tryss shouted instead. "Run!"

And Errance did run.

Straight towards Daran.

The man took a staggering step back, alarm rushing across his face, but he
drew his weapon and prepared for the attack. Just moments before Errance
reached him, two of Daran's men stepped into the alley.

"Errance, come back!" Tellie shrieked, yanking against Tryss's hand.

But he was already upon Daran, ducking under the first sword swing. He
caught the outside of the man's elbow in the second strike and dragged him
around in a spin, then threw him towards the oncoming attackers. Then he did
turn and run as two more of the dark men appeared from the side street.

Kelm took the lead as they fled, skidding to the left and crawling over a tall
wooden fence between two buildings. Galvanized by terror, Tellie went up after,

not even sure how she managed to scale it. Shouts echoed behind them, the voices seeming to roar from each and every alley and crevice like a monster's mouth. Their hearts hammered in time with their footsteps, drumming out the deadly beat of doom.

They broke out of the alley, returning into the lively bustle of the market. The shouts of their pursuers drowned under the squall of the vendors. Lights and colors burst through their vision before they returned to the shadows and dampness of the alleys beyond. Wooden slates crossed the narrow openings between the buildings above them, causing the walls to seem even closer together.

For a moment they paused, taking refuge in the hope their followers had lost their trail.

"Everyone still here?" Errance asked.

"Still here," Tryss gasped in answer for them all.

"I'm here too!" Zizain chimed.

Tellie shrieked again, and this time it was Kelm who covered her mouth. She closed her eyes in frustration, vowing every curse and chain on her ready tongue. If the others blamed her for all their troubles, she would not be surprised.

But the others had no attention to spend on her. They stared aghast at the strange colorful woman perched upon a stack of broken down crates.

"Are you sure you aren't in some sort of trouble?"

With a haggard gasp, Errance stepped towards her. Color drained from his skin, darkening every shadow and scar, and his eyes gleamed a lethal green. For all the beauty he possessed, none of it could be seen now. "Where did you come from? What did you tell them?" he hissed.

"Excuse me?" Zizain returned, quirking her brows.

Errance's hands shot down and gripped her shoulders. He lifted her off the ground and shook her. "WHAT DID YOU TELL THEM?"

The woman dangled in his grasp, hair falling wildly about her face. For just a brief moment, she looked startled. Then she smiled. "I didn't tell anyone anything. And I followed you across the rooftops. Put me down, please, won't you darling?"

He dropped her like a stone, and she landed smartly on her feet without a quaver of fear. "You're a part of this," he snarled. "You're a servant of His Darkness. What are you doing, turning the streets around?"

She gave a saucy wink. "While I'm flattered that you think I have such power, no. But I can lead you through this city like the paths are straight."

Harsh voices rumbled in the distance, too dark and too hungry to belong to anyone save their hunters. And they were coming closer.

"Errance." Tryss stepped forward with a shiver as if she feared attracting the elf's wrath herself. "Errance, we need to keep moving."

With a last murderous look at Zizain, he heeded the threat and took the lead as they fled down the ally.

Tellie looked back at the woman as they ran and saw her staring after them, mouth twisting thoughtfully. But she did not pursue them or leave her place.

On and on they flew, through market street and alley, till Tellie's head spun so that every color and sight that passed by began to look alike. Yet no matter where they went, their pursuers always seemed just behind. What cruel fate set their hunters as hounds on their trail? It was as if some greater hand set them on paths not their own.

As they turned down yet another small side street, this one bare of travelers, a flicker of grey on the arch above the road caught Tellie's eye. It could have been a torn canvas or a bird, but she looked anyway. There across the arched bricks, as a shadow under the sun, lay the shard of Daran's company. Kilkus. A crossbow crooked against its shoulder, and the bolt pointed down towards them, quavering with expectation.

No. Tellie felt her mouth stretched open in a shout but no sound came forth. She felt herself lunging for Errance—

But Errance wasn't there.

He was diving the other way, reaching for Tryss, because the arrow was pointed at her. And when it shot forth, he was sweeping her behind him.

He was the one falling to his knees, the arrow buried in his middle.

Tryss lay collapsed on the ground from the elf's hard shove, and her gaze darted from Errance to the attacker above. She knew what it was, the only thing it could possibly be. A shard. Seeing it with her own eyes, she could hardly believe her own kind could turn into such a terrifying monster. This monster which once had been like her, but had betrayed itself, its people, and been cursed to this existence. She found then, quite suddenly, that she wasn't afraid. She hated it.

She leapt to her feet, knife flashing in hand, and sprang for the wall.

The shard shrieked at her coming, dropping the next bolt before it could reload. It scuttled away like a crab, vanishing across the rooftops.

"Tryss!" Kelm yelled, halting her pursuit. "Help, please, we need help!"

Her heart raced after the shard, but…had Errance been hit? She paused, midway up to the roof, then dropped back down.

Errance lay on the ground. She expected him to rise, no matter the pain, for if there was one thing she knew of him, he was an overcomer. But he was not moving. He could not be dead. The shard would not have shot to kill him, not if he was so important. But then, the shard had not been aiming at him. Her heart plummeted and she raced to his side, turning him over. The stone bolt was buried in his stomach. His eyes stared ahead, unseeing, unblinking. But there was still a pulse in his throat.

"Come on, Kelm," she said with the barest quaver. "Help me carry him. Arms over the shoulders, that's right."

"They're going to catch us," Kelm said. "There's no way we can run like this."

"There." Tellie's fragile voice drifted like mist through the hot air. She stood listlessly a few steps away, face salt-white. She was in shock, Tryss noticed in brief pity, unable to move or help and completely aware and miserable of that. But the girl was pointing beyond them and down the street. Tryss followed the direction to a wooden door in a corner of the turn in the road.

"Well done, Tellie," Tryss gasped, pushing to her feet with great difficulty under the elf's weight. "Hide."

The door was rotting and unlocked so it gave no trouble, and the shade of the little room inside swept over them like water. The room seemed to be a shed, housing nothing but a few boxes of tools, and when Tellie stepped inside, Tryss tried to ease Errance slowly into her arms. If that bolt was jostled, it could do more damage, but if she pulled it out now, it would only make things worse.

"They're going to find us," Kelm growled.

Tryss shook her head. "No. You two stay here, I'll lead them away." A scowl twisted her face at the hint of oncoming protest. "Get inside now!"

She slammed the door behind them.

Shafts of golden light slipped through the cracks of the door, cutting apart the darkness. The two children listened to the sound of Tryss scrambling away, and then there was silence, save for their own wheezing breaths.

"This won't work," Kelm muttered. "We need somewhere we can really hide. We need someone who knows the city."

Tellie couldn't respond. She could barely think, only act, and even then in very small extremes. Except for those shafts of light, everything was pitch black. Her fingers found Errance's sweaty skin, then his shirt, then the bolt sticking out of his back. She curled her hands with a shudder.

The door creaked open, and she looked up to see Kelm slipping out. "What are you doing?" she gasped.

"We'll be caught like rats in a trap if someone doesn't help us," he said. "You stay here."

Before she could protest more, he was gone. Shivering, she scooted Errance's shoulders up on her knees, his head in her lap. When she pressed her fingers against his throat, she could feel his pulse fluttering. Yet somehow, even with his too warm body against her, she felt completely alone. It was like he wasn't even there.

Hot and cold pulsed through Kelm's blood. His breath rattled and his footsteps pounded in his ears as he tore through the streets.

Each face he saw began to blur into the same for he only needed one face and it would be different than all the rest. Where was she? He expected that strange woman to appear again any moment, just like she'd been doing before. But perhaps Errance had well and truly scared her off.

Yes, there was a chance she was trouble. Yes, Errance wasn't willing to trust her. But by the stars, Errance didn't know everything. They were in mortal danger in a foreign city, and any help was better than no help at all.

"Zizain!" he shouted as he ran. "Zizain!" Barely any of the shoppers looked his way as he ran past. He was only a boy after all, and the possible causes for his frantic cry were numerous.

Then she stood in front of him. Whether she'd come from the crowd or dropped from the sky, he did not know, but he reeled to a stop as she grabbed his shoulders.

"Easy there, boy!" she cried. "What's the matter?"

He gulped for air, trying to focus, but everything in his vision smeared. "They—they're after us. H-he's hurt...got shot."

"Take a deep breath, lad," an unfamiliar male voice said. "You're going to have to lead us back to them, and it'll be no good if you faint on us."

A hand guided him under the shade of one of the stalls. Kelm squinted up at a tall man beside Zizain, a tricorn hat askew on his head and a smile askew on his lips. He wore an eye patch, but his other eye twinkled green with danger.

"Now then," the man said. "Do you think you can find your way to your friends?"

The street seemed abandoned, but Daran stood still, waiting for a telltale shift in the sand, for a shadow, for the slightest wave of inconsistency against the stone. His men hunkered around him, swords drawn and teeth clenched, a few of them already bleeding.

A shadow fell over them from the roof above.

With a yell, Daran raised his sword in defense, but he found himself squinting up at the silhouette of Kilkus. "You," he hissed. "Where have you been? Did you get his leg, did you slow him down?"

The shard landed in a crouch beside him, claws gesturing frantically as it chattered a response.

Daran's scowl deepened, and he threw another wild glance around. "I know there's a chema! She's right here, somewhere, been harassing us like a ghost. We can't take two steps without her knife pricking our backs."

Hissing, the shard swung round, peering as if it could see her against the stone. If only it could. If only it was useful and still had any gifting of its previous existence, not this rocky ruin. Perhaps the presence of the chema girl had revived memories of the old friend he once had in Kilkus, because in that moment, Daran looked upon the shard and hated it.

He turned on the shard with murder coloring his eyes. "Well, answer me, spider! Did you shoot the elf?" He paled as he heard the reply and slammed Kilkus against the wall. "You tried to kill her and he took the shot? What if he's dead? You thought of that? Did you? No, no, all you thought about was your jealousy of what you once were, didn't you, you monster, you—gah!" He roared in pain as the knife nicked him again, but before he could respond, Kilkus tore through his grasp and lunged into the air with a snarl.

A feminine scream cried out when the shard landed, and then Kilkus was struggling on the ground with a figure of shifting sand.

"Kill her, kill her!" Daran shouted, shaking his sword above the fray.

A dagger whistled through the air and straight into his wrist. Shouting in pain, Daran dropped his sword and looked up in dismay, squinting into the brilliant sun.

A figure in white leapt down upon him.

Tellie startled when she heard Daran curse, so close by. The men had drawn near to their hiding place, but where Tryss and Kelm had gone was impossible to tell. *Please.* She tightened her grip around Errance. Please, they couldn't find them. She didn't even have anything to defend herself with. Wait. The chemas had given Errance a knife. She felt along his belt until her trembling hands grasped the handle, and she held the knife against her knees. It wasn't much good since she didn't know how to use it, but its sharp presence proved a comfort.

She dropped one hand to stroke the prince's clammy brow. With as much punishment as he'd taken in his life, she could not believe that an arrow would defeat him. But then, none of the torture had been meant to kill him…or maybe they simply had not allowed him to die. Yet he still had his celestial gift; it would heal him just like it had when he'd escaped. Rendar said so, said his delayed recovery only came from the Darkness harassing his spirit—

Tellie inhaled sharply, heart thudding to a stop. All the memories of that strange dream returned in a dizzy rush. Rendar reaching for her hand, her own voice rising in beauty greater than that of this world, seeing her own body asleep on the ground…she remembered that she had been a part of a world dimly veiled.

Shuddering, she touched Errance's brow again. "Come back," she whispered. "Come back, wherever you are." Her hand reached down to his, grasping his fingers hard.

The darkness in the room shifted, becoming no less dark, but somehow allowing visibility. She found herself looking through the walls into the street beyond. Except not really. The street was gone. Instead she saw carved, cold stone stretching away in a terrible tunnel lit by sickly torches. She saw the wooden door in the city of Oolum, and she saw the iron cage gate of Tertorem, both there, both together, both separate. She glanced down at Errance, but it was only the shell of his body. To what depths of this dark dimension had he gone, and dare she try to find him?

Daran's shouts sounded much nearer, and she hunkered back as his men came into view. Through the wall, she could their shapes, could see them in detail, but they were different. They were darker than ever before and tangled in shredded shadow. Behind them came another, a gleaming creature of green, gold, and blue. She was beautiful and bright as a summer day, and Tellie wondered how she'd never seen Tryss this way before.

She watched as the swirling colors that were Tryss danced around the dark men, leading them this way and that. Then the grey, gangly wraith came, the shard. When it attacked Tryss, Tellie scrambled to her feet. She knew she was using her mortal body, for she could feel her fingers gripping the knife.

A flash, small and bright, flew down from the sky and pierced Daran's hand. He cried out and dropped his flailing sword.

Then the man in white appeared upon the roof.

Rendar.

Tellie knew it must be him for who else would shine so bright that she could not look straight upon them. As beautiful and magnificent as a crane spreading its wings, he leapt down beside Daran. He threw Daran aside, and then turned to Kilkus, kicking the shard off Tryss and across the street. Shining like a star he wheeled around to confront the rest of the men, but they were already running, Daran cradling his wounded hand to his chest, and Kilkus scampering after them like a beaten dog.

Tellie heard a jumble of voices, one of which was Kelm, another Tryss, and the third she did not recognize at all. Then the man in white dashed towards her and threw open the door. He reached down and took her hand—

And suddenly, there was no man in white anymore. Well, he wore a white shirt, but there all resemblance to the shining knight ended. She blinked up into one bright green eye, the other covered by an eye patch, a bearded chin, and a rakish smile.

"There we are, lassie," the man said. "Let's get you and the wounded one out, hmm?" He fetched her from the shed with a deft hand and then knelt beside Errance, pulling him up and over his shoulder and back.

Tryss came alongside to help, her hair a tangle around her smudged face. "Careful," she cried. "He was shot through the middle, and the bolt is still in him."

"Yes, yes, so the boy told me. Boy?" the stranger called.

"Yes?" Kelm hurried forward, pale face bright with sweat.

"Take the girl here; she seems to be in a bit of a shock."

"I—I am not," Tellie protested as Kelm took her arm. "I just don't understand wha—what happened."

A hand spun her around, and she found herself staring at the smiling Zizain.

"We'll explain later, yes, doll? Now we must get you somewhere safe," the woman said. "Step quickly." She placed a hand against each of the children's backs and propelled them along the street.

Though the set pace was swift, it was still not fast enough. Daran and his men had run, but how far and for how long?

Zizain did not seem the slightest perturbed by any thought of threat, and she did not slow her firm stride even as they came into an alley that led to a dead end. She marched straight up to the wall and released the children long enough to hook her fingers into a crevice in the stone and pull back with a grunt.

The wall was not made of thick bricks as it appeared, but was instead a thin slab of sandstone. It did not swing open like an ordinary door, but slid backwards into the wall. They all rushed through, and Zizian slid the strange door shut behind them so that all traces of an entrance vanished.

They stood in a street lined with identical houses built of pale, sun-bleached stone, and the brightness and heat emanating from the bricks and the matching sand burned with unbearable potency. Not a sound nor soul stirred the dry-crusted air.

Zizain trotted ahead and up the steps to one of the houses. She threw open the door and disappeared inside with a brisk wave of her hand.

Tellie stepped forward to follow, but then she hesitated. Really, what did they know about these strangers? Nothing at all. But what other choice did they have but to trust them? So she trailed after Kelm up the stair and across the threshold.

Amber light peered in from the slats of a shuttered window and the rickety door, but the pleasant shade of the room and the coolness kept inside the thick walls was a blessing unlike any other. The room was spacious and square, and not a single piece of furniture or ornament arrayed it from roof to floor. A faded purple curtain hung across a door to another room, but other than that, there was not any sign that anyone had ever lived here.

"M'name's Coren, by the by. Captain Coren," the red-headed stranger said as he entered the room and kicked the door shut. He dropped to one knee and carefully unloaded Errance from his back, propping him up against the wall. "Zizain, fetch some water for this fellow here, and while you're at it, our guests could use a drink."

Tellie sat beside Errance, trying not to look at the dark stain spreading around the bolt in his stomach. She looked to Kelm and Tryss for assurance, but they were also the worse for wear. Exertion had dulled Kelm's skin to a sheeny grey, and Tryss's complexion was even more ghastly with bloody scratches across her cheeks.

Zizain had vanished behind the purple curtain but she returned now, carrying a tray with pewter cups sloshing over the brim with water. She gave one to each of them with careful instructions to drink slow, and then she plopped to the ground beside Tryss with a cheerful, "How about washing those scratches, darlin'?"

Tellie took an unsteady gulp of the tepid water as she studied their extraordinary saviors. Zizain and Coren could not have been more different in body—her short, dark, and softly rounded while he was tall, tan, and sharply featured—but they both talked and moved with as little care as a breeze.

Coren pushed off his hat and shook loose a shock of copper red hair that seemed to burn with fire embers. Tellie's gaze traced down from the tips of his unkempt bangs, past his vivacious green eye, to the neat little patch of red beard under his lip. He was, in short, devilishly handsome, and she decided it was not safe to stare. She blushed and looked quickly to the floor when he pulled off his papery white shirt and began to tear it into shreds.

"So…what exactly are you?" she asked.

Coren flashed a quick smile her way. A dangerous smile, the sort that could be worn while charming or killing. "Respectable citizens of Oolum of course," he said. "Captain of the Solitary Star, at your service, and you've already met,

Zizain, dancer extraordinaire."

Having finished tearing his shirt into neat little strips of bandage, he reached out to Errance's shirt and rent the cloth around the bolt a little wider so it could be worked off without catching. He pulled out a knife, and Tellie stiffened, ready to jump to her prince's defense, but the captain simply slit the seams across the shoulders and down the sleeves. The shirt slid down, revealing the scars and the terrible tattoo of His Darkness.

Coren stilled. He stared upon the words and marks slashed across Errance's body, and a shudder ran down his rigid frame. Then slowly, carefully, he stretched out a hand and brushed away the slick hair covering Errance's face.

All color left the captain's skin. He stared upon Errance like he saw a ghost.

Tellie cringed, expecting a torrent of questions, though why he would ask them, why he would recognize Errance at all, she could not guess. Perhaps, this man once served in Tertorem. Perhaps he still did. Perhaps this was a trick, and he intended to turn them back in.

But Coren asked no questions. Though his hands trembled, he silently removed the arrow, cleaned the wound, and wrapped the torso in the white linen. When at last he washed his hands in the bowl of water that Zizain had brought and sat back on his heels, he spoke.

"I am no surgeon, and there is no one in this city whose methods I can recommend. He is yet alive, but who can say what was pierced or what might infect. I am sorry, friends, but I cannot say if he will live or die."

"He'll live," Tryss murmured from where she slumped in the corner of the room. "He has a stubborn way of surviving."

"Of course he'll live!" Tellie exclaimed. "He can live through anything."

"So I see," the captain said, staring dully at the scars. Every trace of his merry ease had drifted away, leaving a shadow of age and regret across his youthful features. He laid his hand against Errance's brow, looking a trace sick at the mere touch. "This sleep is strange. He hasn't reacted to anything I've done, and his spirit should not be this distant." He cocked his head, listening for a distant sound.

And then he bent close to Errance and whispered in a voice low and gentle as evening wind, "Come out of there."

Errance's eyes flared open.

oOo

Far off in his fortress hold, the Voice stiffened as an ice-water chill ran over his body. He rose from his dark throne and passed through the wall onto a terrace pointed west where the faintest glow of sunlight edged the teeth of his mountain borders. He gazed across the vast distance, hands clasped tightly behind his back.

He could no longer see his Prisoner, no longer feel him. The amusing game he'd been playing had been brought to a sudden halt by a player unforeseen.

A tremor of anger ran through his body and through all Tertorem, for there was nothing he hated so much as the weakness he now felt from the presence and power of one man and One.

18

oOo

No…no…NO…cold, wet walls press in around me, pushing the breath from my lungs, and something hard and agonizing pierces my torso. My mind snatches helplessly for the bronzed sands and glaring sunlight that spiral away as I fall deeper into this dark pit. Blood runs down my hands as I shred my fingers against the stone in a useless effort to climb up, to escape. It has taken me again. Where it wills, when it wants. I collapse to my knees in the darkness, panting. I was a fool to think I was free.

And then somebody reaches in and pulls me out.

Coren caught Errance's swinging arm before it hit, and with a dignified series of twists, he neatly pinned him stomach to the ground, arms folded underneath. "Careful there," the captain said, calm as a summer day. "No need to wrench about so when you're wounded."

Tellie spotted it—Errance's right hand squirming free, reaching up to catch Coren's elbow. Before she could even think of the consequences, she darted forward and seized his hand in both of hers. "We're safe, Errance, we're safe! He's here to help you."

His hand paused, trembled, and then fell back to the floor. She blinked in astonishment as his fingers tightened around hers, not in aggression but in desperation. Even so, his grip hurt. His heaving pants echoed in the room and his body shone with a fresh sweat, but he offered no more struggle.

"Where—are we?" he choked. "I was back—Tertorem—"

"You were unconscious, Errance," Tryss said softly. "It was just a dream."

A dream. The eerie things Tellie had seen in that strange vision were as blurry and unclear as a dream, but she no longer doubted their reality. Errance had been gone, really gone, and for just a moment, she had glimpsed where he'd went.

When Coren eased off, Errance pushed up with a wince and braced against the wall, hostile gaze sweeping the room. Each one he studied sharply, with a scowl at Zizain, but when his eyes turned again to Coren, little fear could be seen. Dislike, certainly, but he showed no signs of flight or fight as might have been expected.

"There now," Coren said amiably. "Can you talk or does it hurt too much? All you have to do now is listen anyway. I'm Captain Coren, and at your service if you need it, which judging by the looks of how we found you, I'd say that you do."

"Don't we need a ship, Tryss?" Kelm asked.

She shushed him, then looked to Errance with the same question in her eyes.

Errance did not deign to look at any of the attentive faces watching him. He stared down at his bandaged torso, stroking the bloodied strips with the tip of his fingers.

When no answer proved forthcoming, Coren rocked back and forth on his haunches and studied the ceiling. "Escaping from the city, I take it? Trying to cross the sea? I know some smugglers..." he began.

Without warning, Zizain dropped the tray of water she was carrying. "Oops! My fault, entirely."

Coren threw her a wink. "No need to stop me, Zi, I know what I'm doing." His green eye danced with the spunk of a firefly. "I'm going to be honest here, my strangely marked friend. I am the smuggler of which we speak. It's not something I spread around, but you...you are special, aren't you? So how can I help you?"

Tellie started in surprise at the announcement and scooted a little closer to the wall. Smugglers were not considered respectable, in fact she was quite certain they were on the wrong side of the law. But these folks had rescued them, and if there was any hope of escaping this cursed city, then smugglers could be exactly what they needed.

Errance's eyes narrowed to slits, and bared teeth gleamed under his raised lip. "Why would you help? What's in it for you? " His words broke between breaths, but none could mistake the danger in his tone.

"Would you believe it was out of the goodness of our hearts?"

"No."

"No?" Coren blinked in mock astonishment. "*No?* How very awkward. I take it then you have little faith in human nature. How very sad." The smirk on his face was anything but sad as he held up a hand to his hair and said, "But how would you feel about the nature of elves?"

And he brushed back his hair to reveal perfectly pointed ears.

The silence that fell could have been cut with a knife, and it was a span of several moments before any sound penetrated it, and that was the hushed sweep of Errance's inhaled breath.

"You're no elf," he said.

Tisking, Coren shook his head. "Further proof of your distrust of humankind. And also," he tipped his head to the side, one good eye twinkling, "a singular ideal of what elves are supposed to be. Has it occurred to you that you don't fit the ideal either?"

"Elves don't grow beards," Errance retorted, blatantly ignoring the question.

Coren stroked the tuft of hair on his chin sadly. "You're right. They don't. I had to glue mine on. For you, fellow elf, and only for you—counting your odd troop of friends who I trust merely on our race's merit of keen insight—I will show the elf behind the smuggler."

With a painful wince, he peeled the patch off, leaving a bright red mark on his chin. Then he flipped up the eye patch, revealing a perfectly healthy and identical green eye. "Here you are," he said merrily. "Not so frightening now, am I? Short hair, granted, and shirtless at the moment, but last I knew these conditions didn't disqualify me from my race?"

"Oh!" exclaimed Tellie, very shocked. She exchanged a quick look of amazement with both Tryss and Kelm, but when she looked to Errance, his face could have been carved from rock.

"I never saw you in Aselvia," he said as if it was the most condemning, deciding verdict in the world.

"Of course you didn't! I'm only in my fifties, and you...you left Aselvia some seventy years ago...a few days past the exact date if I'm not mistaken."

There might have been no one else in the world—no gasp of the children, no soft cry from Tryss, no start from Zizain. It was only the two elves in the room and the heavy stillness that hung between them.

Coren's shoulders rose and fell in one deep rush of breath. "I know it's you, Errance. How could I not know? Do you think your portrait no longer graces Aselvia's halls? That stories are not still told of your merry youth? That—" His voice caught, struggling on what he might say next, what impossible answers it might bring, and in those moments, the stunned reverence in his face shone so beautiful that his elven blood was undeniable. "Brights," he breathed, "Everyone thinks you're dead. What happened?"

But there was no answer. Errance sat there, unmoving, unblinking, unfeeling. Whatever walls he possessed had risen to a greater density than ever before. As Tellie watched him, anxious and hopeful for any sign of the elf prince Coren spoke of, she thought he nearly faded, as if withdrawing his spirit nearly withdrew his body as well. It was a strange thought, and when she blinked, he was just sitting there like any person might, except unusually obstinate and reclusive.

"I can explain." The words slipped out of her mouth before she had quite thought about them.

Across the room, Tryss stiffened. "Tellie, I don't know..." She glanced at Coren. "Not to seem rude, but even if you're an elf and even though you've helped us, I don't think we have reason enough to trust you..."

Coren didn't seem to hear or care. His gaze was locked with Errance's in some silent duel.

The vision again flashed through Tellie's mind, the vision of the bright white warrior leaping to their aid. The radiant light that shone from him had been so pure, pure as moonlight. At that thought, she recalled something else.

With a deep breath, she reached up and undid the necklace from her neck. Clenching the strand hard in her hand, she held out the moon medallion. Streams of light gathered in a starburst around the pendant so that the entire room brightened, drawing every eye to its heart. Even if this Coren was just a common pirate, elf and all, surely he wouldn't be such a fool as to grab it right in front of Errance.

To her satisfaction, Coren choked on his own swallow. He hacked and coughed for a bit, before finally gaining control of himself. "Where did you get that?" he gasped

"Oh, do you know it?" Tellie said innocently, turning it on her finger as if she didn't notice anything marvelous.

"I could not claim to be an elf if I didn't know it," the captain breathed, transfixed by the shining necklace. "King Rendar—last I knew it was missing. By all that is sacred, I thought you were just an ordinary girl—"

"Why, thank you."

"—why do you carry something so revered as the moon medallion? It has been lost for decades. Is that really the real thing?"

"It waxes and wanes with the moon," she replied. "If you don't believe me, just look at it tomorrow."

"But why?" he demanded. "Why do you have it?" He looked at Errance as he asked, perhaps expecting the answer from him.

Her mouth opened before she realized her answer seemed laughable. As he said, she was just an ordinary girl. Could she expect him to believe that Rendar would have chosen her for such a task? "Errance is having me carry it for now," she said, ignoring the rest of the questions. "Touch it, please. Just a touch."

With a confused frown towards Errance, Coren stretched out his fingers and brushed the surface of the treasure. It remained bright as ever, maybe it even brightened.

Tellie stared at it, then at him. "We can trust him," she said. Her voice carried such confidence that everyone believed her, except perhaps Errance. She tucked the medallion away, and then, ignoring the ever darkening shadow upon the prince's face, addressed Coren.

"It was a fake death, you see. Instead, the Darkness took him to Tertorem, if you've heard of that. Evil dark place east of here, behind those awful mountains? Anyway, he's been trying to extract the secrets of the Higher World from him, or something like that." The tale felt strange on her tongue, the words utterly inadequate to express the truth.

But Coren accepted it in stride. "Brights," he hissed again. "It's the obvious thing for the Darkness to do, why was his death not questioned, why did they never try to breech Tertorem—" His voice cut off. "They did," he said, rather sadly and to himself. "They tried and failed. But I am sure they did not know he was alive within, or else they would never have stopped trying." Eyes gleaming, he looked to Errance. "So you've escaped. How? After all this time, how?"

"The sewers were my idea," Kelm offered.

"We nearly drowned in the river," Tellie recalled with a shiver.

"I met them in the forest," Tryss said.

"I tripped him in the street," Zizain added helpfully.

"Thank you, everything is perfectly clear now," Coren said, rolling his eyes. He swiveled to face Errance head on and leaned forward. "I want to hear it from you. What happened? How did you escape?"

No answer came. Throughout the conversation, the presence of Errance had slipped further and further away. His face was set, his gaze nailed to an empty corner of the house. There was no sign of any awareness of them, either of their discussion or their sudden silence and expectation.

And then his eyes turned with a snap and met Coren's square. The force of it might have been a slap for the jolt the captain gave.

"Why," Errance said, "would I tell you anything?"

The jovial energy that laced Coren's every word, every movement, wilted under the winter frost in the voice. "I…I thought…"

"You thought?" Errance's smile was like a knife unsheathing, and the room darkened as a cloud passed over the sun. "Tellie is an impulsive child, quick to trust. If I am the prince of Aselvia, as you say, and I have spent my last seventy years amongst demons whose sole purpose was to break me to their will—you thought I might trust you?"

Coren was silent. Everyone else was silent. The silence held the room in a tight-fisted grip, squeezing out air for breath, for thought, for hope.

When Coren spoke again, his voice was low and solemn. "I would have sworn it impossible, but I see with my own eyes the prince of Aselvia before me. The mystery of how or why does not matter, only this. I do not ask you to trust me, but I ask you to believe that I will do whatever I can to see you safely home to Aselvia, for I swear it upon the Truth of Ayeshune."

Something flinched in Errance's face. Not on it, but inside it. Only the keenest of observers in the room might have noticed and no one did. But after a long moment, he nodded just once.

It was enough to break the spell. Tellie exhaled, the fleeing tension leaving her weak and tired, and she exchanged a weary smile with Kelm. Tryss did not smile, but the stiffness in her limbs relaxed and she looked down to nurse her wounds.

"Well, that's that," Coren exclaimed, with a brisk clap of his hands. "As soon as you've breathed enough, we must see to getting you to better lodgings for the night, and tomorrow we may discuss departure."

"Do we have to leave soon?" Tellie said, only just restraining a whimper. "Can we wait until the day is cooler?"

"We could, of course, if you have an explanation for the owners upon their return."

She sat bolt upright, shock tingling to the tips of her hair. "What! You mean this house doesn't belong to you?"

"Indeed."

"Oh, but what if somebody comes back right now?" Her head whirled as she imagined the door opening and the poor owners discovering them all in the living room.

"No fear of that," Coren replied. "These are the quarters of the sale vendors. Their entire day revolves around their booth in the market, and they shall only return at night, if even then. If you notice that the room seems a bit bare, it is because they keep everything important with them. This part of the city is abandoned during the day, and I find it useful for my smuggling business. If the owners happened to return, I'll simply tell them we won't be staying long. I doubt it'd be the first time they've found someone in their house, and once they know we don't plan to steal their goods or slit their throats, I can't imagine they'll have much to complain about. So a few hours, let's say, to give you some rest and to give those pursuers of yours some time to make distance. I'll go run and see if I can find a few shirts to replace the ones, er, lost. And then it's off, my lovelies, off to my own humble home. Or one of them anyway."

The few hours passed by far too swiftly. At some point, Tellie realized she must have dozed off, because she found herself curled up on the ground with no remembrance of doing so, and the lids of her eyes were heavy and hot. Her eyes stared level at sandaled feet, and she looked up to see Tryss kneeling by her side, shaking her shoulder gently.

"Come on then," Tryss said, never sounding more worn. "The captain says it's time to go."

Grudgingly, she pushed to her feet and followed Tryss out, leaving behind the otherwise empty room. When Tellie stepped out of the house, the heat slammed into her body like a wall. She squinted past the glare of the sun to look at Kelm, who looked annoyingly refreshed, and then at Errance, who stood straight and silent without any acknowledgment of his wrapped torso, hidden underneath his new sky-blue shirt and leather jerkin. It was rather refreshing to see him in actual color, made him seem more real.

To enter the streets of Oolum was to again chance a meeting with their

222

hunters. But Coren and Zizain led the way straight back into the thick of the city and the milling crowds who walked unaware of the dangerous game of life and death that danced around them. In the hottest hours of the day, the shopping decreased, and the people sought shelter in whatever shade they could find, drinking water and spirits, jabbering among themselves, haggling over final prices, catching a few winks of sleep. The lack of bustle seemed a bane to Tellie, making their passing a curious thing for onlookers to study.

Coren swaggered ahead of them, for all appearances on his own stroll, when he abruptly did an about-face, whirling his finger in the air. "That ol' lizard, he cheated me of a few coins," he said cheerfully. "Back we go! He isn't going to get away with it."

"What?" Tryss exclaimed.

He drew close, close enough for them all to hear him at a whisper. "It's your faithful 'shadows' back again," he said. "So turn around and go."

Tellie's heart thudded. This was impossible, really, the last straw! What evil fate drew these men after them, an invisible thread binding them together and refusing to break no matter how tangled it wove through the city?

But Coren did not seem to worry, he only continued to walk onward, whistling and hands stuffed in pockets.

Errance lengthened his stride, overtaking the captain. "What is your game here?" he growled.

"We can't just constantly go running about the city pell-mell, can we?" Coren returned pleasantly. "That would get all the wrong sort of attention."

"Is there a right sort?"

"Oh, indeed yes."

"You betray us, you die. I am watching your every move."

Coren chuckled. "Of course you are. I'm a watchable fellow! Follow in my footsteps, friend, and you'll get somewhere."

Zizain had taken the lead, and her hands twiddled with the purple sash around her waist and now it fell away into her hands with a swish. "Boys, how about a tune?" Her rich voice rang out loud in the stuffy air as she paused in front of a band of colorfully clad men lounging in the shade of a merchant's stall. Various musical instruments lay in their laps: lutes, drums, cymbals. They straightened as soon as they saw Zizain, and brilliant smiles flashed across their dark faces. One immediately started tapping his drum and another joined in the beat with plucks of his lute.

It was almost like magic the way the teeming throng lulled in their activities and glanced the musicians' way. Zizain swung her sash around her in an arc, moving those nearby back until there was a wide circle of space about her. Another lute joined in the jaunty tune, and as the third entered the chorus, Zizain swung into the music like she was an instrument herself.

Tellie's mouth dropped open as she watched. She'd never seen anyone dance like Zizain did. The woman's body was fluid, the limbs aflight in graceful bending and swirling, the scarf an extension of her body. The lutes thrummed, and the scarf flared in and out. Her feet moved in flawless precision, leading her across the ground like a bird in curving leaps and twirls. Her dance was the music incarnate, and Tellie had never heard a tune so fast, so full of sauce and vigor.

She turned to voice her admiration to Kelm, but when she saw how he stared at the dancer, eyes as wide as dinner plates and cheeks faintly pink, she lost half of her appreciation of the dance. He didn't have to be that fascinated.

The crowd drew around Zizain like beasts at a feeding trough, squeezing shoulder to shoulder. In their eagerness, Tellie and the others were shoved to the front circle around the dancer, and Errance hunkered into himself as if he could go invisible, only glancing up occasionally to scowl at Coren. But the red-haired elf was wearing a smile as bright as the day, looking very satisfied with himself.

"What are we doing?" Errance hissed at him.

"We're putting on a show, and the crowds love it."

Realization, albeit annoyed, dawned in Errance's eyes. In that moment, Tellie also understood. The people were so closely packed around them there was no way for the hunters to get through, much less see beyond.

As Zizain flashed by, her smile sparkled. She knew how to perform and clearly loved it, conspiratorial reasons aside. The people watching loved it too, clapping their hands to the beat, even chanting her name. Occasionally, a man would try to catch her scarf as it'd whisk past him, but with a quirk of her eyebrow, she'd flick it just out of reach. Then with an impulsive grin, Zizain looped her scarf around Errance's waist and tugged forward.

Errance startled, but remained rock-firm. The crowd hooted with laughter, only seeing that she teased a stiff and scowling young man to join her in the dance. Errance didn't move, but his eyes, glaring out from behind his curtain of hair, smoldered like embers.

With a careless shrug, Zizain let go of one end of her sash and dashed it out towards another person—Coren.

And Coren took it.

The elf sprang into the dance, much to the approval of the crowd. He was every bit as mesmerizing as Zizain, and now the music rose to a level greater than before. They were not two dancers but one, entwining, parting, swirling into a blaze of color. The music sped faster and faster, and then with a roll of drums, it broke in a clash of cymbals.

The crowd roared their approval and surged forward. Tellie and the others might well have been lost in the wave, but Coren and Zizain moved fast and with a few steps they were right beside them so they would not get separated.

After initial acceptance of a job well done, the two smugglers started to shove through the stir, and nobody noticed that the sullen young man, young woman, and two children followed in their footsteps.

oOo

The king of Aselvia was laughing. "Oh Coren," he said, shaking his head. "I never expected to see him back in the story again. He was such a strange one. We never did understand him." His laughter died away as if caught by a breeze, and his expression turned pensive. "And yet..."

"And yet?" the One prodded gently

"Yet he has accomplished more for your sake than many an elf more elegant and fair. Not until I came here did I realize how little we elves do for the world outside our home."

"You were a worthy king of Aselvia." He did not say it as if it were an excuse or an encouragement—merely as a fact.

"Of Aselvia, perhaps," King Rendar said sadly. *"But I might have done so much more."* He did not speak for several moments before a smile lifted his lips. *"Perhaps Errance, who is seeing so much of Orim, will be more devoted to its cause when he is king."*

"Perhaps."

19

oOo

Tertorem gave me this at least—sincerity. I never had to question their intention. They were out to break me, in any way possible. Somehow, while I am with this red-headed jester, I miss that confidence. There is no saying what he will do next or what he is really thinking. His eyes dance far too merrily for me to see anything behind them. I want to call him a liar, the worst of frauds. Yet somehow, I can't. I hate that. I hate that I want him to be real.

Night hides many secrets and knows many fears. It knew the thoughts of the beggars sleeping in its shadowy arms, it knew how many prowlers stalked along its path, and it knew that somewhere several blocks into the poorest part of the housing district, there hid a certain group of tired fugitives.

The little house was full of crates and cobwebs. A close eye might have noticed the hatch in the ceiling, which led to a shallow attic. The space between attic floor and ceiling was so small that one could not even stand up in it, only crawl around or lie still.

Tellie lay on her mat and stared at the thin, blue starlight peering through the slats of a small door to the roof above her. She tried very much not to notice every distant cry and crash, tried to pretend the night did not prey upon her imagination and create ghastly images for each strange sound. After all, she didn't need to be frightened. Tryss and Kelm lay a few feet away from her, and she could hear the shifting of Errance in the room below as he changed bandages for his wounds. So there was nothing to fear, nothing at all. And at last, she fell asleep.

Experienced as he was with sleeping under stars and in inns, Kelm had little fear of nightly noises. The floor was a bit uncomfortable, but he was able to use his blanket for an extra cushion as the air was still plenty warm. So he settled himself comfortably and congratulated himself on judging Zizain right, and did Tellie notice this was the second time he'd gotten them all out of a scrape? Hoping she had, he drifted off to dream heroic dreams.

Tryss lay very still, still enough that the night might not have noticed she was there if the night hadn't been there too. The scratches of the shard burned with a cold fire, and it took all her strength not to fret over them. The pain held the memory of the shard ever near, but she kept pushing it away with a shudder. She hated the city, hated the close, confining walls, hated the way the shadows lurked like predators waiting to pounce. What a terrible thing it was to live in solid stone where flight and hiding were so limited. Thoughts of her endless green forest danced in her mind, but she shook them away with impatience. No, her duty was here to protect the children. And Errance. Errance. What was she even supposed to think about him now? Had he really meant to take an arrow for her, and if so, why? Why for the one he so obviously scorned? It did not fit with any of the behavior he had shown before. And so she fell into uneasy slumber.

Errance climbed stiffly up the ladder, pulled his shirt back over his freshly wrapped torso, and chose the farthest and darkest corner for bed, and when he lay down, his mind drifted...

...but not even the secretive night knew what Errance thought.

oOo

In the taverns of Oolum, the cooling of celestial starlight passed by unnoticed for it was always hot within the crowded bars. Hot and fermented with ale, sweat, and worse—funks of city drudgery.

Daran drew the stench in with each blistering breath, letting it sour in his stomach. The taste of ale on his lips was poor, but he hardly cared for the flavor or the smell around him, only that it fed his ever heating anger. His eyes were nearly glowing orange, though perhaps by the light of the candles, when he looked over the table where his other fellows hunkered.

"One man." He ground the words between his teeth. "One man, and you all ran, the cowardly lot of you."

"You ran too," one of his men growled. He looked like he wished to retract the words, but they were out and on their own.

Daran's hand dropped to his knife, squeezing the leather pommel till it squeaked. "I ran because I was without support. Because my men *fled*. From one attacker. When we are on the *verge* of success! And now, now that elf rat has scuttled loose of the trap again, the minx with him, and the brats, all four of them gone because of just one man!"

No one answered this time. Not one of his own anyway.

But a man a few tables over suddenly stood and laughed, loud and lusty. "A day such as yours deserves better drinks then cheap sewage water. Keeper, a round of Brivani beer for these unlucky scoundrels!"

Scowling, Daran twisted around to have a better look at the stranger who approached. He was a tall, dark man in a dusty, orange tunic and matching turban. The cut of the cloth was fine, but the fabric itself was faded with experience. Daran guessed that came from frequency of use rather than lack of funds. In all his life, he hated the lazy rich, but the rich who didn't mind working hard with what they possessed...well...he had to respect that. So he gave no protest as the stranger hooked a chair with his foot and dragged it to their table in one sweep.

After all, he couldn't pass up Brivani beer, not even for the sake of pride. In young days he'd traveled through Oolum, but had been too poor and weak to enjoy its true pleasures. Now, he should have been pursuing the time of his life, for a knife and meaningful look could buy the same as gold. There was no time for any of that tonight, not with the Prisoner still on the loose. But an offer such as this rich stranger made was not one to refuse.

Nevertheless, generosity did not come without a price. "What's our trouble to you, clothtop?" he snarled.

The man only leaned back, pushing the chair onto its rear legs. "Oh come. You can't whisper a word like elf without my ears catching it." His tapering, brown fingers played at the flap of his collar, flashing for one moment a bronze medallion on his chest emblazoned with a symbol Daran knew well—a slave seller.

"He's our prize, not yours," Daran snarled.

"And someone else's too apparently, or so I overheard. Perhaps had a run in with those scurvy smugglers?"

"Smugglers?" Daran took his mug of beer from the tray a maid offered without removing his intense stare from the merchant. "What kind of smugglers? Who are they? Where are they based?"

The stranger threw back his head and laughed savagely, white teeth flashing in the red shadows. "If I knew that, do you think the thieves would still be crawling about? They've given me more trouble than a shipload's worth of slaves, and I'd name anyone my patron saint if they destroyed the bunch. But no, this is a clever rabble, they use secret tunnels and brilliant disguises. Why, I've heard tell they even disguise themselves as honest citizens of the city."

Daran swallowed his fifth sip of beer eagerly, though he hardly noticed the improved taste in light of the man's story. "The man who attacked us was tall and lean as a whip. Wore a white shirt and had copper red hair."

At that, the merchant snorted. "What? Sounds like they tried to pass themselves as good Captain Coren. Ah, wait till I tell him, he'll be fit to be tied. Will these shenanigans never end? But this I have heard rumor of, mates…some say they see ships anchored far from harbor, and it is my belief that they row out their smuggled slaves."

"Where on the shore do they go exactly?"

The man sat forward suddenly, the front chair legs thudding on the planked floor. A cattish smile curled his lips, and he looked ready to purr. "Ah. I thought you might be interested. It's about time I found men willing to get the job done. Let me buy you another round of drinks, and we'll discuss the details."

The men huzzahed, but Daran shook his head. "No, no, we must be clear-headed in the morning if we're to catch our prey."

"They won't be out immediately," the merchant said with another laugh as he signaled the barmaid again. "No, lads, you only live once and what better place to live than in Oolum?"

Some time later, the tavern door opened, a burnt orange slice in the darkness, and the slave merchant stepped out into the fresh night air. He left the rumble of bawdy ballads and course laughter in the dust of his heels, and his stride down the streets was so purposeful and so sober that neither thief nor harlot sought to sway him.

He passed through many winding streets, neither looking right nor left, nor stumbling once. Without pause, he turned and vanished into the deepest shadows of alley.

A few moments later, Captain Coren stepped back out, and if his skin was browner than usual, who could tell in such lighting? He donned his hat at a rakish angle and then he set off down the street again, whistling and swaying a bit on his ankles, now drunk.

When he'd made his way to yet darker, quieter parts of the city, his whistling and swaying ceased, and he became little more than a shadow blown by the wind. And when come to a certain house, identical among many, the shadow slipped inside and was seen no more.

Coren exhaled once inside the house, and though it was little more than a glorified closet of boxes and crates, he relaxed in it as if it were the most welcoming of homes. With a quick chuckle and flick of his head, he reached into one crate to pull out a rag and started wiping the false layer of brown from his arms.

Ah, such men were easy to fool, and it was a pleasure to do so. But as Coren continued to consider the men he'd hoodwinked, his smile faded and the rubbing rag slowed. The men might have been easy to fool, but it was not the men who were to fear. Throughout his exchange with the villains, his gaze had dropped often to their shadows. Their shade seemed darker and more sinister than most and gave Coren the eeriest sense that someone watched from within.

No, it was not the men themselves who sent such a chill down his spine, but the presence with them, the aura around them...

Many times, Coren had looked east and seen the great, grey mountains so held in fear by folk, and he knew from his days of Aselvia that there was fabled to be a stronghold of Darkness in the lands across the sea. But as far as he knew, he had never met anyone from the legendary Tertorem itself.

There could be no doubt to the markings upon Errance's chest though or the mortal girl's wild explanations...the men pursuing the lost heir of Aselvia were touched by a darkness and power beyond their mortal abilities.

A shudder shook his body, and he at last acknowledged the thought lurking in every corner of his mind.

The prince of Aselvia is sleeping up in my attic.

It was so, so very impossible. Seventy years, seventy *years*, the elf heir had been thought dead, and despite Coren's childhood fancies, he'd always believed it to be so. But Errance was up in the attic above his head.

He released his breath, long and slow. Just wait till the elves of Aselvia found out. What would they think!

What *would* they think?

The rush of excitement that surged through his blood passed as quickly as it came, leaving dread to knot his stomach. By all appearances, Errance had been hidden by Darkness for those seventy years. What had been done to him? What was he even like?

Throwing the rag aside, he reached up to the plaster ceiling and caught an iron ring imbedded above. The trap-door opened, a rope ladder unfurled, and Coren sprang lightly up the trusses to the hidden room. It was very dark, but his eyes had already adjusted to the night on the way home, and pale starlight peered through the slats of the flap to the roof. The figures of Tryss and the children curled in the left corner and in the farthest and very darkest corner lay Errance.

He moved towards him, wishing to exude confidence as opposed to sneaking, but that wasn't exactly easy as he only had the options of crawling on his knees, scooting on his bum, or stalking in a crouch.

As he came within two yards, Errance bolted up with the speed of a snake and stared at him.

Wide awake, Coren thought with a sigh. *Has he slept at all?*

Neither spoke, neither moved, just stared and studied each other. Or rather Coren studied; Errance's eyes did not even twitch. He observed how one of Errance's hands remained under the blanket, and he wagered it held a knife.

"Ah good, you're awake," he said, smiling and settling himself into a comfortable position. "Are the new bandages and ointments helping any?" When no answer came, he rambled on. "I can get you some new clothes tomorrow."

Only silence followed, a very empty silence. In that moment, Coren realized that if he took the wrong move or said the wrong thing, he would be dead before he took another breath. Stiffening, he took a second, sharper look at Errance. If this threat held true for everyone then Tryss and the children could most definitely not stay with him.

But no. The fear straining Errance's body was not for the children, whom he tolerated well enough, nor for Tryss, no matter how mistrust exuded towards her. This fear was of Coren—a man. An equal to his strength, or rather stronger considering the prince's wounds. Perhaps the fear had been there from the start or merely overpowered by the shock of Coren's true identity. This much was true—what the brightness of sunlight concealed, the shadows of night revealed. Errance was afraid of him.

He leaned back on the heel of his hand and scratched the edge of his ear. "It's the city isn't it?" He let a moment of silence lapse, or rather allowed the distant sounds of the city to linger in the air. The howl of a dog, the screech of a cat, the clatter of glass. "You've never been to a human city," he pondered aloud. "You didn't even make it to Dormandy. That place would have been a better impression, at first glance anyway. This isn't the most flattering city of mortal man, but it is among the most honest, so huzzah for that."

He could see the handle of the knife now, and the white-knuckled grip on the hilt.

"I've been to a lot of the cities in Orim, you know! I left Aselvia thirty years ago at the fresh age of twenty, and traveled from Korince to the far North. Really, Korince is not everything it's lauded to be, or rather it is, and that's the problem. Mind you, I haven't stayed away from home the whole time, I'm not that rogue of a child. Time to time I'll go back to visit or meet my family at Dormandy."

"They just let you go, huh?" Errance said, tight-lipped. "When I lived there, leaving was not a popular goal."

"Oh ho, yes, *definitely* not popular. My parents pleaded with me not to go, but in the end, it was actually Un…uh…King Rendar who gave his blessing."

Errance flinched. It took only that name to send cracks through his hard exterior. After a moment, he swallowed hard, and the knife slid back to the floor. "My father? I find that…unlikely."

"Believe me, I was shocked too. Especially after what had happened…well, to you. But he said if I truly believed Ayeshune called me out to human worlds, then I needed to go. Your father is a good man, Errance, he wants to keep his people safe but he also wants them to live to their potential. You know that."

Errance stared past him into the opposing darkness. "Do you know that he's dead?"

Coren couldn't breathe.

No.

Why.

Was it a test? Of course it was a test, but was it true? He doubted the devastation on his face could be seen in the shadows, but his voice shook. "When? How did it happen?"

"I'm the one whose been locked up for seventy years, I thought you might know," Errance said bitterly. "The children came with the news. They're not lying, I can tell."

"I haven't been back to Aselvia in a while...if it just happened, the message or messenger might still be on their way. I hadn't heard he was ill." Had it been an accident? An assassination? It couldn't have been old age! But if Errance didn't know, there was no use in tormenting him with speculation. There was only one thing he could say.

"Errance...I'm...I'm so sorry." With any other person he would have reached across and held him close, but he knew that knife would be planted between his ribs if he tried. He only hoped that Errance would hear his sincerity and believe it.

"So why haven't you been back to Aselvia?"

Coren blinked. The interrogative tone was back, the time for sympathy was gone. He still was reeling from the news, he wanted to go out and learn more and mourn and...but his chance with Errance was now and only now.

He exhaled. "When I came to Oolum...oh...eight years ago...I sort of stuck in roots. And one year in, I rescued Zizain from some slavers. Haven't been back home since as she sticks to me like glue, and I really don't want to try explaining her to my parents, because..."

He noticed that Errance's frozen stance and expression had changed to one that practically screamed judgement. "Because they'd look at me much the same way you're looking at me now, and how encouraging is that?" Shaking his head, he huffed a quiet chuckle. "You can stop glaring, it's not what you think. Zizain's not interested in me like that, or in you, which I thought you might like to know since you bristle if she comes within ten feet. Oh yes, she thinks men very handsome and she's not afraid to make it clear, but she won't pursue any relationship beyond that." His voice drew inwards, hardened to a tight core. "The slavers were sensual sellers. Her own lover pawned her off to them. She was seventeen years old."

With a brisk shake of his head to banish the dark memories away, he continued. "She treats love like one big silly joke, that's how she deals with heartbreak. As for you, you shut everyone out. Who broke your heart, Errance?"

In the last few moments, the tension of Errance's shoulders had begun to fade, but he went rigid as Coren's last words drove in like a barb.

Coren spoke calm and cool, though he kept one eye on the hand holding the knife. "Perhaps it wasn't someone, but something. Something that someone didn't do. A cruel action. A failed ideal." He saw each of his suggestions hit home, the pain of them revealed in Errance's eyes. But he looked for one in particular, one scar more vital than all the rest.

Errance opened his mouth, and then seemed to change his mind, for he shut it again and looked down, refusing to make eye contact.

"Anyway," Coren leisured, "if you ever feel like talking to someone about those years, I'm here. It's not like you can talk about them with anyone else. Nothing you're going to say is going to shock me. This city was spawned of the Darkness, and he's got people here just as evil as in Tertorem." He leaned closer. "And I *am* an elf of Aselvia, I am one of your people, like it or not."

No response.

With a yawn, Coren scooted backwards and reached for the roof hatch when Errance spoke.

"Do you really want to know?"

A fatal challenge could not have been spoken with more peril. Cold, laced with mocking and contempt. An uninvited chill crawled down Coren's spine, and he stilled, hand tightening on the latch. His elven prince would speak, not to unburden the sorrows of his soul, but to test Coren's mettle. And if the taunting lilt of his tone meant anything, he did not believe Coren could truly take it.

For a moment, Coren wondered if he dared to hear, wondered if he should have been so bold to claim knowledge in all the dark ways. He wondered if he should perhaps invite Errance to come talk up on the roof, away from young ears. But he could hear the light snores of the children and knew they must be deep in sleep after such an exhausting day. And Errance would not speak again if delay came now.

He came back near and settled himself to wait, not prompting any beginning, for he knew Errance would start when he wanted to and not before.

No matter the heat still baked into the stones, the aura around Errance was cold, and when he spoke his voice was colder still. A hard, uncaring sound, devoid of emotion. A common ear might have thought it the voice of one who had never loved in its life. Coren recognized it was the voice of one who had loved too much.

"They all died that night," Errance began. "Every elf with me. Lord Reyin was last, killed before my eyes. My clothes and belongings were left scattered in the gore of my companions, and I was taken to Tertorem. I was told the conditions of my captivity from the start. The moment I submitted myself to their service, agreed to read and reveal the secrets of the Moonscript, the torture would end, and I would be set free. Lies, of course, and young fool though I was, I saw them as such. So I was given over to the Darkness's commander of war and pain, Lord Raduer. And from then on life smeared into one red blur of endless agony. Perhaps they meant to break me in one fell snap. But I did not break. Because there was no choice for me. At that time, I was still naïve and innocent enough to think that even if I had wanted to obey, I wouldn't be able to read the Moonscript because Father would not allow it."

The bitterness in the last lashed out like a whip, but Coren did not flinch under its sting. Steadily, he kept his gaze locked with Errance. It was not so much a struggle for him, he kept his spirit calm and cool, but he could see fire and smoke ever building inside his companion's soul.

"I survived the first decade. But that did not faze His Darkness, for he had constructed a three-part plan to break me, and without delay he set upon me a new master, the lord of slavery and shame, the one they call Ajahleish. There I was taken from mindless torture to humiliation. After that, an ever enduring torment of pointless work, hot and dry, surrounded by other slaves and lurking taskmasters. No shred of righteousness was left in any prisoner, eventually all turned on me, and we were enemies surrounded by our enemies. It was in that time I discovered the true power in my celestial blood. Instead of breaking down like all the men around me, I grew stronger. I healed from each wound given me, and though there was always new pain to cripple me, yet I hardened and grew. I started to think of myself as a hero, wondered if I might escape. But there is no place for heroes there, and no strength that matters against the will of—"

His voice suddenly broke. So cut of stones his words had been, and now they cracked. Alarm and confusion blazed into his eyes, and his jaw tightened to hold in any other unexpected weakness.

Coren did not blink. He simply watched. But inside, his heart lurched against his chest. *So*, he thought. *You thought to disturb me with your tale, you thought I would flee from it, or else show a hidden delight that would prove me evil. But you do not know what to do with a steadfast heart. You sense my compassion, you sense that I care. But you do not know what to make of it, and your heart has responded when you thought it so hard. Oh, Errance. Do you not even remember what it is like to be loved?*

Errance no longer returned his gaze, instead staring down into the dark corner of the room, his face withdrawn to hide in shadows. But the hand holding the knife could still be seen by a little light and it quivered.

When he spoke again, his voice was husky. Halting. Walking warily upon thin ice. "Having broken me with pain and shame, His Darkness then sought the crippling stroke. To seduce me in my weariness, in my weakness. Tertorem changed. It took on a glamour of intoxicating beauty, a world boasting wonders rivaling even Aselvia. All pain before had been for their pleasure, and it would be no different here. But she who is known as Etiserdis…has power to corrupt the mind, to make you believe enslavement is what you desire. But I fought. I clung to what good I knew, and would not yield to what lies their forked tongues hissed. So they took all that was pure and lovely and made it sordid. The truths I'd been taught were twisted till every dream I'd once had lay ruined. They set me at war within myself, my mind against my body, and when they started meddling with my mind, it was my heart against everything else, and that shriveled day by day."

He was gone now, lost in the memory of his torment, and perhaps he no longer realized he spoke aloud to someone, for he no longer tried to conceal the shaking of his voice, the suffering within it.

Coren sat still, his fingers curled hard into fists till the nails were digging into skin.

"I at last understood there would be no rescue," Errance whispered. "That I was doomed to suffer as by their will, and that I could not escape, not even...not even through death." His breath caught, then released in a rattling swell. "I...I was devastated. I did not care about anything anymore, and though I still did not fully submit, I gave up fighting back. Then I knew Prince Errance had failed indeed, and that the secrets of the Moonscript and my people were in mortal danger."

A spasm of pain contracted Coren's face, and he finally dared to exhale. Throughout his conquests he had seen many shattered spirits. He did not see or sense anything in Errance that he had not seen or sensed before. But never, never had he ever met a soul with so much pain in it, so high a score of defeat. Yet still he knew they had not reached the true core of his broken heart.

"How did you regain your strength?" he asked.

Suddenly snapped back into reality, Errance laughed, short and sharp. "I didn't," he said. "I died."

"Except," Coren said, brow wrinkling, "not really."

Errance's eyes blazed in the darkness. "No, I died. That boy, the tattered remains of the Prince you saw painted on walls—he—died. When I could not sever my spirit from my body, I suffocated it, buried it with despair beyond any equal before or since. I do not remember the next decade of seclusion they say I spent. Perhaps they thought my subconscious would writhe in solitude, but they were wrong; there was *nothing*."

After a few more moments, the prince continued, voice steady again, though still teaming with an underlying fire. "And then someone else awoke. It awoke in the mines, and there was pain, and there was rage, and there was meaning. I killed two hundred and thirty-seven men that first year and lost count after. I was a mountain of fire come to life from dormancy. They locked me in seclusion again, this time with a demon outside to speak lies and pervert my mind, but I withdrew again, though not so deep as before. There I regained self-control and a strange sense of pride. They had done their worst—but I had been reborn stronger than before. What could they do to me that they hadn't done already? In a way, I was above them. I wouldn't give in; I couldn't die…what was left?"

With a swift shake, he straightened and his voice became brisk, unfeeling. "Whatever strategy they'd had was now in shambles. I suppose they were thoroughly tired of me, because the next warden set in charge of Tertorem was a mere mortal man who only thought himself dangerous. I soon taught him otherwise. At the end of his ten year reign, Tellie and Kelm arrived as neighbors to my cell, and the Voice returned to Tertorem."

"The Voice," Coren interrupted, "Wait, who's that?"

Errance stared at him as if he had grown a second head. "What do you mean who's the Voice? He is the most powerful and revered of all the demons of His Darkness."

"Never heard of him."

Errance's brow furrowed incredulously. "Strange," he murmured. "He is the one held in most dread."

"Not the Darkness?"

A slight scoff caught in Errance's throat. "You never see the Darkness. According to rumor, he dwells in a black sphere called the Nyght that floats over Tertorem. The Voice is his mouth, his eyes, his ears, and his actions. It's the Voice that reports to him and who receives orders. He is…the worst of them all. Every turn of the decade he would come to see how I fared and turn me over to my next master. But this time…this time, he declared himself the new warden. But we…escaped. The children and I."

"You never see the Darkness?" Coren repeated, his tone disbelieving.

"No."

"Are you certain? They say he takes the form of a wind black as death—

"I've never seen him," Errance said, but the firmness to his voice sounded queer, and Coren was sure he saw a flicker of…uncertainty?

Nothing more was spoken for a long while after. They simply sat there in the dark, light fading in and out between the wooden slats as somewhere far above clouds passed over the moon and stars. But in that stillness hung expectation. An emptiness of words unsaid. For Errance was not finished, Coren knew, but he dared not encourage him to continue, for any encouragement would surely be taken as pressure.

"I don't know how I didn't give in." The words were whispered. A secret shameful confession. His hand slowly uncurled from the knife and rose to wrap around his other arm. "Perhaps if I had known in the beginning how long or hard it would be. It was a strange duty...to protect people I had never met. Sometimes...sometimes I am angry they still live perfect lives free of Darkness while I suffered to preserve that perfection. But maybe I was never protecting them. Maybe I was only protecting my own pride."

The air around them inhaled, even it understanding how hard it was for the prince to speak those thoughts. Swallowing, Coren looked to the floor, unable to see how very still Errance's face remained. Those words he had spoken—who knew how many countless times they'd tangled in his mind, and yet he refused to show any relief that he had at last voiced them.

So much said, so much revealed. But it was only a scratch on the surface after all, only the smallest of leaks in the pain pressured within him. Who would be able to stand firm if the dam he'd built ever broke?

Errance's eyes hardened again, the look of loss retreating to hide behind his walls. He made a small, scornful sound to mock the vulnerability that had slipped free. "Any questions?" he said, sardonic to perfection.

"Just one. What about Ayeshune?"

The look that flashed through Errance's eyes was as brief and as violent as a strike of lightening. It told Coren everything he needed to know.

"That's all, Errance," he said quietly. "Thanks for talking."

He rose and reached for to the hatch, climbing out of the dark, cramped room and onto the roof, the vast night overhead. A cool ocean breeze swept across the roofs of Oolum, and he turned his sweaty face into its path. Every muscle in his body trembled, trembled with an anger as red as his hair and blood. But he took breath after deep breath, willing the liquid fury to sink down and wait. Righteous wrath was all well and good, but there was no righteous outlet at hand.

Instead, he looked up into the sky and the stars sparkling brighter than the purest diamonds. The west wind bore aloft the scent of sea salt, a more welcome perfume to him than any expensive oil.

He noticed then that he was not alone. A small silhouette sat on the edge of the roof, moonlight illuminating blowing hair. He went and sat beside the figure. He did not speak, but he looked so he could see those dark eyes bright with reflections of starlight floating deep inside. Zizain was a beautiful woman, but more beautiful at night for of those hours she was queen. He looked away before she could feel his gaze upon her.

Zizain spoke, barely moving her lips. "You spoke with the prince, yes?"

"Yes," he answered, pulling one knee up so that he could rest his chin on it.

Then a growl rumbled out of his throat. "He was long gone by the time I was born, Zi. But oh, the stories told of him. Stories of a bright, adventurous youth with a laugh that could warm the coldest hearts and a smile anyone could trust. A boy with a spirit brave and bold that strove hard to learn every skill of art and battle, but whose heart still remained kind and pure. Not a perfect boy, even the stories admitted he had a streak of rebellion and other normal faults. But a boy better than most. When I'd see the paintings of him, I *knew* that all those stories were true. And that that bright young boy should be that mutilated man down below us…"

Coren clenched his jaw, but breath hissed out between his teeth. Until that moment, he'd prided himself for control. But by the stars, *Errance*! His prince, his king! Tears began to thicken his throat, and he could barely speak.

"And yet when I heard what he just told me…I realize we should have nothing at all. He should be a raving monster, devoid of any mind. He says his former self died, and perhaps it did, perhaps for a time he was nothing but a monster. And yet nobility and some memory returned, no matter how he might deny it. That streak of rebellion could not have been able to take him this far."

"Then what did?" Zizain asked.

Crossing his arms, he craned his neck back till he stared straight up at the stars. "The celestial elves have a powerful light dwelling within them. They can pull it out to craft, strengthen, and heal. Since Errance is only half celestial, he doesn't have the power to pull his light out, but it is is inside him. I can only guess it sustained him throughout all those years, healing his body and stabilizing his mind. But other than that...he's empty. He doesn't have anything else. If that fails him one day..." His voice trailed away, and he stared off into the distance where silver caps of waves ribboned the midnight sea.

Zizain gave his hand a soft squeeze. "If he's the prince, doesn't that make him your cousin?"

"Yes," Coren said shortly. "But don't tell him. Somehow I doubt he wants to know."

20

oOo

For a small breath of time, the burdens on my soul eased as I let them down, spoke them aloud, pried their grip from my throat. But I could not loose it all for though his eyes are seasoned beyond his years, the truths hidden in darkness would snuff any light, and I do not want the bright spark in his eye to go out. He does not need to know the power of Darkness.

"*Tellie. Tellie, it is time.*"

She shifted, trying to squirm deeper into sleep and let the voice fade away. Was that Mister Norne—no, no, of course not, that was a very handsome voice. Errance or maybe Coren? No, not them either. That's right, it was Rendar, the elven King Ren—

She bolted upright, blanket flying.

There he knelt across the room. As he came towards her, she shrank back.

He halted, surprised. "Are you afraid of me?"

Coloring, she cleared her dry throat and peeled her tongue away from the roof her mouth. "No! No. It's just...it's just one usually doesn't dream when they're so tired."

With a quiet chuckle, he said, "Have I not told you that this is no dream?"

"Yes, well..." She trailed off unhappily. The last time Rendar had appeared could certainly be explained as a dream. Maybe even this time she could excuse it as a dream. But that experience she'd shared with Errance in the streets of

Oolum could not be denied. "Well. Well, then what is this, Rendar! What's happening and why is it happening to me?"

Sympathy filled his eyes and he reached out his hand. "I'm sorry, I did not explain well enough last time. Or perhaps you were not ready to understand. But come with me now and your sight shall grow."

All at once every exquisite detail of their previous time together rushed back into Tellie's mind. The terror of the darkness, the thrill of the singing, then the exhaustion and collapse. After all the activity of the day, she doubted she could muster the strength for another battle.

"Do you want me to help Errance?" she asked weakly.

He shook his head. "Coren is helping him tonight."

"Coren!"

"Indeed. A noble elf, though very different from the rest of us. Tonight, he is helping Errance release a little of the pain rotting inside."

"Errance is confiding in Coren?" Tellie said, shocked more than ever. She'd thought Errance wouldn't trust Coren ten leagues away.

"Do not think Errance desires isolation, even if he believes it himself. He is starved for friendship, and no matter what his mind may deny, his heart recognizes Coren as kindred," Rendar said. He stood, and Tellie's stomach turned as she saw he could rise to his full and terrible height in the low-roofed attic without changing size. She really shouldn't be allowed to dream such impossible things.

When he took her hand, she felt a slight change, as if the morning sun was just beginning to rise. She glanced around the room and she saw the figures of her friends just like she might have normally, except...except not. There was more. She could see further in. Beyond the first layer of their bodies and into the glowing core of their spirit. It wasn't noticeable at first, only when she really looked for it. And there was something more about them, but it was utterly different to her mind, so she shook it off.

What did she look like here, deeper in? She stared down at herself, brow furrowing and suddenly her sight changed. It wasn't like anything she knew. The best she could compare it to was looking into a mirror. But there was no dark room in that reflection nor anything that could be remotely called a place. In that strange reflection she saw...things...about herself. No, not things, for that would give the impression of something tangible. But looking at them in that reflection, she began to feel them in her own state even where she stood, though when she looked quickly over her shoulder, nothing was there.

"What is it, Rendar?" she demanded. "What's this around me?"

He arched a silver brow, mouth curling in slight smile. "Ah, so your senses are already attuning to this realm. Those, Tellie, are the prayers of people who love you. Leoren and Casara worry for your safety."

Everything within her inhaled. She could barely breathe, let alone talk, but she felt the wings of her heart slowly unfold and swell. "What?" It didn't matter if she said the words aloud. All her being expressed the question, the desperate hope.

For some time now, she'd begun to doubt if the elven couple had truly cared for her, or if her imagination had simply made up what she'd wanted to believe. But they were praying for her, and the touch of their thought was warm and comforting.

"The Unseen," Rendar said, "is the realm of our spiritual selves. All are a part of it, all affect it, but few are those who see it. Those who have this gift are called Walkers, but do not misunderstand, they are no more powerful in spirit than any other, they have simply been called to see beyond the mortal veil. I was one in life, and after death, I am still one, for it is a gift of the spirit. And you are one as well. Called by Ayeshune."

"So let get me this straight," she said, very carefully. "This is not the realm of the dead."

"Absolutely not. The Awaiting Souls rest elsewhere. But I have been given leave to still walk here in the Unseen, for I have many prayers to wrap around those I love who are yet living on the mortal side."

When he spoke of his prayers, another scale fell from her sight, and her gaze was drawn to Errance. Or rather to that which surrounded him. She sensed fervent love of such that she had never known. It was too personal for her to look closely, but a close look was not needed to be overwhelmed with awe of the many and powerful loves that enveloped the prince of Aselvia.

And there was hers. She hadn't consciously ever prayed to Ayeshune about Errance, but her thoughts and hopes for him had been recognized. A small daisy chain amongst grand jewelry. It was really rather abashing; what could her simple love and prayer do for him when he already had such powerful pleas and protections in his defense?

"So," she said with a quick shiver. "What are we going to do then?"

"It is time you understand what we're fighting for."

"We're fighting for Errance."

"But what is Errance fighting for?"

Tellie didn't answer, suddenly muddled. Yes, yes, the Darkness had been after him for that Moonscript, and all that imprisonment and torture had been the means to an end, not just for entertainment. What was in the Moonscript that evil sought it so hard?

"Come," he said, lifting her to her feet and leading the way through the veil walls. The world spread out before them, the city of Oolum sweeping across the sands to the swaying ocean shore.

As Tellie looked across the clustered buildings and towers, she fancied she saw each and every soul who dwelt within, and within them was more to see, but it was all too much for her to understand. Still, she saw how the quiet of the night proved false. Always, always there was energy and battle lacing through the city, prayers and curses carried on secret roads, dark and light, in strife and conflict.

Without her notice, the world had become small and far away like a toy city spread out on the floor. She wondered if it was because it had shrunk or she had grown, but the next moment it hit her with a sensation of a slap that it was because she was now high above it. Somewhere in the sky, perhaps. And for a girl terrified of heights, it was quite the most awful realization she'd ever had.

Or at least it would have been if there was not such an assurance that she was quite secure and stable, which was peculiar to be assured of when one had neither body nor ground to stand on. Instead, she found safety in Rendar's hand, and so focused on that instead of the little world below.

That was when she noticed the bright lights floating around them. They were too far away to discern, but she thought they might be fireflies, except some were too big, and anyway, they were far too white as if they were stars. Stars. Oh no, it couldn't be, she really couldn't be up walking among the stars, now could she?

"Where are you taking me?" she whimpered, clinging tighter to his arm.

"We have reached it now," he replied, pausing. "We have come to the top and very edge of the Celestial Cleft and at this distance those of the Lower World must remain until the renewal of days when the Higher and Lower shall again be as one."

It all sounded very fancy and above her, but all at once she didn't need an explanation to understand. Because she saw it. There across far fields and sparkling streams. She saw...

...a white, gleaming city. The great celestial city of Korsical.

Her legs began to waver, her chin started to quiver. For a moment she could not breathe, and when she could, it was to gasp out, "Please. Please turn me away. I cannot do it on my own."

Rendar at once turned her away, cradling her shaking shoulders with his arm. "What is it, child, what is wrong?"

To her bewilderment, she began to cry. Which was a most unwanted and annoying thing in the presence of an elf king. "Because it's so beautiful—it's perfect. I can only imagine what I know, and I don't know or imagine anything like this. So this isn't a dream, it's real. And I don't know why I'm crying, because this is really quite wonderful, but it's so strange and—oh!" She cradled her head in her hands. "Oh, my head hurts."

One of Rendar's strong but gentle hands slipped behind her head and two of his fingers pressed against her brow. The pain faded away, and Tellie found herself much calmer and able to think. "How'd you do that?" she asked.

He laughed and shook his head, before turning to look back at Korsical.

Warily, she looked back as well, but seeing it had now become much easier. Still impossible. But it was the most wonderful impossible she'd ever seen. Just looking at it gave hope...hope for impossible dreams and impossible love. Looking at it, she knew that such dreams could come true and that such love was real.

"It's perfection, isn't it?" she whispered.

"Nearly," the king said with a sigh. "A land untouched by the stain of sin...still flourishing in the way created by the One. And for that reason, the Darkness desires it. The celestials denied his lies and continue to deny him day by day...but he believes if he can find a way into the Higher World and corrupt their land, he will also be able to corrupt their hearts." Turning, he looked her straight in the face, and the air swelled with the passion of his words. "It has not been revealed whether or not the Higher World shall last till the end of mortal days. But if it is left to me, the fallen of my kind, to protect their purity, then I would do so to the last of my light."

A shadow passed over them then or perhaps the nearby stars dimmed. Now such a heaviness came to his voice as if it was burdened under mountains of iron. "I never thought...I'd hoped...that Errance would not have to be involved. But I was not there for his birth, and he came too early, too soon. To save his life, his mother passed on all the light I had given her to him and died from the sacrifice. So he was gifted with Celestial brightness, a full half measure instead of the little we had originally planned. I had hoped, since he was the vision of his mother, that he would not be sought for his celestial light. But the Darkness knew too much of us...guessed too well the reason for my wife's death. And so he seeks to use Errance's inheritance to learn the secrets of the celestial and to ruin them if he may."

After a sober silence, Tellie looked back to the bright kingdom and tried not to imagine shadows creep up its walls and decay crumble the fields. The thought was too horrible to bear, so she looked away and into the stars to chase away the dark images.

That was when she noticed the stars were coming closer. Not only closer, but walking. And if they were walking, perhaps they were not stars at all. Perhaps they were…

Five people stood around them an instant later, clothed in the silk of starlight itself. Even more beautiful than Rendar were they, wise and powerful, crowned in hair of living silver and adorned with the aura of righteousness.

Like the city had been before, they were impossible for mortal eyes to stare at without being blinded, but Tellie's eyes were no longer mortal here, and she gazed upon them with wonder, not fear.

And the greatest, most terrible thing of their awesome glory…was that they looked completely comfortable with it. Not haughty, not self-concerned. Simply happy and content, unaware of their perfection.

She found she could not be afraid of them, because all she wanted was to be like that…good without any want of being evil. She looked into their eyes and she saw her best friend because they loved her even though they surely did not know anything about her.

But that thought was wrong, because the next moment, she realized they knew a great deal about her indeed. She saw more then, saw that despite their innocence, they were not ignorant. Knowledge deepened their eyes, for while their spirits were not enslaved by sin, they had seen it, watched it burn the Lower World, and were all the more hateful of Darkness for it. That was strange, she thought—that hate could be so pure and right.

When they spoke, it was not in the common tongue, but in some language she'd never heard. That didn't matter here, she understood it just fine.

"Is this the one, Rendar? The little lamp for our Errance?"

"Yes," Rendar said warmly, laying a hand on her shoulder.

Tellie looked around askance for the lamp of which they spoke, but one of the bright beings knelt before her and took both her hands. She stared stupefied into his brilliant eyes and wondered if she could get lost by looking into them too long.

"She is very like him," the bright one said.

Like who, like Errance? Oh, for pity's sake, would people stop comparing her to him, they were nothing alike.

"You're celestials, aren't you?" she managed.

"We are."

"You aren't...you aren't dead too, are you?"

"Dead!" The kneeling one straightened, fixing Rendar with an upraised brow. "What have you been telling the girl!"

Rendar sighed, "I have tried to explain. No, Tellie, they are not dead, they are Walkers whose bodies still live on your side of the immortal plane."

"Use words like that and no wonder she's confused," another said, highly amused. It was a woman, and she turned a familiar smile on Tellie. "Our physical bodies still live in the Higher World, but in the Unseen, we walk upon your world and pray for its healing. The Darkness knows and fears our presence and thus seeks to rip us from the roots. Errance has suffered much for our sake, and we have long sought his redemption. You are the first answer to our prayer."

"Wait," Tellie said, alarm rushing up her spine. "You walk in my world? During the day? When I'm sleeping?!"

"We do not spy," they laughed. "But we are keen on such battles between the light and the dark. We heard your song the other night and it pleased us well!"

"Oh." Her stomach curdled. They'd heard that. How embarrassing.

"It was straight from your heart and that is what makes it powerful," the shining lady said. "But it can be more powerful still. Rendar, why have you not trained her?"

"May I remind you this is only her second time here?" Rendar said, setting a hand on his hip. "I know I fell, but I did not completely lose my feathers."

"Well, keep singing, child, and your voice shall grow stronger," the lady said, setting a hand on Tellie's cheek. "Soon your voice shall be powerful as Errance's in his youth, when his song could ring from the mortal world to the corners of our courts."

"Wait." Tellie rubbed her head. The world might have just turned upside down. "Errance. Singing? But men don't sing! Not nicely anyway!"

There was a moment's silence, and then every elf turned and looked at one particular celestial male with grins on their faces. He shrugged dolefully. "Now my feelings are hurt," he sighed.

"Oh!" What she would have given for an Unseen ability to reel words back in. Blushing furiously and trying to hide it behind her hands, Tellie groaned, "I didn't mean any of you, I just meant, well, I haven't heard very nice singing from men." She'd been quite convinced they were only capable of bawdy ballads and monotonous march tunes. Really, could she display her ignorant country girl stock any worse?

The celestial woman withdrew something from her robes that looked a little like a lute, but far more refined, and she tucked the edge of it under her chin, her other hand hovering a small slender staff over the strings. "Listen, Tellie. Listen to the sound of the glory of the heavens and the sorrow of the earth, of the rending between them, and of the great healing to come. Let your heart be opened, and your song will be sweeter than ever before." She drew the rod across the strings, and a keening wail dove to the depths of the soul, then suddenly soared to the height of hope.

Tellie listened, awestruck, and as each elf lifted their own instrument, from harp to flute to chime, the music swelled up in a wellspring inside her, and the words flowered to knowledge in her mind. When they reached the second round, she opened her mouth and let the first words sweep into hand with the music. The celestial man began harmony with her, and she felt as if a strong arm had come up under her voice for support.

She barely understood the words she spoke or the story she told. But she felt the power and glory in the music and she knew, she believed, if she let the music carry her like a bird on the wind, it would take her away to another place. A good and happy place. A place she wanted to be.

21

oOo

Sunlight, no matter how soft, startles me awake. Which means I was sleeping. I flinch and curse myself for such foolishness. How could I have found peace to sleep here in such a wild city with any manner of evil? Yet I had slept, and I'd have suspected something had been slipped into my drink except I am left with none of the aches that follow. I am yet alive and untouched and after a moment of tense listening, I can hear each steady breath from my companions. So I carefully allow the tension across my shoulders to ease. I sink back onto the warm wood and listen to the song of morning.

"Good morning!" Coren crowed. "The sun is rising, the day is still young, and it is time for you to continue the perilous flight for your life!"

Groaning, Tellie flung her arms over her head and burrowed deeper into the blanket bunched beneath her nose. She was quite sure she'd be useless at standing. Not even the hard days at the Nornes had left her limbs this stiff. But the noisy clatter of Kelm's descent on the ladder jolted away the last hope of sleep, and so she wearily pushed up and smoothed out her rumbled clothes. The chema fabric did not seem to retain much sweat or dampness, which must have been a mercy in the jungle, but it was still unbearably clingy and uncomfortable to sleep in. With two successive yawns, she clambered down from the attic and joined the others waiting in the brightening room below. Truly, it ought to have been a sin for them to look so awake when she was so tired.

"So," Coren said, leaning against a few crates, arms crossed. "One can never be too careful in this kind of business. I sent your hunters to bed with some heavy drink and I do not envy the headache they shall have upon waking. But to avoid a trail of gossip, we are splitting up today. Zizain shall take Tryss and Errance and I shall take the rascals. And my most favorite part—" He paused grandly, throwing off the lid of the top crate and digging inside like a child set loose on a treasure-chest. "Disguises!"

He flung out the most elaborate, most expensive garment Tellie had ever seen. It was all shiny purple and trimmed with gold tassels and lavishly embroidered in a set of tunic, leggings, and head wrap.

"I have been just waiting," Coren said, "to put someone in this lovely."

Errance snorted. He hadn't moved from where he guarded the wall, and his pose indicated disinterest of the whole affair. "I'm sorry for whoever that is."

Coren smiled kindly at him. "Indulge in self-pity. It's you."

Errance's head jerked up like a puppet on string. "What! No!" he protested in a voice stung with disbelief. Even a swift glare at Tellie and Kelm could not stifle their giggles. "No. Absolutely not."

"Absolutely yes," the captain replied, tossing him the clothes. "You see, you were my biggest problem, because you are so noticeable."

"He's a looker, all right," Zizain said. "He'd be less noticeable if we put a bag over his head."

"Thank you, Zizain, your input is always so helpful," Coren said with a grin to contradict the frowns from Errance and Tryss. "Anyway, no more tall, dark, and mysterious stranger. Say hello to ridiculously rich merchant. A traveler all the way from Brivan and thus so thoroughly dressed to keep out the sun and sand on the road. "

Again, he reached into the crate and drew out a soft pink bundle of fabric. "Now then," he said, looking to Tryss. "Zizain informed me you are a chema, which I failed to notice yesterday. Part of the tribe I've heard rumor of in the jungle east of here?"

Tryss stiffened, her fingers curling. "Is…that a problem?"

"Oh no, unless you can't go invisible with non-chema clothes on. Can you?"

"I can."

"Really? Fascinating. I don't pretend to understand the science of it, not a bit. Now I know blond is not your natural hair color, so how about being a brunette for the day?"

Her mouth dropped open and her hand flew to her hair, though if in shock or offense or both, who could tell. "This has been my hair color since I was born! Chemas don't have natural color, they reflect what they see or want. I don't need to disguise myself so very much, the hunters haven't even seen me!"

"All right, all right, good point. Now go change up in the loft, thank you."

"What do I get to dress up as?" Tellie said, bouncing on her toes. Why, this was enough to forget all dangers, she hadn't played with costumes since she was in the orphanage.

"You and Kelm will be my cabin boys," he replied. "I'll be taking you down to the wharf."

She froze in the midst of fingering a silky veil hanging from the crate. She stared up at him, dismayed. "I—I'm a girl."

"Not today!"

Kelm exploded into a snort of laughter, and she glowered at him. Trust men to have no feeling about this sort of thing.

The captain gave them each a white shirt, brown breeches, and sturdy shoes. Sometime already that morning, he had fixed up packs with rations, a bedroll underneath, and water flasks for their belts. He slipped each pack into a brown burlap bag, calling them 'cargo' for the ship.

"Errance," Coren said, serious for the first time that morning so that every eye in the room fastened upon him, even Errance, who until then had not ceased in frowning and fingering his outlandish costume. Coren held a long and slender object wrapped in fine cloth. "You need a sword. I see you already were given a bow and a knife, but that won't do you much good if you're surrounded."

Errance stared. Faint color rose in his cheeks. "I haven't held one since…"

"I know. That's why I thought it'd be best to give you one that's familiar." When the captain threw back the cloth, light gleamed off the blade in a flashing star. The metal shone white and curved from a silver hilt with the flow of water. There was something too unnaturally bright about the blade, as if it glowed from the inside.

The same glow reflected in his eyes, Errance stepped forward, wonder upon his face. Running a finger down its surface, he murmured, "An elven sword. But wouldn't it be—"

"Mine?" Coren shrugged. "Yes, it would be, but I haven't carried it since I entered this city. I'd be mugged or at least questioned for carrying this beauty around." A twinkle lit his eye. "I doubt people will give it a second look on a high-class merchant."

Errance slowly accepted the sword, looking at Coren with a curious expression—almost a smile. He inspected the hilt and muttered, "The mark of lordship." He looked up sharply. "You're a lord?"

With another flippant shrug, Coren laughed. "Runs in the family. Now, do you remember any of your training at all? Do you know how to fight with it?"

"I can kill."

After a sober pause, Coren's mouth tilted up in bitter understanding. "Then it should serve you well."

The ladder creaked as Tryss climbed back down into the room with a swish of soft cloth. When Tellie turned to look, she went nearly cross-eyed with jealousy. The young chema woman wore a filmy rose robe that wrapped and floated around her body like mist. A sheer veil of matching hue draped over her face and golden hair that, now undone, cascaded past her waist.

"Oh," Tellie breathed. "You look beautiful."

Tryss held the wafting veil back from her face with an impatient tug. "What exactly am I supposed to be?" she asked, a suspicious redness coming into her face that looked so different with the tribal paint oiled off.

Coren had the good sense to look abashed. "Oh, ah, yes, you'll be the merchant's slave girl."

"That merchant?" Tryss jabbed a finger at Errance.

"Yes."

"No," Errance said. He said it with a will that had been forged by seventy years in the hottest fires and heaviest irons, not in the end destroyed, but strengthened.

Coren's smile reduced that will to the petulance of a child. "Yes. You don't have the luxury of nursing your insecurities." To the others, it seemed a strange thing to say in the face of such strong opposition, but Errance deferred to the captain in silence.

"Don't you have anything else I could wear?" Tryss demanded.

"Nothing that quite matches his dress," Coren said carefully. "You might not be his slave girl—you could be a favored wife!"

Tryss let the veil fall back over her face in an attempt to hide the burning of her cheeks.

"Never mind," Tellie whispered. "You do look lovely."

"Trust it to be the attire of a slave girl."

After a short while of taking turns in the attic, they were all fitted in their attire. Tellie inspected herself as best she could, tugging fitfully at the white shirt and loose leather vest that fell over her. She patted at her head to make sure her brown hair was still bound up under the scarf that wrapped around her scalp. The dirt rubbed onto her cheeks itched, and she wished she could wash it off. "Are you sure you can't tell I'm a girl?" she asked.

"Not a bit!" Kelm said cheerfully, earning a righteous glare.

"All right, then." Coren bound a belt strung with a sheathed sword around his waist. "We'll meet at the docks by the Flying Crane shop. I know a ship that will take you to the Dormandy port."

Tellie swallowed. Now that they'd come to it, the idea of sailing frightened her. Floating in the middle of a merciless world of water that swayed up and down and again. She trudged out after Kelm as they all left the shelter and stepped back into the world of bright sandstone.

Already Zizain was leading Tryss and Errance down the street, chattering about who knew what, and as Tellie forlornly watched them go, a strange sensation seized her mind, a feeling that she ought not to let Errance leave her sight. Even having him obscured in that outfit was unnerving, giving her urges to run and see if it was really him under the hood and wrap.

"Aye, my lads, we're off," Coren said, calling her back to reality.

Lad. Thank goodness it was only for one day.

Though Tryss had heard Coren's claim that Daran's men were indisposed, she could not shake the fear that hung as close as her shadow. If Errance was truly such a prize, wouldn't the Darkness have sent more than a small company of human men to capture him? For all they knew, Daran was just a decoy, a false front. They had not even ventured far into the city, but she already felt as if danger watched them, seeing right through the ridiculous disguises, but whenever she'd turn to look for it, it couldn't be seen. Sweat beaded her skin, whether from the heat or fear, she could not tell. She did not consider herself a coward, but how could she face an enemy that would not show themselves?

She measured each breath she took, willing herself to remain calm, but alert. Trying to keep an eye on every person at once proved an impossible task. In the jungle, she was used to having her vision obscured, but at least she knew how to pick up threats from the nearby animals, the signs predators would leave in their area. Not here. Here everything was exposed…and more impossible to see.

If Zizain, a supposed seasoned smuggler, had any such fears, she certainly wasn't showing them. As if music echoed in her mind, she all but danced as she led the way through the streets, bobbing between stalls and exclaiming over wares with the sellers, yet still always managing to keep one step ahead of her followers' steady pace.

With every second that passed, Tryss regretted leaving Kelm and Tellie with Coren. They were smart children, but they trusted so readily. Even Errance trusted Coren more quickly than she dreamt possible. So Coren seemed to be an elf. What of it? Weren't elves as capable of treachery as other beings?

Perhaps, she reluctantly admitted to herself, her anger did not derive so much from Errance's corporation with Coren, but from his distrust of her. What had she ever done to earn his continuing resentment? She felt it every day, every hour. She felt it even now as she walked close behind him. Though to be fair, she wasn't any happier about playing his slave girl then he was.

Yet he'd taken the arrow meant for her. She glanced at him again, unable to detect any pain in the way he walked. Coren had not seemed concerned over his ability to move, but it seemed impossible that such a wound could have healed overnight.

Her own wound, though only in the shoulder, was bothering her a great deal. They'd changed the bandages on it again and cleaned the deep scratches, but it still burned and chilled by turns, often sending her into waves of dizziness—

A figure in the shadows. A dark cloak. A glint of steel.

Tryss grabbed Errance's sleeve and pulled him back. Cover. In such a crowded area, why wasn't cover easier to find? There, a shop. Keeping a firm grip on the prince, she darted through the shop door. In a moment, Zizain bounded in after them.

"If I knew you were so keen on shopping, pretty one," Zizain said, "I could have showed you many a shop beside this one."

"I thought I saw one of Daran's men," Tryss explained in a whisper.

Her fingers stung as Errance jerked his sleeve out of her grasp. He leaned against the open door and scanned the crowds. Tryss didn't have to point the suspect out to him—after a second, he turned back and mumbled, "Not one of them."

"Easy to mistake," Zizain said, seeming to see Tryss flush under the veil. "There's plenty of clandestine characters hereabouts." She glanced into the shop beyond. "We should probably keep going."

"Ah, so you are here, at last!" a rich voice rumbled.

Tryss leapt back in surprise, only just remembering not to blend into her surroundings. She turned around, noticing the shop for the first time. A large round hole in the roof let in sunlight that revealed shelves of pottery and fine vases. And coming across the floor was a robust man with a golden sash encompassing his vast belly.

"I thought you would never come!" he said, throwing his arms out wide as if he was going to embrace Errance.

Errance must have wondered the same thing because he stepped back so fast he almost trod on her feet. She scooted out of the way, keeping a wary gaze on the wealthy man before them.

The man frowned, taking in their defensive postures. "What is the matter? Have you not brought me what I asked?"

Before Errance or Tryss could speak, Zizain bounded forward, dropping in a neat little bow with her hands pressed together. "Pardon me, Master Hathon," she said brightly. "There has been a mistake. I am acting as translator for this foreign merchant and his lovely slave girl."

An understanding look crossing his bulbous features, Master Hathon nodded. "Forgive me, forgive me, I mistook you for a slave seller I was expecting. He had promised me a new slave-maid and he is three days late in arriving."

His gaze veered over to Tryss, and she looked away, suddenly feeling more exposed in this enclosed shop than out under the open sky.

"Would the merchant be interested in selling his slave girl?" Mastor Hathon asked. "She is fairer than many I have seen." His hand stretched out towards her veil, reminding Tryss of the talons of the crested eagle that would snatch monkeys off their branches. She took a step back, heart leaping.

The edge of Errance's hand smacked into the man's wrist with a sharp crack. With a yelp, the merchant snatched his hand to his chest and looked at Errance, appalled. "What was that for?" he exclaimed. "He nigh broke my bone!"

Zizain darted forward between them, hands upraised. "Ah, forgive him, forgive him." She shook a finger under Hathon's nose. "What have I told you about sticking your hands where they don't belong? Maybe this teaches you a lesson, yes?"

Clutching his wrist, the merchant glared at Errance. "He could have indicated in some other way he didn't like his property touched. You had better explain to him manners, Zizain."

"Ah, but you did not understand your own trespass." Zizain leaned in, cast a conspiratorial glance towards Errance and Tryss, and whispered, "You do not understand the power of love."

"Love?" His chin folded in confusion. "I thought you said she was his slave girl."

Zizain purred a knowing chuckle, and if possible, her accent deepened. "Ah, you base man. Yes, yes, true love between a merchant and a simple slave girl. Marriage would never be permitted, yes? So they have run far, far, far from their native home. He abandoned his home, his family, his fortune—for what?" She jabbed the merchant in the belly. "Love, Hathon! True love!"

Tryss realized her mouth was hanging open and hoped the veil concealed it. How could Zizain stand there, such blatant lies rolling so easily off her tongue?

The merchant shifted uncomfortably through this passionate prattle. Coughing, he gestured towards the door. "Yes, well, I would never be a man to stand in the way of true love. Were you here to buy something, hmm? No? Then perhaps, I should get on to my customers. Wonderful to see you, Zizain. May you and your friends have a blessed journey." After nearly walking them out, he bobbed a bow and hurried back into his shop.

"Poor man," Zizain sighed a few moments after they'd left the shop behind. "His dear slave girl was spirited away by smugglers or so they say." She flashed them a broad wink.

The veil pressed against her lips as Tryss sucked in a sharp breath. "Zizain," she muttered, "you're absolutely—"

"Brilliant?" Zizain gave a sage nod and continued trotting ahead. "I know, darling. I know."

Shaking her head again, Tryss cast Errance an apologetic glance, wondering if he felt as flustered as her.

But he wasn't there.

She skidded to a stop, eyes searching back and forth wildly. "Zizain," she cried, heart rising to her throat. He could not have fallen behind. In that costume he could not be overlooked. Where could he have gone? It did not seem possible that someone could have snatched him away without them noticing.

With a sharp glance around, Zizain's mouth curved down in a frown. "I see," she said only. "He made a run for it then."

Not even fifteen minutes had passed and already Tellie panted in the morning sun and itched from the sweat that pooled under the burlap bag slung across her shoulder. Yes, it was just as she suspected—being a boy was not at all pleasant.

"Pretend the bag is heavy and walk bowed over with your head down," Coren had instructed her. "It'll hide your…ah…gender better."

Pretend the bag was heavy? If he had any consideration for her *gender* at all, he wouldn't have put so much in it! Had all the food and tinder boxes been put in her bag? Watching Kelm stroll briskly, she guessed the only thing in his bag was clothes.

Coren abruptly halted in front of a colorful booth and flipped a few coins to the vendor. "Three iced lemon drinks," he said, propping his elbows upon the counter and crossing a foot over his ankle.

Exchanging a confused look with Kelm, Tellie bit back questions as the merchant poured a pitcher of yellowish liquid into three cups of crushed ice. Coren handed them each a drink and led them over to the side of a building where he comfortably settled down on the ground.

Tellie sat beside him, setting her sack aside. "What are we doing?" she demanded.

"Eh, lad?" Coren raised a skeptical eyebrow at her, and Kelm snickered.

Blushing, Tellie realized how feminine her voice sounded. "What are we doing?" she repeated, trying to imitate Kelm's voice, which made him chuckle even more. She bit her lip in frustration. "I mean, why are we stopping?"

"You're a wilting flower," the elf teased. "You were practically falling over in the heat." His eyes softened and he added, "Besides, I wanted you two to have some good memories of Oolum at least. I love this city."

Tellie cast an appraisal at the stirring crowd around them. "But it's so noisy." She caught sight of a slave train trudging through a crossroad. "And corrupt."

"That it is," he agreed. "But I like the noise, the constant bustle. As for the corruption, it can become discouraging. But Ayeshune brought me here for this very reason." He heaved a gusty sigh. "I'm thankful for Zizain. And there are a few other people about who help us. Still. More support would be appreciated."

Tellie glanced down at her cup. She'd heard of lemons, a foreign fruit that grew in the east, but she'd never tasted it. It was said to be terribly sour and only good for flavor over dishes such as fish. Cautiously, she took a sip. An explosion of zesty sweetness burst inside her mouth, making her tongue tingle. She coughed in surprise, her eyes watering from the unexpected tartness. Yet it was sweet! So very, very sweet and cold. Delighted, she took another swallow.

Coren smiled as he glanced both at her and Kelm as they gulped down their drinks. "Be thankful for the honey. Otherwise you'd be gagging." Sipping his own drink, he said, "So how are you two coping on this journey?"

"I'm fine," she replied. There seemed little else to say.

"It's been swell for me, all sorts of places I've never seen!" Kelm said enthusiastically, but the sparkle in his eyes dimmed an instant later. "Except for those people pursuing us, I'm still trying to figure them out, and there hasn't been much time to think or people who are willing to fully explain. What are they, an ancient kingdom of evil magicians? That man…that thing…that seemed to be charge…he was a nightmare!"

Tellie squirmed, wishing she'd told him more, but then she wondered how much more she even knew. There was so much she was just taking as it came and still so much more she did not understand. In the presence of the enemy, evil was the only identity that mattered, and she'd been loath to question further since. Not with Tryss, who seemed to know little on such matters, not with Errance, who knew too much. But maybe with this man, who had charged the evil so fearlessly.

"Oh!" For the first time, Coren looked disconcerted. "Oh, them. That. Thing. Yes. Where do I start? Um. Do you happen to be believers of Ayeshune?"

"Sure."

"Uh-huh."

It was the only decent answer to such a question, after all.

"I see. Well...so before Ayeshune formed the world, he created ministering spirts to serve the new world and its people. But the greatest of their number saw the power of God, mistook humility for weakness and sought his own way." As Coren spoke, the stiffness of his words eased into the same swaying cadence Rendar had used in his storytelling. "But outside of God, what is there? Only himself, and that was a small and frightful thing. So he took that emptiness, that rebellious solitude and formed it in shadows of Ayeshune's creations— introducing the same separation and eternal death for the children of God."

"So," Kelm said nervously, "then he succeeded...gaining power to challenge Ayeshune?"

"Brights, no!" Coren scoffed. "Anything useful he has is borrowed, didn't you hear? Ayeshune has only to take it back with a flick of his finger and the Darkness with be left with just that, only less."

"Then what's Ayeshune waiting for?"

"Us, of course! Removing the stain of that dark devil entirely would leave many as an empty husk, spinning into the void as well. Rather hard for a lot of folk. Rather hard on Errance, steeped in shadows as he is. Rather hard, I daresay, on you if you come to the end of life with only a basic knowing of God and no friendship, no faith for salvation. End will come, Kelm lad, but Ayeshune's mercy is very patient, and I'm glad of that, aren't you?"

Kelm didn't answer, only scrunched his face as if thinking very hard.

So Tellie spoke, swallowing a thick gulp. "How come the evil seems to have so much more power than us?" It wasn't an entirely fair question considering her celestial visitor of late, but was it too much to ask for a miracle while assuredly awake?

"Why? Why? Because the Darkness is a cheater, a trickster, a fraud, desperately taking shortcuts to win the game. But the game's done, and he's lost. Ayeshune is the past, the future, the now, and if he doesn't want you to be at your destination it might be because he has something in the journey. He's out for your care, dear child, not your convenience."

He sprang to his feet and gave a jolly laugh. "Come on then! Somehow I don't think your Errance would approve if we're late!"

But Coren need not have worried about Errance tapping his toe for them by the Flying Crane shop, because he and his harem were not there by the time Coren and the children arrived. And as minutes passed, he still did not come.

So they sat on the porch under the shop's sign and waited beside the bustling docks. The constant screech of the crane's metal wings on the sign rang in Tellie's ear and she glowered as the wind spun the wings round and round. The crane's steel eyes gleamed in the sunlight with something like malice, and the screech of the circling gulls seemed to come from its parted beak. Huffing, she tried to ignore it swinging above her and leaned back against the wooden support of the trade shop.

The funk of fish and sweat coated the air she breathed, and beyond the shrill squeak of the crane's wings, the ships in the harbor groaned under the tramp of men hurrying up and down the gangplank.

She glanced over at Kelm, whose sparkling eyes adored the surroundings, and then at Coren, who picked at his sleeve. "Don't you think they should be here by now?" she asked, crossing her arms.

The words hadn't even finished leaving her lips when Kelm cried, "There they are!"

Pushing through the crowd came Tryss and Zizain, and even from that distance, the anxiety on their faces could be clearly seen. Tellie's stomach plummeted as she looked for Errance and saw no sight of him or anything remotely purple. She froze where she stood, watching Coren run out to meet them and speak in tense conference. Tryss broke away from Coren and Zizain's exchange and approached the children with a pale face.

"Where is he...?" The question fell in a quaver from Tellie's lips.

"He disappeared." Tryss pressed a hand to her brow as if she held off a headache. "It looks like he left on purpose."

"What on Orim for?" Kelm exploded. He stormed up to Coren, little caring how he interrupted the discussion. "How do we find him, Captain?"

The words swirled in Tellie's mind but the moment they made sense, she raced to join her friend. "He can't do that to us, he just can't! We have to find him before they do. How could he have gone, the ocean is right there!" She jabbed a finger at the frothing harbor. "Aselvia is somewhere across it, he can't just leave!"

"Calm down," Coren said. "Zizain, stay with them. I'll go find him."

"But—" Kelm protested.

"Stay here," the captain ordered, glaring with the sort of force that stops a landslide. He turned on his heel and stalked back into the crowd.

With a terse smile, Zizain ushered the three of them back under the shadow of the trade shop. Scowling, Tellie leaned against the wooden wall, twisting her fingers together. The crane sign screeched above, mocking the tick of a clock with each swing in the wind. She counted each second in the minute so that each minute passed by achingly slow. Determined not to go insane, she cast aside the creak of the sign and counted each heartbeat instead. Here within her heart she could think a little clearer than in her muddled mind.

Errance had seemed so afraid—yes, afraid, she could see past his hard exterior—in this city, so how could he just set out alone? With his pursuers nearby, no less! Her eyes scanned the passing crowds, but her mind was so far separated from her sight that she very nearly overlooked the figure draped in shining purple that appeared in the milling throng.

"Errance!" she yelped, pushing away from the shop wall.

The figure startled at her call, turning on heel towards them. The head wrap concealed anything his face might have shown, but his rigid posture told enough—he'd happened upon them by pure accident. And without a pause, he turned and ducked back into the crowd.

"No!" she shouted, leaping forward. "Come back!"

She was darting after him without bothering if the rest followed her. She would not lose him, not again, she swore to herself as she squeezed through the sailors, danced between the market stalls and scampered beneath two burly men carrying a large crate. Everything around was too tall, too much so she sprang for a pile of crates and stood on tiptoe to peer over the bustle. Just on the other side of the shipyard, she glimpsed the purple swish of a cape vanishing down an alley. She leapt down and squirmed through the crowd, jostled and squished in the effort till she reached the other side. The alley was empty, but she sped down it, hoping to catch another trail before it was too late. The alley took a sharp turn, and when she rounded it, the waiting sight ground her pursuit to a halt.

There he stood at the dead end of the street, cornered in by three walls too tall to climb, and his only escape blocked by her. His head rested against the wall and his hands hung limp at his sides. She stared, stung by the defeated slump of his shoulders. He could have just as well been waiting for someone to thrash him.

"Tellie...Tellie!" The voices of her friends chimed softly in the distance, coming closer by the moment. She felt, rather than saw or heard, them arrive.

Errance turned to face them, folding his arms across his chest, shoulders braced on the wall at his back. The wrap around his face had come undone and hung down his chest. The light in his eyes glinted like shattered glass.

"I'm not sailing," he said.

They stood in stunned silence, untouched by the rest of the world bustling behind them. The shouts of sailors and the groan of timbers faded. Even the unreasonable statement did not matter. Only the hardness of his voice mattered.

"Golly," Kelm gulped. "You could have just said so."

A crease bent Tryss's brow, carved in by Errance's declaration. "...what?" She blinked, the crease clearing briefly, only to reshape into a glower. "*What? It's the quickest and safest way, are you telling us you are going by land? Do you have any idea how long that will take?*" Her words jumped out between each frustrated breath. "I...I don't even know if I could guide us safely!"

"I don't recall," Errance said, every word cold and chipped, "asking any of you to come." He whisked his hand back the way they'd come, towards the sea. "You may go by ship."

"NO!" The word broke like a thunderclap from Tellie, so strong and so desperate that even she jumped at the force of it. She staggered a helpless step towards him, flinching at how he withdrew harder into the wall. "No, we aren't leaving you!" She turned for the affirmation of the others, and though she found it in Kelm's vigorous nod, she was dismayed to see the hesitation on Tryss's face.

"Tellie," Tryss began, "I promised to keep you children safe, and the ship is the safest way. If he insists on going alone—"

"Then I shall insist on going with him!" Tellie exclaimed angrily. She turned again to Errance, eyes widening. "Please, Errance. I promised your father I'd bring you back!"

It was perhaps the best thing she could have said, although she didn't realize it until pain flashed across his face.

"You should go with Coren and Zizain," he said in a low voice.

"Well," Kelm replied, casting a glance about, "that won't work at the moment, because neither of them are here."

"See," Tellie pleaded. "We need you now. If you want to leave this city without them, fine, but you can't leave us behind. Friends have to stick together."

He did not move anything but his eyes and those slid so subtly one could barely tell how keen he looked at each figure before him. Two country youths and an uprooted young woman. They would be easy to shake, he surely knew that. Easy to leave behind.

But he took a deep breath and said, "Do not slow me down." Then he turned, not quite meeting Tryss's eyes, and stiffly asked, "Do you know where the North Gate is?"

Tryss glanced at the sun with a wince, but it was a little too centered in the sky for any clear direction, so she shrugged and said, "The docks are on the west, if we follow these streets up, we should encounter the north wall and find the gate."

With a nod, he brushed between them, pace swift but steady, and so they fell into step behind him, glancing over their shoulders with not a little bit of guilt for leaving the good smugglers who had been so kind.

Of course, they never thought to look up, because people so rarely did. Coren sat atop the round roof of a lookout tower above the North Gate, gazing upon the small figures vanishing into the hills outside Oolum. Every trace of joviality had vanished from his face, leaving behind an elf very weary with the world. His eyes shone wet, defying the dry dust in the air.

"I'm sorry he did not wish to say good-bye." Zizain sprawled down beside him and handed him another ice drink. "But his mind seemed quite made up."

"I know," Coren said. "I was there above them the entire time and heard everything. I only wish I could have taken the children oversea, but they would not be parted from him, and they might well follow him to their doom."

"Eh, he seems like the type who could take them safely to your pretty elf-land."

The lines in his face deepened. Taking the last swig from his cup, he said, "Errance isn't going to Aselvia."

His matter-of-fact tone drove Zizain up to a sitting position. She gaped at him. "You think the hunters are going to get after them that fast?"

"I'm not speaking of interference from those pursuing them. They won't get there because Errance is terrified of returning," he said flatly.

Slowly, Zizain blinked, then stared out into the rolling hills as stunned as if she'd gotten smacked. "Why do you think that? It is his home."

"That was his home. He's spent almost three-fourths of his life in Tertorem. Now that he finally has the chance to return to the love and life he knew, he's afraid it won't be the same. He's right. It won't. He's afraid that when he goes there, he'll be more out of place then the lowliest urchin of human-kind. He wasn't afraid of the ship, he was afraid of reaching Aselvia too soon. And unless something dramatic happens, he won't go in when he gets there. He's only saying that he will, but he won't. I can see it in his eyes, even if he doesn't realize it yet."

"But what about Tryss and Kelm and Tellie?" Zizain sputtered, starting to sound indignant. "He just can't wander around with them forever!"

"No. He'll find them places they can stay once they get back over to West Orim. After he finally shakes them...I don't know what he'll do."

Bemused, Zizain leaned back on her elbows and chewed her lip. The blue sky beyond was hazy with sand and was beginning to blur from her concentrated stare. Then a knowing smile spread over her face and she said, "So Captain Coren...what are you going to do about it?"

Coren never broke his gaze off the horizon, but an answering smile curled his lips. "I'm going to Aselvia, and I'm telling them their prince is dawdling on their doorstep and they need to go and drag him in."

Zizain grinned. "I'll tell the lads to prepare your ship."

"Thanks. I should be there before they are even halfway to their destination. I need to be quick. Errance is running out of time."

22

oOo

I ran. I was chased. I was cornered.

And yet the anger in their faces was not hatred. The young girl had tears in her eyes. I can't remember the last time I made someone cry. I should have run for it anyway. I'm sure I could have lost them, and it would have been better for everyone. Don't they know that danger haunts my footsteps, a danger that doesn't need to concern them? I wasn't prepared for them to pursue me so desperately. Not because they wanted my harm, but...they wanted to remain by my side. It is a strange, unfamiliar feeling. I could not deny them. And so we're stuck together, headed to...somewhere.

I n all the great stories...the epics told in books...the tales remembered by grandfathers...in every one of these inspiring legends of heroes traveling vast journeys....no one ever mentioned how badly one's legs and feet started to hurt.

Tellie did not consider herself to be a weak girl. But after the last few days of travel and especially the recent chase, the muscles in her legs were very sore indeed, and the gentle, rolling hills were not so gentle as she walked up and down and then up again, the entire while clenching her teeth against the pain.

To their west side a road ran along the coast, but of course, Errance did not want to take the road, he wanted to head along the sea in his own private path which meant every single hill.

As they ventured deeper into the hills and valleys, they paused to take the time to discard disguises and don the other outfits Coren had given them in the packs. Errance exchanged his purple nightmare for a set of dark clothes, Tellie shuddered out of the boy attire into a rosy, country girl frock, and Tryss all too gladly took back her own chema clothes, a little worn and torn, and left the pink gown as a puddle in the grass. Kelm remained in the sailor boy attire, looking more confident for wearing it.

At every peak of a hill, she could see the ocean glittering to their left. Terrifying as a voyage would have been, she was still frustrated with Errance for refusing it. Who knew how long this route would take and what dangers they'd encounter along the way.

Strangely, Tryss seemed as tired as her. At first, she thought she was staying behind to keep her company, but as she took pause after pause, breathing heavily, Tellie began to get worried. "Are you all right?" she asked at last.

Tryss held a hand to her shoulder and winced. "The wound I got from the shard. It…it aches."

"Should we have a look at it?"

Tryss cast a glance ahead at the boys but they were just going out of sight into a dell. "All right." She sat down in the tall grass and carefully peeled the cloth back from her shoulder.

Tellie gasped. "It's grey!"

The red scratches were edged in grey, only intensifying their nasty appearance. Remaining color drained from Tryss's face as she looked upon it. "It wasn't that bad a few hours ago," she said faintly. "I thought the color was a little odd, but…"

"Is it infected?" Alarm rattled in Tellie's head. "Do we need to go back?"

"Don't…don't be silly. I just need to treat it. The sun is beginning to go down anyway. We might as well make camp."

Tellie called for the others. When they saw how far they'd gone ahead, they grudgingly came back rather than make the girls go all the way to them. At first

Errance did not agree to the idea of stopping while so much light was left in the day, but Tryss's pale face and the children's chorused complaints about their aching bodies soon decided the argument without him. There were no trees to make an ideal camp, but they sat down in the shaded side of a dell and loosed the packs from their shoulders. Several streams ran through the hills to the ocean so Errance and Kelm took their kegs and fetched more water while Tellie helped Tryss inspect the wound more carefully.

A small hiss slipped from Tryss's lips as she sponged her torn shoulder with a wet cloth, but there was little to clean for no fresh blood came from the ghastly scratches. She took a small pouch from the pack prepared by her people and ground the little leaves within to a fine powder between her fingers.

Tellie bent forward on her knees for a better look. "Wounds don't look like that usually, do they?"

"No."

"Why is it doing that then? Errance, have you seen anything like it?"

Startled that the elf had arrived so silently while Kelm was still trooping down the hill, Tryss tugged her shirt back onto her shoulder, wincing at the haste.

"I have not," Errance said. His brows were knit in quiet intensity. He sat in a crouch, stirring the beginning embers of a small fire. "Have you considered the curse?" he asked.

Tryss froze.

"Curse?" Tellie echoed.

"Chemas can turn into shards," Errance said.

"Tryss is turning into a monster?" Tellie practically shrieked.

"Who's turning into a monster?" Kelm demanded, reaching the camp.

Tryss's hand curled into a fist. Her pale face reddened. "I'm not a monster," she said, and a hard edge sharpened her voice. "It's not...it's not some disease to be spread around."

"Do you know how chemas turn into shards?" Errance challenged.

"Do you?"

He hesitated. "No," he said finally.

She was beginning to tremble as she clutched her shoulder and leaned forward. "I am not a monster," she said again. "And I'm tired of being treated like one. I'm away from my home, taking care of two children and a strange man who glowers at me every chance he gets. We could have stayed with Coren and Zizain, we could have gone over the sea, but instead we're out here, so if you could stop thinking the worst of me for once—"

She suddenly broke off and spun away, lurching forward on her hands and knees—and proceeded to be sick to the stomach.

Tellie and Kelm drew back in dismay. It occurred somewhere in the depths of Tellie's mind that it would be kind to go and hand her a cloth, but then, there wasn't much good in two people being sick.

Then Errance was kneeling alongside her. A moment ago, he'd been sitting very still under her tirade, but now he was there with hardly a flicker of a shadow. Without a word, he lifted her up and slipped his knee under her sternum. She didn't seem to notice or else was too sick to care, but she braced against his leg as another heave shook her slender body. His face expressed nothing, neither disgust nor sympathy. But he caught the loose tendrils of hair hanging about her cheeks and swept them back with a deft hand. They remained thus until her shaking and coughing ceased.

"Would you stop that," she mumbled, wiping her mouth.

"Stop what?"

"You know. The arrow, the accusations, the…this. Stop being so confusing, will you?"

He didn't answer.

After a moment, she pushed away and looked at the wide-eyed children. "I'm not turning into a monster," she said weakly. "Grandfather said it was never certain what changed a chema to a shard, but that it wasn't a sickness."

They ate their meal in silence and then huddled down into the grass as the sky began to darken and the air cooled. Tryss huddled in a ball, murmurs of pain slipping free now and then.

"Could you heal her, Errance?" Tellie blurted. "The light within you heals you, and your father could withdraw it. Can you?"

He sighed heavily. "No. I've tried to pull it out many times, even when I was back in Aselvia, but a half portion is not powerful enough."

"How's that?" Kelm asked.

"It is not passed through blood exactly," he murmured. "It's a gift. Exchanged by spouses and passed on by mother to child. My mother had received the gift from Daava...I was only meant to have a small portion."

It was very hard to hear him now, and Tellie had to strain for every word. Though thrilled to finally have him reminiscing, she wondered why he opened up now, what aches had split his heart unseen.

"But I came too early, and Daava was up North that day. So she gave me all that she had been given. And she died. It has sustained me through all these years. And now he's dead." His voice strangled. It came forth again in the most trembling of whispers. "Why is he dead, Tellie?"

She swallowed hard, staring at the stars for all she was worth, hoping an answer could be found written among them. "I...I don't know. They said he faded. They didn't know why. Though...some said...it was from grief."

Without a word, he rolled onto his side, away from her, and did not make another sound.

Hot tears filled her eyes, turning cool on her cheeks. She wished she had some word of comfort, some way to heal his hurting. But in the end, she had nothing to say because she knew there was no help for such pain. After all...she'd killed her parents too.

Dawn brought little comfort or healing for Tryss was more waxen than ever and little beads of sweat dewed her forehead. Tellie, not completely inept as a nurse, kept soaking a rag with fresh, cool water and dabbed her face, but whatever relief that brought could not bring any strength into her limbs.

"She can't travel like this," Tellie said anxiously, looking to where Errance's silhouette stood in the dusky morning glow. "And none of her herbs are taking effect!"

There was no indication he heard her, so she bent back over Tryss's feverish brow with a sigh.

"You could always carry her," Kelm suggested.

Errance turned at that, eyes narrow and bright. "What?"

"You know, on your back."

Cough rattling from her throat, Tryss shook her head in fretful disagreement. "H-hanging onto someone's back for dear life sounds just as...impossible as walking."

"That's easy," the boy continued, not at all offset by rebuff. "You just tie her on."

"Oh!" Tellie rummaged through her pack, flinging out a familiar long scarf of gauzy pink. "Would this work?"

Tryss stared, sickly eyes momentarily clearing in amazement. "Tellie...I threw that away."

"I know," she said, bashfully twisting the silken scarf about her hand. "But it was too pretty to leave behind, so I took it. It would be more comfortable than rope, wouldn't it? And we might need our rope for something else."

Errance considered in silence, every thought concealed behind that invisible wall he could raise. Such an achingly long amount of time passed they began to wonder if he'd moved on to other thoughts, when he abruptly said, "If there's no other way." He dropped to one knee beside Tryss, facing away. "Help get her on, Kelm."

Despite Tryss's slurred protests, Kelm hefted her up and propped her against his back. Tellie ran over with the scarf, and between the effort of all four of them, they had Tryss slumped against Errance, arms over his shoulders, legs bound securely against his hips, and scarf wrapped around waist and shoulders coming to a knot at his chest. Tellie tied the knot in a pretty bow, which Errance promptly undid with a scowl.

"We'll rest in the shade during the midday hours," he said as he straightened. "And then we won't stop until the light has faded."

They grumbled at that, but not too loudly, for his gaze swept back the way they had come, back the way their hunters would come in pursuit. So they swallowed their miseries and prepared for yet another day of grueling journey.

oOo

The miner chipped away at the stone, making as much progress as the wind against granite. His bent back pulsed with an unending pain that had become as constant as the grimy air he breathed. No spirit shone out of his eyes, not anymore. For no longer was there anything to live for in this grey world of stone and broken dreams.

The Prisoner was gone.

Perhaps they had finally killed him, the miner thought. He supposed he should be happy for the Prisoner's sake, whose desire for death had been etched into his face as clearly as the marks he bore. But he could not help but feel sorry for himself and all the other prisoners. None of them could remember a time the Prisoner had not worked beside them, unwithered and unbent by the relentless toil. He'd been their last reason to hope, their last glimpse of another world. No longer could they admire his proud, emotionless face. No longer was he there to protect them from the overseers' mad will. He was gone. And he would never return.

The miner found it his turn to be one of those to cart the chipped stone back up to the entrances and send it rolling down the steep slopes. Yet not even the outside air could lift his spirits for though it was crisp it was laden with malice so thick he could barely inhale.

The fortress of Tertorem drew his eye against his will. The spires rose like thorns from the rocks, and suspended between the two tallest hung the Nyght. The dark clouds in the sky whirled to a point above the sphere, and though its black surface never varied, the miner could see that the Nyght was full of wrath. The storm clouds cracked in thunder and lightning so that the entire sky writhed with an eerie green glow.

The Darkness dwelt in the Nyght, so it was said. If it was so, then the Darkness was angry.

Shuddering, the miner dumped his load and hurried back inside, not bothering to watch the stones rattle down the hill to break upon shattered bones.

He could only pray that the Darkness's wrath would not fall on them.

23

oOo

The landscape is endless. Golden dunes and silver sea stretch out on one side, the shadows of mountains on another. I knew the world was vast, but I'd never had the chance to see it until now. It is not as stunning or dramatic as my homeland. But it is still strangely beautiful.

Four days. Four whole days of walking across those tiresome hills, crossing sandy stream after sandy stream. It seemed impossible that one could survive such monotony, but now they all stood as living testimony on the brink of a hill, looking towards a changed world. The crisp ocean breeze left their hair stiff with salt and crystallized the sweat in white patterns upon their skin. Ahead, the valleys and hills rose into steep gullies and jagged mountains, the sand and grass giving way to scree and shrub.

The road for the common traveler remained skirting the sea and no other path dared branch off into the treachery of the mountains. But none of them wanted to travel along the road so they climbed up into the mountains with no guide but intrepid will. The going was slow as they scrambled up ledges and narrow rock paths, often using the scraggly trees as an aid, but the struggle was welcome after the dreadful plodding across the plains. Wild goats startled from thickets and bounded to a safe height so they could stare down at the strangers who'd invaded their homeland.

By the time sunset spread its saffron hues across the sky, they had made good progress into the wild. A tangle of trees rose up all about them, the glitter of the sea shining through the thicket.

Tryss's health had leveled, neither improving nor declining. She was still weak and feverish, and the wound was refusing to heal, the same grey shadow haunting her skin.

When night fell, Tellie curled up on the ground, a crumpled cloak folded under her head. She peered up through branches into the sky where stars gathered so thickly she might have sworn a fog floated overhead. Only in the halo of the moon did the stars die away, fading in respect of her radiance.

The moon medallion mirrored the sphere above with such perfection that Tellie could have believed she held the lady of the night in her hand. During the day, the medallion was pretty, but when darkness fell, she often wondered how she was even allowed to hold such a precious piece.

It belonged to Errance. It bothered her that he would not take it. Rendar had passed on in this world; surely that meant Errance was king now, and thus should take the medallion as his birthright.

Rolling over, she looked to where the elf sat on a fallen tree, taking the first watch of the night.

There were some old tales that said the true nature of a man could be seen under the moon's glow. In that light, Tellie thought he looked fairer than he had ever been. The rays of moonlight casting through the trees softened him with a pure, holy glow, the light and shadows dancing across his body in vivid contrast. One knee was drawn up to keep him from sliding down the log and he rested an arm upon it, his other arm braced against the wood. His face turned to the sky, and his gently stirring hair was so awash in moonlight that it almost shone white.

She rolled back over so that Errance wouldn't feel her shameless stare and wrapped the cloak tightly around her. But fear shivered through her body at the sensation he'd vanish simply because she'd looked away. With Tryss sick, he wouldn't leave them again, would he? The terror of his abandonment of them still haunted her, drove her mad with confusion. They needed him and he needed them, couldn't he see that?

Exhaustion pressed her eyelids shut, the haze of sleep enveloping her. But in the moment she fell asleep, *she became more alert than ever. This time she could feel the weight of her slumbering body and the pressure of her closed eyes. With an impatient shake, she rose out of it, looking expectantly for Rendar.*

He stood a few feet away, staring at Errance.

"Rendar?" she said, approaching him hesitantly. He did not respond, so she came to his side and waited.

Rendar's breath caught. "He almost seems like himself here...under the shelter of the trees and the moon."

On the contrary, he seemed nothing like himself or at least not the Errance she knew. But who was that Errance even? Did she know him at all, any side of him? "I don't understand him, Rendar," she said with a sigh. "You said something about our spirits being similar, but I've never felt more distant from anyone before. I mean, I thought I knew him, thought he survived through protecting. And he does that sometimes. But he also left us." She stared up at the king, biting her lip. "I thought he cared. About us. About returning home. But he doesn't seem excited to return home. We'd already be there by now if we'd taken the ship."

At last, Rendar turned his gaze from son to her. "Sometimes, child," he said, "it's the people we love whom we fear the most."

She blinked. "But that makes no sense, Rendar, none at all! All my life, I've been searching for people to love me! I'd never run away from them; I long for them!"

Something like a sigh or perhaps a sob caught in Rendar's throat. "You are so alike," he said, turning away with a swift jerk of his shoulders.

"What? But I just said—"

"Tellie," he interrupted. "Are you willing to see Errance as he truly is?"

She paused the moment before she said yes, a sudden fear gripping her. How dreadful would it be? Could she be able to withstand the pressure of his pain and devastation? Would she be able to look into his eyes and know the secrets of his soul? "I...I believe so. I think. I must."

"Then I will create a dream for you," Rendar said. "It will not be real, but perhaps it shall reveal the truth."

"All right." She nervously twisted her fingers, pushing aside the wish for someone at her side like Tryss or even Kelm.

Rendar's hand lightly pressed against her shoulders and turned her again to Errance. She gasped. There upon the tree sat a boy no older than seven. He seemed to be waiting for someone, swinging his leg with restless abandon. She'd seen this Errance before in what she now realized was her first vision into the Unseen.

"Rendar, you can't mean that's all Errance really is," she protested.

He shook his head sorrowfully. "No, no, that is simply what he was. My memory of his spirit come to life. Only memory, not real, but still true." Lifting his chin, he called out in a clear but trembling voice, "Errance!"

The boy's head spun towards them. "Father!" He sprang off the tree and ran towards Rendar. He barely came to his father's waist, but his slender arms reached up in yearning to be caught up high. Such life sparkled in his body, even in the bounce of his silken brown hair.

Tellie watched in muddled shock, unable to reconcile the boy of the past with the man of the present. They were nothing like each other, not at all. And yet when the memory of the boy turned and stared at her with an uncertain crease in his brow, the expression belonged to Errance.

"Errance," Rendar said. "I should like you to accompany Tellie for a while."

A smile as bright and sweet as the crescent moon lit his face, and the sight of it stabbed Tellie through the heart. No, that smile was gone forever from Errance. This boy was truly just a figment of bygone years.

Errance, though her mind rebelled at calling him that, reached toward her and caught her hand. "Come on," he said.

She began to follow, but paused at the sight of a winged, grey animal the size of a small cat clinging to his back. "What is that?" she gasped.

He spun around to look, the creature swaying on his back. "What's what?"

The creature was staring back at her down its narrow muzzle, blue eyes narrowed in annoyance. Its tufted ears were lying against its head. "I'm a daisha," the creature said, teeth showing.

"Good heavens, it talks," Tellie said, clutching a hand to her chest. She felt she would have been more frightened had it happened in real life. A vague part of her remembered she'd heard of daishas before, but she was fairly certain people said they were extinct.

With a fragile flutter of its wings, the creature sprang to Rendar's shoulder and eyed Tellie with a sulky glare.

Errance laughed. "Don't you know what a daisha is? They're people too, you know. Anyway, hurry up, I have something to show you."

The world around them had transformed into an entirely different sort of forest than she'd been in before. Bright mist floated in the still air through the lacy hemlock trees that brushed past her face as Errance led her up a mossy incline. The dewdrops glowed at his passing, and it took Tellie a moment before she realized with surprise that in this dream he was the one wearing the moon medallion, and it reflected a full moon.

He led her straight up to a crevice in a rocky cliff side and slipped in. She pulled her hand out of his at once. "Oh!" She took several steps back. "Ah, little...little Errance, I don't want to go in there."

His head poked back out to stare up at her. "Why?"

"I'm bad in caves," she said. Or any dark, cramped place for that matter.

"But there's a surprise," he insisted. "It's not dark and scary, believe me. It's my favorite place in the world." He paused and tilted his head as if weighing his claim again, but she took a deep breath and nodded. This was just a dream after all, and she could be braver here.

She crouched and wriggled her way through the opening after him, relieved to discover it was not so restricted inside. She followed the glow of the medallion deeper and deeper. She did not quite notice that the wet rocks under her feet gradually turned into wooden boards that creaked with each step. That is, she did not notice until she realized the glow ahead of her no longer belonged to

Errance.

She froze. "Errance?"

He did not answer.

Trying to calm her racing pulse, she dropped to her knees and crawled along the floorboards till she neared the light which turned out to be a broken board in a wall. She seemed to be an attic, and the light came from the room below. Curling her legs underneath her, she bent and listened.

"Such a shame," a woman's voice said. "So young, so much yet to live for."

"And the child has completely recovered?" another woman said.

"She did, by some miracle. But it might have better for them if she hadn't."

Everything stilled. In silence. In disbelief. In horror.

Tellie's breath rushed back into her lungs with the violence of a storm. A terrible mistake had been made. This had nothing to do with Errance. This was a memory of herself when she was but five years old. Again, she sat in this attic hearing what she was never meant to hear. She covered her ears, desperate to block out the voices, but still they came.

"How do you mean?" the other woman asked.

"They might have recovered if they hadn't tried so hard to keep her alive." The woman clucked her tongue. "A crying shame, that's what it is."

"What's to happen to the girl anyway?"

"Well now that it's certain she doesn't have the plague, I'll pass her on to the orphanage..."

The voices faded away as the woman finished cleaning the room below and walked out the door.

Tellie huddled on the floor, her shoulders shaking with suppressed sobs.

"Tellie?"

She nearly screamed to hear the child Errance's voice again, so near. He stood across from her, his hands on his hips.

"Where'd you go?" he demanded. "We're almost there."

She shook her head, eyes burning. "Where did you take me?" she asked hoarsely. "How...Rendar, something's wrong, it's all wrong."

The boy dropped down beside her in concern. "What's wrong? Do you need me to go find Father?"

She reached out and grabbed his arm, able to see him perfectly despite the darkness around them. "What do you see? Are we still in your cave?"

"Of course we are." He stared at her like she'd gone mad. Perhaps she had. Perhaps she hadn't been strong enough for whatever Rendar had prepared for her, and this was the result of a snapped mind.

The world around her changed again. Errance was no longer there, and she sat instead on the dusty ground, her knees stinging with dust in scraped flesh. Chills ran up and down her body as she recalled this scene as well, one of many.

Slowly, she lifted her eyes to the boy who'd just pushed her down. He stood there, older and wickeder looking than perhaps he had been in real life, but no different from how she'd always perceived him. A boy named Nad who'd rounded together some of the orphans to make her the target of their games.

"Don't get too close to her, Nad," one of the other boys called. "She might give you the plague!"

"Yeah," another jeered. "If you don't watch it, she'll kill you just like she killed her mum and dad."

"I did not," she shouted before she could stop herself. Tears could no longer be held back, and they streaked pale lines through her dirty cheeks.

"They wouldn't have died if they hadn't had you," he taunted. They all laughed and began to dance around her in a ring, their chanting reeling around her.

She cowered into herself, hoping that this too would melt away if she ignored them hard enough. "Go away," she whispered. "Just—"

"Leave her alone!" an indignant voice cried.

Her eyes flew open to see the child Errance duck through the cavorting children and into their ring. Could he actually see them now? It was apparent he could as he charged straight up to Nad with fists clenched. Undaunted by the elder boy's towering height, he lifted his chin and ordered, "Let her go at once." His eyes flashed with all the fire and force of a king.

For a moment, Nad seemed startled, but then he drew back his fist and smacked the little prince across the face.

Tellie cried out in protest as Errance stumbled back and collapsed. He lifted himself up on one elbow and gingerly touched his broken lip. He stared at the smeared blood on his finger with more curiosity than repulsion. Nad and the others closed in around him like wolves.

With a growl, Tellie surged to her feet and caught Nad's shirt. "Don't you dare touch him!"

Nad spun towards her, his face knotted with anger. But before her eyes, the anger melted like wax, reforming into mortal dread.

"She has the Flags!" he wailed, wrenching out of her grasp. All the bullies scattered, staring at her in dismay.

When she lifted her hand before her face, she saw the red blotches across it, and her vision blurred till the splotches wavered like the flags for which they were named. The plague. She had it again and she would destroy everyone around her. Shadows rushed in once more, and the figures of her torments began to writhe and gravitate around her till they flickered out of existence.

Closing her eyes and covering her ears, she screamed. Her knees folded, and she hit the ground hard, forehead slamming into the dirt.

With all the beauty of a sunray slipping through a storm, Errance's voice echoed through her muffled ears. "Tellie? Tellie, are you all right?"

His delicate fingers touched her arm, and she recoiled. No, NO, he could not catch it. "Stay back," she ordered, leaping to her feet. The hurt in his darling eyes smote her, but she smothered the guilt. If he died because of her as well…she would never forgive herself. "Just stay away from me!"

She turned and ran, plunging deeper into the shadows. The chanting still followed her no matter how hard she ran; the blotches still remained no matter how deeply she scratched at them. But she could not run forever, and in the end, she fell again.

Cold, wet stone rested under her body, and she realized she'd returned to Errance's cave. As her hiccupping cries faded, she became aware of another *sound—the pure bubbling of a spring. She turned and found herself at the edge of a pool fed from an underground river. The surface near her remained smooth and still, and a brightness seemed to reside within it.*

Trembling, she leaned out over the surface to see her reflection. The blotches no longer marred her cheeks, but she did not even notice. She could only stare disbelieving at her own face. Surely she'd not aged so much since she'd last looked in a mirror. The shadows in her skin, the tightness of her mouth, and the heaviness in her eyes did not belong to her. They belonged to a tired, broken soul.

They belonged to Errance.

Another figure reflected in the water, and she whirled around to face Rendar. "What happened?" she demanded, her voice harsh and choked. "What sort of dream was that? You told me I'd understand Errance."

"Do you not?" he asked softly.

Her gaze began to drop back down to that terrible reflection, but she jerked it back up. "That's not me. It can't be."

He settled alongside her, stirring his fingers in the pool and watched the ripples dance away from him. "It's a more honest glimpse of yourself than you've ever dared look at. No matter what you may pretend, deep down inside, it is always there." The gaze of his reflection met hers.

"But if that's true," she whispered, "I can't be the only one. You always say I was chosen, but my pain doesn't make me special. There are a lot of girls like me. Everyone gets hurt."

"Just so," Rendar said. "But perhaps you were chosen for this role not just because of how you could help, but how you could be helped in return. Your family circumstances are...in part our fault."

"What?"

"You went to live in Denji inn because you were related to the owners. Your grandfather was the ambassador of Dormandy, and he was cousins with the current innkeepers. He died that night."

"Yes," she said, shivering. "I've been told that."

"I did not know it until long after, but his unexpected death brought financial ruin for his family. His young son was raised in poverty and, in turn, married a poor woman, and they had you. I cannot help but think if I had known this, I could have helped and perhaps prevented the sickness from ever touching your family."

Tellie swallowed. "It's not your fault," she said bravely. She certainly would not be telling Errance. He blamed himself for enough deaths already.

"Still," Rendar said. "I believe this is one of the reasons Ayeshune brought you to us. So we could help what we had hurt."

He rose, and his hand knocked the side of the cave wall. Instantly, the stone chamber lit in thousands of brilliant blue lights clustered to the side of the walls like moss, shimmering with the pulse of life. Tellie gazed at them in awe, never noticing the pool, stone, and even Rendar fade till she found that the little blue lights were the stars above her, and she sat in the camp with the others once more.

But she'd not returned to her body yet so she hurried over to where Errance, the real Errance, was now sleeping. She knelt beside him and whispered, "It's your favorite place in the world."

A crease bent between his brows.

"Their glow gathers brightest in the bubbling spring, but when you touch the walls, all the lights flicker to life," she continued. "I think they might be alive, but I don't know, because I've never seen anything like them. They are like stars and how beautiful they glow in the darkness. You might never see their true beauty except in that cave. You lean back and listen to the water's song, and the lights shine for ever and ever."

She watched as the lines in his face smoothed like the ripples in the spring, and for a breath, she saw the boy in his face again.

She crept away from him and returned to herself, where peaceful slumber with natural dreams claimed her once more.

24

oOo

Memories long forgotten drift through my mind again. The warmth of my father's hand, the company of a winged creature, the sparkle of a starlit cave...An ache seizes my heart, almost stirring me from sleep, but I accept the pain because it is better than other thoughts more troubling. In this unexpected and strange moment of peace, I can almost imagine myself back there—in a land of laughter, daishas, and dreams.

Tryss had insisted she walk on her own the next morning, and so their pace was slower to give her a chance. They kept to the ridges just above the road along the sea, and thus far they had not seen any travelers. It was a wild and lonely part of Orim, drawing ever nearer to the North. The air was getting colder, and every once and a while they glimpsed taller mountain peaks further in, dusted with snow.

And then, a company appeared on the road.

"Get down," Errance ordered. "It's unlikely they'll see us up here, but still."

They nestled into the bushes and watched as the small figures, horses, and carts gradually grew larger. One enormous wagon centered the group, and as it drew near, they could make out a giant, barred cage hauled by oxen.

"Look at the size of that thing," Kelm whispered. "What do they have in there? Do we even have a creature in Orim that large? Can you see what it is, Tryss?"

She squinted. "No. It's grey, furry, but it's all curled up, and I can't get a good—" She paused. "Errance, are you all right?"

It was a funny question for the sick member of their group to ask, but when Tellie and Kelm turned to the elf, it was easy to see why. He'd gone as sickly white as the ocean foam.

"It's a daisha," he breathed.

"Sorry, a what?"

"A daisha." A ragged growl was curling in his throat. "That's my daisha."

"Hold it," Kelm said. "You don't mean those winged beasts that went extinct, do you?"

"Yes," Errance muttered. "Only there was one left. She—I know her. I knew her."

Tellie stared at him. She'd never heard this tone from him before. So desperate, so panicked. A vision of last night's dream swept before her mind—a small, soft, grey creature with judgmental blue eyes clinging to young Errance's shoulders. It had talked, but that had surely just been part of the dream, right?

"Are you sure it's the same daisha?"

He glared. "I just told you there was only one left. She was in the care of my people. We were raised together, and she was with me that night…but she escaped. She should have gone back home. What is she doing here?"

"Whether she's the same one or not, we have to do something," Kelm said. "Looks like they're headed to Oolum, and while it would be great to have Coren and Zizain's help, we can't go back. So we have to stop them here."

"I know," Errance snapped, turning his back against the turf and pressing a hand into his face. "Let me think."

There was a moment of polite silence that lengthened into bored impatience. "I think it's obvious," Tryss said. "I can blend in and sneak down."

Lifting his head, Errance stared at her, no small amount of confusion lining his face. "But…you're sick. You shouldn't."

She shook her head with a huff. "I can work through it. All I need is a distraction. That's the dangerous part. Think you're up for it?"

He raised a brow in answer.

"We can help," Tellie jumped in.

"Absolutely not," Tryss said. "I just said it was dangerous. Those are armed men and if they realize you're a decoy, they could attack."

"But there's a lot of them, and you can't be sure they'll all pay attention to Errance," Kelm reasoned. "We're guaranteed to be a distracting enough force for you to swipe the keys, and once the daisha is out, it will be chaos. They have no way of knowing we'd be part of that. Besides, I already have a story."

"And that is?" Errance asked.

"We're runaways! Tellie and I will go racing down to them for help and you come after us as our grim pursuer! That way, when things go wrong, it only is natural that we would run, and of course, you would be after us. The perfect cover to get in and get out."

"Genius," Tellie agreed.

"It could work," Errance muttered. "But I don't see why I have to play the part of the villain."

Tryss stared back and forth between them and then sagged with a groan. "If we're actually doing this, you're going to have to be so, so careful. There's no telling what might go wrong. Errance, you have to keep them safe. And if something goes wrong before I can unlock the cage, I'll forego the plan to protect the children, understood?"

He nodded.

"All right!" Kelm rubbed his hands with glee and met Tellie's eyes. "Are you ready?"

They climbed over the ridge and began picking their way down to the road, fast enough that they would be seen as in a hurry but not so fast that they'd lose control and break their necks. Tellie could almost imagine Tryss slinking alongside them, though she had no way of knowing for sure. It was strange, but she was actually excited by this. An inane notion no doubt as the men they approached were certainly trouble, but for whatever reason, she didn't feel frightened, and it was all she could do to keep a smile from her face. She could not smile or laugh or do anything of the sort, so she pulled up all her feelings of fear from their previous pursuits and tried plastering them across her face.

They had not been noticed yet, but as they neared the ground, Kelm began hollering. "Help! Heeeelp! He's after us, misters! Help!" They leaped down the final few paces and sprinted towards the traveling band who had stopped to turn and stare in surprise. Their hands had gone to their weapons but paused there in uncertainty when they only saw two youths waving wildly.

"Help us, sirs!" Tellie cried as they pulled up to the men, panting, but not so close as to be grabbed. "He's coming!"

"What is this?" The man who appeared to be the leader of the group shoved his way to the front and fixed them with a withering glare. "Where did you come from; I don't recall a village in these parts. And who is he?"

"There he is," Tellie moaned, spinning around to look back up the mountain. "It's too late. Please, sirs, you can't let him take us back."

Everyone looked up the slope and watched as Errance came striding down. Unlike the children, he did not come down in a hurry, but he came with purpose, the sort of purpose that water has when carving stone through the centuries. His lone figure was intimidating, all in black, hand loosely set on the sword at his side, stride confident and sure.

He reached the road and came towards them with the same unwavering force, and the men, many as they were, seemed suddenly nervous.

"Hold it right there!" the leader barked. "Name your purpose."

Errance paused, his dark expression fading to something more negotiable as he held up his hands. "Sorry, gents, but that's my niece and nephew. They've gone and run away again."

"Lies!" Kelm yelled. "We're not related to you! We don't even look alike!"

"That's right, sir," Tellie said, turning her very best pleading face towards the leader. "He's the madam's dog, and he'll beat us if you let him take us. He beats us every day!"

"I do not!" Errance said, and the incredulity and insult of his entire being was so genuine that Tellie flinched with guilt. She hadn't recalled his side of the story being part of the plan, but a distraction was a distraction. Shaking his head, Errance set his hands on his hips and looked at the children with nothing short of disappointment. "I'm sorry, gentlemen, I have no idea where they come up with these tales. They think they can just forgo a hard day's work and run where they please. Well, I'll won't have it. Tellie, Kelm! Apologize to these fellows at once for bothering them, and then you're coming back with me."

"It's not true," Kelm retorted, although he sounded far less convinced himself and more in awe at this twist of events. "We're poor orphans, and they'll work us to death."

During the argument, which had the entire band of men transfixed, Tellie snuck a glance behind them to the enormous cage. The creature inside had lifted her head and she watched them with foreboding intensity. Her nostrils flared if she caught the scent of something and the edges of her mouth curled to reveal sharp teeth.

And then the lock on her cage clicked and the door swung open with a gentle creak.

The sound of the creature's roar, followed by the shaking of the cage as she burst from its confines, was anything but gentle. She knocked over the closest men in one pounce and then leapt into the air with an enormous buffet of her long, leathery wings. The men shouted in dismay, all scrambling for their weapons. The oxen bellowed and bolted, dragging the cage along behind them.

As planned, Tellie and Kelm darted behind Errance for safety who was already backing them up towards the ridge. Yet their movement was hampered by the pure shock of the daisha's attack, and they watched in half amazement, half horror as she swooped down amid the flurry of arrows, grabbed a man in her paws and then carried him back up into the sky. Within moments, he was a small dot flung towards the ocean. The daisha hovered for a moment in the air, unconcerned of the arrows showering her, and then dove again. The men panicked then and fled after their horses, dropping their weapons in an attempt to improve their chances for escape. The daisha followed them, her roars seeming to contain some sort of insults. After a moment, she tilted one wing and banked back the way she had come. Towards them.

"Back," Errance said, and then again, louder. "Back!" He shoved them behind him, raising his hand towards the oncoming beast, but right before she reached them, she dipped and struck at the ground.

There was a sharp scream.

Whether by instinct or pure fear, Tryss abandoned all semblance of camouflage and appeared under the claws of the daisha. The creature thrust off from the ground, nose tilted towards the sky, the chema girl caught fast in her paws.

Tellie and Kelm cried out as one, but Errance dropped his sword and launched forward. He leapt as the daisha lifted off, only just catching the end of her back paw. She squawked in surprise, flight stumbling.

"Put her down!" Errance shouted.

The daisha screeched, but with a clumsy flap, she returned to ground, Tryss pinned beneath her, and Errance rolling clear of the landing. The creature shook her head, then her neck snaked towards Errance viciously.

"Idiot!" the creature roared. "What was that? I was saving your life!"

"She's not an enemy!" Errance pulled himself up into a crouch as he faced her. "She was the one who opened your cage, if your nose had half a brain!"

"Half a—! You little kit, don't you know who I am?"

"Don't you know who I am?" Errance yelled back at her snapping jaws.

She paused. After a moment of cold silence and colder consideration, she pulled back onto her haunches, paw easing its press on Tryss. Her light blue eyes narrowed.

Shakily, Errance got to his feet. His face had gone white, but his eyes were filled with desperation, not fear. "Don't you?" he asked, voice collapsed into something soft and tremoring.

"I already know you're an elf," she said. "I have *half a brain* in my nose to know that. And I know who you remind me of." Her ears flattened, as if she didn't like what she saw. "Are you some relative of Errance then? What are you doing all the way out here?"

He exhaled slowly. "I'm not a relative. I *am* Errance."

She recoiled, letting Tryss go. The chema girl scrambled away, but the daisha did not even notice her. She began to pace, her tail flicking the sand angrily. "That's—liar. You—he died. Everyone knows that. I was there that night."

"But you didn't see it, did you?" Errance said, and his voice was strangely gentle. "When you flew, you didn't stop until you were too tired to keep going, did you? And you probably huddled in a tree for safety. If you went back, you found everyone slaughtered."

"Stop it!" Her teeth clashed, her eyes were wide. "I was just a kit, I barely even knew how to fly!"

"I know," Errance said. "I'm not blaming you, Daisha, I'm glad you fled. I always wondered if you survived."

For a moment more, she hesitated. And then a low wail keened from her throat. "Errance." Her wings and ears both drooped, and she crept forward in hesitation. "It is you, isn't it? It…it is!" Her head closed the remaining distance with blinding speed, nearly knocking him over. "Great STARS, Errance, how is it you?"

He gasped for breath, pushing her great, fondling head away from his face. "I could ask you the same question."

"That is NOT fair, you're the one who's supposed to be dead." Her attention whipped briefly towards Tryss and the children who all jumped in fright. "And why are you with these smelly little creatures?"

"It's too complicated to explain," Errance stammered. "I was imprisoned, that's all."

"All! I've thought you dead for this long and that's all!?"

"Yes," he said, trying to stay on his feet as she wound about him like a happy dog. A creature of her size behaving anything like a dog made it rather hard to stay upright. "I'm trying to get back home now and—these are my companions and…guide. But what about you, why were you captured? Why aren't you in Aselvia?"

The daisha suddenly stopped frolicking and lifted her head to its highest extent, staring down the road, her ears perked. "We should retreat into the mountains," she said at length. "In case those louts return for a second match."

Errance glanced in the same direction as the daisha and nodded.

Tryss struggled to get to her feet, breathing hard.

"Tryss, are you all right?" Tellie ran to the chema's side, giving the daisha a healthy berth. She wasn't quite ready to face the reality of the talking—actually talking—monster yet. It was better to stay focused on what she could handle.

"Did I crush the skin-blender's bones?" The daisha asked, sounding more curious than concerned.

"She's already been sick," Errance said. "Took a scratch from a shard."

"In these parts?" The daisha stuck her nose towards Tryss, sending both girls cowering backwards, and drew a long sniff. "Ah. The Shadow Infection. It will eventually run its course, but it does cling to chema kind."

"So you're familiar with it?"

"Darling, I've been living up North where chemas and shards both are common. So yes, I know a thing or too."

"What about a cure?" Kelm hazarded.

The daisha's head swung around to him, diamond pupils narrowing.

He flinched, but did not look away.

"There is an herb that could help drive the sickness out sooner," she admitted after a long moment. "The chemas call it some fangled word, translates as kiss or something, and it grows up in the mountains. We might be far enough up North to find some."

"Could you look?" Errance asked.

She sighed, wings dropping. "We just reunited, and you're already sending me off again? Fine, fine, but you had better find a good hiding spot in these mountains while I'm gone." She crouched towards the ground, muscles coiling, but Errance stepped towards her, an uneasy look on his face.

"You'll come back?" It wavered between the sound of command and question, but there was desperation to it either way.

She gave him a toothy grin, as fond as it was frightening. "My dear. You're alive, and I've found you. There is nothing that is going to keep me away." Her wings pounded against the earth, sending grit flying and branches shattering. They covered their faces as her takeoff buffeted them for a while longer and then settled in a cloud of dust.

"Well, you heard her," Errance said.. "We've got to get further up into the mountains."

"Hold it!" Tryss snapped. No color had returned to her skin since she'd been attacked, and now she was shaking. "You're going to trust that creature? Just like that?"

Tellie stared, also wanting an answer. After so much distrust, it didn't seem possible Errance would just accept the new company. He stood still, face a perfect blank. Even she could come up with reasons not to trust this beast. Perhaps she was bait the Darkness was using, after all, it was convenient for them to run into her here at this time. Even if he did know her once, who could say what she was now? It had been so long, and they had been but children, so was that any basis for trust....

"Yes."

Tryss blinked and took a step backwards. "I..." Her voice faltered.

A new expression set Errance's jaw. A determination. A choice.

If it was now that he would choose hope over doubt, faith over fear...if he for once wanted to believe in something good rather than something evil...who were they to discourage him?

Tryss's shoulders sagged. "All right," she said, with a helpless flutter of a hand. "If she does bring back some herbs that will help me, I'll be grateful. But I don't still understand why she singled me out to begin with."

"Chemas and daishas have never had good dealings with one another. And the last of her kind was wiped out by a chema ambush when she was but a kit," Errance said coldly.

"Another sin I must be blamed for." Her mouth tightened.

"It's not...it's just she may not trust you for a while."

Tryss gave a sharp laugh. "The feeling is mutual. But whatever her character, I suppose none of us have much choice except to humor her at this point."

The sun was beginning to set by the time the daisha returned. As instructed, they had gone further into the mountains, and there they found a cave nestled amid the forest. It was deep enough to start a small fire without fear of being seen. The trees were the first indication of the daisha's arrival, rustling as she circled above them. She landed in a nearby clearing, then came stalking through the trees. A small goat hung limply from her mouth, and she dropped it by the crackling fire with a pleased snort.

Tellie drew back her feet, staring at the dead animal. Wonderful. The daisha even hunted like a beast. It wasn't hard to imagine her crushing them in those strong jaws.

"Did you bring the herb?" Errance asked.

"So direct, and for a little skin-blender too." She shook her thick mane. "Yes, yes." She lifted a paw, clenched tight around wilting greens, and deposited them next to Tryss's huddled body.

After the creature had swept away, Tryss began sifting through the plants. "Tellie, Kelm, come help me with this," she said. "I'll show you how to make a poultice."

They scrambled over in an instant. Whether or not she actually needed help, who could say, but distance from the daisha seemed a good idea.

Not that it mattered, her mission complete, the creature was now only fixed on Errance. They sat across from each other by the fire as the elf began skinning the goat.

"What do you think of her, Kelm?" Tellie whispered.

The boy peered over his shoulder. "I...I've heard some stories of the talking beasts who flew across the sky, but I never actually thought...it's just..."

Yes, exactly. Of all the things encountered in their unexpected adventure, this was by far the hardest to take. Far easier was it to believe in beautiful elves and demons with endlessly dark eyes as opposed to a furry, winged animal that actually talked with a great deal of intelligence.

Oh, yes, that creature talked. Endlessly. If Tellie had ever worried she talked too much, she felt less guilty now. And Errance listened. Listened ever attentively! He didn't do much of his own talking, and after a while, Tellie's curiosity began to creep up.

"Excuse me," she said, scooting a little closer towards the fire.

The daisha stopped mid-sentence and looked at her. "Yes?"

She wasn't sure if it was bravery or brashness that had inspired her to attract the creature's attention. "I was just wondering…if we could be introduced." Clearly, Errance wasn't going to do it for them. "I'm Tellie, and this is Kelm and Tryss. What is your name?"

"The Daisha. Make sure the 'The' is attached, I won't respond otherwise."

"That's it?"

"That's what?"

Tellie turned to Errance in amazement. "Errance, didn't you or Rendar name her?"

"Oh, they tried," The Daisha scoffed before he could answer. "Some flowery elvish name, I'm sure, best forgotten. As soon as I was old enough to talk, I made it clear I wanted to be known simply as THE Daisha. If I was to be the last of my kind, then let the whole world know."

"How sad," Tellie said.

The Daisha turned a diamond eye her way in a reproving manner. "Not at all. I'm quite satisfied being The Daisha."

Tellie blushed. "That's not what I meant. I mean…how sad it is that you're the last of your kind."

"Oh." The Daisha suddenly looked sorrowful and she released a gusty sigh. "Yes. It's very sad."

"How lonely you must get."

"Yes. Very lonely," she said, more sorrowful still.

"Do you get hungry?"

"Yes," The Daisha moaned. "Very, very hungry."

"That's a surprise," Kelm muttered.

The Daisha fixed him with a hard stare. "Excuse me? What do you mean by that, young man?"

Whitening, Kelm stumbled over his words. "Ah, it's just that…just that…"

"He means you've gotten fat," Errance said.

The Daisha's jaw dropped. Her head swung towards Errance. "Well! Excuse me! Just because you have a trim little waist doesn't give you any right to mock mine!

The other three cast nervous glances Errance's way. Surely he would excuse himself or apologize. It seemed most unwise to offend a creature of her proportions.

Errance stared at The Daisha and for a moment his face constricted as if he sucked in his breath.

And then he laughed.

Tellie, Tryss, and Kelm stared in stunned silence. His laughter rang like silver stars, full of amusement and unashamed joy. It was beautiful and uplifting, and it paralyzed them.

The Daisha looked more offended than ever, but the elf didn't seem to notice or care.

Tellie couldn't believe her ears or eyes. Was this the same Errance, the elf who questioned everyone's moves and actions like the world was out to kill him? He whom, when she'd first met him, had looked like he'd never smiled in his life? No. No, this was the child in her dream.

"You promised me a flight when you were big enough, you know," he said, still grinning as his laughter died away. "Now I daresay you're too big to lift us both off the ground."

"Really! As if! I could carry you to Aselvia and back this very night!"

Errance's smile faded. "But not all of us."

"All four of you?" The Daisha stared at the others, looking especially sharp at Tryss. "Certainly not!"

301

"It's all right, I wasn't planning on flying there anyway."

"But you need to return to Aselvia at once!" The Daisha cried. "Everyone must know you're alive! And if your pursuers are still after you—"

"It's fine," Errance snapped. "We lost them a while ago. We'll just travel together, there's no need to sweep me away. As you can see, I've already recovered, so there's no reason to rush."

Tellie tried to close her gawking mouth. For just a moment she'd felt a jolt of fear that this winged beast would take Errance away from them. His refusal warmed her heart, and then confused her the next instant. Already recovered? Since when was he treating his imprisonment so lightly? Did he not want The Daisha to know?

The meat had been roasting over the fire during the conversation, and Errance tested it with a knife. "Food's ready."

They scooted closer and accepted their portions, blowing on the roasted skin.

"Want some?" Errance asked The Daisha.

"Ah, cooked meat is a rare luxury for me these days, but no, I am afraid I am—" her eyes narrowed "—watching my weight. Apparently." She cast an appraising glance over the other three. "This is certainly strange company you keep. So you told me you'd been captured by our enemy in Tertorem. How'd you end up with them?"

"Kelm and Tellie escaped prison with me. We encountered Tryss's village in our flight, and she…she helped care for my wounds."

"Did she." Embers gleamed in The Daisha's eyes as she studied the chema girl. Clutching her freshly bandaged shoulder, Tryss glared back. A sudden softness filmed The Daisha's eyes and she cleared her throat in a raspy purr. "Well then. I suppose she has my thanks. How is the herb, little skin-blender?"

"My name's Tryss," she said shortly. "And it's fine. I think it's helping."

"Good." She turned back to Errance and continued to converse with him, leaving the others to silently finish their dinner and prepare for the night.

The cave floor was full of stones and roots, and worse still, Tellie had to choose between using her cloak as a cushion or a blanket against the mountain chill. But after several minutes of uncomfortable shifting, she nestled into stillness and watched the firelight dance in strange shapes upon the stone walls.

Their new companion would take some getting used to. A discussion hadn't come up, but it seemed already determined that she was coming with them. And somehow, the distrust had faded over the evening. She made Errance smile. She made him laugh. In such a brief time, she had done what none of them could. It seemed both unfair and reasonable at once. She was part of his golden past, an untainted memory. And Tellie couldn't begrudge his new happiness, it would be too selfish.

I hope The Daisha doesn't snore was her last coherent thought before she drifted into slumber.

In the dreaded hours between night and morning, Kelm found himself wide-awake. Considering the impressiveness of their new comrade, it was a surprise he'd ever gone to sleep at all. The fire had died away into drowsy embers, and he saw the slumbering shapes of Tellie, Tryss, and the gigantic Daisha. But where was Errance? He pushed himself up and looked towards the entrance of the cave. There against the canvas of starlight woods, he could see the dim silhouette of a figure. Cautiously, he crept towards the person, hoping it was the prince and not some unwanted visitor. The night's pale light illuminated the person's features as he drew near.

Relieved, Kelm straightened with a heavy sigh and trudged out the final few steps to come along the elf's side. "You can't sleep either?" he asked.

Errance shook his head.

The boy climbed up on the rock beside him and stared out into the trees. He pulled out the small knife from his belt, picked up a branch, and began to shave the wood away.

"Errance," he began hesitantly. "Have you ever wanted to marry a girl?"

"Excuse me?"

"Marry a girl," the boy said, and without waiting for an answer he plunged ahead. It was indeed a random question to spring on the prince, but it had been on his mind for some time, and there wasn't anyone else with whom to discuss it. "It's just that I like Tellie a whole lot, and she doesn't pay me much attention. And what if she doesn't want to marry me?"

Errance sat blinking in muddled shock. He twisted around to get a good look at Kelm's face. "You *like* Tellie? Like *that?*"

"What's not to like?" Kelm asked, eyes round. So what if she had a firecracker temper? He liked it.

"Well," the elf said awkwardly, rubbing one sleeve. "Aren't you a little young to be worrying about that?"

"I suppose," Kelm sighed, his shoulders sagging. "But gosh, Errance, I've got to worry about it sometime or she might just go ahead and marry someone else. How do you impress girls?"

Thoroughly shaken by two unexpected questions over such a small period of time, Errance was reduced to stammering. At last he took a deep breath and said evenly, "Impressing women has not been my concern."

With another hefty sigh, Kelm said, "Yeah, but you're sure good at it anyway." Not noticing the start this gave the elf, he stared at the sky with furrowed brow for another few minutes. "What about falling in love, has that ever happened to you?"

For a moment, it didn't seem as if Errance would answer or if he'd even bother trying. But when he looked down at Kelm's earnest face, his expression changed into one of consideration.

"If I did, I don't remember. So either no or it wasn't important. When I think of home, I usually just think of my father…and all I'd have said to him."

"Oh." Kelm looked crestfallen. "Your father…he meant a lot to you, yeah?"

Errance was silent. But then he whispered, "He meant the world to me."

The boy nodded sadly and waved the whittled piece of wood in his hand. "My pa taught me how to carve when I was a boy. Said it was good to keep busy. And it…keeps him close."

"You seem skilled," Errance noted. "Considering there is hardly enough light to see by. When did he die?"

"Well," Kelm said, shifting. "I don't think he did. He dropped me off at the orphanage when I was nine. Said he couldn't take care of me. I think he felt...sorry...He drank a lot, you see, and that changes folk. People said he turned to drinking and rage after my ma died giving birth to me. But I don't think he *wanted* to beat me, so he said the matrons would give me a better...future."

Errance stared at him. "...Your father," he said.

"Uh huh."

"Your father beat you."

"Only when he was drunk."

They said nothing more for a long time, simply stared at the star-filled sky spread out before them, scarfed with streaming grey clouds lit on the edges by moonlight. The Daisha growled in her sleep behind them and Kelm jumped, but when he saw Errance didn't, he pretended he hadn't either.

"Say, Errance," he said. "How'd you get so strong?"

"Brutal slave labor, celestial resilience, and stubborn determination."

"Oh." Kelm twiddled his thumbs. "Is there a way more suited to me?" he asked hopefully.

Errance's eyes followed the path of a shooting star, but the corner of his mouth lifted in a wry smirk. "Growing up might help."

25

oOo

Having part of my former life return to me feels so surreal. It was so long ago, and we have both changed, The Daisha and I. Yet it's all still there. The friendship, the trust. I'm glad His Darkness had never known of the bond we shared or he would have ruined that too. Like he ruined everything else.

In other circumstances, Coren might have found it amusing that his own people were so suspicious of his appearance. Granted the guards who first found him and Zizain after they'd crossed the border were fresh-faced youths who he didn't remember seeing before, but even their captain, who he did remember, had stared. If his short hair and clothes were this shocking to strangers, he couldn't wait to see what his parents thought.

But if he was fair, they had a right to be on edge. Aselvia's border had always been protected by an invisible shield of light set in place by King Rendar—only a native of the land and anyone they invited could pass through. So it was reasonable that the guards could have at first feared that with Rendar's death, the shield had gone down. Coren did not believe this was the case. He was quite certain he'd felt the shield as he'd passed through, like a breath of fresh wind. The light Rendar had poured into the royal swords had not dimmed nor had the light in Errance, so it seemed that what had already been given was to remain.

It was strange to come home to an Aselvia without King Rendar. He could feel the grief running through the roots of the land, could hear it in the silence of the city, could smell it in the misty air.

Once the guards had escorted him into the palace, he waited in a small wing, because there was no need to go to the court, and he didn't want to see the empty throne. Of course, through his youth, the throne had usually stood empty because Rendar had better things to do than sit in it. But an empty throne in which Rendar would never sit again. That. That was different.

Rendar had always been a good uncle to him. A little somber, a little strange. But kind.

Coren cursed under his breath. *Couldn't you have waited a little longer? Did you have to die at all? You were* this *close to seeing your son return.*

"My," Zizain said, lounging across a couch and stuffing her mouth full with the grapes a servant had brought into the room. "This place is amazing, why ever did you leave?"

Coren looked around at the intricately painted walls hung with dried greenery. He could smell the fresh evergreen and the damp earth blowing in through the open lattice window. His heart hurt. Maybe that was another reason why he'd always been so reluctant to return home—maybe he hadn't wanted to realize how much he'd missed it.

"Coren?" An elf woman stood in the doorway, her lavender eyes wide with shock. "Coren!"

"Hello, Maava," Coren said, but got no further since the wind was knocked from his lungs by the woman's leaping embrace. He staggered back a step, but managed to hold onto her as she wrapped her arms around him and began to weep.

After a few moments, she pulled back, swallowing down hiccupping tears. "You came back. Because of Rendar?"

He winced. "Well. Yes. Yes, and more. You see, it's about…well, is Daava here, I'd rather explain with both of you at once."

"He's not here, he's…" She paused and stared at Zizain who perched on the edge of the couch, smiling shamelessly through the whole reunion. "Oh…I…I did not realize you brought a guest home."

"Oh yes," Coren said, far too fast. "Um, yes. Maava, this is Zizain, a friend...um...a friend from work. Zizain, this is my mother, Casara."

"Brights!" Zizain cheerfully swore. "Elves really do age as well as they say!"

"Oh," Casara said, looking anxious. "Um, thank you?"

"What were you saying about Daava?" Coren asked, eager to move on.

Contrary to Zizain's observation, he thought his mother did not look well. Her fair complexion was bleak and her usually thick brown hair hung listless. He'd never seen her like this, even in his wild youth when he'd driven her to distraction.

Her slim fingers were trembling as she took both of his hands in hers. "Coren...much...much has happened in these past few days. There is something I must tell you. It is better that we sit down."

"Oh, good," Coren said. "I was about to suggest the same thing."

"It's about your cousin."

"Yes, we've met," Zizain said, popping another grape into her mouth.

Casara went white.

Afraid she might faint, Coren reached out and caught her, throwing an exasperated look at Zizain who had the decency to look abashed.

"You know then?" his mother gasped. "You found him?"

"Yes, in Oolum, but how did you know he's alive?"

"A letter from Rendar...right before he died." Tears were spilling down her cheeks, and she shook in his arms. "Coren, where is he? If you found him why isn't he with you!"

Coren sagged. He wondered even now if he should have taken drastic measures to make sure Errance came home. Perhaps he should have knocked him over the head or slipped something into his drink. But he hadn't wanted to break Errance's trust like that, and anyway...he wasn't sure he could have bested or tricked a man who'd spent seventy years surviving attacks.

"Maava, you must understand. He's been a prisoner for a very long time, and I only just found him recently escaped. He's very...well, he will be very different then you remember him."

"Still handsome, but ornery as a hornet," said Zizain, then clamped her mouth shut with an audible click when Coren gave her another look.

Casara inhaled slowly. "We...we knew that would happen. It's been so long. Poor boy. Did he run from you then? Did you come back for help?"

"He has said he's coming," Coren said hesitantly. "But yes, I did come back so we could go and meet him and make sure that he arrives safely. He took the route around the cape."

"By himself? What about a girl? Was a young girl with him? Rendar was so strange right before death, he declared a human girl we met would find the next king and then—"

"Oh yes, Tellie! I forgot you've already met."

A small cry broke from her, and she buried her face in her hands. "She's alive, thank God! We were in Denji, and she was taken by servants of His Darkness. Your father has been out looking for either one of them...we hoped somehow they were brought together."

"She seemed to be in good health and spirit. And she's not the only one with him," Coren said. "There's a boy and a chema woman too."

Casara stilled, a disturbed expression clouding her eyes. "A chema...why is a chema with him?"

"There's a tribe that lives in the jungle near Oolum, quite different from the Northern folks, I'd say. Don't worry, Maava, she seemed an intelligent and compassionate young woman and was really the only reason I let Errance out of my sight at all. She's serving as their guide and caretaker."

"Coren, I'll tell you what Rendar told us, and then you must tell us everything. I'll call an emergency meeting of the council, and then you can explain all."

It was a new experience seeing Coren so out of his element. Zizain couldn't decide between amusement or pity every time he stammered or hesitated or nervously scratched his jaw. This insecurity was strange to observe.

She supposed he didn't know how to explain her. Most people in Oolum assumed they were a couple and it wasn't an issue there. They were a couple of partners in crime, but that was it. Clearly, an assumption of anything further was not appropriate here, and maybe Coren could explain that, but there didn't seem to be an opportune moment. In the beginning of their friendship, she'd teased him mercilessly, trying to prove he was as corruptible as other men. No success. He was unshakeable and she'd grown to love him for it.

The council seats spread in a crescent from a great tree, and from the tree's roots rose a white throne. Zizain guessed that it would be empty throughout the meeting.

"Coren, take your father's chair," Casara said, gesturing to the seat at the right hand of the throne, before sitting at the left.

Zizain began to sit down next to him, but he caught her arm in alarm. "That's General Reyin's chair," he said.

"Is he coming?" she asked.

"No...he's....we leave it empty to honor his memory."

How many dead people would be coming to this meeting? She had enough grace to keep the thought inside, but another quip slipped out. "Shall I sit in your lap then?"

Coren went red to the ear-tips. He would have laughed it off any other day, because he knew she only teased to try and get a reaction out of him. She certainly got one this time, and not only from Coren but from his mother's concerned inhale. Poor man. For the first time in her life, she felt the urge to blush. "I'll just wait till you're finished with your meeting," she said lamely, tugging hard at her earring.

"No," Coren said, recovering. "You sit, I'll stand."

Zizain sat, feeling a bit awkward about it even without the elf woman's stare fixed on her, but she figured she owed it to Coren to not make any more of a scene.

It was then that rest of the council began to arrive, and she forgot the embarrassment in exchange for the fascination of each appearing member.

One tall man with thick black hair strained with white especially caught her eye, and not only for the white, but for the scarf wrapped around his head and covering his right eye. His ageless, ancient features immediately gave her a new understanding of why humans liked to call elfkind immortal.

She tugged Coren's sleeve. "Who's that?"

"Damarik, our head healer," he whispered.

She stared without any shame only to discover he was looking steadily back from his one dark eye. Not a judgmental or shocked stare, just arcane and wise and penetrating—

She hastened her inspection to the next seat as Coren muttered their names in her ear. "And that's the army's lieutenant…um…Valryd, I think…standing in for Commander Maril."

"Where is our elder priest?" Casara said.

"He had already gone into the woods for his evening prayers," Damarik said, his voice as calm and deep as lake water.

"That could be a while then." She hesitated. "Well, the rest of us are here. Thank you for coming so quickly, councilmen. As you can see, Prince Coren has returned, and he brought us news of Errance. He met him in Oolum."

Everyone seemed to have something to say to that and precious little could actually be heard. "Is he safe—why hasn't he come back—how did you meet him—has he really been—what does—"

"Hold it!" Coren threw up his hands. "One at a time, eh?"

"Is he captured or free?" one elf asked.

"Free, but only just recently. He's been held in Tertorem, like Rendar told you, I hear."

"So how is he physically?" Damarik asked, concern rippling his composure.

"Well…like Rendar, he has an absurd healing ability. I saw him freshly injured while we were in the city together and it hardly slowed him down. As for scars, he had several horrible ones, but they were fading. All except for two tattoos. One that I recognized as the mark of the Red Three. The other said…Property of His Darkness."

The tension coiled tight as a noose.

"And is he?" Valryd asked.

A hiss of pain escaped Casara and she gave the man a strained glare.

"It must be asked," the lieutenant persisted. "If he has been in the clutches of Darkness this long, who knows how much it has changed him. Is he…is he…" But even he could not finish.

"Has he accepted the Darkness as his master, Coren?" Damarik said quietly.

Zizain rubbed her brow. She could actually feel the pain pouring off these folk and it was uncomfortable.

Coren's jaw clenched. "He is….much darkened…but he is a fighter. He's not…not evil, if that's what you're fearing. He's just…hurt and angry…and afraid. I could not convince him to come with me directly. I believe he feels unworthy."

"He does not know," Damarik murmured, touching the wrap upon his face. "As a child he saw only our perfection. This is the consequence of hiding our history. He does not know that we understand. He does not believe healing is possible."

"Exactly!" Coren exclaimed. "So we have to go out there and show him! Let him know that he's as loved as he ever was! He's coming from around the sea. So we need to contact my father and the army. If the army was headed to Tertorem, we must have just missed each other crossing the sea. I did see an unusually large fleet of ships on my way over, so that must have been them. If we send a message, they can start traveling in Errance's footsteps and we can come from above, and somewhere in the middle, we will find him."

"Tertorem."

Everyone startled and turned.

Zizain observed a newcomer pace into the council, a bit smaller than the rest of them. His sandy hair and brown eyes matched the shades of his simple robes, and she thought his face the most unremarkable of the elves she'd met thus far. "Who's that?" she hissed at Coren.

"Oriah, our elder priest," he whispered back.

A priest, was he? A holy man? There weren't many people in Oolum who'd dare to call themselves a holy man, but Zizain had always gotten the impression that they should look rather extravagant and regal.

"What about Tertorem?" Casara asked.

"We must go and join Leoren at the foot of the mountains."

"Hang on," Coren said, turning ashen. "I sent Errance's pursuers on a false trail. Are you saying he's back in Tertorem already?"

"If that is so, have we missed our chance?" Valryd cried. "We have besieged Tertorem before to no avail! What will be different this time?"

The priest gave a sad, small smile. "Ayeshune revealed a vision in the Unseen as I prayed tonight. I saw the mountains dark against a pale horizon. The message has been spoken. We must go."

26

oOo

Kelm has been positively giddy over this secret plan he shared with us in the last few days. He acted as if I couldn't keep a secret. Honestly.

"Tellie, wake up." The voice was a little distant, and at its second call, she mumbled and rubbed her eyes. It took her a moment to realize that the morning sun had already risen and the forest was aglow and sparkling and that the others were already gathered around the fire. They were all staring at her intently.

"Sorry," she said, pushing herself up. "I overslept?"

"Oh, we went ahead and let you," Tryss said.

"Since it's your birthday!" Kelm burst out. He'd been holding back a very obvious grin and now it exploded all over his face.

"What?" Tellie exclaimed. "But it's not—I mean—" Her thoughts tripped over one another in the effort to sort themselves out. Her birthday. She'd already had it, but she'd spent it in a prison. That was the sort of thing to drive away any thought of celebration, and it had been too chaotic for her to think about it afterwards. And yet Kelm remembered.

"I told them you'd missed it," he was saying. "It's been one thing after another, but now that things have settled, I told them, and we all planned on how to surprise you." Both he and Tryss came over to tug her to her feet, and a flower crown was set upon her head.

314

There was a delicious smell coming from the skillet over the fire...egg, mushroom, meat. It was so like something she would have eaten back home, and her mouth watered as she was led over and grandly sat down. "I say," she said faintly and that was all.

"I know," Kelm said. "Tryss outdid herself. The flowers were her idea too." He shoved something into her hands. "This...this is my gift."

Head still spinning from the heavenly aroma and wonder of everything, Tellie looked down at the wood figurine in her hand. It was a magpie, perfectly carved. "I say," she gulped again. "This is probably your finest work yet, Kelm. How long have you been working on it?"

"Oh, off and on," he said carelessly, and then blushed when she leaned over and gave him a hug.

"We are not well acquainted, little lady," The Daisha said, "but I too wish to celebrate, and this is my gift." She lifted her wing and pulled forth...an entire bush, pulled up by its roots, and set it next to Tellie.

Dumbstruck, Tellie looked at it and wondered what she was supposed to do with a bush, but then she noticed the small berries clustered among the slender leaves. "Oh blueberries!" she exclaimed. "A whole bush of them! Thank you, The Daisha." She plucked a handful and tossed them into her mouth, receiving sweet and sour flavors in a burst. "Um, everyone can help themselves."

Tryss dished out the food, and they all began devouring it, blueberries punctuating throughout.

As they drew to a finish, Errance who had not said anything yet but was wearing a thoughtful expression, cleared his throat. "You...you once asked me for a memory of Aselvia," he said. "I answered cruelly. So...ask again. Ask anything you like."

She stared at him, her last bite of food dropping back to the plate. "Really? I mean...are you sure?"

"The Daisha has brought back some memories I'm certain of," he said with the ghost of a smile. "Go ahead."

"Er." Her heart thudded. "How about...well, where does one live? In trees?

Houses? Do you have a palace?"

His lips pressed together as he thought. "A mix of all that, I suppose. Many live out in the forests and mountains, some houses built on ground, some in the trees. We do have a city, Telvar, and the palace is there. The stones of the palace are all white and covered in growing vines. The land is very green, and there are many rivers falling down from the snowy mountains to pool in lakes."

"That sounds lovely," she breathed.

"Anything else?"

This was a special day! "Er...I know celestial elves have that light and chemas can change colors and so on...is there anything special an earth elf can do?"

Errance sighed, his face scrunching. "We are very good at making things grow and supposedly our very presence encourages the land to be fertile and beautiful. Haven't really noticed this effect, it certainly did not help me in Tertorem. But Aselvia is beautiful, so there you are. We smell like evergreen, how's that."

"You do?"

"Well, we're supposed to, I don't know that I have the scent anymore."

"Yes, you do," The Daisha said, and since nobody was going over to sniff him, they took her word for it.

"Do...do you have any other family waiting for you?" It was a hazardous question, and she flinched as soon as she spoke it. He was kind to open his memory to her, and this was probably too personal.

He stared past her into the forest, the sunlight and shadows flickering in his eyes. "Aunt Casara. I guess Leoren counts as my uncle now." He paused. "I...I have a grandmother."

"Really?"

"Yes...she...was never well in her mind. But we got along." A shadow began to cross his face, but he straightened and shook it off. "So there you go, three questions, three answers, Happy birthday."

She grinned. "Thanks." Turning, she gripped Kelm's hand. "You're simply wonderful, Kelm. Thanks for everything."

It was the perfect day. From the crisp morning pace, to the afternoon soothed by the stream and shade, to the dusky purple shadows of evening, everything whispered peace and contentment, all fears swept back into corners. The danger that pursued them…that seemed far, far away.

The light slipped past the horizon, and the stars began to come out in multitudes. With supper still warm within their stomachs, the travelers stretched out on their bedrolls and wrapped up in blankets near the fire to keep off the mountain chill. The Daisha took up first watch, her massive form still and proud as a statue outside a monastery.

Once she hit the bedroll and had wiggled to a comfortable position between the roots and rocks, it did not take Tellie long to fall asleep. But now of course, as she had hoped, the deeper she slept, the sooner she slipped into the Unseen.

Opening her eyes, she looked up into a sky ablaze with colors never seen in the mortal world, where the stars told stories as clearly as illustration.

Excitement thrilled her heart as she wondered what new thing Rendar would teach her tonight. Such incredible things she'd been learning! Seeing emotion, motives, inner hearts. If only she had such eyes while awake, the world would be a much more manageable place. When she sang, she sang with the soul, till her voice became more lovely than she ever dreamed. Rendar taught her about the weapons of the enemy and how to strike back.

Tonight, Rendar was not there to greet her.

Frowning, Tellie looked around the brush and trees. Where was he? How could she have entered the Unseen without him to call her in?

The light of the stars and the moon overhead suddenly dimmed.

She looked up to see a shadowy substance, as supple and flowing as a scarf, drift across the sky, coiling like smoke. But a chill preceded it, one that she could feel in her sleeping body and around her spirit form. The curving darkness dipped downwards in aggressive speed, and the trees swayed violently, trying to uproot themselves and run. It was not smoke—it was wind. Wind as dark as a

317

void.

Tellie took a step back, not afraid as she knew she should be. Rendar would be here soon...wouldn't he?

The black wind descended in a fog, enveloping her in darkness.

All right. She knew she should be afraid—no, not afraid, but cautious.

Still, the wind was now soft and warm, like a blanket. There was always something deeper within, Rendar had told her, and as she peered into the shadows, the sensation took her that some great wonder was concealed just beyond her sight. It set all her curiosity to burning, shoving away better sense. She felt calm, unnaturally calm. A small voice whispered in her head that it had been silly to ever feel afraid of darkness.

Who are you, Gifted Stranger?

She heard the voice without speech, without sound. But it was caressing as silk, as strong as iron.

"Who are you?" she asked impertinently, her fear continuing to fade by the moment.

It laughed in a soft purr. Do you not know? Very well, I shall tell you a little, if you in turn tell me a little about yourself. I am a Weaver, a weaver of lives. I am a Dreamer, seeking to rise. In that, we are alike, are we not, trying to reach impossible things? Here one can see the hidden depths of men, and I look for an ally to accomplish my dream. And we both meet over this elven prince, for he is part of your dream as well, is he not? But what is your dream exactly? That I am curious to know. For I have wandered the Unseen for countless years, and yet you have slipped my eye until of late, which is an astonishing thing considering your power and grace.

It was a terrible lot of words to take in all at once, and Tellie blinked hard, trying to shake the warm thickness that had seeped into her thinking. The compliment was rather nice to hear. It was sometimes discouraging that she did all this Unseen business with nobody to recognize her.

"I...um..." She'd shared her dream so easily with Rendar, but this wasn't Rendar, and the harder she tried to see through the dense darkness, the thicker

her head became.

But the very thought of her dreams revealed it to the presence, and its voice was pleased, amused. You have tall dreams for a mortal orphan girl. Elven home, elven parents…you take nothing but the best I see. What else might you dream? Ah. Elven love. He *is* pretty, isn't he? You're a mite too young for him though, but perhaps you dream he'll notice you when you blossom womanly fair, and he is yet as young and beautiful as ever.

"Oh no!" Tellie said, amazed that she could blush yet redder. She suspected if she saw the color of her own spirit, it would be blazing in fire. "That's not it all. Well. I mean, I suppose I have felt a bit sweet on him, but I know it's silly, and anyway, I've been wondering if he and Tryss might get along, and I quite approve of that, and really, I'd just be happy if he was my br—" She halted in confusion. Why was she babbling unguarded words to this entity?

Yes? *crooned the voice.* Do go on.

"I shouldn't," she stammered. "I shouldn't be talking of him to strangers."

No? *Hurt surprise surrounded her.* But you speak of him to strangers all the time. Chemas, smugglers, wild beasts…why should you hold such prejudice against me?

She frowned. "If you know so much about me already, why do you bother asking me more?"

I only first took note of you when you proved yourself so able in fighting the Darkness.

"You're dark," she said, slowly backing away, though she didn't seem to be going anywhere in the surrounding cloud.

Dark? No, I am not dark, I am Unpainted, I am the substance of Dreams Yet Unrealized. There are so many things I hope to see done, but until then I must remain unfinished, just as your dreams have not yet come to pass. What do you think, Young Dreamer? Will we together make our dreams true?

She continued to back away, her frown beginning to etch severe lines into her face. Something was wrong. Something was terribly wrong, and worst of all, she could not see it. Whatever was within was hidden by that darkness, and she could not tell its true identity. It was inside her mind, clouding everything, even rational thought. *"Where's Rendar?"* she demanded, the words coming out with difficulty.

Rendar? Why would you call upon one who is dead? I summoned you tonight, not a king of bygone history.

In that moment, she heard a shout. It sounded as if it was miles and miles away, and muffled as if a rag had been stuffed in it. But she heard the words clearly. "Tellie! Tellie, get out of there!"

Rendar. It was Rendar.

The shroud clouding her thoughts tore free, and she gasped like unto the blind seeing light for the first time. There had been nothing hidden under those shadows...it was merely what it was—Darkness.

All the fear came rushing back—and with it, anger. "Liar! I know what you are!" She shook with fury. "How dare you try to deceive me? Go away! Go away!"

Go? Where would I go? You're the one remaining inside me.

"Then I'm getting out," she panted. *In her panic, she forgot everything. She forgot song, light, and hope. All she felt was determination to leave. A fine force, but useless without strength to carry it through. She leapt forward, clawing at the cold, scalding blackness. She could feel it sucking at her like a leech, a vampire, and the sensation made her scream. The wind around her began to spin, increasing in its strength till it was a whirlwind. The terrible force of it lifted her off the ground. She tried to catch at something—anything—but only emptiness surrounded her. "Rendar!" she shrieked. "Rendar, help!"*

The wind spun her around till she felt she would tear apart, and her limbs flailed, pulled each way. Darkness was fear. Darkness was Dreams Denied. And she knew that Rendar would not be able to penetrate it.

And in that horrifying realization, only one word came to mind. Her breath was so stolen away she could not speak, could not even force her lips to form words. But her heart screamed it nonetheless.

Ayeshune!

The Darkness ceased.

For a few breaths of time, she huddled, shivering, eyes squeezed shut. Had she somehow fallen out of the Unseen? No…it had been night when she had entered, but now light glowed from beyond her clenched eyelids.

And she was quite certain someone was holding her.

Tentatively, she opened her eyes.

Stars of light danced before her vision, golden as the sun one moment, crystal rainbows the next. And as the light began to clear and she saw who it was that held her, she felt as if she lived her entire life in black and white and only now saw color. No, she felt she had never seen anything before, but was a child first coming into the world. The sensation was terrifying, thrilling, full of wonder, and full of fear. But instead of trying to run from the overwhelming emotion that flooded her, she cuddled deeper into the encircling arms, some unknown sense softly telling her that the fear could not disperse from fleeing, but by coming closer.

"Tellie."

She dared not speak, wasn't sure if she even knew how.

"Why are you here, Tellie?"

She had to answer. But what could she possibly say in return to such a question? Swallowing hard, she rasped, "I—I—I don't know. I needed help so You came."

"How did you come to be here?"

"I was trying to help Errance. I've been trying to help him since we got captured. No, since I first met the elves. At the Nornes."

"And why were you at the Nornes?"

"B-because I'm an orphan."

The glorious embrace cradled her gently. "You are no orphan, Tellie. You are My child and I am your Father. I am the One, the Creator of worlds. I have guided your life since before you were born."

Tears, perhaps from draining fear or dawning hope, rolled down her cheeks. "Your child? How…how can I be such a thing?"

"I am the Father to the lost who are found. You have acknowledged me since you were young, yet have not understood what I am."

At that moment she realized that the lonely wish of her heart, which had still ached even on the journey with her friends, could not be felt here at all. It was if it had never been.

"Ayeshune," she whispered. "Father."

She had called him that before. The orphanage matron had directed all the children to address the God they did not see as Father, and so they obeyed without much conviction. What a wonder it was to call him Father and believe it. She rested in his arms, amazed and delighted by the complete peace and satisfaction.

But then he spoke. "Tellie, the Darkness is still present. He plagues Errance even as we speak."

Confidence swelling up inside, she straightened and said, "I can take him if you are with me."

He chuckled. "Indeed you could. But not now. You need to wake Errance up."

Bewilderment wrinkled her features. "Wake him up?"

"Yes. Now."

The light was gone. The warmth vanished.

She was lying on her side under the trees in the night. Blinking, she knew she could not deny what had just happened with the marvel still pulsing through her blood. But it was gone so fast. He'd told her to...

The cry shook every breath in her body.

She gasped as she scrambled to push up to a sitting position. "Errance!"

He lay dead asleep, but he thrashed on the ground, gasping for breath. Tellie shoved to her feet, but Tryss and Kelm were already up and running for him.

Kelm reached him first, calling, "Wake up! Wake up!" As soon as his hand touched Errance, the elf's arm flung out, caught Kelm, and threw him away.

Tryss and Tellie froze.

Errance struggled to inhale. Words broke from him in a burst. "No! NO, p-please, *no!*"

Her heart pounded in her throat, but the rest of her didn't move. *Oh, please Ayeshune, please have him wake up,* she pleaded. Surely she could have done more in the Unseen. There she was brave—not frozen like this.

The next moment, there came the sound of great shifting, and the colossal form of The Daisha sprang over the dead fire and straddled the writhing body of the prince. She clamped him down to the ground with her hand-like paws. "Errance!" she barked. "Awake immediately!"

"Let go, let go, let GO!" Errance screamed.

Without waiting another second, the Daisha's huge pink tongue shot out of her mouth and slurped over the elf's face.

Errance gasped again, but this time in shock instead of agony. His eyes fluttered open. "Daava...?" he gulped in confusion.

"No, but you may call me Mummy," The Daisha said cheerfully, nuzzling his chin with her nose.

Sighing in relief, the others clustered around The Daisha's shoulders and peered down in concern. "It's us, Errance," Tryss said wearily.

His reddened eyes focused with recognition and when his body slightly relaxed, The Daisha stepped back.He pushed up onto one elbow, shoulders bent inwards. "They had Daava," he choked, voice thick. "They were torturing him, and I could not break free, could not stop them...my greatest fear...they've done all they can to me, how can I bear watching them do the same to those I love?" The frantic stream of words slammed to a standstill. He closed his eyes and pressed a fist into his face.

"It was just a dream," Tryss whispered. "Nothing more."

Reeling, he struggled to his feet, and though they moved to catch him, he lurched out of their reach to a nearby tree where he retched.

The three of them fidgeted, but The Daisha watched her elf with deep intensity. When his heaving stomach at last sank into a quivering balance, he stood with his bowed back to them, bracing on the tree with an arm. His voice came quiet and strained. "Just...just leave me alone for a little while."

They nodded silently, and he stumbled into the dark forest. After his crashing through the brush faded away, they turned back to their camp. But they could not settle there—Tellie trembled, Tryss sat with her face in her hands, and Kelm tugged incessantly at his sleeves. The Daisha paced about the camp, looking constantly in the direction Errance had disappeared and sniffing the air. At last she came over to them and stuck her nose in each of their faces. "All right," she snapped. "I demand to know exactly what they did to him in that prison."

Tellie cleared her throat. "We really don't know anything about what he's gone through," she said. "But when something like this happens..." Her voice broke. "I don't even want to think about it."

Snarling, The Daisha flung her head away. "If any danger comes near my elf, why I'll...curses! Curses! The most abysmal of curses on all who have hurt him! May their teeth fall out and may their wings wither! I shall tear them all to shreds!"

Tryss made a sharp shushing motion with her hand, and they turned to see Errance returning, slump-shouldered. He dropped to his knees beside the fire and stared at it with as much heat as the coals themselves.

"Just a dream," he muttered.

"That's all," Tryss assured.

"All?" The word was sharp as a knife, and they flinched.

Errance's hands clenched and unclenched as if they sought something to strangle. "All a dream? Sometimes I wonder." His breath came quick, and his skin shone deathly pale in the firelight. "Ever since I've met you, ever since I've escaped, I've wondered if it was real or just another hallucination. I've had them before. They've spawned from my mind alone or I've had them forced on me. There was always something in the enchantments they created that I could tell was false, but they might have gotten better. For all I know, none of this could be real. But then what is real?"

Tellie stared at him in growing alarm as his words grew more feverish and rushed together. She wondered if she should say something, should do something to stop him. The Daisha was beginning to growl in her throat.

Starting to shake, Errance ranted on, "For all I know, my life in Aselvia could have just been a story they created for me, something to taunt me. There could be nothing but darkness, nothing but pain, nothing but—"

"Errance!" Tryss cried, reaching out and grabbing both his arms. "Errance, enough!"

He pulled away from her, trembling, but the Daisha reached out a long paw and caught him against her fluffy chest. She craned her neck around to nuzzle his cheek with her nose. "There, there," she murmured, making motherly, shushing noises that were strange coming from her predator mouth.

Kelm and Tellie exchanged frightened looks and crawled a little closer. Tryss, after searching through her bundle, pulled out a few leaves that she offered to Errance to chew, but he didn't seem to notice.

"Errance," Tryss said. "You can't let yourself start thinking that way."

"But it's true, isn't it?" he whispered, staring into the fire. "All of this could be false."

"No!" she snapped. "No, it could not be. The Darkness could not have created the love you remember from your childhood, nor could he have invented the adventure we're having. Its goodness is beyond his creation. This is true and real, and you know it."

With a shudder, he dropped his head against his knees and didn't respond. They watched in helpless dismay, wondering if perhaps he was about to cry and if the world might end if he did.

Tryss lowered her voice to a soft and gentle tone, and asked, "Can I make anything you'd like to eat? I can heat some water."

He shook his head.

"Another good lick across the chops should do him," The Daisha said confidently.

Errance hunkered deeper into his arms. "*No.*"

"What about music then? I can play my pipe and…" Tryss offered.

"No."

At last, Tellie found her voice, though it came out small and weak. "I..." She cleared her throat. "I could...I could sing for you."

"No, no..."

"I could whittle," Kelm offered.

Tellie rounded on him in disgust. "Why in Orim would he want you to whittle?" she exclaimed.

"Why in Orim would he want you to sing?"

"Why...!" She opened her mouth, outraged.

"Both of you, silence!" Tryss ordered.

But she needn't have spoken because in that moment they all went silent as Errance gave a choking chuckle. Slowly, he raised his head and rubbed his hands down his face with a deep groan. "No," he sighed. "I don't think the Darkness could ever *imagine* what you two decide to bicker about."

Tellie and Kelm blushed, not quite sure where to look.

After that, no one spoke for a long while. They sat there and listened to the mountain crickets chirp, the wind shiver through the branches, and The Daisha's breaths rumble warm and deep.

"I don't know what came over me," Errance said at last, barely above a whisper. "I don't usually allow myself to think like that. I don't dare or else I'd go insane. I have to believe this is real...believe or else collapse."

"You're exhausted, physically and mentally," Tryss said. "It's little wonder you haven't had an attack like this earlier."

At that, Tellie's mind flashed back to her ordeal in the Unseen. While the One had comforted her, the Darkness must have unleashed himself upon Errance in full force. "I'm sorry," she said.

He glanced up, frowning. "This has nothing to do with you, Tellie."

Nothing to do with her. Of course. Because she couldn't possibly have a significant effect on his life. She stifled a sigh.

"Will you be all right now?" Tryss asked tentatively. "I could stay up with you, if you like."

He shook his head. "No. No, go to sleep. We all need it."

No one could argue with that, but even when they'd settled back onto their bedrolls, they kept watching as he eased back down onto his blanket. His hands folded tightly over his chest, and he gazed up into the sky without blinking. The Daisha curled up behind his head, griping and cursing the whole while. When she laid her noble head by his own, he smiled slightly and stroked the ridge of her brow. It seemed to calm her and soon she was snoring.

One by one, they all dropped back off into sleep, till only Tellie remained awake. Once again, her vision in the Unseen began to fade. Not so much that she forgot what happened, but that the intensity was less vivid, the reality less believable. But she knew she had seen Ayeshune, the One and Only. She knew this, no matter if the rest diminished. She knew it to be true by one thing.

Peace.

Sighing deeply, she cushioned her head in her arms and fell into a sweet, dreamless slumber.

Morning dawned bright, shining through the dewdrop scalloped leaves. Tellie awoke to the sound of a trilling bird. Stretching, she sat up and looked over the camp where the other sleeping forms were huddled. She breathed deep, filling her lungs with the fresh air.

And that was when she realized Errance was gone.

27

oOo

The nightmare hit me hard. Punishment for daring to think I could someday be happy again. I have been bound too long to live in freedom. What I have felt in these past few days is not meant for me. It is sometimes better to give in first before you are taken by force. And if that is my fate, I cannot keep anyone near me.

"Where's Errance?"

Tryss startled awake at Tellie's cry, scrambling to sit up without tripping in her blanket and braid. She looked first to Errance's empty bedroll and then around the rest of the campsite, but there was indeed no sight of their elven heir. The Daisha began to bound about the camp, wings and tail smashing against the circling trees, her fur bristling.

"Daisha! The Daisha! Stop, you'll ruin any tracks!" Tryss shouted, reaching out to grab Kelm and Tellie before their scrambling could do similar damage.

They all froze, swaying with dizziness, and cast anxious glances into the surrounding forest. In the quiet, they could hear the birds and the creak of wood, but nothing else.

"Perhaps he just needed a little privacy," Kelm suggested. "He's done that before."

"He's also left us before," Tellie said. "If he was just going to be gone for a while, he should have left a note or something. No, he's gone, because now we have The Daisha to protect us. Oh, it was that awful nightmare; I just knew something like this would happen!"

Tryss turned, took Tellie shoulders and gave them a firm little shake. "Tellie, you must calm down. Now."

The young girl blinked at her stern tone, but she obediently shut her mouth and was silent, though her exchanged glances with Kelm were as nervous as ever.

Taking a deep breath and pressing her hands to her head, Tryss forced herself to think, which became a little easier when The Daisha stopped romping about the woods and paced back to the camp, nostrils flaring. "All right," she said, lifting her chin. "The Daisha, will you search from the sky while I take the ground?"

The Daisha lifted her doe-like ears with pride. "Not to seem rude, little skin-blender," she said, not seeming to notice how Tryss frowned at the title, "but I'm sure I could handle the search well on my own."

"I'm sure you could," Tryss said stiffly. "But while this is not my forest, I'm good at tracking, and while I might be slower than you, more people covering the search have a better chance of success."

After a pause, The Daisha nodded and then waddled out to a clearing where she could spread her wings and take to the sky.

Tryss turned back and saw the two children looking at her expectantly, the very images of calm and dignified anticipation. But when she looked at them without speaking, their faces melted into worry.

"Aren't Kelm and I searching too?" Tellie asked.

She shook her head.

"But Tryss," Kelm protested. "You just said the more who search, the better."

"Only if they know how to search. You two would get lost, and then there would be more trouble on my hands," Tryss snapped. "Now stay here and don't leave!" She hated her sharp tone, had always hated using it on her younger siblings, but it was effective. Both Tellie and Kelm sat with a thump on a nearby log and looked up at her with wide eyes.

She turned to leave, but her conscience tugged her back to their unhappy faces. "Don't worry," she said, patting a hand to their cheeks. "Errance probably just went out for some peace. He might come strolling back here any time, and then you all can have a good laugh about it."

At the sound of tree branches rustled by the wind of The Daisha's takeoff, Tryss set out on her own search, circling the camp close to the ground for any sign of footprints or broken foliage. She caught one trail and pursued it, but whether it was Errance or a deer that'd been bold enough to pass through camp that night she could not be sure until she reached its end. But that trail led to fern squashed down flat where an animal had bedded, and so she hurried to the next possible path.

The unknown forest seemed bent on causing endless frustration with broken branches and stirred soil scattered across the forest with no apparent reason, and she began to feel wholly inadequate to the task of tracking.

Despite her encouragement to the children, a knot grew in her stomach as she considered why Errance disappeared. If he'd been anywhere near and was not attempting to sneak away, he certainly would have heard their commotion and come back to be sure they were safe. But if he had left…why would he leave? How could he leave—now, in the middle of nowhere, still so far from Aselvia? Back when she had first met him, she'd considered him a strange, callous man, quite capable of deserting them. But now, after these days where their unlikely company had hardened into comradery, she was furious he would do such a thing to them—not to the others anyway.

See them safely to their homes, the Ancient had said. Such a quest held heavy weight to it. When first given it, she could scarcely believe that such an honor had been bestowed upon her, yet she had not doubted her ability to carry it through. She'd pitied the elven prince and considered bringing him and the children back to his homeland a thrilling adventure. But Errance changed her mind not long after. When he frightened her, she'd sworn she would look after the children and let him fend for himself, and that was all that duty and honor required.

Duty and honor be dashed! When he had first tried to escape, she assumed it was only his stubborn desire to go home alone. Now, she was not so sure. If he had another intent in mind...*Oh God, let me find him in time.*

A dark shadow sailed over her, and a trumpeting voice called, "There he is!"

Startled, Tryss looked up to see The Daisha fly overhead. She broke into pursuit, leaping over logs and branches.

Tellie hated to be excluded. After Tryss left, it did not take her long to begin pacing the camp, twitching her hair, and leaping eagerly towards every noise.

Kelm remained sitting on the log, but he pulled out the little pocket-knife the chemas had given him and began whittling. He frowned at his friend as she stalked back and forth. "Will you stop that?"

"It's inconceivable!" she cried, flinging up her hands.

"Do you even know what that means?"

She ignored him. "How could he leave us like that? You men are impossible!"

Despite being packaged into generalized mankind, Kelm adopted a reasonable tone and said, "The Daisha and Tryss will find him."

"They can only go so many directions at once. Why, he could get hundreds of miles away if they took the wrong route."

Shaking his head, Kelm bent back over his whittling, but he straightened in alarm as he saw Tellie make a decisive turn into the forest. "Hey!" he exclaimed. "Where do you think you're going?"

"He might have gone this way," she said, planting her fists on hips.

"Tryss told us to stay here!"

She lifted her chin and pulled the Moon Medallion out from under her collar. "I was given this for a reason, Kelm. I was told to find the next king of Aselvia. Well, I found him, but it won't do any good unless I see him safely to his homeland. It's my duty to find him."

Kelm scowled, but he saw she was quite resolute. "Bother it," he grumbled, rising to his feet. "That explanation better sound good when you're telling it to Tryss."

"I assure you, you don't have to come," Tellie said, very dignified.

"I assure you, I'm coming."

The Daisha's flight had led to a small plateau at the rocky feet of the mountains. She'd disappeared out of sight on the top of it, but it was not so tall that Tryss couldn't hear the ensuing argument as she tried to scale the steep hill. Their words were indistinguishable in their effort to be heard. The Daisha roared with the gnashing of teeth, but Errance, not at all intimidated, threw fiery retorts back at her.

When at last Tryss reached the top of the slope, she saw them facing each other near a ledge.

The Daisha noticed Tryss approaching them first. Her head poked out towards the chema. "There you are! Try to speak some sense into this obstinate creature! If he doesn't get reasonable soon, I'm picking him up and carrying him back to camp—upside-down! See if I don't!"

His face flushed red with anger, Errance swung around towards Tryss. But to her surprise, as soon as he saw her, the color in his cheeks paled and pain leapt into his eyes. He turned away to face the cliff's edge and crossed his arms.

Tryss hesitated, all courage stolen at the daunting curve of his set shoulders. She cast a pleading glance at The Daisha, but the creature really did seem angry beyond reason and had stomped away to the other side of the hill, though her ears still cocked back in their direction.

Now that she had found him, she hardly knew how to approach. Everything she thought to say felt wrong. She recalled the story she'd told Tellie, about the hurt monkey who'd hurt her in return. There was truth in it, wisdom that needed to be shared. But it wasn't enough. Errance was more than what her fear and pride had been willing to box him into. She could hardly make sense of him, so often did he contradict, yet the glimpses of something beautiful had awakened the desire Tellie spoke of—finding the colored glass behind the grime.

"Why did you leave us again?" she whispered.

She did not know she'd spoken aloud until he answered.

"Can't a man take a walk without women demanding him back?"

It might have been humorous, but there was such venom to the words, Tryss flinched. "Evasiveness does not become you," she said, unable to keep the hurt out of her voice.

"On the contrary, it has always served me well." But his back bowed under a heavy weight.

"What did we do?" she pleaded. "Where do we go wrong? Why will you not stay with us and see this through until our destination? Did I offend you again? And if so, what is my offense?"

Errance slowly turned. "Look," he said, voice measured. "I did not leave because of anything you've done. Tellie and Kelm have brought back life I thought was lost to me. And you…" His gaze dropped. "I admit, I misjudged you at the beginning. I was wrong to treat you so."

"Why did you?" she asked. "I know my people's history does me no credit, but my grandfather worked so hard to distinguish us from them, and I—"

"The only beauty in Tertorem was ever meant to deceive and harm me," he burst out.

The words on her tongue trailed away, leaving her mouth hanging listlessly open. Her lips trembled as she tried to find some sort of response. But there could be no response, not to the raw pain of his voice.

"Anything right was made wrong. Any truth twisted to betray me," he said with a heavy pant. The anger in his voice faded to a dull ache. "I suppose the only thing worse than a new perversion is a ruined idealism. Yes, I did resent you because of your race. But I resented you more besides." He held up his hand to halt her interruption. "Please…understand why you are so different. The children…their presence is new and unexpected and unlike anything there. The Daisha belongs to my innocent past. Why did I not trust you? Perhaps I did not think you truly would harm me, but you reminded me of something that had. Perhaps I thought you were too beautiful to be true."

She blinked. He'd called her beautiful. Yet it didn't sound like a compliment, so she could not take it as one. Taking two deep breaths, she summoned courage for what she needed to say. "You fought your captors for seventy years. You desire to prove evil wrong. But have you not thought that others wish to do the same? Give us a chance to care for you, don't keep running away." *Let me prove wrong the conception you have of me*, she silently added. *To be more than the sins of my people and the fear tangled inside you.*

He breathed a bitter laugh. "You do not know how many times I gave that chance only to be betrayed."

"But everything was done in darkness there. Here there is light. If you run from both, where can you go?"

He turned away again, but Tryss walked around him until she stood directly in front. Her hands grasped his arms, and though he winced, he did not pull back.

"Errance," she said, forcing her voice to be steady. "Errance, you are not a slave of His Darkness. You are the prince of elves, soon to be king, and there is a beautiful world to call your own. You are noble and brave, and you inspire everyone around you. Can't you see that? Tellie adores you, Kelm worships you, and I—" She halted, unsure of what she meant to say. "You protected me. Even after everything you've gone through, you still protect."

Errance looked quietly at her, and she had a sudden savage wish that he wasn't so horribly good at hiding his emotions. "That is why I'm leaving you," he said at last.

Tryss stared at him, hot tears threatening. "*Why?*"

He heaved a breath and looked down. "The Darkness will always hunt me. If we ever reach Aselvia without being caught, which I doubt, he will try to take me even there. I can no longer be with you. I was a fool to stay this long."

"And leave us out in the wilderness? Thank you for that!"

"You have The Daisha. I'm sure you could reach your destinations without trouble, and as for the forest your grandfather wants, the elves will surely spare you some. I'm a danger to you, not an asset."

She stepped back, stunned. He had known. Somehow, he had guessed that there had been more motives then just benevolence. "Our wish to help you is *sincere*, Errance. Where then do you intend to go?"

He shrugged and did not answer.

Anger blazed to life in her gold and green eyes. "Errance," she said, voice coming choked out of a tight throat. "You cannot aimlessly wander forever. What are you looking for, death?"

Errance's gaze dropped down to the ground, and Tryss knew that even if he hadn't decided on it, he had considered it.

For a minute all she felt was anger. How could he think that, after all they had done for him! But the more she looked at him, the more she saw how much pain filled his posture, she just felt her heart break. "Why, Errance?" she whispered.

His head snapped up. "The only thing keeping me alive these seventy years was the will of my captors! I hated every breath I took! You expect that all to change over a few days?"

"Yes!" she cried. "Yes, because you have hope, and you have light, and you have us! You aren't just a prisoner anymore. You're a king. Your people need you. We all need you!"

But he was shaking his head, face fixed back to the ground. "I can't risk your lives," he said, barely moving his lips.

The Daisha gave a snort, and they both jumped, having forgotten that she was there. The worthy beast strode forward and arched her neck, proudly gazing down on them. "Well," she sniffed. "Very noble of you, I'm sure. But you'll just have to risk our lives a little bit longer, because I have my eye on you now, and nobody outfoxes The Daisha." She lifted her chin and looked very grand.

Tryss sputtered a laugh, but Errance's brow furrowed and his hands clenched.

The Daisha saw his reaction and brought her nose down to nuzzle his neck right under his ear with a snuffling snort. His mouth curled up against his will and he jerked back, shoving her nose away. "Daisha, enough!" he sputtered.

The Daisha continued tickling him with her muzzle, saying, "Daisha? What a strange name."

"All right, all right, THE Daisha!" he gasped, bending over and clamping his hands around his neck.

She pulled back and gave him a toothy smile. "Remarkable," she smirked. "Such a delight to know that you're ticklish."

Errance glared at her, but a sparkle had returned to his eyes.

"Well then," The Daisha said, spreading her wings low to the ground. "Get on, and we shall return to camp."

Her words hung in the air, for a moment unable to be accepted into understanding. They blinked, taking a step back.

"You mean," Errance breathed, "ride?"

"Did I stutter?" She raised her nose with a regal air. "Did we not talk about it as children? I did promise to fly you all over the world, I seem to recall." She folded her limbs beneath her and tucked her wings back to provide the most convenient mounting.

Errance lingered a little longer, fingers flexing. He tentatively stepped forward, braced his arms upon The Daisha's withers and vaulted onto her back. For a moment he clung there as if he'd forgotten how to ride, which was entirely possible. Breathing heavily, he straightened, his hands clutching large clumps of her fur.

"Hold with your legs, not your hands," The Daisha instructed. "You may have a grip on my fur if you must, but do *not* pull." She nailed her gaze to the hesitating Tryss. "Well, don't be shy, dearie. You are certainly the first chema to be offered a ride from a daisha, and you may be the last. So snap it up while the offer lasts."

Tryss stared, grabbling with her mind. As of a few days ago, flying had been an unattainable thought. Everyone had the dream sometimes when watching birds, but she had never been acquainted with the legend of daishas and so had never dreamed of riding them. For a moment, she thought to tell them to go ahead without her and she'd make her way back to camp on foot. But no, she was no coward, and if this was another way to establish trust with Errance, then she would take it! So with an uncertain smile, she clambered up behind Errance. At once she was seized with doubt at the wisdom of flying in the sky without any real securement, but she held her tongue.

With a shake of her head and maned shoulders, The Daisha coiled to the ground, wings rising high above till the tips touched. "Hold on, my lovelies," she said and then sprang into the air.

Tryss's breath left at the launch. Throwing all decorum and tact to the rushing wind, she wrapped her arms around Errance and clung for dear life.

The Daisha shot up, each powerful wing thrust sending them further and further from the earth. With a final heave, she leveled in the sky, her enormous wings spreading on either side, the thermals catching under them and holding her aloft.

"There now," The Daisha said, looking over her shoulder. "That wasn't so bad was it?" She chortled to discover that Errance lay flat against her back, his arms wrapped around her neck, and Tryss mirrored the image on him. When The Daisha bent her neck about and nuzzled his brow, he pulled his face from her fur and shakily straightened. At that moment, Tryss remembered herself and sat up as well. "How are we feeling, young winglings?" The Daisha teased.

"Can we go back for my stomach, I think I left it on the ground," Errance gasped, quite pale. But even as he spoke, a smile curved his lips.

"How are you?" The Daisha looked pointedly at Tryss.

"Mm," Tryss replied, the sound shrill despite coming from behind sealed lips.

"Delightful." The Daisha snickered.

She tilted a wing and sunk into a low skim across the forest floor, the leaves a living carpet underneath. Every color of green and brown flashed by in blurs, songs of birds heard in brief moments. If they hunkered low against The Daisha's withers, the wind parted around them, only catching the ends of their hair. As they glided on, they began to relax and look around to better see the trees and sparkle of water occasionally below.

"Oh look," The Daisha said, dropping even lower and turning to circle back to a glade they'd passed. "It's the little ones."

Tellie and Kelm, hurrying across the ground, jumped in surprise when a voice sounded above them, a gigantic shadow following immediately after.

"What are you doing?" Tryss called down, the annoyance visible on her face even from above tree level. "I told you to stay put!"

"You're riding The Daisha!" gasped Kelm, even as Tellie squealed, "You found Errance!"

"Yes, they're riding me, and yes, we found him," The Daisha said. "Now you two sit down right there until we are done, and I really do mean stay put. Or else you'll have *me* to deal with."

Obediently, Tellie and Kelm sat, staring up in wide-eyed wonder, their hands shielding their faces against the wind of The Daisha's pulsing wing-beats. With a last severe look, The Daisha swung out of her hover and took to the sky.

Tellie sighed in relief, wiping her wind-blown hair out of her eyes. "Thank goodness, I was getting so worried."

"I couldn't tell," Kelm grumbled. But his frown faded as he gazed after the winged creature. "Flying," he muttered. "Incredible. I should like to do it myself."

She didn't seem to hear, staring instead into some starry-eyed thought. "You know," she remarked. "I really do think Errance and Tryss look sweet together."

"Oh brother," Kelm groaned.

When they left the children behind, it took a few seconds for Tryss to move past her frustration of intrepid youth to realize that The Daisha was showing no intention of landing, but instead climbed higher into the sky. "I thought we were landing."

"You assumed. A common inclination amongst you two-leggeds. Quite silly of you. I said nothing of landing yet. I said I'd give you a ride, and a ride I shall give you."

"You would, of course, set her down if she wished it," Errance corrected.

The Daisha huffed. "If we must be all considerate, yes,"

"No, carry on," Tryss said. She didn't fancy admitting any fear in Errance's ears, and so far she'd handled heights rather well. Nevertheless, she took a deep breath and clenched her teeth as The Daisha's ascent grew steeper.

The pump of her wings lurched their seats, so they had to rise and fall with the rhythm to keep balance. The air grew colder the higher they went, and when at last The Daisha leveled again, a few clouds floated beneath. Seeing those wisps of white over the far forest sent Tryss's stomach swirling, and she closed her eyes and pressed her forehead against Errance's shoulder. He did not seem bothered by the height, but instead stretched out to see better.

"So why did you run again, Errance?" The Daisha said, sounding strangely like a teaching mother.

"They told you why," he said curtly. "Evil pursues me."

"As far as I know, that evil was nowhere near when you ran. So you couldn't have been running from them. Try again."

He didn't answer. Tryss could feel that familiar ice stiffen his body, sealing himself in and everyone else out.

"Seems to me there was nothing but friendship and freedom around when you fled. Is that what you feared?"

"I…"

"Of course it was," she said, arching her neck and glancing back with a fanged grin. "Freedom is terrifying."

With that she folded her wings against her body. For a moment, they hung weightless and silent. And then The Daisha's nose tipped earthward, and her body arched into a dive, and the world pulled them down.

The wind shrieked by so that Tryss could not even hear the sound of her own scream though she felt her throat ache with it. Her eyes watered, and her head and ears stuffed out sound. In no way could she see or hear if Errance made any sound of fear, but she could not help but feel the shock and terror rush through his limbs.

The Daisha bolted through the sky, and then as the world began rushing frightfully near, she suddenly unfurled a wing and shot to the side.

Tryss's stomach dropped back into place with a plunk, and the end of the drop sent energy pounding through her body. She did not know whether to laugh or to cry to discover she was alive, but life was a gift, and it never seemed clearer than that moment. So she spat hair from her mouth and tossed back her head and laughed. The sound sped The Daisha faster than ever as they raced upon the roads of the wind.

Errance unfurled from his fear-stricken grip against The Daisha's shoulders and his back eased under Tryss's arms. She could feel his swift breath rise and fall under her fingers and then inhale suddenly as their mount bent so far sideways they had to cling with all their might to stay on. And then everything coiled inside him—the remaining fear or growing joy, who could say—burst from him in a shout.

At that sound The Daisha's flight became even more merry, dipping and twirling like a swallow chasing the breeze. Only blue filled their eyes, bright, purest blue of heaven's own water. The weakness of the terrible drop scattered away, leaving behind only light exhilaration.

This was as akin to understanding freedom as an experience could be. Tryss felt it even when she had not looked for such a feeling, and so she knew Errance felt it as well. That The Daisha knew its way and loved it, and so had taken them to know it as well. And yes, there was terror, but they only needed to trust that she would not let them perish, and then here at the end lived such a joy.

Tryss still laughed as she held onto Errance, and he glanced back at her, his eyes alight and lips parted with breathless pleasure. It was only a short look exchanged, but it sent a deep gladness into her heart. This amazing joy, this dream come true...he knew that she saw it and that she shared it with him and yet he did not mind. Perhaps he would trust her more after this because they had done such a thing together.

She wished it would last. That such a peace and faith would go on forever. But eventually, they would land and the journey would go on. If they reached

Aselvia, then perhaps all would be well. But in her heart, she knew he would flee again before the end.

28

oOo

Only a little while ago, I had sunk back into the familiar haunt of despair. But now, I soar above it, unbound, unburdened. Who knew that one could fly above their troubles. If they are down below or trailing after me, I refuse to look. Only these moments matter. This singing wind, this everlasting sky. It is unlike anything I have ever known, and my heart longs to stay forever. While up here, I close my eyes and allow myself to taste it—hope.

"Can't I have a ride?" Kelm pleaded for the third time.

Errance and Tryss had not returned till that afternoon, and since then their journey had progressed at an energetic pace so that they covered ground at a swifter rate than any day before. The rich colors of late afternoon set in, casting the first shadow of evening, but Kelm was set on flying before dark.

At Kelm's latest and most persistent remark, The Daisha slithered through the trees, her wings tucked close to her body, graceful limbs gliding over the rough ground like it was silk. Her long neck snaked forward so that her head poked over the shoulders of Kelm and Tellie. "Ride?" the creature mocked. "Because I give Errance and Tryss a ride, you think you are instantly entitled to one as well?"

Kelm batted at the small tuft of fur at the end of her chin. "Aw, come on, The Daisha."

"My wings are tired," she said pathetically. "My back is permanently bent."

"Stop sniveling," Errance called back.

Smiling, Tellie threw a glance up at The Daisha's offended face. "All Kelm wants is one small ride."

"Yes," Kelm said. "And Tellie can ride with me!"

"Wait—what?" That was definitely not all right. Helping out a friend was all well and good, but there were limits to loyalty. The sky lined the limit for Tellie. "No!"

"Aw, why not? It would be fun."

"Fun?" She wrinkled her nose. "It would be terrifying. You know how I hate heights."

"B-but I don't want to go alone," he stuttered.

No matter how puppy-eyed and pathetic he looked, a shudder ran through her as she imagined the world dropping away below with only a smooth grey back to ride on. No. Not for her.

"I can ride with you," Tryss offered.

When Kelm's face lit up, Tellie almost regretted her fear of heights. It could be fun to do something so daring and dashing with her friend...but no. Too terrifying.

The Daisha puffed a long-suffering sigh. "Oh, very well," she groaned. "If you are so set on it, I suppose I could give you a quick little flight." Yet behind the veil of annoyance, her eyes twinkled. Tossing her head, she headed towards a clearing and Kelm hurried after, all flushed with excitement.

Tryss began to follow, but hesitated and looked back at Errance. "You'll stay here?" She raised a meaningful eyebrow and nodded towards Tellie.

Errance nodded.

"We won't be too long." She smiled and waved, before running to catch up with the other two.

Sitting down on a moss-cushioned log, Tellie stretched out her legs and propped up her chin as she watched The Daisha vanish beyond the curtain of rustling leaves. After the wind settled, the forest lapsed into sudden serenity. A strange quiet that had not existed often in the presence of their company.

Sighing louder than needed, she shifted to look at Errance who leaned against the tree and gazed out into the forest like a perfect statue. After a minute, he shifted and withdrew the sword Coren gave him, running his hand down the blade again and again. Over the past few days, Tellie often saw him do this and each time she watched as closely as she dared. The blade truly did shine with some inner light, but she hadn't found courage yet to ask why. Trying to awaken Errance's nostalgia never really worked, but she hoped he found it himself in the perfect curve of metal and the designs etched therein.

She could hear his hand smoothing down the blade. It took her a moment to realize why this was odd. She heard the sound because there was nothing else to hear. The silence of the forest went beyond the mere stilling of their company— there were no sounds of birds or insects.

The silence was dead.

"Errance." Scalp suddenly tingling, she began to inch up from the log.

Too slow. Too late.

She did not see, only sensed the shadow dropping down towards her from the branches above, but all she had time to do was huddle and cover her head.

But Errance had already reached her, yanking her forward and away even as he thrust himself upon that which pounced. She tumbled into the ground and moss, thrashing in panic to find footing. By the time she scrambled up and turned around, Errance and their assailant struggled upon the ground in locked battle.

It was the shard, Daran's shard. She had no way to be sure it was the same one, but it was only one she had ever seen.

She screamed in terror, shock, anger, alarm. Only a second after did she fear the sound would draw any other of Daran's men nearer, but surely if the shard was here, the others were not far behind. Swinging about, she looked for a tree limb, anything she might use in combat, but before anything could be reached, a terrible shriek sounded just behind.

She spun and saw the two wrenching apart, the shard scrambling along the ground, and Errance thrusting himself up on one knee. Blood ran in rivulets down the prince's face and neck, but his grip on the elven sword adjusted and found control. He swung the blade high above his head and it blazed in a shooting star as it arced down.

Tellie forgot to close her eyes. She flinched instead as the sword drove into the shard's chest and into the ground beneath. But there wasn't any blood. The ghostly flicker in the monster's eyes winked out, and wisps of darkness curled out of its shadowed sockets and sagging maw.

Errance staggered up, swiping his shaking hand across his brow, which only smeared the scarlet across his too pale face. He lurched toward her and seized her shoulders. "You listen to me," he snarled. "You are going to run until you out of this forest and in the open where The Daisha can see you. She's our only chance."

"Shouldn't we hide?" she whimpered. "The Daisha can't carry all four of us, can she?"

"She will have to. Now run and do not stop. Do you hear me?" He gave her a hard, short shake. "Don't. Stop."

Birds exploded out of a nearby bush, squawking in dismay. A dark figure rose behind the brush. Another of Daran's men. He didn't leap to attack, but stepped forward to test whether they'd run or fight.

Pivoting with deadly grace, Errance faced the awaiting foe, holding the blade loose at his thigh. "Go," he said with the authority of a commander, a king.

Tellie stared at their enemy, head spinning. The shard was dead, here was one man, but where were the others? Why weren't they attacking all at once? "You…you will be coming after me?"

"I said, GO!"

Her trance of fear shattered into splinters of glass. She leapt into flight, racing away from the clearing, setting all her will on escaping the forest. She forced herself to ignore the ring of steel clashing behind her. Find The Daisha. Find The Daisha. Find The Daisha. The trees and ground blurred out of focus. When she tripped on a root or rock, she simply got up again and kept running.

Branches tore, stone crumbled. She scrambled down ditches and up cliffs.

Then another man leapt out in front of her. With a scream, Tellie dashed to the side, falling into a gully. Rocks scattering before her feet, she slid down and jumped for the opposite side. A heavy figure landed right beneath her and grabbed her ankle. Twisting, she jabbed her other foot at the attacker's face, and his hand swiped to grab it as well.

A dark blur caught the upper rim of her eye, and she looked up in a wrench of fear, but it was Errance. Her attacker, perhaps glimpsing the sudden relief upon her face, let go and spun to face the elf. Tellie seized the moment and kicked the back of his head. It was not much of a kick, but enough to send him a surprised step forward and out of control.

Errance leapt, knee thudding into the man's upper chest, knocking them both against the gully's side. His elbow smacked aside a grasp at his neck, and then the blade of Aselvia sliced deep and true.

Tellie sank against the bank, chest burning for breath, but Errance hauled her up again.

"Keep moving," he said, his own breath unsteady, and she feared that he might be wounded, but a quick glance did not tell nor could she look any further. Keep running. The end of the forest could not be far now. Out on the hills, they would be visible and surely they would see The Daisha up in the clear sky. Perhaps their friends were already alert to the danger and coming as fast as possible.

Three men were accounted for, Tellie realized in a distant corner of her mind. That left Daran and one other. Why had they spread out? Why were they attacking her when they wanted Errance?

If she'd stopped to consider this, she might have come up with the answer and insisted on staying by Errance's side instead of taking a longer lead.

If she had stopped, she wouldn't have turned around the large boulder barring the way and run straight into the arms of one of the hunters. Before she could scream, before she could wrench away, a hand clamped over her mouth and an arm pinned her own to her sides. She stiffened, disbelief jarring every sense within her.

"Finally," Daran's voice muttered from somewhere nearby. The man holding her jerked off her feet and carried her several yards back from the rock. The arm around her body released for one brief moment, but only to draw a knife and hold it against her throat.

No. No, no, no.

Errance came around the corner. And saw her. Saw them. He skidded to a halt, eyes flaring.

"That's right," Daran said, saturated in smugness. He left his sword hanging by his side, standing with supreme confidence. "Don't take a step closer or she's dead."

Errance's eyes narrowed to slits, snapping back and forth to Daran and to the man holding Tellie captive. The hand gripping his sword tightened till the knuckles turned pure white and every vein stretched against skin.

"You ran her right into our little trap," Daran taunted. "How noble of you. I hope you're decent enough to let her live. Put down your weapon, and we'll spare her."

Errance took one small step forward, and the man holding Tellie dragged her several steps back. And then he at last looked at her.

Their eyes locked, and she shuddered to see that not a single veil concealed his spirit. The pain and sorrow in those eyes was raw, swiftly turning red. She realized then that she had never known for certain if he cared for her even really liked her. But now she knew. She knew that love was his deepest core, that it had driven him to refuse freedom for years. And with that same love he would give up that freedom to see her live.

NO! Fury roared to life inside her veins. She threw herself back, then forwards against her captor's grip. She felt the knife blade nick her throat, but she knew that only came from the struggle. The hunters wouldn't dare kill her if they didn't want Errance upon them. She needed to scream for The Daisha, praying she was near enough to hear. She bit the hand over her mouth. She knew that if she could break free, Errance would spring and save her. Savagely, she gave another twist and felt her captor's hold slacken.

Something hard slammed into the side of her head, and lights exploded in front of her vision. *Perhaps Ayeshune has come to save us*, she briefly hoped.

Instead, darkness fell.

For a terrible moment, Daran watched all his ambition teeter on the point of a knife. He knew that if the girl broke free, the elf would be upon them and chances of outmatching him were slim. Yet he could not take a step to help his man restrain the wench because that too would expose them to attack. So he stood tense and watched, sweat beading on his brow.

The knife knocked against the girl's temple, and her eyes crossed and then fluttered shut. Her body went limp as a broken dove.

The thrill of success returned in a heady wash. Daran exhaled with a muttered curse and set all his focus on the elf. He'd heard the surest way to capture the Prisoner was by threat of other life and so far it proved true. "Drop that sword," he snarled, "and get over here."

The sword fell with a light thump upon the earth. The elf's steps to him were slow but steady. The instant Daran touched him, the thrill of success traded place with terror of failure. He jerked the elf to him, whipping corded rope around his wrists with shaking hands. Finishing, he breathed again and turned his head toward the forest.

"Kilkus! Narg! Hurry it up, Blath, we caught the vermin," he hollered.

Nothing but the rustle of leaves answered.

"They're dead."

Daran's hand tightened on the elf's arm, and he stepped to the side to get a better look at his prisoner's vacant face. "What?" he demanded, skin crawling at the north cold chill in the prisoner's tone.

"I killed them," the Prisoner said.

Whirling around, Daran looked at the elf's sword that he had thrown aside. Blood and dark shadow stained its blade. Kilkus—the monster, the chema, the friend—gone for good. Narg and Blath had been a dependable sort, good in a pinch or for a pint. And here stood this pointy-eared beast announcing their deaths as he might have mentioned the time of day. Daran's shock erupted into fury.

"You ghoul!" he snarled. He drove his fist into the prisoner's stomach, and as the elf doubled over, he slammed an elbow down between his shoulder blades, dropping him the ground. "I was required to bring you back alive— nothing more!" He drew back his foot to kick, but he paused, because the prisoner's shoulders were shaking, and a strange noise rattled in his throat.

"Are you crying?" Daran asked in disbelief. So much for the unbroken legend.

The elf turned his head so that his cheek rested against the dirt. He was laughing. "Pain," he gasped. "How I've missed it." He collapsed into another breathy spurt of laughter.

Cold, clammy fingers touched Daran's spine. Was the elf mad? Surely so, but he had never expected the madness to manifest in such a strange and…terrifying way. Terror. No. No. The tickle of cold quickened, turning into a tongue of fire. The fire burst into rage, white-hot hatred. He would not be intimidated by his own prisoner! This was his moment of triumph, of truth, and for once he would show he was master!

He delivered the kick with savage force.

Errance struck.

The elf prince rolled to the side with the speed of a snake and the strength of a lion, knocking Daran's feet out from under him. He kept rolling till he reached the sword and then looped his wrists around the blade and severed the bonds with a jerk. Launching up, sword in hand, he whirled back to where Daran attempted to stand and threw himself on the man's back. His knees pinned the man's arms to the ground, and he slid the sword under Daran's neck.

Grunting for air, Daran began to struggle, but he froze when the blade bit keenly into skin. Panic numbed his limbs. It could not end like this. Not after everything.

The other hunter had taken several paces back, dragging Tellie's body with him, his knife still at her neck. His eyes were wide in his pale face, but his body was coiled to strike. "You kill Daran and she's dead!"

"Kill her and you are both dead," Errance snarled.

Silent, they eyed another, weighing their own threats. The man pulled Tellie tighter and Errance ground Daran deeper into the dirt.

Flecks of earth caught in Daran's eye, and he wrenched his head about till he could lay it sideways. Every dreadful oath he willed upon the entire race of elves. "You can't win this one, boy," he spat. "We may not be able to kill the girl if we want to live, but we can maim her until you submit. Lorm, take her eyes if he doesn't drop this sword in ten."

The sword bit harder to his throat, the hand holding it trembling. "Anything you do to her will be done to you tenfold!"

The truth of the threat turned Daran's bones cold, and his heart faltered. Had he not heard the legends of his prisoner, how he could kill even with both hands chained above his head? Was there any method of torture the elf did not intimately know? But no, Daran would not be threatened by his own prey.

"Do it," he growled, teeth baring. "But vengeance isn't going to heal that girl. You want to be responsible for her blindness...the scars across her fresh little face..."

It was a gamble. A dreadful gamble playing on a heart this prisoner should not even have.

And it worked.

With a gasped curse, Errance dropped the sword. He rocked off Daran's back and bowed over his knee, hands digging into the dirt.

Daran pushed upright and found the rope again. But he had not taken so much as a step toward the elf, when Errance said, "You have the girl. That's enough of a chain."

No, it wasn't. It was a chain as long they didn't let their guard down for even a second. Daran knew the risk was high and so did this elf. Yet this was not the time to argue. There was no telling when that strange flying creature would return.

Grinding his teeth, he tucked the rope away. "You realize if you try to escape the girl is of no use to us."

Errance swallowed. "Yes."

Nervously glancing at his accomplice, Daran sidled to the elf's side. He took his arm again and pulled him up, shoving in the direction of the deeper forest.

For a moment, Errance did not respond. His eyes flickered to Tellie one last time and then the blue sky peeking between the boughs. And then his shoulders sagged, and he walked where his captors willed.

oOo

As the sun began to set and shadows blanketed the forest floor, The Daisha soared back into the clearing with much groaning and griping.

"It wasn't that bad, was it?" Kelm said with a laugh. His skin still shone several shades paler than normal and his hands shook, but the grin would not leave his face. Flying. Incredible—more incredible than he could have ever dreamed.

"My wings are wilting!" The Daisha snapped. "When I die of exhaustion, I hope you're satisfied!"

"Oh, enough of your griping," Tryss said, swatting her playfully. "You enjoyed every minute of it or else you wouldn't have given us so much time." She slipped to the ground as soon as they landed and swept towards the glade where they had left the others, calling, "Sorry we took so long!"

"I sure hope they've got a fire going," Kelm said, shivering.

"No smoke scent. They must want me to freeze to death," The Daisha complained, extending neck high into the air and drawing a long sniff. Her nostrils flared and her body went rigid. "Tryss," she said voice low and alarmed. "Tryss, come back—"

There was a sharp cry, muffled, horrified.

Gasping, Kelm rushed after Tryss, The Daisha overtaking him with a single bound. But Tryss was already racing back towards them, eyes wild. "They're not there," she panted. "They're not there, and that creature is!"

"What creature?" Kelm and The Daisha demanded at once, shoving forward.

"No, Kelm, don't look," Tryss exclaimed, grabbing him. But it was too late. He stared down at a stiff, grey body scantily clad in dark armor, fingers tipped with claws, and hideous face contorted so that the fangs were clenched in a leer. It had no eyes anymore. Just empty sockets.

"Is that…isn't that that thing?" Kelm whispered. He tried to bend in for a better look, but Tryss pulled him away.

"A shard." The Daisha poked the body in disgust.

"It's not just any shard," Tryss whispered. "That is the one from the band pursuing us. Daran found us. Tellie and Errance must be hiding."

"Or they got caught," Kelm said shakily.

"Don't! They have to be nearby. The Daisha, what can you smell?"

"Dead blood," The Daisha said, moving over into the brush and pawing a body free of brambles. "Another of your enemies, I take it. My elf kills cleanly."

She sniffed again, and after a few tense moments, her eyes flew wide. "Both of you, quick, onto my back!" As soon as they leapt on, she bolted from the ground with speed unlike any yet experienced. Her body sped like an arrow over the forest top, wings slashing the air. When she dove back to the ground, they were nearly unseated at the hard landing.

"Sorcery!" The Daisha cried. "The foulest stench of all!"

Kelm stared at the circle burnt black into the earth's surface a little distance from them, smoke still rising from its lines. "What is it?" he whispered. But he already knew. He'd been blindfolded the last time he'd been near such a mark and so of course had never seen it. But the tremor in the air shook his bones in the exact same way.

"A Nyght portal," The Daisha growled. "They have been taken back into Darkness."

29

oOo

Wind sings a sad and cold lullaby. The sound of it shivers the soul and awakens the senses.

As the song grew louder in Tellie's ears, her consciousness uncurled and began to reach out in the darkness. Her body ached from lying in an arched position over a hard ridge that swayed and jerked. By instinct she began to struggle, but a dart of pain stabbed through her head, and she stopped in bewilderment. Something had happened, something terrible, but it was hard to think through the pain splintering her brain. Holding her breath, she opened her eyes. All she saw was the ground passing underneath her. She was being carried on someone's shoulders like a sack of feed. How humiliating! Once again, she started to squirm.

"Well, well, that didn't take long," a voice growled. "You should have hit her harder."

"Never mind that," said the voice of the man who was carrying her. "She's heavy anyways." He roughly slid her off his shoulder, grabbing her arms before she could start hitting him.

Oh, she remembered everything now in all its dreadful clarity. She glared at her captor, hating his dark, beady eyes, hating the stubble on his jaw and neck, hating the scar on his chin. Some paces away Errance stood resolutely still, Daran just behind him. But where were they? How long had she been unconscious? Last she knew they had been in a grove of trees, but now—she craned her head, wincing at the pain, and saw jagged cliffs rising up all around.

"Lost, little girlie?" the man said, shoving his repulsive face far too close to hers. She thought to slap him, but he'd already straightened. "We're back home sweet home."

No. Tellie's heart and stomach plunged in a sickening drop. How could they have returned to Tertorem so quickly? Unless…they used a portal. Again. Just like that, all the effort of the last few days, the weary but satisfying journey—it washed away in a torrent of despair.

Her captor's hand prodded her shoulder, and she stumbled forward, reality shriveling her spirit. What had been the point of everything if it had just led back to here? The sky was gone, forest and rivers were gone, Tryss and Kelm and The Daisha were gone. Instead she walked with enemies in a matrix of sharp stone, and when they reached the end of the path, they stood on a ridge overlooking a desert of ash and bone.

She realized she had never seen more of Tertorem than the dark interior. But now, as she looked across the deathscape, her gaze drew to something nearer to them, something so frightful, her eye had refused to acknowledge its presence.

It rose from the roots of the mountains like a crown of death, sharp spires piercing the roiling clouds above its savage triumph. It seemed chiseled out of the very stone, few doors and windows glaring with squinting eyes down on the land as if it scorned the sight. A true castle of horror, like no other. But most terrible of all was the Nyght, floating above in defiance of mortal comprehension.

She had never seen it before, this sphere suspended between the tallest spires, which was said to contain the very essence of the Darkness himself. Now as she looked upon its remorseless ebony surface, she knew she looked upon the death of every dream, beauty, and hope that had and would ever exist in this hopeless, cruel world.

She wanted to cry. And then she wondered what good that would do. None. So there was no point at all.

Every fear and reverence filled Daran's soul, pushing out breath, as he beheld the edifice of Tertorem again. The terrible awe never failed to stun him, the terrible desire never failed to stir. A tremble shook his body and a laugh stirred deep in his belly. He had done it! He had brought back the Prisoner, according to the command. He would be forever remembered and glorified in all the eternal reign of the Darkness. Perhaps he would become the next warden of Tertorem! Perhaps in time he would be second only to the Voice himself!

His eye wavered from the prison to the Prisoner, and elation turned to disgust. There that elf stood, eyes glazed and body lifeless…and unbound. To think that he had actually allowed such a thing. Arrogance restored, Daran reached out and jerked the Prisoner close, looping a cord around his wrists and tightening till the skin turned white. Shoving him aside, he turned next to the pale little girl.

Grabbing the roots of her hair, he twisted her head up to look at him. "Enjoying the view, pretty?"

"Let go of her," the elf said. Quietly. Without looking at them.

Scowling, Daran straightened and stared. The Prisoner had an endless supply of nerve. "Watch it, scum. You're in my territory now."

The Prisoner looked at him, his calm expression gently disturbing. "I've been here since before your parents were born. I *said*, let go of her."

A chill of lifeless fingers pattered across Daran's shoulders. He shuddered involuntarily and turned away, releasing the girl. "Forward," he growled. "The Darkness waits for his prize."

The march down the death-ridden mountain felt far longer to Tellie than their entire journey of several days past. Sharp shards sliced at her boots, and in no time the leather began to peel away, causing her to wince with each step. A thick, choking film lined every breath. Every so often, they passed a few bones scattered amongst the shale. Once, they came upon a decaying body of some poor prisoner, left where it had dropped dead. Her stomach turned at the sight, and she looked away.

On the slopes of the encircling mountains, she saw paths strung with dark figures leading up to gaping tunnels. Mining work, she supposed dully, such as that at which Errance had once toiled. Was there any point to it besides spirit-breaking labor?

Though the journey was long, they reached the foot of the fortress all too soon. Passing through cowering sheds and shacks of sagging wood, they came to a stair and then up and up they climbed, following its zigzag pattern till they were high above the plain. Tellie's legs burned with agony from the strain of the ceaseless climbing, and it took all her will not to scream and sob in frustration.

When she could, she glanced behind at Errance, trying to guess how he fared. He marched up the steep stairs without apparent effort, even while his captor labored after him. His head was erect, his shoulders straight, and his gaze level. Truly, he carried himself like a king.

King.

The moon medallion, still concealed underneath the collar of her dress, became unbearably heavy. He would never wear it. He would never return to Aselvia.

Neither would she. The pain of that realization stung sharp. For some time now, stronger than she realized, she had counted on Aselvia being her home. She'd counted on Leoren and Casara still being open to her. That she could finally learn what it really meant to be part of a family, loved and wanted. She'd counted on her dreams coming true.

No longer.

Deep within Tertorem, at the very heart—if such a place could hold a heart—waited the throne room and he who sat on the throne. The chamber had changed since the warden's rule, turning from a simple room of stone to something...else. The hall was longer now, the sides closer. Pillars stood at intervals against the sides and the surfaces between sometimes seemed to be walls or sometimes looked like halls leading away or else looked like windows peering into the fathoms of the dungeons. There were no torches anymore, just an eerie and still half-light. Despite the tightness of the hall, a sense of vastness pressed down upon anyone standing inside and if they dared to look up, they would know why, for the ceiling could not be seen. Above, there was only a far-reaching blackness.

The throne itself was no longer a basic stone chair, but an artifact of broken shards and bones melted together. And on it sat the devil himself, the Voice of the Darkness. His hair drifted now and then as if touched by a breeze, though not a puff of air stirred the corpse-cold chamber.

A poisonous fire kindled in the shadow of his eye as Daran and a set of guards pushed Errance and Tellie through the entrance onto the slick hall floor. A savage hunger flitted across his face, a desire for nothing more than to spring and tear them apart. But he smiled instead.

"My lord," the Voice said, rising and raising his arms, cloak cascading down his back. He rushed forward and swooped into a deep bow at his prisoner's feet. "King of Aselvia, you grace me with your presence." When he looked up, his ink black eyes laughed.

Errance winced and looked away. "Was it real?"

"What, did you think I fabricated it? Of course it was real," the Voice assured, knowing that reality of his journey, now snatched away, would be a far more devastating truth.

The life in Errance's eyes was only a faint and quiet flicker. "How did you find me?" he asked softly.

"Find you? Oh, come now. Were you ever far away, dear child?" Chuckling to himself, he took an appraising step back. "I pray your little stroll about the world enlightened you. I can see it most certainly did your health well." He came close and cupped Errance's face in his hands, tilting it this way and that like an artist inspecting his most prized sculpture. "In that short time, you nearly returned to the height of elven beauty and strength. One would barely know your previous state except for those little *deltha* tattoos through your eye."

Without warning, his hands dropped to Errance's neck, seized the collar, and ripped the shirt open. Errance staggered forward at the violence of the action, but the Voice steadied him with a hand. "Oh yes," the demon said, tapping a finger on the Prisoner's chest. "There's this mark too. I hope you didn't forget it."

Tellie stared, appalled. What the Voice said about his health was true, she had not really noticed how vast the change was until she saw Errance here in only days since he'd last stood in the same place. His starving body had filled out, the muscles nourished, the skin calmed. A body of perfection... except...except for those dark etchings scrawled into his chest. She *had* forgotten. But Errance had not. Not with every breath that strained the skin still raw and red around the words and symbol burned into him.

She took a step forward. Though no concrete plan had formed in her mind, she knew with upmost conviction that she could not stand by and watch the demon torment him. Had she not walked in the Unseen and driven the Darkness from Errance's dreams time and time again?

But as she stepped forward, she felt a ribbon of the Voice's consciousness flick towards her. And she stopped dead in her tracks.

After all, she was just a small girl. These were not dreams. Just a cruel reality. She had no place in this story, the dealings of darkness and high immortals were all beyond her, and she was just a mistake that should cower in the corner because in the end she could make no difference. The thoughts swarmed in, perhaps not fully her own, but still in control. The shadows embraced her as she slipped back.

"You have a choice, my prince," the Voice purred, his tone as smooth and compelling as silk. "If you aren't careful, I might be persuaded by some of my friends to return to you to them."

The threat struck true. The final shred of color fled from the prince's face, and shuddering, he bent his head down between his shoulders.

The Voice gave a friendly laugh and patted Errance on the cheek as if he was reprimanding a child for being afraid of a harmless thing. "I understand. Those wretched demons of mine are so difficult to control. But I'm here now, and we can speak reasonably. Just because you're back in...well, hell...it doesn't mean your former treatment has to continue. All I ever wanted is for you to read a book. Is that so hard?"

The elf tensed, ready to reply, but the Voice halted him with a hand. "Ta, ta—wait. I know how this goes. How it's always gone. And I'm getting a bit tired of repetitive scenes, aren't you? I want you to think this through very calmly. You've had time to grow calm, yes? A little walk out in natures does wonders for a soul. So think—to read the Moonscript, you must return home. Your most cherished dream, home. So determined to leave it as a youth, so determined to return now. Ah, but that does not matter. If that is your wish, who am I to deny you? So home you go. You could stay there indefinitely after you tell me everything that is in the Moonscript, because you are now king. I would not stop you, I would not care."

He strolled over to a table that may or may not have been present before and took up a pitcher, pouring water into two glasses. The water twinkled in a song of silver stars. The Voice took a swallow with an appreciative sigh and then he held out the other glass to Errance.

Errance ignored it.

Eyes narrowing, the Voice grabbed the prince's jaw in one hand and squeezed his fingers tight into the hollows of his bone. The second he pried Errance's mouth open, he poured the glass's content inside. Before it could be spit back out, he clamped his prisoner's mouth and nostrils shut. For a long while, much longer than one would have thought was possible, Errance held the liquid in his mouth, and the Voice began to hum a jaunty little tune as he waited. Then the elf's shoulders and stomach started to tremble with desperation for breath, and at last his throat convulsed in a hard swallow.

The Voice released him, all pleasant smiles again. "There, see? It was just water. The only harm done was that which you gave yourself by being so stubborn. All I wanted to do was help you, and you refused without my insistence. That's what this really is all about. Now I know you have refused to read the Moonscript for so long because you believe the Higher World must be separated from the Lower, but that is honestly wrong!"

He swept into his throne, throwing out a hand. "I mean, really, how unfair. The celestial elves should not be treated with such favoritism. A perfect world, bah. The people in the Lower World have more trials so they are the ones who should have more privileges. And anyway, trials have proven to build character and birth wisdom. The more you experience, the more powerful you are. You know this. Why should the celestial elves be kept in ignorance? You act as if these elves would lead horrid lives if they were exposed to this world. How so? Your people in Aselvia live in beauty and grace, though you call this world broken. Why should the celestials be made so separate? Is it not imbalanced? I want walls torn down. I want everyone to be made equal and given what is due. Don't you see, Errance? Can't you see it clearly?"

Tellie hunkered in the dark corner of the room and the longer she listened, the faster her head spun on the end of a string. How right the Voice was! What a shame it had been that there had been such a misunderstanding all this time. The Voice wanted to be fair; he wanted to create equality for all.

Errance's voice, cold and clear, cut through her ensorcelled thoughts like sharpened steel. "Yes, I can see it, Voice. If I reveal the secrets of the Moonscript, and if you are able to penetrate the celestial shield, then the elves therein will suddenly and brutally be exposed to your evil. Do not pretend you'll strip their protection and then leave them alone. You will attack, and they, a people of peace and not of war, will be defenseless before you. The elves of Aselvia will come to aid them, and there will be a terrible war where thousands will die. If they manage to drive you off, you'll simply retreat into darkness, dragging hundreds of prisoners with you. Captive elves, Celestial and Aselvian, to be tortured at the indulgence of your demons. My own horror story—played out in hundreds of fresh lives. You think I have had seventy years to change my mind? I have had seventy years to realize why I cannot! I'll never read the Moonscript and your plan will never succeed." Out of breath, Errance lifted his face and looked the Voice directly in the eyes. "Not on my life."

"Not on your life, perhaps," he conceded. With fluid grace, he spun and strode over to Tellie before she realized that the inevitable was happening. Her heart leapt as his hand came to rest on the top of her head.

"Not on your life, but what about hers?"

Errance went as pale as the moon itself, a tremor running through his body. "There is nothing I can do to save her," he said in a low voice.

"Are you quite sure?"

The elf's eyes glinted. "The lives of others are not mine to bargain with."

"Of course they are," he snapped. "You're the king, that's what a king does."

"A king," Errance said, slowly and steadily, "protects his own."

"Is that what your father told you?" The Voice's face contorted into a snarl and he lunged forward. Grabbing Errance's hair, he wrenched his head back to look up at eternal darkness above. "Your father is dead," he hissed in his ear. "It's time to make your own path."

Breathing hard, Errance closed his eyes. "The only life I can offer," he whispered, "is my own...to do whatever you wish with it."

The Voice threw back his own head and laughed. "But Your Majesty, we've already done everything we've wished with it."

Grimacing, Errance forced the next words out as if they tore out his soul with them. "There are those who would take pleasure in the fact that I offer myself freely."

Smile frozen on face, the Voice spoke through clenched teeth. "But we're not talking about their pleasure, are we? We're talking about mine. And the only thing that would please me is if you read the Moonscript."

"Well, I WON'T!" Errance shouted. "Torture me to the end of my days, kill all my friends, ruin the world, I don't CARE! I shall *never* reveal the secrets of the Moonscript to you!"

Tellie gasped and looked up in terror at the Voice. Whatever fury those words ignited would be unleashed on her. Couldn't Errance at least attempt to save her, wasn't she worth the effort?

The thought bit her conscience an instant thereafter. He had attempted, offered a sacrifice of himself that was surely far more terrible than she could know. And he could do no more because that was their reality. They were both doomed already so why bring the celestials into it? Even if an exchange could be made, was she truly so selfish a person as to want her life over thousands of others? She had seen it from afar...the miraculous beauty of the Higher World, so should she not feel a great conviction to keep it safe?

Impending loss hung in Errance's eyes, and she would not strengthen its agony any more. She'd be courageous in death. Heroic, even.

She wondered if all heroes trembled so violently.

But the Voice cast not a glance her way. That smile remained fixed on his face, growing more awful with every second. His breath hissed out between his teeth in ashen smoke. "Yes," he whispered. "Yes, I believe you. Nothing will change your mind, will it? You have driven my Darkness to his wit's end." He heaved a pathetic sigh and smoothed a hand down his face like a man who has given up on an age-old dream.

Frowning, Errance stepped back, sensing a trap.

The Voice cocked his head as if listening to something and then gave a decisive nod. "And so, I am afraid that if you will not give me your gift...then I must take it from you."

Errance's expression sickened, and he swallowed hard, but he tilted up his chin and spoke without waver. "Others have tried that before and their efforts failed. My light cannot be found in my body nor can it be consumed."

The demon's eyes turned back to him first, rolling with dark glee. "Oh, Your Majesty. Yes, it is not in your flesh, in your blood, or even in your mind. No, it is something deeper. Something woven into the very fabric of self. It is a part of *you*." His teeth bared in a carnivorous grin. "And you, precious, are MINE."

He lunged, hand out-stretched like the jaws of a striking snake, caught Errance's throat and slammed him to the wall. The prince choked and struggled as he was lifted off the ground, clawing uselessly at the arm that held him.

"I gave you," the Voice hissed, "every opportunity to come to me willingly. I have suspended this so that you may survive. But now you will learn my power. Fool! Have you not known until now who I am?"

The pupils of his eyes pooled out, clouding like ink in water. Veins rose black and thick under his skin, and then darkness began to bleed from his being, spiraling in tendrils of wind. The ribbons of darkness whirled without focus for one moment, then turned to the prisoner pressed against the wall. They darted forward and vanished into Errance at his heart, and the brand burned there flared in shadow. Something like smoke could be seen curling under Errance's skin, spreading out in ravished hunger.

Not a single cry escaped Errance's lips, but his eyes were squeezed shut and his mouth stretched open in soundless agony. Such a dreadful silence it was, broken only by an infrequent gasp of desperate breath and a deep, underlying thrum.

Tellie stood rooted where the Voice had left her, staring in disbelief and horror. She did not know for certain what was happening, but it was surely a war of will. And as Errance's body became slick with sweat, she feared it was a war he would lose. She had to do something, small and useless or not, she had to stop this!

Not one guard moved to stop her as she sprang forward, for they were all cowering in the corner in awe of their terrible master. She did not know what she would do when she reached the Voice, only that she must distract him, and if that required ripping off his cloak or climbing atop his head, then she would do it.

She slammed into a wall.

Reeling backwards, hand to face, she stared in confusion at the path ahead. Not a single barrier could be seen and when she stretched out a hand, she met no glass or anything solid. But the second she tried to step through, resistance met her with solid force.

There are some places where both the mortal world and the Unseen become nearly one. Rendar's words floated back into memory. Tertorem…of course this would be such a place. And if the veil between here and the Unseen was so very thin...

Closing her eyes, Tellie willed herself to feel other forces, other threads of reality, weaving invisible around her. Surely here where they converged so strongly, she might slip through.

She felt a loosening, a thrill akin to dropping a heavy burden. She felt as lightweight as a feather, and she didn't even notice how carelessly she let her body fall to the ground behind her.

Eagerly, she leapt towards the Voice, then paused. She was forgetting all the lessons Rendar had taught her. Combat darkness with its opposite, drive it back with light. She thought of every pure beauty she knew, of every love that lasted, of every hope that shone. Delicately, she probed her mind forward towards the Voice, determining to stand between his power and Errance—

An abysmal force snatched hold of her mind and sucked in like a vortex consuming all that drew near it. She tried to dig into anything beyond his reach, but the terrible presence filled the entire room in choking smoke. She could feel her own body aching from the strain of her spirit, and she sensed life draining out of her as if her throat had been slit.

No. No, she had to be strong; she had to free Errance from this terrible, consuming power. Dizzy with racking pain, she struggled forward, but something grabbed her and pulled her back. The maelstrom of darkness stuck to her like glue, and she screamed as she was jerked out of it.

"Tellie!" a voice cried.

She writhed in the stranger's grasp before realizing the voice was not unknown. Opening her vision to the world again, she stared up at Rendar. Relief pulsed through her. "Rendar!" she gasped. Light as a feather, she clung to him in fear of blowing away altogether. "You're here. We—we can do it together. We can defeat the Voice—he must be stopped."

He took her shoulders with such firmness, she stared up at him in surprise. "No, Tellie," he said.

She blinked, unbelieving. "What?"

368

The pain in his eyes was that of an open, bleeding wound, but he shook his head.

She wrenched against his hold. "No! No, Errance is hurting, we've got to stop the Voice."

"Not this time, Tellie. This is beyond you. This is beyond me. We cannot help."

"I can do this!"

"Not this time," Rendar shouted. "You must not put yourself in this! You are barred from the Unseen."

Rendar vanished. Tellie found herself lying on the ground, the stone stretching out before her eyes in a grey, cracked plain. Her head ached abominably from where it had struck the ground. She pushed herself up to her hands and knees, arms chaffed and burning. But she fell back to the ground an instant later.

For Errance screamed.

A raw, anguished cry pulled from his stomach by a hook. It was a sound like that of something ripping, on the verge of giving way and toppling ruin. His body arched against the wall, trying to escape the darkness coiling within him.

And then suddenly the Voice let go, and the black ribbons withdrew into their master. Errance dropped to the ground with a thud. Choking on pain and blood, he doubled against the wall as if he could hide in it.

The Voice, skin grotesquely stretched over his skull, wheeled away with a savage roar. "Take him away!" he barked at the guards. "Take him and the girl and lock them back in their cell!"

The guards remained rooted in horror so before they could snap back to themselves, Tellie forced herself to her feet and ran to Errance's side. This time, no wall barred the way, and she fell to her knees beside him.

His quivering skin shone sickly pale and changed from white to green to blue in moments, and when she brushed aside his slick hair to see his face, dark veins bulged out on his temple and brow. "Er-Errance?" she whispered, softly touching his arm but he jerked away.

The guards came then, roughly taking him up, and another seized her by the shoulders. She submitted without a sound for she saw that they were bringing her wherever they took him and that was what she needed—a chance to be with him alone.

So close! So close and yet still too dangerous! The Voice of His Darkness prowled in the hall, breath whistling between his teeth like wind through a cracked window. He spun and stalked to the throne, slamming into it with such force that a less study seat might have broken. Seventy whole years had not been without its purpose. For the allotted time, he would have patience. But that time was over, and his patience withered. From the beginning he had known that if the prince could not be coerced, another possibility existed. A chance he'd lingered in using for its risk was high.

Everything about a person could be found knitted in their spirit, and somewhere in the Prisoner's complex fabric hid his celestial light and the power it wielded. But one cannot reach in and rip something out without damaging everything around it. The Voice knew well that the act would destroy the elf prince—a pity, but an acceptable one—but it also could possibly destroy the power as well. And if that was lost…all would be over.

The prince's grasp on his gift was still too strong. The Voice ground his lip between his teeth, calculating. As he'd said, any one of His Darkness's demons would eagerly return to the care of the Prisoner, and that certainly could lower Errance's morale…but it was all so repetitive. He needed something new, and while he thought of it, he needed Errance kept in discouragement and exhaustion and that meant…

The slightest movement drew his eye to the source with a snap, pinning Daran to his place like a fly on a needle. The man blanched under the hellish glare, raising a hand to his face in futile defense.

"You."

"Your Lordship?"

Tilting his head, the Voice steepled his fingers to his lips. "My hunter who brought in the prey. But you never had your chance to break the legendary unbreakable Prisoner. He made you look quite the fool, I imagine. They all do, don't they? The strong, the beautiful, the fortunate…how they lord it over the lesser and how you would love to grind them into the ground. You have your chance now. I don't care how brave that boy thinks himself. Pain wears everyone down. When I am ready to summon him again, I want him completely incapable of resisting."

So that he might uproot his power like a sprout from fresh soil. And as long as the gift could be gained, so what if the body died?

30

oOo

Ever since Tryss left, the chema village had been overcast with a spirit of fear and sadness. Fear of the shadow that stretched over their sunlit trees in the morning and sadness for the home they were pressed to flee from—the only home that many of them had ever known. And many missed Tryss, wondering if they had seen the last of their children's guardian eagle.

But no one expected Tryss to return so soon and in such a manner.

She came storming into the village on foot, accompanied only by the boy Kelm.

It was not the entrance she'd originally planned, at first only thinking to arrive as soon as possible and thus landing in the fire pit clearing on The Daisha. But The Daisha would hear none of that, insisting she would be shot and screamed at, and anyway, her appearance would only distract from their true plight.

It was amazing how fast The Daisha had flown and how quickly the ground they'd covered in days was eaten up in hours by the straight course of her wings. But it was still too long. Too long and too terrible. She was sick with horror, and poor Kelm looked ready to faint, so pasty grey was his skin.

The village children spotted them first and dashed throughout the village, shrieking the news of the arrival. In moments nearly all the folk were crowded around, crying out questions and greetings. But Tryss could hardly see them, could hardly feel them as more than gnats biting at her skin. She pushed her way through the tangle until she found her grandfather, the Ancient, who was the only one in the gathering who looked sad because he already saw what no one else did.

"They've been taken," she gasped. "Taken to Tertorem. I need to speak with the council."

An uneasy silence fell over the people as they understood this was not a happy return. One by one the council members stepped to the Ancient's side and looked with somber eyes upon her.

Somehow, even though her breath was still short and her mind lay in shattered fragments, she told them all and how it had ended. When she was through, tears pricked the back of her eyes, but she vowed to stay strong. "Please. I know we're not warriors. But we have to rescue them."

Throughout her speech, the elders had remained silent. Ominously so. She'd hoped the passion of her plea would rouse them so that they were nigh interrupting her to head off into battle, but instead they just stared and blinked with sorrowful eyes, even her father.

Sighing wearily, the Ancient stood. He came forward and took her hand. "My dear granddaughter," he said. "It is said that there is no way through those grey mountains, save by the Darkness's will."

"I don't believe it," she snapped. "There has to be some way. Are we not followers of Ayeshune? Are we not descended from the chemas of ice and cold who live in the North Mountains? Can we not become invisible in our surroundings?"

"What then, Tryss?" another elder asked. "If by some miracle, we did pass through the ring of mountains, what would we do next? We do not know the workings of that dark demesne."

"Kelm's been there."

"Outside the dungeons?"

The tears burst past her will and started rolling down her cheeks. "We have to do something!" she cried. "You all decided to help Errance before! Why, because he was the prince of Aselvia? Because he might be able to find us a new home? He is more than that, he is a friend and a person in desperate need. And Tellie, a child! How could you possibly stand by and let them remain in Tertorem?"

The Ancient pulled her shaking form into an embrace. Bowing to the other elders, he led her away from the mute, staring crowd. "Ah, my dear, tender one," he murmured. "If there was anything I could do, I would do it. Alas, this body fails me. But I cannot decide for the rest of the tribe. You have presented your plea to the council. They will discuss and weigh the cost of it."

"The men of our village must help," she said angrily. "Aren't two lives— even one—worth saving?"

"Do not judge them harshly," he soothed. "You must try to see it from their side. You ask for the lives of two at the cost of most our men. Without the men, our people will diminish and perhaps disband altogether. You ask for the lives of our entire village. And they believe it would be in vain."

Tryss stared at him, shaken. Slowly, she lowered her head and nodded. The decision of her tribe was not hers to make. She was responsible for her choice alone—and she knew the decision she had made.

oOo

The cell door clanged shut, shaking her bones. But the moment Tellie found her footing after being thrust into the cage, she spun back around and grabbed the bars. This was not how it would end; this was not the fate for her life. "You won't win!" she shouted. "You can't keep us here forever!"

The guards walked off, not paying her the slightest attention. Not that it mattered. She wasn't yelling at them anyways. She wasn't quite sure who she raged at. The Voice. The Darkness. Anybody who bothered to hear.

She slumped against the bars, strength bled out. For now, she was here. And Errance was here in the same cell, so that was all that need matter at this time.

His soft moan brought her around, and she was kneeling at his side the next instant, feeling for him in the pitch black. When she found his head and shoulders, he jerked back as if from branding irons.

Tucking her legs to the side, she leaned against the bars and tried to think over the thunder of her own beating heart. Strange that the guards had locked them in the same cell. They hadn't bothered to chain them either. The men were shaken, she supposed. But it could be more than that. A flicker of hope flared to life inside her. Perhaps they weren't so abandoned after all. "Are you with me, Errance?"

He didn't respond.

For all she knew he could have lapsed into unconsciousness. She touched him again, and this time he was still, only the faintest swell of his skin giving evidence of life.

"Come back," she whispered. "You're strong, stronger than them." She winced as she recalled the sight of him, white as death, collapsing to the floor. No, she would not think of that. She would think of his courage, of his determination.

But it was so hard to think of anything past this ever tightening prison, to remember what had been before. It seemed they had never left, that their great journey had only been a passing dream. Even the life that came before was ghostly, and all her dreams were waning. There had been a little stream she liked to visit in the wood, hadn't there? The cook at the orphanage had sometimes snuck her an apple tart. Oh, but it was so far away. And anything in the future was stolen away, her family, her beloved long-sought family—

No. She'd had a family. For a little while. Not only her parents who had loved her so much that they died for her sake. But these people who she had journeyed with, they'd become a family without her noticing until now.

"Do you know, Errance, I always dreamed of an older brother?" She held her breath, waiting for the slightest inclination that he'd heard her, but there was nothing. Gathering her nerve, she continued. "I always dreamed he was great and strong and would come to my rescue, chasing troubles away. He'd ride up to the inn, scornfully wave the Nornes aside, and then we'd set off on such adventures." She laughed. "I don't suppose the Nornes seem so terrible now. But the truth still is…that you're like that brother in so many ways. You've protected me again and again and led me on a path where only heroes tread. One thing you should know about this brother, just so you can live up to the role. He never gave up, no matter how hard things got." Her voice wavered. "So you can't either. Please, please, don't give up now."

Time inched by, and she paced about the cell, checking each bar and stone for weakness. At times it was easy to forget that Errance was with her in the surrounding cage. *I wish Tryss and Kelm were here with me*, she thought, not caring how selfish the wish was. *Tryss would know what comforting thing to say, and she would hold my hand. And Kelm wouldn't give up. He'd say something silly and make me laugh.* Things always look so much brighter when Kelm is around. He was always there for her, even when she hadn't wanted him. She wanted him here now. She wanted him by her side more than the entire world.

"Tellie…" Her name scraped out of a dry throat, but it sounded more beautiful than birdsong.

"Errance!" She dashed to his side, accidently jabbing a knee into his ribs.

"You…you are here?"

"Yes, yes, I'm here."

He muttered something into the ground that she didn't suppose she wanted to hear. Then he rasped, "He was in me. Clawing…shredding. In the very core of my being. He saw, he knew—everything. He was tearing me apart." His voice broke in panic, words running into each other in their terror.

"There now," she soothed. "He's not here anymore. We have a moment of respite. And we'll find another way out, I promise."

The shivering of his shoulders abruptly stopped. "No," he said.

"What?" She wondered what he'd thought she'd said to give such a response.

"There is no way of escape."

"I suppose you thought that before Kelm and I came. But we found a way."

"No," he said. "We didn't."

Chills ran down her spine. Perhaps he simply suffered from the same lie that had tried to ensnare her mind just minutes ago. The Voice had been meddling in his mind, after all. "Yes—we did."

"Then why are we back here?" His contempt slammed into her, solid as a ram.

Biting her lip, she stood. "Yes, we were caught again, but this isn't the end. If anything, we're stronger now than before."

"He'll be back," Errance muttered, almost talking to himself. "He'll be back, and I don't have the strength to resist him. Defending myself took all the strength I had. It's over."

"No, it's not!" She clenched her fists fiercely. "Ayeshune will help us."

Errance surged to his feet. She did not need to see him to feel the heat of the wrath that suddenly exploded within him. "*Ayeshune?*" he snarled. "Since when has he ever helped?"

Stunned, she backed away, her own anger dimming in the fear of the unexpected violence so close by. "You don't know that you're saying," she stammered. "Ayeshune cares."

"Ayeshune *cares?*" Errance shouted. "Oh yes, he cares! He cares about his glorious purpose, his greater good! And people like me are left to writhe in agony, screaming for deliverance, and does he care then? Does he? DOES HE?" Out of the darkness, he grabbed her by the shoulders and gave her a shake that rattled every bone in her body.

"Errance, let go!" she gasped. "Y-you're not yourself!"

"*Myself?* You know nothing of me! You have no *idea* what I've gone through! None of you do! It's over, I've lost, and there is nothing anyone can or will do! It's OVER!"

He let go as abruptly as he'd grabbed her, and as he stumbled across the cell he groaned and crashed to the floor with a heavy thump.

Shaking out of control, Tellie stumbled away and hit the wall. She slid down to the ground, tears running down her cheeks to drip from her quivering chin and onto her drawn up knees. It was not his fault. She repeated that to herself over and over. He was right; she had no understanding of his pain. And pain was what caused this, he had not meant to hurt her, he couldn't have.

What of his words about Ayeshune? Had he meant that? It was too terrible to be true. She had been held in the arms of the Almighty and she did not believe he could be the indifferent god Errance spoke of.

The cell bloomed into visibility about her—the stone, the bars, the body of Errance huddled in the corner. A form of light shimmered quite near, but she did not raise her head to look.

"I thought I was barred out," she said, a bit coldly.

"Only for that time," Rendar said. "Only so you did not destroy yourself."

She looked to Errance, mouth twisting. "But he was nearly destroyed. What will happen now? Is he going to recover?"

Rendar walked into her vision, coming to Errance's side. He knelt in a billow of robes, and it seemed that he gathered his son up in his arms, cradling head to his breast, though surely that would not be seen in mortal sight. "If given time," he whispered. "But the choice is ultimately his."

She leapt back up. "Then we'll give him that chance! So how do we get out? You know, don't you? Ayeshune knows!"

Rendar did not look up. "Escape is possible. But only for you. Errance cannot, will not go."

It was a reality she did not care to hear, not from Errance, not from Rendar. "He came with us before, why should now be any different?"

"Because now, he understands the truth."

"What truth?" Tears again filled her eyes, and the shining form became blurred.

Rendar's words were terribly quiet. So very still and soft they hardly seemed to come from his mouth at all. "He is a prisoner of His Darkness. And the only true prisoners of Tertorem are those owned not only in body, but also in soul."

"How can that be? Errance hates the Darkness more than anyone, and you raised him to follow the One Light!"

"Raised in it, yes," the elf king said sorrowfully. "But believed in it? Did he embrace it for himself, trust in the One? No. No, he was too independent and too

proud and...and...and—" His voice broke, and he huddled lower into the body of his son, shoulders beginning to shake.

Tellie stared, then took a tentative step forward. "Rendar...?"

His sob sent her skittering back like a young fawn. The great elven king, celestial, solemn, and wise was weeping, tears pouring from a loosened floodgate. Not merely tears, but a breathless wail that racked his entire body. She could only stare, eyes round and misty.

"*I—blame myself,*" he said through heaving breaths. "*When he was young, I sheltered him completely from the outer world, even as he grew into a man. I had wanted to give him the paradise lost in my youth, for why should he suffer for the sins of his forebearers? But when he persisted in the desire to see and know the rest of the world, I knew I could not keep him forever. But when I let him go, I did not see that this—this—would happen. I had not seen that in my effort to give him perfection I had blinded him from the need for salvation. What thought for God had he save that it be his father's religion? And when"—*his voice curled with disgust—*"has religion ever saved a soul?*"

"*This is a punishment then?*" she cried, blood turning to mountain lava. "*Yours, his?*"

"*Punishment?*" Rendar looked sharply up, tears fading away. "*Consequence. If one rejects the light, how can they help but be in darkness?*"

Looking down again, he stroked a hand along Errance's bruised brow. "*Tellie. If there was any way that I could have saved him, I would have done it. I led the forces of Aselvia in attack against Tertorem soon after Errance was taken, and though my people believed it was simply a strike back against the evil that had slain my son, I had a hope to rescue him.*"

She stared, then blinked. Blinked hard. "*You mean—you mean you* knew? *This entire time—all these seventy years—you've known where Errance has been? Rendar, how could you? He loves you so much! How could you just leave him?*"

Rendar's eyes snapped open. She took a step back, startled by how alike they were to Errance's in that moment. But behind the pain, anger, and sorrow swirling there, there was a calm assurance she could not comprehend. "It's time you understood," he said. He leaned forward and took her hand.

The next moment she felt the world rushing past, much like when they traveled to the brink of the celestial cleft. And then she found herself on a mountain peak overlooking the entire expanse of Tertorem, the razor sharp mountains, the solid walls. She looked at them, and she saw that they were a part of this world—the Unseen. "I don't understand," she stammered. "I thought the Unseen merely overlapped our world. But this..."

"That is how it is meant to be, Tellie. But the Darkness has grafted his kingdom to be one and the same. Tertorem may feel solid and strong, but it belongs to and so is bound by the rules of the Unseen. The Darkness cannot keep what does not belong to it. You were an orphan when you were first here, lost and alone. Now you are a child of the One. Its chains no longer apply to you and so you are free to leave."

She stared out at the decimated world, heart sinking. "And Errance..."

"For months, we held the mountains under siege, but could find no breach or pass. One elf fell while trying to scale a cliff. I only just reached him in time to save his broken body. I looked upon the sorrow of my people's faces who had already lost so many loved ones and now faced losing more, and I knew I could not spend their lives in folly. So we returned to Aselvia. I locked myself in my room for weeks on end, pleading...raging...with the One for my son's deliverance. In the shadows, the Darkness himself appeared, daring me with a deal for Errance's release. But I knew how such deals ended and somehow found the strength to refuse. Because all along I knew...even if I had thrown down the walls of Tertorem, swept my boy into my arms, and taken him back to Aselvia..."

"He would still be as much a prisoner of the Darkness as he ever was," Tellie finished softly. She understood those strange moments now, those times Errance's spirit had fled back to this evil place. He would have been still here, in Tertorem, even in the midst of his home and his people.

Slowly, the prison walls closed back in around them, mountains fading *away.*

"You wonder why I died?" Rendar said softly. "Know then that I did not leave him. Many times I came here in the layers of the Unseen, and I sacrificed what I could of my spirit to give him strength."

"You mean all the times he healed...it wasn't just his light? It was yours?"

"Yes. I could not stand for his gift to be wasted here, so I spent as much light through the Unseen as I could, fading day by day in the real world." He gave a sad laugh. "My poor people. They could not understand why I weakened."

She shivered, remembering the confusion of the elves over his mysterious illness.

"But in the end," he said, "Salvation could not come from me."

"Is there no way he can be rescued then?" she asked hopelessly. "Why was I brought to him? Was our escape truly just a trick?"

Stepping back, Rendar studied her with gentle eyes. "It was the Darkness's intent to tease him with the taste of freedom. But do you think it was in his plan for you and Kelm to care for Errance so tenderly? Did he know you would be taken in by the chemas, saved by brave and gentle Tryss? Was it just a coincidence that you should come across Coren and Zizain, The Daisha, people uniquely eligible to help Errance? My dear Tellie, the Darkness has forgotten the saving power of love. He now only twists it for destruction and underestimates its strength. This beautiful journey...it was not the Darkness's crippling stroke, but God's saving grace."

"Then what happens now?"

"Know this," he continued, hands clasping behind his back. "I have seen and experienced many impossibilities. Errance has come from a legacy of broken people—myself, his mother, his uncle—we all fell to darkest depths and yet were restored. The grace of the One is infinite. I have been promised that the time for Errance's fate is at hand. The ultimate choice will be given him. What he will choose we do not know nor can we control."

He knelt, taking her shoulders. "But you have a choice of your own to make. You have done a great thing for Errance...you have loved him. But for now, you must let him go. These bars, these prison walls are not meant for you."

"But if I leave," she whispered, "is there nothing else I can do?"

"I do not know. Ayeshune may yet have another path for you. But I have been sent to let you out."

Fearfully, she gazed out at the black maw, the light of the Unseen only penetrating so far. "Alone?" Her voice sounded so small, so easily swallowed. "Without Errance...all alone?"

"Tellie." His voice was the sternest she had heard yet. Stern, yet also the most compassionate. "Who are you following and placing your trust in? Errance? If so, then stay. But it is Ayeshune who has called you to this mission and it is Ayeshune who now calls you away. Who do you have faith in? Whom do you trust? If the One opens the door, does he not have the strength to carry you through?"

The Unseen vanished as suddenly as if she blinked. There was no sign to show that it existed...none visible. But as Tellie stumbled forward her hand caught against cold iron and the door creaked open.

With a delighted shriek, she whirled to Errance and, unable to help herself, called, "Look! Errance, look, the door! It's open!"

A pause, then flesh scraped against stone. "What?" murmured a voice, dazed and barely audible.

"Come on!" She swung the door back and forth, letting it squeak on its hinges so he would know she spoke the truth. Maybe this one last hope was all that was needed to prompt him to faith. She heard him inhale, she heard him begin to sit up.

Then silence.

And then a release of breath and all hope. "What's the point?" he whispered. "I'll only be taken again. Why torture myself? I will never be free."

Numb, she stared into the darkness where he lay.

"You're right," she said at last. "If you believe that, you never will be."

Turning, she faced the open door where the darkness leered, willing her to collapse and succumb to its embrace. Then she broke out of its crushing hold and flew to Errance's side and hugged his startled, resistant body.

"I'm sorry, Errance," she gasped. "But I'm making my choice. Follow me soon, I beg you!" Before fear could stiffen her limbs once more, she flung herself out of the cell and staggered against the opposite wall.

She'd done it. She was out.

What next?

It was unlikely that escape could be found through the sewer passages again. Was there any possible way that she could sneak through the labyrinth of the fortress and then escape over the mountains? How would she survive? For a moment, she nearly wanted to run back to the cell with Errance. The chance of her escaping was ridiculous, no, impossible.

Warmth bloomed against her skin. Her fingers flew to her neck and discovered the spider-silk thread of the necklace. Catching it up, she pulled the moon medallion out from under her top and stared at it. The light shone in only a slim crescent, but it shone nevertheless.

Even upon her second capture she hadn't been searched, perhaps because she was not expected to still carry it. After all, why would a simple orphan girl be trusted to carry something so precious?

One word rested in her heart, unfurling into power.

Follow.

She was an orphan no longer.

Holding out the moon medallion, she began wandering down the dark pathways of the prison, not knowing where she went, not knowing how long till she would be discovered. She simply trusted in the One for it was all she could do.

31

oOo

Chemas were creatures renowned for their stealth and secrecy, but never once had Tryss suspected she would hide from her own people. She could not actually disappear from their eyes like other races, but she took care not to be noticed as she snuck from the hut in which she'd taken refuge and went off in search of supplies. First, she restocked her arrows and added a few more knives, and then she crept to the healer's hut and gathered up what medicines and wrappings she thought might be needed. What might be needed…oh, she shuddered to guess what state Errance or Tellie would be found in, if they could be found at all.

She couldn't say good-bye. That stung. When first sent off, she'd waved farewell with little fear that she would not see her family again. Now she left on her own with little chance of coming back, and she could not tell them because they would surely not let her go.

Shaking away the growing fear and pain, she headed out into the jungle. Kelm lingered on the borders of the village, having refused to enter once he heard that a rescue effort was not being mounted.

"Kelm," she whispered.

He turned and looked her up and down, eyes rekindling with hope. "I say…are you…"

"I'm going myself. I'll go back to The Daisha and see if she'll try to take me into Tertorem."

"I'm going with you!"

"Absolutely not. You need to go to my village and stay safe. This is my choice." Anything else she wanted to say to was drowned out by the explosive roar of the boy's voice.

"Your choice? It's my choice too! I mean…what other choice do I have? I don't even have a family! Tellie is my best friend and Errance is my hero…there is no way I am staying behind! If you don't take me, I'll find a way of my own!"

She could not deny the truth of that or doubt his determination any more she could her own. Asking the tribe to keep him would only succeed in having her caught as well. With a frustrated breath, she nodded. "I understand. Perhaps we have a better chance together. Come on then."

As they headed back to the clearing where they'd left The Daisha, they heard the sound of swinging branches, breaking bracken, and savage snarling. Tryss skidded to a halt, pulling Kelm to the ground. "Wait here," she hissed.

She slid through the undergrowth, faintly pleased to back in her familiar jungle. She peered out between broad, waxy leaves into the glade where The Daisha stood in irate posture. The creature's head snapped back and forth, her eyes following something small and altogether not dangerous. It took a moment before Tryss saw it—a flash of black and white wings.

"Come just a bit closer, you fiend!" The Daisha cried out. "And we'll see what a pretty bird you are then!"

Sighing, Tryss rose from hiding. "Never mind, Kelm," she called. "It's just a bird."

"Just a bird indeed!" The Daisha's head snapped around to her, offense wrinkling her lips. "If you'd been watching for any length, you'd see that it's a devil in feathers. It's been terrorizing me for nearly an hour! You were taking so long, and I was about to have it for a tasty snack."

Kelm stumbled into view, brushing twigs from his curls, and all of a sudden, the wings flashed white again, and the bird swooped low over the boy's head, strong beak catching a lock of his hair and sharply tugging as it passed by. "Gah!" he yelped and ran under the refuge of The Daisha's wing. "Stupid magpie!"

"Ignore it," Tryss said, which was easy enough to say since the bird had made no attack on her. There was no time to mind bothersome birds, not even strange ones that she had never before seen in her jungle. "The Daisha, we will have to rescue them alone. My tribe is not coming."

"Not a bit surprised," The Daisha sniffed.

She winced, but there was no defense against the bitter truth. Setting her teeth, she swung onto The Daisha's withers and looked around to see where Kelm had gone. The boy stood underneath a tree, tossing stones up at the offensive bird, who bounced from branch to branch, squawking and bobbing its long tail.

"Kelm, forget it."

He gave a final shot, then trudged over with a scowl. "Figures one would show up after starting this entire mess."

"Starting it?"

"Yeah. It was a stupid magpie that stole the moon medallion and took it back to the elves. Tellie wouldn't have gotten into so much trouble if it hadn't. And I about killed myself trying to reach a nest—"

But Tryss wasn't hearing him anymore. She stared at the fluttering bird, skin tingling. Was it no mere chance that a foreign bird should appear now?

"The Daisha," she said slowly. "Follow that bird."

"Good." Stretching out her wings, The Daisha bared teeth at the magpie. "Fly for your life, you little monster."

As if it understood her, the magpie shot into the sky and began racing across the treetops. In a flash, The Daisha was after it, her great wings closing the distance between them in a matter of seconds. Yet the bird didn't seem to notice its own peril but flew determinedly on. The forest blurred underneath them like rushing water, and soon they came to the end of it altogether and sailed over the rolling hills, pale under the starlight. The magpie continued, the white on its wings flickering like the stars above.

"Look there, Tryss," Kelm said, pointing. "At the foot of the mountains…are those tents?"

From the distance, it at first looked like a cluster of trees in the bare hills, but one could see things glittering and flashing amongst it. As they drew nearer, they could make out the dark green tents and see the horses and folk. They had not seen the camp when they'd flown to the jungle, but the rolling hills could hide many things, and perhaps this company had not been camped long judging by how many figures still hurried about.

"Any idea who they are?" Tryss asked.

"Smells like evergreen woods," The Daisha said, and when that was apparently not a sufficient answer, she added, "Elves, of course."

"Elves?" Tryss and Kelm cried together. "But how did they know…how did they come here?"

"I suppose you should ask them," she replied, circling to land still some distance from the camp. "And when I mean you, I really do mean you. I've grown since they saw me last and I don't want to startle them, so I'll wait until you've established contact."

"Kelm, do they know you?" Tryss asked, gazing nervously towards the company as she dismounted.

"No." He swallowed hard. "Tellie never introduced me. I don't know if these are even the right ones."

"They're elves," The Daisha said, staring at him as if he was the stupidest boy on earth. "They're deadly, but they're not likely to kill you on sight."

"They better not," he muttered. "Otherwise, I'll be really upset."

Heaving a sigh, Tryss took his arm and pulled him forward. It felt like it took a terrible long time to approach, but they were able to observe much more of the gathering as they drew near. It was a camp of war, the tent flaps tied open for the figures rushing in and out, the sound of armor clinking and gleaming weapons being sharpened. Dark banners stitched with shining trees and stars swayed in the slight wind.

Tryss called out a greeting before they had quite arrived, but the call was lost amid the snort of horses and the blur of elvish voices, so they were forced to walk straight into the bustle.

And quite suddenly every elf stopped, every horse pricked its ears, and every weapon hushed. They all stared stunned at the meek figures who had so quietly invaded their midst. An instant later every hand sprang to sword, and Tryss and Kelm were surrounded by a forest of blades and arrows.

Tryss inhaled sharply, tugging the boy close to her. "No, we're friends," she cried. "Please, who is your leader, we came with important news."

Not inclining to answer her, a captain of the company spoke swift instructions to a soldier in their own tongue who dashed off into the shadows of the shelters. They did not have to wait long…a tall figure in a white shirt came hurrying through the crowd and as he came close, he broke into a run.

"Tryss? Kelm?" the man exclaimed.

Their mouths dropped open in shock. "Coren?"

It was the smuggler, there was no doubt about that, for no other elf could be caught wearing that roguish apparel of a sailor.

Nor did any elf's shadow follow with such a vigor and mind of its own, twinkling with its dark, brown eyes and saucy smile, calling in a distinct Oolum accent, "Did you kids get lost?"

Coren shouldered through the last of the retreating elves, his smile as wide as the sky. "I'd say they went the wrong direction." His eyes skipped over the disbelieving stares of Tryss and Kelm and searched beyond. His grin dropped away. "So he's gone then?"

"He was taken. Yesterday." She somehow managed to choke the words out despite the confusion and hope and disbelief spinning her mind. "Tellie and him both."

"How are you here, Coren?" Kelm demanded. "We left you only days ago…why are you here, and how did you get all these people?"

But Coren shook his head, snapping out a few words to their surrounding guards who immediately retreated. "Never mind that for the moment. Come with me, I need you to give a full report to the commander."

He turned and swept away, Zizain again at his heel, leaving them little choice but to follow in his wake. The elves parted before them, staring with shining, inquisitive eyes. They marched up to the central tent, which like the others was open, and within it was set up a table and hung with lamps that filled the curtained chamber with a fire-hearth's glow. A tall, elegant man bent over the table, his long blond hair brushing the map upon its surface. As they entered, he straightened and surveyed them with a quiet and unsettling depth.

"Tryss and Kelm, this is my father, Lord Leoren," Coren said, with a jerk of his hand.

The chema and boy stared, both somehow managing to not slack their jaw. The elf lord did not look old enough to be any grown man's father, let alone Coren's. Coren, the red-head rascal of Oolum…son of this refined creature?

"Daava," Coren said. "These are two of Errance's companions. It is just as Oriah said. The Darkness has already caught Errance and Tellie again. But this is Tryss, of that chema tribe I spoke of, and Kelm, Tellie's friend."

Leoren inclined his head gracefully, but a heavy weariness hung in his eyes. A disabling grief that continually plucked at his attention, allowing nothing else to be received in full concentration. "You arrive at an opportune time, friends. It is strange that we should meet."

"More than strange, your lordship," Tryss stammered. "That you should be here is completely baffling. Coren only met us a short while ago."

"I told you going by ship was faster!" Coren said, tossing up his hands as he began to pace the floor. "I reached Aselvia a few days after you left…I had every intent of bringing a company to intercept Errance and secure his travel home. But when I arrived, I found my father had already set out for Tertorem…turns out Rendar had known about Errance's location. He figured Tellie would be there too."

"You know Tellie—" Kelm interrupted. His eyes bulged a second later as he guessed the answer. "Are YOU the man who was going to adopt her?"

"That was my hope," Leoren said softly.

"Anyway," Coren continued impatiently. "While I was there, one of our priests had a…well…it's bit hard to explain if you aren't familiar with…you know…spiritual realms…the Unseen world? Anyway, I suppose you could call it a vision. A message from the One himself, telling us to assault Tertorem once more. I guessed that Errance had been retaken, and so I set out with a company to join my father here."

Leoren sat heavily in a chair, his head in his hands.

Looking at him, Tryss thought him much older than he first appeared. Indeed, she had not known an elf could look so tired…Errance didn't count, for even exhausted a ferocious energy had burned in his gaze. The poor man. He had only had a few days at most to process the survival of his crown prince and now faced losing him again.

"When we combed the Tertorem mountains for weakness," the elf lord murmured, "I thought it was only Rendar's desire for justice concerning Errance's death. In the years that followed, he'd lock himself away for days…maybe even weeks….I wonder if he was here….trying to find a way in. And if he could not, what chance do we have..?"

Coren slammed a fist into his palm. "Because we can see Ayeshune's finger in all this! He is guiding the pieces to their positions….everything is aligning, our board is set. If there was ever a time to discover the way over those cursed mountains, it is now and—"

He suddenly stopped. And blinked. And spun around to face Tryss and Kelm with a confounded expression. "Half a moment. You said they were caught yesterday? I rather thought you'd have made better progress on your journey. How'd you two get back here so fast?"

Tryss's mind stuttered and she blinked at him.

But Kelm had found his tongue. "We flew of course. And as for getting over the mountains, we already figured all that out—we have The Daisha!"

Tryss was never sure how much time passed, because everything that happened afterwards could hardly be measured, but she found herself again sitting in the tent, now curled up in a chair and looking at the faces of the elves while they in turn stared at the face of The Daisha.

390

The Daisha lay halfway into the tent, the curtains draped around her shoulders, and she chattered on cheerfully, quite unperturbed by the stunned looks upon her.

Tryss sipped the flask of warm tea given her by a woman with brown hair and lavender eyes who she guessed was Lord Leoren's wife. Finally, she began to feel alive again, no longer lost in the fever that had propelled her from yesterday through night to another night again.

It was funny, she thought, but Coren, daring and intrepid man as he was, looked the most sick about The Daisha, while Zizain wore a dazzling smile that cared little about her own confusion and shock. Lord Leoren did not wear an expression of unbelief like his son for he'd known the creature in her youth and surely remembered to what size they grew, but he did look quite dazed or at least as dazed as a man of his sophistication could hope for.

"Anyway," The Daisha went on, clasping her fingered paws. "I say it is providence that has brought us together again, although I do wish it was under happier circumstances. My Errance is still alive, and no one, no one, can simply snatch him away and not expect me to do my utmost part in rescuing him."

Leoren's eyes fluttered shut as he bent his head into hand. "Two impossibilities in only a few days…"

"They tend to happen all at once," The Daisha comforted. "So let's get the third out of the way and scale those mountains, yes? My wings are large enough now to lift me to those heights."

The elven lord nodded, brushing back his doubt and exhaustion. "What do you propose? You cannot fly us over the peaks one at a time."

"That's easy," Coren said. "She only needs to fly up a few of us with ropes so we can secure them to rocks and send down a ladder for the rest of you."

"That could work…but it's so simple."

"Everything's marvelously simple when a daisha is your friend," the good creature quipped.

"And while we draw out their forces," Coren continued, "The Daisha flies Tryss and Kelm to the fortress to search for Errance."

"What?" Startled, Leoren looked to him with a jerk. "You suggest sending in the boy?"

"I'm the only one who's been inside," Kelm protested. "I've the best chance of recognizing places…they didn't blindfold me all the time."

"That place is demonic. There is no telling if anything is going to look familiar to you. No, Coren, we cannot have children involved in this."

"With all due respect, sir…your lordship," Kelm said, stiffening his back. "Those you'd call children are already involved. My friend Tellie is in there, and she and Errance need all they help we can give them if this rescue's going to be successful. Anyway, I am fourteen and that's almost a man."

Coren leaned against the table and smiled. "He has a point, Daava. Many human cultures would consider him so."

Before Leoren could respond, another shadow cast in the room, and they turned to look at the elven guard standing in the tent door. "Lord Leoren," he said. "We have new arrivals come from the jungle. More of her kind." He gestured Tryss with a nudge of his chin.

With a gasp, she stumbled to her feet. "My tribe…?" But fleeting hope dashed a moment later with the thought they had more than likely come to bring her back. Her hands curled. Well. She was not going back, and in this mighty company, there wasn't much point to their protest.

"May I speak with them first?" she asked, bowing a little to Leoren. If they did cause a scene trying to convince the folly of her actions, she hardly wanted them all to witness it.

"Very well."

Leaving behind the resurrected argument of Kelm, she hurried after the guard through the midnight draped camp. The elves gathered in an agitated throng on the borders of the camp, perturbed to have so many unexpected visitors at once, though these ones at least they had seen coming. Or at least Tryss hoped her people had given the elves the chance of seeing them approach.

A cluster of about fifty men stood outside the camps borders, and as Tryss drew near enough to see detail in the torchlight, she recognized the foremost man as her father. And a few of her uncles. And beyond them, the faces she could see belonged to the most able men of their village. If all the shadows revealed the same, then over half of the tribe's men had come…and they had come arrayed in what armor and weapons served their most perilous hunts.

She quickened her pace, heart rising on wings in her throat. "…Da?" And by then she could see the answer to her question, the war-paint striped across their faces and bare arms. They'd come to fight. For Errance, for Tellie. For her.

"You came!" She threw herself into her father's ready embrace with a glad cry, nestling deep against his heartbeat. "I thought—"

"My stubborn cheedee…" He cupped her face in his large hands, shaking his head in somber pride. "Your dedication to your friends convicted us all. If you would risk your life for them, we cannot let you risk it alone. Though I see," and here his eyes rose cautiously to the onlooking elves, "that you are not quite alone."

"The Aselvian elves, Da. Errance's people." It was perhaps a bit silly to say since no one else in Orim could so perfectly match the idealized stories of the reclusive elves. "We are discussing our plan of attack in the main tent. Come, I'll introduce you."

And taking his arm, she lifted her chin with pride and led the way.

oOo

The girl was no longer in the cell. A cowering guard slunk to the Voice to tell him the news. Daran had found the cell door open with the elf still inside. Though interrogated, the elf would say nothing about the girl's disappearance. Of course. Because he was stubborn that way.

The Voice of His Darkness took the news without comment or action, merely turning away.

It had been a long time since a child of his Great Enemy had entered his demesne. He'd underestimated her, written her off at their first meeting. She was just a little thing—but her frailty seemed to make her cling all the greater to her faith making her more powerful than she realized.

And now as he sent his thought peering into every corner, every crevice, every chamber of Tertorem, he could sense nothing. Blinded. Blinded! Even within the shadows of his own domain!

But the elf had not gone with her. That, at least, was an encouraging sign that the Darkness held predominant sway over the prince.

What was the girl doing? Was she wandering around listless in dark tunnels...or did she have a plan?

The Voice wheeled about so fast, the guard nearly dropped to the floor in fright. "Bring the Prisoner to the Well," he said. He'd find the girl himself—but first, he'd make sure the prince was somewhere she would never find him.

32

oOo

Now was not the time to panic. In all Tellie's years so far, she could think of several more opportune moments for flailing and hysterics, mainly in the toddler years, but the time for that was not now. Instead, she reminded herself that she could in fact breathe, even though her chest and back were pinned between two unmoving walls of stone. Tight spaces. Add that to her growing list of fears.

At first her escape through the tunnels of Tertorem had been very successful. The medallion's light shone each step ahead, and she'd followed its glow through rot-riddled cells until she'd reached a freshly broken crevice in the wall, caused perhaps by a recent earthquake. The glow had reached inside so she'd followed with only the slightest tremble. The passage widened and narrowed at turns, and finally she'd been forced to her belly to wiggle through a small hole.

And that was when she'd gotten stuck.

Heart rattling, she lay still against the cold stone, feeling the rocks close in around her. The moon medallion rested in her palm, glow faint. As the hours of her journey had passed, she'd begun to notice that the sliver of the moon was vanishing altogether. It would be gone soon. "All right," she whispered to herself. "All right, I can do this. Please, please, please, Ayeshune, help me do this." Releasing a long breath, she began wriggling her shoulders back and forth and using her feet to push forward. She felt the stone tear through her dress and skin, but didn't dare stop.

Then her head and shoulders burst out into open air, and with a final shove, she squirmed free and somersaulted down onto the ground. The hard landing knocked the final shred of breath out, so she lay sprawled on the jutting stone, whispering groans of pain and prayers of thanks.

When she finally found strength to stand up, she reached for the moon medallion and…it had gone. She seized in panic for one second before her frantic hand combed the necklace strand and found the medallion's shape still under her fingers. No longer visible, but still there.

New moon.

But she could still see in this small, rocky cavern she'd stumbled into. It could be the Unseen or it could be…she noticed the dim glow flickering behind the turn in the wall the same moment she heard the sound of chipping stone. Striking metal, rattling of rocks.

Sucking in another breath, she crawled forward to peer around the corner. Beyond reached a long tunnel full of jagged rock and haunting echoes. A few torches cast fingered, grasping shadows down its length. Scattered in the shadows were carts, picks, shovels…and people. Bent, broken people.

There was one not ten feet away from her. A more miserable manifestation of life she'd never seen. In another reality, he might have been middle-aged, but here time had given rule to death. His back arched, his bones jutted out from his lacerated skin, his body was covered in dust and sweat that matted his beard.

She stared in horror, and without any intention, let out a small whimper.

His head jerked up and his red-veined eyes swiveled around. Alarmed, she pulled back out of sight. But with a slight scuffle, his head peered around the corner to stare down at her. Biting her lip, she made sharp, shushing motions with her hands, eyes wide and pleading.

He just kept staring in incredulous disbelief. "What are ye?" he rasped.

"Tellie," she whispered. "I'm Tellie, please don't sound an alarm."

Muttering something under his breath, he said, "Are they sending little girls into the mine now? But ye can't have been here long by the looks of ye."

"I'm not supposed to be here at all. I'm escaping."

His haggard face drooped, and he placed a quivering hand on her shoulder. She forced herself not to flinch away as she saw his fingers were all swollen and smashed. "There's no escaping this place, little lass," he murmured.

"Actually…" She studied him hard, considering her options. So far he hadn't given her away. And despite all the horrors wreaked upon his body, some kindness still lingered in his eyes. "Actually, I've escaped before. This is my second time out. It's easy as a choice, really, though I suppose the decision itself can be hard." Heavens, give her time and she'd be spouting riddles like Rendar.

Throwing an anxious glance over his shoulder, he crawled nearer. "Are ye an insane little thing?" he asked, almost sounding curious.

Would I know it if I was? Aloud, she said, "I…I'm a follower of Ayeshune. This prison can't hold me."

He only stared, a stupid animal look on his face.

Struck with a sudden idea, she asked, "Do you know Errance? He used to work in the mines. Tall, brown-hair, blue-eyes, pointy-ears, scars through the right eye?"

The miner drew in a sharp breath, and before she could blink, he'd grabbed and pulled her deeper into the shadows, away from the prying eyes of the torches. "Ye know the Prisoner?" he growled. "Ye have seen the Prisoner?"

"If he matches my description, yes, I assume so," she gasped, astonished by the strength in those broken hands.

Slowly, he let go of her, relief and hope illuminating his wearied features. "He was taken from us," he muttered. "Our last hope. What have they done to him? Is he yet alive?"

Somehow, she had taken the impression from Errance that no one existed in Tertorem except to hate and punish their elven prisoner. But she should have known there would be other captives who'd been inspired by him, for had he not affected her the same? She wondered if he even knew or if he'd become that blind to any kind of love.

At the sight of the strange, loyal love, she poured out in brief the tale of their escape and adventure and then how he was caught again. "Now," she finished, "I don't think he has much time left. And he wouldn't come with me. He's lost all reason to fight. If I can get out of here, I'll find our friends, and then…I don't know what I'll do exactly."

The man leaned back against the rough wall, a spark in his once vacant eyes. "Do ye think he might fight back one last time if…if given the right push?"

"Well I—"

"He was the only one of us who ever fought more than once. He fought for himself, he fought for us…he fought. We did nothing." The already puffed and reddened whites of his eyes turned yet redder as they pooled with tears. "If we fought for the first time…would he stand with us?"

Tellie stared, hardly able to hear her own thoughts over the thundering of her heart. "But. What could we do?"

"Nothing!" The old man threw back his head with a cackle. "We shall all fail and perish miserably in the attempt."

"Oh." She hunkered against the wall, wondering why she'd let hope get piqued by a raving skeleton.

"But," the man said, and he spoke low with reverence, "we shall do it nonetheless."

"How?" she protested. "What do you mean by 'we'? Do you mean you and me?"

Without an answer, he grabbed her wrist with that terrifyingly strong grip and tugged her forward. "Come—come, girl! He merely held onto memory, but you are the memory itself…they must see you!"

She started to dig her heels into the ground, but the man's bewildering passion tugged her heart forward and the rest of her could not help but follow. Though the man's back was crooked, he gave every effort of standing straight as she came alongside him. And together they stepped out of the shelter of the shadows and into the center of the tunnel.

Here, she could see them all clearly. Not men, not women. Ghouls toiling into the oblivion of a mountain's throat. They were not alive, their bodies merely moved. And they moved, one by one, to turn and stare at the young girl standing before them.

They stared without understanding. She, a mortal young maid with bright eyes and vibrant life, could be no more believable or beautiful than a celestial. Yes, she was grimy, clothes torn, eyes deepened by sorrows more profound than her innocence at first suggested. But there in that forsaken place, in a ruin between worlds, many saw more—they saw brightness and beauty that no darkness could dim. A candle that no wind could blow out.

An answer to forgotten prayers.

And she watched as light returned to their eyes.

They stood, stumbling towards her. None of them dared come too close, as if she was a rainbow that would flit further and further away. Perhaps nothing was more grotesque or out of place than the hope and eagerness in their broken-down bodies.

Instead of fleeing in fear, she stood her ground and looked over them, pity pouring into her heart. Errance might have kept some trace of beauty, but in his core, he was no different from them. Just as she had been no different.

"It's a lie, you know," she whispered. "This prison, these chains. There is no darkness that light cannot overcome. You only need the courage to believe it."

The miner stepped alongside her, snatching up a pick and shaking it above his head. "They've taken our hero. They'll crush him like they've crushed us all. Enough! Enough, I say! They may own our lives, but they won't decide our death!"

"Here now!" a harsh voice shouted on the borders of the mass. "What's this about, refuse?" An overseer shouldered his way through, and as he caught sight of Tellie, he staggered in shock and reached for his sword.

His fingers never touched the hilt.

Like an ocean wave, the slaves moved as one, silent in their onslaught. The overseer vanished underneath their bodies.

Tellie jerked away, even though she couldn't see a glimpse of the killing, not sure how her stomach could threaten to be sick even while her blood thrilled at retribution.

The overseer's death, something only before accomplished by their hero, ignited a horrific fire within the miners. There was no turning back now, only charging ahead, and they exchanged their silence and murmurings for wild, animal cries. As they stormed down the tunnel, the sparks of their fury ignited every slave they passed, till the very mountain shook with roaring rage.

Tellie and the old miner followed at their heels, and as they broke out onto the open mountainside, the man turned and gripped her by the shoulders. "Go find the Prisoner," he panted. "Tell him of what we've done. Let 'im see. Make 'im fight."

Rendar had made it very clear she was to escape and that Errance would need to make a choice on his own. But well, she had escaped, and he never said what she was supposed to do afterwards. As for Errance, maybe this was the fateful turn for his decision. Surely it could not be wrong for her to try.

oOo

Coren sat upon the sharp ridges of the mountain peaks, watching as the elves and chemas alike climbed the robes anchored by The Daisha and her passengers. There was a passage through the mountain here, but the wall to it had been far too slick for anyone to find. Now those who had reached the crest gathered in the chasm, tensely listening to their lord's plan of attack for another time.

The captain's eyes wandered to where The Daisha waited with the two figures upon her back. Even now, he questioned his support in bringing Kelm along. But as a smuggler he'd learned to take whatever chance, whatever hope, though this was indeed the most daring rescue he'd undertaken yet. It was more than a rescue. It was a war, and neither Tryss nor Kelm were warriors.

Neither was Zizain. His thoughts drifted back to her with a sigh. If the last image he would have of her was such an indignant scowl, he'd never forgive himself. But, as he'd explained, she could have no place in the main battle as she'd never killed a man before. Of course she'd pointed out that he hadn't either, but Coren was convinced he wouldn't have a qualm once engaged. She was used to helping those rescued find relief and recovery and so would be better waiting with the elves and chemas who stayed behind in a healing camp for the aftermath of the battle.

Or this was the reason that he'd given her.

He didn't dare tell her that his heart would never recover if she died in the battle.

Focus. There was a fight ahead, and it was to save the heir of his country. He had to focus.

He wondered if he'd have the nerve to tell Zizain the truth of his feelings if he survived.

oOo

The horrors of Tertorem dwelt in layers, some known only to a few, some changed only by one. The chambers and secrets within were limitless, and the Voice of His Darkness knew them all. Each had its own specific purpose, and the one he came to now was called the Well.

By first appearances, it was simple. A small circular room lit only by a sputtering torch bracketed to the wall. In truth, he would have done away with the torch all together, but the wretched mortals did need to see their own steps. The sickly light perished the instant it touched the opening void of the Well in the center of the floor. And in that deepness dwelled the very essence of every despairing dream.

The Voice waited, leaning against the post upholding the bar from which the chains dropped into the pit. He smiled when the guards at last arrived with his prisoner. "Oh dear," he said with an apologetic chuckle as he appraised Errance's sagging, battered body. "It looks like the guards got a bit carried away." He reached out and lifted his face upwards, running a finger along an open cut in his cheek. "Can you tell they missed you?"

The elf's eyes remained utterly blank.

For a moment, the Voice felt a twinge of fear. Had his infiltration proved too much after all? He dug his fingernail deep into the cut. Errance flinched, and his eyes refocused with a sparkling anger. It was gone the next second.

Satisfied nonetheless, the Voice gestured to the guards to begin shackling the chains wound around the pulley to Errance's wrists. "Something I want you to remember, Your Majesty," he whispered. "The more you resist, the greater your destruction. When I return, I am holding nothing back. It's your decision whether you will be yourself or a slavering imbecile at the end of it." He looped an arm around Errance's torn shoulders. "Now then…sweet dreams."

With a thrust of his arm, he shoved the prince off the edge into the Well. The chains rattled violently as they unwound and then seconds later jerked to a halt. Casting one last glance into the consuming darkness, the Voice turned and left the chamber.

And it was in that moment, that he felt the breech.

33

oOo

Killing should not be so easy. Coren felt a tad of guilt as he withdrew the blade from the belly of the first Tertorem guard he encountered. The assault of their greatest enemy's fortress should also not be so easy. But perhaps in years of success against invasion, the Darkness had grown lax and arrogant, his men lazy and incompetent within the walls. For the army had crossed the high mountain pass and picked their way to the very foot of the castle without a single encounter.

Now, as soldiers and guards and servants poured out of their barracks to defend against the attack, they were cut down by arrows or blade hardly before they knew what was happening.

Almost sad, at least if the men here were not the crop of the world's wickedness, only caught off guard because they had felt secure in enjoying the fruits of their evil. The surprise would only last so long, and then Coren was certain the battle would become far more intense. Who could say what manner of secrets and powers the Darkness kept within his nest? They had hit a stone against a hornet's lair and were only yet facing the first stings.

"Pull back," Leoren called, signaling to the crags from where they'd climbed. "We have to draw them out, keep his attention away!" His green eyes snapped in vicious brilliance, and he suddenly sprang behind his son with a shout, flashing out his sword to cut down an attacking soldier.

So much for my meek and mild-mannered father, Coren thought with another surge of guilt.

So far they had a good chance of keeping the upper hand as long as they kept the higher ground, the rocks providing shelter. If the Darkness thought this was the focus of the attack, he might be blind to other movements.

But somewhere, high up in the clouds, their true hope waited for the opportunity to strike.

"A bit stuffy up here, isn't it?" The Daisha called.

Neither Kelm nor Tryss answered, trying not to smell even as they struggled for breath. The atmosphere above Tertorem was thick with grey clouds, filled with an acidic mist that stung the skin, the eyes, and the lungs when one dared inhale.

"Please," Tryss wheezed. "It's poison, we can't stay much longer…"

The Daisha dipped beneath the cloud cover to study the ground and Tertorem far below which looked little more than a child's castle from such a distance. "A few moments more. The elf army has entered the edges of the fortress, but there's mass confusion amongst the men of the Darkness and they haven't engaged yet."

Thunder rumbled far too near overhead, and Kelm hunkered deep into her fur, eyeing the brooding cloudscape for a strike. He couldn't have chosen a better time to hunker, for it was then that The Daisha dove. He squeezed his eyes shut in the glorious rush and when he dared peel them open again, the spires of Tertorem flashed by.

Tilting her wings, The Daisha started to circle, looking for any suitable place to land on the fortress itself, which showed little sign of access.

"There." Tryss pointed to where a branch of the wall met the side of the mountain. A narrow path ran along the edge.

An arrow zipped past with a shrill whine.

"Quick to catch on, aren't they?" The Daisha remarked. "Ha, poor little fellows, arrows aren't strong enough to pierce my hide." She evaded the next two that flew past with ease. "When I land, you two will have to run, all right?"

"Right."

She swooped down, her claws grabbling on the cliff that ran alongside the narrow path, and Kelm and Tryss jumped for the ledge. Shoving against the stone, The Daisha launched off and dashed away from them, disappearing down into a lower level with a fell screech.

The distant sounds of battle could be faintly heard over the howling wind. Shuddering, Kelm looked around at the sharp rocks, wondering if they would suddenly come to life and attack. Now that they were here, the fortress loomed larger than life, and the fact he had never once seen the outside weighed even worse on his mind. He hadn't stayed unconscious as long as Tellie, but had been blindfolded, and while he remembered a great deal of walking and talking, he'd been in too much stress to recall anything of use for finding a way inside.

Tryss took his hand and placed it on her arm. "Don't lose me," she said. "I'm disappearing." Her image melted away, leaving Kelm seemingly all alone on the cliff edge. The feeling of her warm fingers on his arm did nothing to abate the terror. "Come on!" she shouted and tugged him forward.

The path along the mountain to the fortress was narrow and unstable. Kelm had never been afraid of heights before, but it took all his willpower not to shake as he edged against the mountain wall and refused to look down at the steep drop of shale below. The wind was no help, constantly buffeting against the rock and then sweeping away with a tug at the limbs. He'd never felt quite so alone and small.

Part of the path crumbled and gave way before him, sending rocks skittering down. Tryss let out a sharp cry. "Careful! This road isn't stable!"

Sucking in a deep breath, he clung tighter to the rocks and focused on their destination—where the trail along the mountain ended and turned into a battlement walkway of the fortress.

A brilliant flash of lightning blinded his sight and the crack of thunder that immediately followed seemed fit to bring the cliff down on top of them. With a yelp, he flinched away…and then he was overbalancing, teetering on the edge, the ground crumbling beneath his feet.

"Kelm, no!"

Two hands grabbed his arm and jerked him back to safe ground, but even at the moment, more of the path gave way. Tryss's hands slipped from his arm, followed by a small scream. That scream was lost amid the shriek of storm and stone.

He dropped to his knees, hunkering against the rock. "Tryss? Tryss!" Nothing but the storm answered him. Inching forward, he stared down the slope, trying to see what path the rocks had fallen along, but the wind had swept away all the dust. And he could see no sign of her.

Not daring to stay on the ledge a moment longer, he crawled the rest of the way to the solid stone road and stared down the wall again in an effort to see her. "Tryss!" he shouted again.

"Where did you come from?"

Gagging on his next call, Kelm jerked upright and stared at the soldier who had just come around from behind a battlement turret.

"We've got a runaway!" the man shouted over his shoulder to who knew what reinforcements and leapt forward, drawing a short blade.

Not even waiting to see how many people would be in pursuit, Kelm jumped to his feet and charged up a set of stairs to the walkway above. Every leaping stride felt as if it would be his last as shouts sounded behind him and the wind threatened to trip his feet. But he sped along, taking a new turn or road whenever it was offered. A short tunnel carved the way through mountain outcrop, and when he came to the other side he found a vast view of the fortress and the plains beyond.

Since he heard no sound of his pursuers, he took the moment to catch a breath. Brights, that had gone all wrong. He had no way of knowing if Tryss was still alive, and if she was, how would they find each other again? Maybe The Daisha…if he could get her attention…

A roar of voices thundered over the wind. He scrambled up to the top of the parapet to see over into the valley just underneath. Among the ridges of the mountains, a river of people was pouring out from dozens of cave mouths. For a sickening moment, he thought they were enemy soldiers. But the next instant he saw that none of them wore armor, but flailed shovels, picks, and whips like wild men. When the first few Tertorem guards were swallowed up in their assault, Kelm dropped back down to the ground in shock.

The slaves were fighting back.

"Why now?" he wondered aloud.

"We're doing it, little lass!" the miner shouted in triumph.

Tellie wished she could shout with him, but her concentration was too occupied by not falling and facing death by trampling feet. The vicious energy of the seething throng was both terrifying and exhilarating. Now that their spirits had been awoken, nothing could stop the slaves as they clambered across the mountainside, ignoring the narrow paths, slipping and sliding on the loose rock.

Tellie climbed her way to a stairway leading up into the levels of the fortress, and turned to watch the mob of slaves continue their rush downhill, making straight for the quarters of the slave-masters that dwelt at Tertorem's foot.

"Go to it, lass!" the miner's voice called one last time, before being drowned out in the inarticulate rage.

Shuddering at the slavers' approaching doom, she turned away from the sight and started up the stairs as fast as her legs would go. As she reached the first level, a new sound swept in on a gust. A sound of ringing blades and battle cries.

Afraid of what she might see, she climbed up a stairway to the top of a high wall and stared out to the southern edge of the citadel. Upon the grey shadows of the fortress's base, glimmered a forest of silver figures, blue and green banners flickering out amongst them. Dumbfounded, she leaned in for a better look.

A sudden nausea gripped her stomach, and she stepped back, only just realizing that the wide walkway on which she stood did not have anything barring her from a long fall to death. Carefully, she knelt down before raising her eyes to study the army again. "Who…?"

She watched a distant shape shoot through the air, darting to and from boardwalks. A glad cry burst from her lips. "The Daisha!" Delighted, she clapped her hands to her mouth. "They've come! Is that the elves? It must be—it is! Oh, Errance will have to come now!"

"Will he, indeed?" a voice growled.

Gasping, she spun around and stared down into the face of Daran. He stood at the bottom of the stair with a sharp scowl and an even sharper sword. "You weasel," he said. "I might have known you'd wiggle your way free."

She backed away, looking to her left and right for the next stair down. There wasn't one. Daran stalked up the steps to the top and headed towards her, his firm footfalls closing the gap of her fluttering retreat. The hooded shadows of his eyes and curl of his mouth paralyzed her somehow, and he was already far too close when she turned for a full-out run.

But too late.

His hand snaked out and caught in her curls, dragging her back towards him. "I've had enough of you, you useless brat!" he growled, swinging up his blade. "I've had enough of your running!"

Run. Flee. Escape. No. NO.

She too was tired of running.

A snarl ripped from her throat. She twisted around and leapt straight for his face, her fingers grabbling for his eyes, and her teeth snapping at his nose. As she collided into him and bit down hard, Daran howled and staggered backwards.

Gravity seized them both.

The red rage swept clear of Tellie's mind in a surge of terror, and she thrust off him as the fall began. She leapt for the wall, but his fingers were still in her hair, and as her feet touched stone, she felt herself pulled back off with him. She dropped to the stone, fingers seizing the ledge just as she slipped off.

Daran's hand tore from her hair, and she heard his scream spiral down below to end in a soft, sickening thud.

She clung to the wall's edge, shaking from the effort and shock of what had just happened. With a little moan, she tried to pull herself back to the top, but any remaining strength had gone slack. Already, she could feel her cold fingers losing their grip.

"No…no, no," she whimpered.

"Tellie!" A terror-filled call rang in her ears, startling her so badly she almost let go then and there. "Tellie!" Footsteps pattered up the stair, and she looked up to see Kelm peering over the edge. "Tellie, thank the One!" He dropped to his knees, caught her hands, and pulled her back up onto the wall with a heave.

For a moment all she could do was huddle against the ground, soaking in its solidity. Kelm's arms looped around her, and he half dragged, half led her down the stair. But as they reached the bottom of it, her legs gave out. "Wha—what are you doing here?"

He crouched beside her. "We came to rescue you! What are you doing out here? How'd you get out? I can't believe it! You actually took on Daran and won! I couldn't believe my eyes, and then you fell over and I thought you were gone. Daran sure is. Yech. Not a pretty sight."

"Stop it!" she gasped, voice cracking. "D-don't say that. I d-didn't mean to k-k-kill him. He wasn't supposed to…fall…down." Quivering, she pulled up her knees to her chest and began to cry. She didn't dare wonder what Daran's last thoughts were, what it must have felt like to fall.

"Hey, hey there, Tellie, it's all right, I didn't mean to upset you." Kelm wrapped an arm around her shoulders in a comforting hug. "It's all right," he repeated. An awkward kiss brushed her cheek.

Well. That snapped her from shock in a hurry. She straightened with a deep blush. She sniffed back a few more tears and pushed to her feet.

"Where's Errance?" Kelm asked, hovering beside her arm as if he expected her to drop again.

"I found another way out, and he stayed behind," she explained, stumbling along in determination. "He's spent, Kelm. But I convinced the slaves to revolt and maybe the fight will strengthen his heart somehow. What about you? Did you bring this army?"

Kelm reddened and looked away. "Coren brought the elf army, and Tryss convinced some chemas to accompany us. And The Daisha found a way through the mountains. I haven't done much of anything."

"You saved me," Tellie mumbled.

Not seeming to hear that, he went on. "And I lost Tryss. She fell down a hill in camouflage, and I wasn't able to find her."

"Where?" Tellie demanded, paling. "Do you think she...."

"I don't where she is," he said miserably. "I think she's all right. I hope. But I had to run."

Biting her lip, Tellie shoved back the fear. "I'm sure she's fine. She has to be. Come on. We'll find Errance and get out of here."

oOo

Despite all the cold piercing her body, Tryss could feel one wash of warmth on her brow. A warmth that was also a bit wet and sticky. The rest of her body ached like she'd fallen from the highest tree in the jungle and had hit every branch along the way. What could have...

Her eyes flared open as memory rushed back in. Tertorem, the storm, the path, then falling, and a crack against her head along with a flash of sickly light. Gasping, she shoved up on her arm, only to collapse back down on the sharp rocks.

Argh, what were the north chemas thinking to keep their home up in the mountains? Falling down a cliff was ever so much worse than falling out of a tree. She sat up more carefully, cradling her head as she looked back and forth for bearings. Yes, there was the path and the fortress up the steep incline. Where was Kelm...how come he had not waited for her? Her stomach, already sick, lurched to an unfathomable depth. Oh, let him not be captured. Not that.

But the fear gave her the strength she needed. Snarling, she struggled back up to the path, not caring how the wind tried to pull her back or how the stones spitefully gave way. She gained the high ground and leaned for a moment against the wall.

Tellie and Errance were somewhere inside and her best guess put Kelm in there too. So what if she was alone and injured? The shadows would be an excellent cover even if she didn't create a disguise all her own. All she had do was find them and then…she'd figure out what to do from there.

The first entrance she found had no door to close it, only a narrow black chasm in the face of the fortress. The moment she stepped through, the world went dark. And she knew she had gone far deeper into Tertorem than a single stride could have covered. The blackness weighed down in a heavy curtain upon every sense, every thought. For a moment, it was all she could do simply to stand and remember she could still breathe.

Then another step. And another. God help her, she would keep moving.

As she forced forward, a gradual perception of surroundings came to her…the depth of despairing souls caught in cages, cages of all sizes and shapes and torments. No matter how close they hung near to another, they were trapped in their own miserable solitude. She could not see them, but she felt them…felt the overwhelming loss and emptiness of shattered hearts.

It sent her gasping to her knees. She hid her head in her arms and blended into the blackness. This—this was Errance's prison. She'd perceived it, but she had not *known*. She not even come close to understanding the horror he struggled to escape from. "I'm sorry," she whispered, throat dry. "I'm sorry. Please, Ayeshune, please let me find him—let me find the children. Set captives free."

With a surge of purpose, she shoved to her feet. No matter how many twists and turns this labyrinth threw at her, her path would remain true. So she walked.

And the wretched, entrapped souls glimpsed a bright figure of springtime hues drifting through their midst. Some saw it only for a fleeting moment and then forgot, but others gazed after it long after it disappeared, treasuring the sight within their heart and recalling other beautiful things lost to them long, long ago.

34

oOo

In the depths, in the darkness, there dangled a prisoner, and once upon a time, he had been a prince. He knew this not because he remembered those happy days but because in the blackest of nights it had been the only thing that kept him strong. When they'd tortured, taunted, and humiliated him, he had sworn to himself over and over again that no matter what they tried to mold him into, he was born to be a king. A man of pride, of honor, of grace…not a slave of shame and suffering.

Icy burning spread from his wrists where spiked shackles bit into skin, blood crusted his face, and his body throbbed with each heartbeat. Torment. Never ceasing, always creeping closer, deeper. The knowledge of what was to come clawed at his mind, demanding notice. The Voice would try again. If he just gave in he would not have to face that terrible battle again.

But wait—hadn't the Voice said that the more he fought the less there would be of him at the end?

There then was the answer. He had to fight. He must have his spirit torn to shreds, for he knew what his fate would be when the Darkness finished with him. He would be tossed away to the demons and their minions like a bone to a pack of starving wolves. Each ten years had felt like eternity…what then would eternity feel like? He needed to destroy himself in this one method possible. There must be nothing left of him at the end, just a shell so that he would never again…

…never again hear the joyful ripple of Tellie's laughter or see her curls bounce on her shoulders. Never again see Kelm roll his eyes or watch him lengthen his stride to match his own. Never again feel Tryss's arms tight around his waist or feel her cheek pressed against his neck…

No, no, *no*. Life and love had been stolen from him that dark night seventy years ago. He could not, would not think that way, for there was no hope. Terrified at where his mind might leap next, he focused on the present. He hung from chains in frigid, scalding darkness, his body again broken. Nothing existed beyond this nightmare twisting through him.

Tell me of Aselvia, Tellie had pleaded.

A single sob tore from his throat, spiraling out into shadow and swallowed whole without an echo. He did not remember Aselvia. If he had before falling into this abyss, even those memories were shades and shards. It was lost, all lost, as it had been in years past when the flame of his soul had flickered so far down the wick as to drown in its own wax. He did not know his homeland, his people, or even who he was—

"Daava!" The little boy, blue eyes full of tears, sat up in bed, soft blankets bundled to his chest, and called anxiously until a door adjoining to his opened, and a tall man with white hair swept to his bedside.

The father sat on the bed and cradled his boy to him, long, elegant hand clasping the small one. "A frightening dream?"

Hiccupping back a sob, the little boy nodded and huddled in closer. His father stroked his hair and whispered, "There, there, my little one. A foul dream cannot hurt you. Very little can hurt you unless you give it that power."

The child drew back, small brow puckered. "But Daava, I fell yesterday and scraped my knees. It hurt, and I didn't give it anything."

His father smiled. "That's true, isn't it? We can be hurt physically. We can be hurt emotionally. But then there is you. *Not your body. Not your mind.* You. *Pain will want to change who you are. It will want to force you to become something you're not. But if you fight hard enough and stay true to the One, it cannot destroy you."*

The boy gazed solemnly up, his fair, young face thoughtful. *"Who am I, Daava?"*

The father's eyes glowed with love. *"You are the prince of Aselvia. You are the heir of the kingdom. But most of all, you are my beloved son."* He cupped his child's face in his hands and kissed him on the brow. *"Never forget who you are, Errance."*

His breath broke from his chest with a shuddering gasp. That...that was pure memory. A memory true and untouched by the filth of lie and illusion. He could not remember the last time he recalled something of his past so clearly.

All at once, he was frantic for more, desperate to find something else he knew had belonged to him. Love could not exist here but it had existed, and he needed it, he needed—

The memories came, fast and relentless.

He was a young boy straining to pull a bow to its limit, sighting down the shaft to a distant target, with Lord Leoren calling instruction from the side. As a young man, he sat on a bench leaning against a wall, breathing heavily from a sword duel. His father stood next to him, sword tucked under an arm, smiling down at him. They'd bested Lord Reyin that day, or Reyin had let them, or Daava had cheated a little bit as evidenced by the bolt of light that reflected off the blade into Reyin's eye on a day when the sun was covered by clouds.

He remembered how his father always spent time each day with him, as if knowing how short the time would be. He remembered how he sat at his father's right hand during feasts, a coronet smooth against his brow and the moon medallion resting upon his chest. Then how his father promised they would one day enter the secret room together, and he could at last read the Moonscript...

Newer memories started flooding in—Tellie trying to coax a smile onto his face, Kelm asking how to impress women, The Daisha nuzzling his ear, Tryss saying, "Your people need you, Errance. We need you."

Never forget who you are, Errance.

He had to get out. Everything could not be simply over. There had to be a way.

For a few breathless moments he hung there, forcing himself to recall what he could of the chamber above him. There had been a bar and pulley, letting the chains down into the void like a bucket into a well. It was not covered.

Gathering all his strength into his core, he swung himself back and forth to build momentum. On the strongest swing, he flipped himself upside down so that his body ran up the length of the chains. Trembling from the terrible strain of supporting himself on his shackled hands, he began his next move. The pain of the spikes cutting into his wrists and the pressure in his shoulders threatened to overwhelm him. A small scream escaped before he could bite it back. He clenched his teeth, swearing silently. Would all his stamina unravel now after that snap?

Quickly, he shifted his weight onto one wrist, slackening the chain of the other. Catching his foot in the loose chain, he wrapped it up in a secure hold and then did the same for the other. When his feet were firmly twisted and supported in the chain, he swung and pulled himself up again, no matter how many lights burst in front of his vision.

Right side up once more, he clung to the taut chain, the length from his wrists to his feet dangling loosely around him. The dancing stars seemed to flicker out, nausea churned within him, and for a terrifying instant he thought he was going to lose consciousness. *Please…no…*

But as he rested there, the chains under his feet as solid as any ground, his trembling body began to calm from the effort. He had no idea how long he stayed there, willing every muscle and bone to stop screaming. The celestial light inside him flickered as erratically as his heartbeat, threatening to go out.

After his heart slowed in its hammering, he grabbed one chain with both hands. Sucking in a deep breath, he pulled himself up its length, hand over hand, slowly dragging the rest of chains behind him. With no support under his feet and the heavy chains draping below, he wondered if his shoulders would tear out of their sockets the rest of the way. They should. He knew that the only thing holding him together and giving him strength was his celestial gift. And it could fail him any moment.

But it would not. It could not.

He climbed higher and higher, taking care to be as silent and still as possible as he neared the top. There would be little time. As soon as the first shred of light touched his knuckles, he surged. Up the chains he darted and grasped the wooden beam. Heaving with all his might, he flung a leg over it and straddled its length. The guards, leaning lazily by the door, spun around with shocked shouts. They leaped towards him, right into range. He caught up a length of chain and flung it out over their shoulders. Then with a jerk, he pulled them forward, and they unbalanced, tottered, and then toppled into the abyss.

Long after their screams had faded, he clung to the beam, his head sagging over the edge. Not an inch of strength remained in him, he knew if he tried to move he'd slip, and the darkness and weight of the chains would drag him down into that deathly drop again. So he only hoped no one had heard the cries and come running.

Finally, the frantic pounding in his chest settled, and he gathered himself up again for another effort. Crawling across the beam, he reached the supporting pillars and climbed down to solid ground. But no time for relief on that. The heavy chains pulled against his wrists, teasing him back to the edge. He found the gears of the pulley and pressed the chain links in between their teeth. The crank refused to turn on his first attempts, it took his fifth lurch and strain to roll it and then—the chain links snapped and the dead weight sped off like a snake across the floor and plunged silently into the pit.

He stumbled to the door and stared up the stairwell, not daring to remember how long it had taken to come down, not that he would be any great judge of what the distance was now. But he'd only made it a few turns up the stair when the clatter of footsteps echoed above. No turning back, no stopping, nothing could get in his way. Taking a sharp breath, he sped around the corner...and...curses, he had misjudged the distance. The guard, still several steps away, stared at him in mute surprise that swiftly morphed into a snarl of rage. The man drew a sword from his belt and jumped towards Errance, but the prince ducked aside at the last moment. He caught the guard's collar and wrenched him back onto the steps with a crack, then twisted the sword from his grasp and ran him through before any recovery could be made.

He went to move onward, but his legs collapsed on the first try. Panting, he pressed his brow against the wall and tried to steady the scattered fray of his mind. What…what was he even doing? He knew he couldn't escape, he knew it, so why try this another time?

He already knew how it ended, it always ended in one way because there was no other way…no…other…way…

Unless…

Not even daring to think it through lest it prove wrong, he jostled the guard's body free of his jacket and slipped it over his bare torso. If this would be his final stand, so help him, he would not face it half-naked.

Forcing himself up, he took the next step and then the next. Don't stop. Don't stop. Never stop. The beat hammered out in his heart, giving strength to his legs, and soon he was running, breaking free of the stairwell and set loose in the narrow halls.

The rush of air past his ears was cold and sorrowful, just as it had been long ago on a night when he rode for his life and ran straight into death. But back then he had not known where he was going…he knew now. He knew and he would not be afraid.

"Errance? Errance!"

The girlish cry tripped his pace, sent him lurching to a halt and staring back with wide eyes. Tellie…she couldn't be here. She'd left, just as she should have. But here she was now down the hall, trotting towards him with a look of hope and excitement. Kelm was beside her too, and that was not right. Kelm had not been brought here a second time.

It was a trick. A trap.

"Stay back," he rasped. "Stay away!" He turned and ran again, ignoring their wailing cries and pursing footsteps. It was all just an illusion, a way to lure him from his purpose.

Errance…you are running the wrong way.

This voice was still and small, a strange calm in the midst of his chaos. But he drowned it out with an inward scream. "Leave me alone, leave me!" He saw an iron door barring his way, but kept hurtling towards it without breaking speed. "Darkness, if ever you wanted to do me a favor, do it now!"

He wrenched open the door and flung himself through into the shadows beyond.

"Errance!" Tellie threw herself against the door, only to stumble back with a cry of pain. She grabbled for a handle, a knob, a latch, anything that might open it. But whatever had let the elf prince through was gone now, and she could not make the stone budge.

Even so, Kelm joined her, and together they pushed and huffed and pounded against the iron, calling Errance's name. When nothing prevailed, Tellie sank against the wall, rubbing a sore shoulder. Why must he always run…and where was he running in this place if he'd given up hope of escaping?

Frowning, she leaned harder against the door and closed her eyes. Kelm started to say something, and she shushed him sharply. She just needed silence for a bit. Here, if she concentrated just so, she could still sense the thin veil between the Unseen and the mortal realm. If she could just reach out with that special sight that gazed past all substance, she could peel back the stone, the shadows, the sorrow, and she would see…

"No!" With a haggard gasp, she jerked backwards and fell to the floor.

Kelm was beside her in an instant, grabbing her by the arms. "What's wrong?" he yelped. "What did you just do? Are you okay? Talk to me, Tellie!"

She shook her head, tears streaming down her cheeks. How could she explain that which she barely understood? Except she did understand, however impossibly. She had never been to the place where Errance had gone. And yet she knew its presence all the same.

"Errance has gone into the Nyght."

35

oOo

It was dark.

Only not.

Errance stood on the very brink of a precipice, looking out into the belly of the beastly sphere that he'd watched hover above his world for more days than he had seen the sun or the moon. It was both less and more terrible then he had expected.

For one, he could see. Although the encircling surface was as black as ink, everything within it was lit in a pale shade. So he could see thousands of broken fragments floating soft and silent throughout a prison so vast, so small. When he first saw the debris, he thought it nothing more than the broken teeth of sharp rock or glass. But the closer he looked, the less he was sure, and so he stopped looking.

Instead he looked to the center where the largest suspended stalactite hung, and upon it stood a lone and ghastly figure. The figure stood with his back to him, though surely he had summoned him here.

Clenching his teeth, Errance waited for the next bit of rock to float by and then he leapt upon it. It swayed under his weight, and he clung to the surface. When it settled, he carefully rose and jumped for the next. This one was larger; it did not mind how he caught its edge and scrambled to pull himself onto the top. But now there were no pieces anywhere near and though he waited, breath whisking in and out of his lungs, none came any closer.

"Don't give up." The Voice of His Darkness, still not bothering to turn and face him, inspected his fingers in patient waiting. "'Tisn't like you to just give up."

A fragment came a little closer, tempting. He leaped, but just as his hands touched, it skimmed backwards. He barely caught hold and slammed into the hard rock-face. As he hung, vision spinning, the surface of the stone looked back at him like the surface of a mirror. Only...it wasn't his face. But it was a face he knew.

He cried out and lashed himself up to the top before he could see anything more. Too late. The stone was glowing now with that same sickly half-light and the images within were searing into his thought even while his eyes squeezed shut.

"You like them?" The Voice said, as droll as a keeper of the finest antiques. "My collection. Of broken dreams. I daresay there's a bit of yours in here, like this little sliver, so hard to find anything left...but there are others you might recognize better. Or if you don't, shame on you, because you had a primary hand in breaking them. Who did you just see? One of your loyal elven guards, I suspect? Funny, he'd already lived so long and yet his life was still so incomplete."

"Shut up," Errance whispered, pressing his hands hard into his head in an effort to shove the images away.

"What's this one? Oh, yes, this belongs to that doe-eyed, little orphan girl who thinks you're a hero. Too bad you didn't tell her what you really are before she pinned all her hopes on you." The sound of His Voice was so very clear, as if speaking right in his ear instead of lengths away. "And here, I don't think you'd know this one, but this man, an enlisted guard in my service, had very fine dreams, lots of ambition, most of them even good once upon a time. Maybe someday he could have returned to those good dreams. Of course, we'll never know now because, oh yes, you killed him."

He wouldn't stop. There was only one possible way to make him silent.

He crouched as the stone drifted near the center stalactite and then he leapt.

It was almost too far. His fingers tore as he caught the side of it, but he pulled up and rolled to the solid, unmoving ground.

"Nice of you to drop in," The Voice said.

"Well," Kelm cried, "is there any other way to get to the Nyght?"

"No." Tellie paced, raking her hands through her hair. "Didn't you see it when you flew in on The…" Her mouth dropped open and formed into a silent 'O'. "The Daisha! She can reach it! Come on!" She grabbed her friend by the arm and led him pell-mell back through the corridor to the entrance by which they'd come in. The outside storm was a shock after the dead silence of the halls, and she staggered at the force of the violent wind. "Daisha!" she called, fearing that her voice would be drowned out, "Daisha, where are you?"

They scanned the visible sky, fortress, and mountains desperately for a sign of The Daisha and it was not long before they spotted her. She was hard to miss, cavorting about the towers and battlements, always one wingbeat ahead of the arrows and spears that sped in pursuit. She'd dash in and out to grab unfortunate soldiers and toss them away.

"She's not hearing us," Tellie wailed, after they'd yelled and screamed several times to catch her attention.

"DAISHA!" Kelm shouted, his young lungs finding a power as to be nearly deafening.

This time the creature's head twitched, and with a tilt of her wings, she soared over their station, muttering loud enough for them to hear, "That's funny, never heard of anyone called Daisha before…"

"The Daisha, come here right now before your wings rot off!" Tellie shrieked.

She plunged down, her front paws wrapping nimbly around the border wall, and flashed a blood-stained grin. "No need to get snippy. You called?"

"Errance! He's gone to the Nyght, that dark globe in the sky. He's going to get himself killed!"

The Daisha's ears turned back disapprovingly. "*My* Errance?" she said, eyes narrowing. "I didn't think he was so stupid."

"He's desperate. He has got to be stopped. We need to fly up there and figure out a way in!" Tellie pleaded.

"We most certainly must," The Daisha agreed coldly, turning her head to stare at the distant Nyght. "And when I say 'we' I apply it to myself in the most singular form of the word." With a powerful thrust of her wings and haunches, she launched into the sky.

"No!" Tellie cried, reaching after her in dismay. Kelm caught her about the waist and pulled her back as she leaned dangerously out over the edge.

"She's right," he said, holding her tight as she struggled. "We would only hinder her."

She couldn't argue, she couldn't say anything at all, only watch through fearful tears as The Daisha's figure became a blur racing towards the remorseless heart of Tertorem.

Errance staggered to his feet, keeping a careful distance from the Voice who had not moved from where he stood.

The demon watched him from the corner of his eyes, a small smile tugging across his lips. "Now this is an intriguing mystery. Why would you bother escaping again if you were only coming to turn yourself in? It can't be that you've finally sided with me after all these years…"

Aches pulsed through every nerve and muscle of Errance's body, but he straightened. "It has been more than enough," he whispered. "It's time for an end."

"Whose end?" The Voice asked.

"Yours," Errance said, and even before the word had left his lips, he'd drawn the knife hidden in the guard's jacket, and he sprang—

Tellie and Kelm watched in dismay as The Daisha, now looking so terribly small, scratched against the Nyght's surface. She flew up and down, hammering at it with her paws and body at several points. And then she turned and flew away, flew away as if she needed an ocean of a distance.

"Is she giving up?" Tellie exclaimed, dragging nails against her cheeks. "She can't give up!"

But Kelm's face whitened. "Oh," he said. "Oh. No. She can't really…no, that's too dangerous. She'd couldn't. She is."

"What? What is she doing?" There was no need for an answer. She could see it happening that very moment. Her heart rose in the breath before the plummet as she watched The Daisha rise into the sky, stall, and then fall in a grey streak towards the Nyght.

—the Nyhgt shattered.

Black glass exploded through the air in flying knives, and the dark surface webbed with bright, blinding natural light. Bursting through the darkness, shards crumbling around her, came The Daisha.

She did not so much as falter as her front paws extended and caught Errance, jerking him off his feet. With three more powerful thrusts of her wings, she continued right on, barreling through the other side in a cloud of glass flakes.

All of Tertorem stilled. Everyone standing within its realm felt the sudden intake of breath within their own chests, felt the change under their feet. Whether man, elf, chema, or shard, they all looked up as one to the towers where once the Nyght had hung. But now it fell in a rain of ash and death.

And streaking out of its ruin, in pursuit of the beast who had shattered it, came a dark and terrible wind.

"Daisha, no, NO!" Errance screamed, writhing in his friend's grip as she hurtled through the air. The rush of her speed rendered him nearly helpless and he did not know if she could even hear his gasping cry. Forcing his head around, he looked behind them and saw what was coming after.

"Let me go! You can't save me!" he shouted. "You idiot, please, drop me, let go! You can't win!"

But whether she could not hear or just ignored him, it was apparent The Daisha believed she could win, and not only could she outrace the wind to the mountains but lose it in the process.

It was perhaps her very determination that blinded her to the realization that the spires and arches she flew through were not ending. She didn't seem to notice that when she flew straight, they went in circles. When she flew up, they flew down, down, down, into an arena of smoke and shadow where the walls of Tertorem rose up on every side.

"This is his realm, you can't escape him—not with me!" Errance pushed against her paws, trying to break free. "Daisha, let go of me and save yourself!"

Suddenly, The Daisha dropped, without warning, without reason, without intention. She spread out her wings to slow the fall, but even her wings folded in on themselves. At the last possible second before impact, she whirled upside down and clutched Errance to her chest so that her back and shoulders crashed into the ground.

All was strangely soft and silent now that the wind no longer rushed by. Just a quiet world of cold stone.

Errance wrenched out of The Daisha's grasp and rolled to the ground. Struggling up, he cried, "Now go! Get out of here, you—" His words strangled in his throat as he saw how motionless she lay. With a gasp, he collapsed to his knees at The Daisha's side. His hands ran over her heaving shoulders and neck, the soft grey fur matted with blood and slivers of the Nyght's exterior.

Trembling, he crawled up to where her head lay against the ground, her nostrils flaring with each breath. Gently, he stroked her jaw. "Why'd didn't you listen to me?" he whispered.

Her beautiful diamond-blue eye flickered open and looked reprovingly at him. "You didn't say *The*…"

And her eyes closed.

The dark wind spiraled down, its terrible length coiling into the form of the Voice. He watched from across the arena in mock respect, hands folded quietly in front of him.

Errance didn't turn. He simply huddled over The Daisha, looking as fragile as a child beside their dying mother.

"What a pity," The Voice stepped up behind him, stroking a hand across his shoulders. "She was the last of her kind, wasn't she?"

For one breath, Errance was still. Then his hand shot back and grasped the Voice's wrist as he spun around, knife leaping into his other hand—and he plunged the blade into the demon's chest.

The Voice shuddered, fingers convulsing. His eyes widened, then slowly looked down into Errance's own…and then those pupils ruptured like ink in water. With a rush, his body melted away from around the knife and spread out in a flood of consuming darkness. The weight of it sent Errance to his knees.

"You fool!" The Voice of His Darkness laughed. The sound came from everywhere, in every breath and beat of the surrounding malevolence. It rose in a towering roar, too monstrous for the arena to contain. "You fool! You think you could kill me? I *am* the Darkness, I am not bound by life or death. Did you really think you could kill me?"

Errance collapsed under the thundering dark, the knife skittering from his limp hand. He bent over his knees, brow pressing into the ground.

"Did you?"

With great effort, he shook his head.

"No." The thunder gentled, drew in closer in a tight and suffocating embrace. "No, deep inside you knew it was futile. So why did you even try?"

No answer.

"WHY?"

"I had nothing else left!" Errance yelled.

The silence was stuffed with deep satisfaction, and the swirling void knit around and through him in a meshing net. "Nothing else left," the Voice said softly. "You never had anything to begin with, did you? But why is that surprising? You're all but worthless. Have you made yourself out to be a hero through all this? You, a hero? What have you to be proud of? Your heritage has fallen into dust, you forsook the teachings of your people. Your purity stolen, your mind enslaved, your hands red with the blood of man upon man. What would the elves think of you now? You are one of the filth they are so careful to avoid, lest they are contaminated. Yet despite all this, people placed faith in you. Tellie...Kelm...Tryss...this creature...They were willing to risk everything for you. And you've let them down. You've brought them here to die. Were it not for you, they'd be living peaceful lives far from here where I would never have noticed them. After their deaths there will be no one who cares for you. Just as well...that way you can't betray them."

Errance shuddered, wrapping his arms around his head. "L-leave me."

"Why?" the Voice purred, the cold shadows of his presence soft as a caress. "I am the only one still here. After everyone else has forsaken you, I am still present. After all you have done, after all the pain and evil you have caused, I am the only one who still wants you. You were mine from the beginning, Errance."

The Darkness closed in, draining, consuming, and then filling every sense and every breath. For one final moment, Errance struggled against it, knowing that if he didn't now he would never have the strength again. But there was no strength left within in him and in that fleeting gasp of time, his heart reached out for only one thing.

God, save me.

Light burst forth.

36

oOo

With a shriek of terror, the Darkness drew back, unable to bear its complete opposite, its overcomer, the one thing that might vanquish it.

It was the light of dawn after the longest night when the sky above the mountains softens and the clouds brighten into spun gold. It was the light of the morning creeping through the sleeping garden and turning every dewdrop to a diamond to adorn the waking flowers. It was the light of the sun in the summer, so white and so vivid that it warmed the entire world.

It was the light of fire, the forger's fire, a burning, purifying, and terrifying light.

Errance, curled into a ball upon the ground, wished then to wrap himself up in the shadows that had only moments before sought to swallow him whole. It no longer seemed such a terrible fate as compared to this. *You fool*, his mind gasped. *You weak fool. You fall under one only to surrender to the other?*

As he lay there trembling, the pain of the light lessened, but not because he had found some resistance against it, but because the source had softened to a measure he could stand.

"Why do you cower?" The voice was like the light itself, warm, gentle, piercing. "Did you not call me?"

I wish I hadn't. Aloud, he said, "And I've had respite, so let me go."

"If I let you go now, you will be destroyed."

His mind screamed like claws on glass at the sadness of that voice. "Like you care?" he gasped. "I have been destroyed long before now. Where were you when I needed you before?" He bit his tongue too late, pushing his face harder into his hands. *Needed?* He...hadn't needed anyone, not ever.

"Was I not always beside you? Have I not always come when you called? And have you not always pushed me away?"

"I didn't want you! I just wanted out!"

"Out where?"

"Anywhere else! Back to my life!"

"The life you chose to leave. Would you have found what you wanted had you returned? You have been lost far too long, Errance. You were empty, even when you had everything."

Gritting his teeth, he lashed back, "I wasn't evil! I dare say I was even good. At the least, I did not deserve this fate!"

"This is the fate of the lost. The Darkness does not care if you are good or evil, only if you are vulnerable. And you had no protection, for you had rejected me already."

"And if I was yours, I would have been safe?" he asked viciously. "If I was your servant, would I have been safe forever, never having to fear anything? Do not lie, Daava may not have told me much of his past life, but I know it was fraught with pain, though he ever served you." Bitterness tanged his throat, barely letting him speak further. "Even in the shelter of his kingdom, you allowed my mother to die!"

"Such was her gift of love to you. This world gave itself to death long ago and now is shadowed with sorrow and pain. Those brave enough to live and to love within it are blessed in my name and their eternity is treasured in my hand. But Tertorem is the prison of death and it binds the soul far tighter than the body. You know this, you have felt it. But even its bars cannot keep you from my love."

"Love!" Hands dropping away from his face, Errance lifted his chin and stared into a darkness sealed across his eyes. He gave a little laugh, shrill with anger and disbelief. "Love? You let me stay in that prison for seventy years, tortured, devastated, degraded, broken! How dare you speak about love? You do not understand what I went through! Are you not God, so great and glorious and above us all? You are a lie! I HATE YOU!"

And he would die. As soon as the words left his mouth, he knew he would die. He fell back to the ground, arms sheltering his head once more as he waited for retribution to fall. It could not be fear that made his limbs shake, for had he not desired death for so long? And yet tears streamed down his cheeks, for he could see nothing beyond that death save more death.

But there was no brilliant stab of light, no wave of sundering power. There was only a still and small silence.

"Errance."

He would not turn. Never.

"Errance."

Slowly and painfully, he turned with a scrape across the ground. Drawn despite the struggling of his spirit, he lifted his tear-blurred eyes from the broken rock to the shining heart of the light.

He looked upon the One. The One who could cup the world in his hands, magnificent and holy, beyond all mortal restraint and comprehension....

...he looked upon a Man who bore all his scars.

Moments sometimes could be measured by a tick of a clock. Others hang suspended in forever. For Errance, it felt as the latter, as he sat and he stared and he tried to understand.

The scars were not merely those he'd borne within a few days, a few weeks, or even a year. It was every scar he'd received, far too many to count, far too many for one body to contain at once. And not all the scars were of flesh. He could see the rents across his heart, the fluttering rags of his soul. He could see that all the blood streaming down that body was not merely his own, but the life-blood of those he'd taken, both innocent and not, but blood nonetheless. The scars went on and on in layers upon layers that his vision ached to comprehend.

When he at last he tore his eyes away, his own body shook without control. "That shame is mine," he whispered. "W-why…why would you wear it?"

"I have done more than wear it. I have taken it upon myself."

"How?"

"Am I not God?" The echo of Errance's accusation rang back with the faintest amusement. Not cruel, merely chiding.

"But why bother? I have done nothing but hate you for all these years, so why would you care to share my suffering?"

The One cupped his own chin in his hand and looked down for a few moments in quiet musing. The normalcy of such an action was somehow far more unsettling than any display of cosmic energy.

"Do you believe your father loves you?"

Wincing, Errance looked away. That…why must the question he most feared be asked? It was a question he could never even hope to answer, not anymore. "I don't know. I'm not sure he could after seeing what I've become."

"Let me tell you something about fathers. True fathers, who understand the beauty and preciousness of the life they have helped create. They love their child before it has done anything to earn such affection. If then their love is based without condition, how could their heart be changed? So then, did your father love you?"

"Yes?" Errance's mouth trembled, and his eyes fluttered shut. It was true. He could doubt himself, but how could he have ever been so awful as to doubt the trueness of his father's heart? "Yes."

"Then let me tell you something about myself." A body couldn't hold the majesty of the One, and hands and feet were far too humble for him to possess. And yet footsteps quietly padded alongside Errance, and a figure knelt in front of him, and hands gently cupped his face.

Unfathomable eyes stared into the prince's own. So simple in flesh and blood, but in their depths, the galaxies danced. Those very same eyes were bright with tears. "I am your father's Father. I spun the world from my fingertips, each beautiful thread bound to my heart. No matter how many tear away, how matter how the canvas frays, the day is soon in coming when the picture will be remade. Prince, prisoner, you do not even know who you are. But I know who you were meant to be. I would have you as a son of mine and heir to my kingdom for I loved you since before I wove you in the womb. Will you not believe that now?"

As Errance looked upon him, it seemed then that he saw even more than the scars. He saw the hope in Tellie's eyes, the kindness of Kelm's smile, the gentleness of Tryss's touch, the strength in Coren's hand. The shining of the stars and the green of the grass. Everything that was good and lovely and true. Everything that he had loved and everything that he had lost. It was here, here within the One from whom it all came.

He had never been neutral in his battle against the Darkness. He had always been its slave, running farther and farther away from that which could save him.

A lie?

The only lie had been the one he'd told himself.

Your pride will be the death of you, he recalled his father once saying. So it had been. A long, painful death, chained by his own determination to win a battle that he'd already lost. But in every life comes a chance for change. In truth it was there all the time. But only sometimes was it clear to see.

Breath stuttered from his lips. "Forgive me."

And he collapsed into Ayeshune's arms and wept. Wept for the anger, the agonies. The sins and the shames. But as he wept, the pain that had long clasped claws into his heart loosened and fell as a vanishing wisp across the ground. And in its place, the bloom of everlasting hope unfurled.

The celestial opened his eyes with a gasp. He looked around the circle where he and his comrades sat and found them all staring at one another in like astonishment and blossoming joy.

"He is saved," one breathed.

"Rendar must know," another cried. "Someone must go into the Unseen and tell him!"

"Oh, I think he already knows."

"Tell the whole city!" the celestial man leapt to his feet with a glad shout. "Brighten every star, sing every song, they all must know!"

A hand caught his arm, and he looked down at the eager face of a maiden. "Yes," she said. "But first...tell Erran."

Whereas first the light was like fire, it now soothed with the coolness and flow of water, sweeping away filth and leaving the skin and soul shining clean. Errance held still in the constant embrace, afraid to move lest the spell be broken. The pains that had become part of his very fabric were gone in this presence, and he hardly knew what to think or to feel or to do. Was there any weight left to keep him grounded to the earth or would he blow away on the first breeze? He could take deep breaths, feel the power of his heartbeat instead of the ache...it was like...like...

"Did I die?" he asked softly. "Is this why it feels...so strange?"

Ayeshune chuckled, the rumble in his chest loud against Errance's ear. "In a way. You've been reborn and unchained."

"So..." He pulled back, eyes cast to the ground. "I am to return. Back...there."

"Why are you afraid?"

"I'm not," he said, then flinched because it was a lie. "I just...I am tired of struggling and this...I know this peace cannot last back there. And I have failed everyone who loved me. If you would just take me now...I...my father, he was the one I desired to return to the most and now he's gone...and..."

Ayeshune cupped his face in one large hand and tilted it up so they looked one another in the eyes. "There is much life in you yet and your future has the hope to be full of power and wisdom. There are many in that world who need you...and through you, great glory may come."

Errance blinked, his mouth opening and shutting several times over. He squeezed his eyes shut, fighting the terrifying thought of leaving this safety, this comfort. "Send me back then," he said, the words scraping roughly from his throat. Better to do it fast before he could become any more afraid.

"First," the One said. "There is one who wishes to speak with you. One whom you love."

The strong, gentle hand turned Errance's face to the side then, and as Errance squinted into the gardens of light, he saw a tall figure take shape and come forward, the light gathering into colors around him until he could see...

"Daava..." he whispered.

37

oOo

The Darkness skulked in the cracks of stone and the rubble of rocks, outside the reaches of the light, unable to see through the brilliance beyond. Hissing and twisting like a serpent, he paced in impatience and fear. His greatest prize had vanished within that celestial embrace, and now he could only wait in trepidation for the result.

Surely the prince could not last long in there. Oh, the Darkness knew the state of his soul, triumphed over it moment by moment. Perhaps…it was a terrible thought…perhaps his great Enemy had taken the elf to destroy him rather than let him be used for a wicked purpose. After all his hard, careful work, that *would* be how it ended. Yet perhaps he could find some satisfaction in thinking on the Prisoner's miserable fate.

Wait. Voices. Coming from the heart of the light and drawing steadily nearer. He squinted into the brightness and spotted a familiar figure. The Prisoner! Somehow still alive and coming closer. He'd take him now; it was the last chance, now—now!

He sprang, darkness ripping through the brightness, heading straight for the soul where he could coil in safety—

—but there was nothing but light. The blackened cavity of Errance's soul could not be found. Only the light, allowing no place for Darkness. Horrified, he shrieked and writhed, desperate to get away but finding himself weaved in from all sides. "Mine!" he screamed. "He's mine!"

Errance stood firm, trembling only a little, and finding support in the hand on his shoulder. "No longer," he said, and his eyes glinted with the same sharpness as swords. "It's over, Darkness. I am not yours. The Moonscript will remain hidden, and the celestial kingdom shall remain free from your touch."

For one second in time, the Darkness was still. In that instant he saw it all. He remembered what he once had been, when light was not agonizing. He remembered his pride, his ambition, and his fall. For even though he'd become Darkness itself, devoid of all else, still he desired the perfection he had lost forever. So alluring, so satisfying. The celestial realm beckoned to his unquenched thirst, his unsated appetite. Now after all these centuries, he looked at the one who was the key to his desire—and he saw upon him a seal that he could never break. A lock he could never open. A life he could never own.

With an earsplitting screech, the black wind drew into a sharp spiral and shot into the air, a shockwave spreading out from its contrail over the entire expanse.

To its very roots, Tertorem trembled.

Errance swayed as the ground shook underneath him, but was steadied by Ayeshune's hand. The One turned him about and looked proudly upon him, brushing a finger across his brow. "Go now," he said. "This fortress has lost its strength and it will fall. You must find your friends and bring them to safety."

Taking a deep breath, Errance nodded and clenched his fists. His gaze drifted beyond Ayeshune's shoulder where he could still glimpse visions of paradise between the rays of light and somewhere there stood a tall figure who watched with a tear-glistening smile. Someday…

"I am ready."

—and Errance was left alone on his knees by The Daisha's side, exactly as he had been before.

But he wasn't the same.

The world wasn't the same.

The world was falling down.

For the moment, that hardly mattered. What shook his reverie more than the shattering walls and crumbling floors was the sight of The Daisha all still and silent upon the ground. Exactly as he'd known it would, the grief and weight of the mortal realm slammed into his heart, and he collapsed against her with a hard sob.

The Daisha twitched. Jerked. Errance reeled back as her eye opened, rolled about a bit, and then focused with intense sternness. She raised her head with a scowl. "There you are!" she said. "Did I fly fast enough? You look different. What in Orim is all this beastly earth-quaking about?"

She stared at him, then rolled her shoulders in irritation. "Are you going to answer me or you going to just look at me like a complete idiot?"

"B-b-but you were dead!" Errance stuttered. "Or were dying." He gestured to her fur still matted with glass shards and blood.

"Oh," The Daisha said with an indifferent sniff. "Mere flesh wounds. Don't you know that daisha hides are tougher than leather? Few things really get deep past all this fur anyway."

"Then why did you fall?" he exclaimed, his voice breaking with frustration.

"Why? The world was going backwards and forwards. And then I couldn't breathe and hardly move. I felt like I'd turned to stone. It was a very nasty trick, whatever it was."

"The Darkness," he answered in disgust. He leapt to his feet, startling her so that she sat up on her haunches. "His powers are broken now. Where are the others? We have to find them and leave this place."

"Where exactly did the Darkness go?" The Daisha demanded as he leapt onto her shoulders. "And what exactly happened—ouch, watch where you're sitting—to you?"

"No time," he gasped. "We have to fly."

Grumbling, she lowered her body and spread her wings, but at that moment they heard a distant cry. Errance twisted around and stared off into the unstable walls. "That sounded like Tryss!"

"That's because it is Tryss, silly man."

There was a rattle of stones falling, and then a small, grey figure rolled out of a crack in the distant wall. Brushing aside grit and dust, Tryss pushed to her feet and staggered towards them. "Errance? Daisha!"

The Daisha reached her in three bounds, muttering something about slow two-legged persons, and Errance reached down and caught her hand. He braced as she scrambled up and he pulled her in front of him.

The Daisha launched into the sky as the first part of the wall fell to the ground and obliterated. Struggling for breath, Tryss leaned back against Errance, trying to turn and see his face. "You're safe? I was looking for you in the tunnels, but I ended up here and—" she broke off with a gasp. "Where are Tellie and Kelm? Tertorem will fall on top of them!"

When the shaking first began, Kelm ceased staring after The Daisha's disappearance and grabbed Tellie's arm. "Tellie!" he cried as the wind rose to a piercing shriek. "We've got to get back down to the elves!"

Her eyes remained glued to the stormy distance, lips forming soundless words.

A sudden crack thundered above their heads, and they looked up to see one of the tower foundation crumble, and the great spire began to tilt over. "The whole place is coming down!" he shouted. "Come on!"

"But Errance—The Daisha—Tryss," she wailed, pulled after him against her will.

"I said, come ON!"

A deep rumble vibrated the earth and the slope below them split apart, gas hissing forth from it. They raced down the path, stones bouncing around them. But before they had gone down the next level, there was an eerie roar and the ground turned to rubble beneath their feet. As they started to slide down, Kelm grabbed Tellie by the waist and lunged for a wide outcrop still fixed in place. Gasping, he pulled her onto it, and they huddled against the surface as the entire mountain about them continued to disintegrate. All they could do was sit and watch as the avalanche rushed past and more and more of their rock was exposed.

"It won't stay secure very long, I imagine," Kelm said, trying to still his shaking limbs. Gingerly, he reached out for her hand. "I should have got us down sooner, Tellie."

She stared at the destruction, eyes vacant. "It's my fault."

"What?"

Drawing her knees up to her chin, she wrapped her arms around her legs and tried to ignore the chill of oncoming doom. It was somehow more peaceful than she imagined, even with all the chaos surrounding them. "I was told to escape, that I couldn't help Errance anymore. But I went ahead and decided I knew better. And now we're both going to die. I'm sorry."

"Oh." Kelm blinked, and rubbed his brow hard with the heel of his hand. "Well. We might have helped anyway, so I don't mind. At least we're...you know...together."

She nodded and opened her mouth to reply, but a powerful roar stole all her thoughts away. It wasn't the roar of the falling mountains...it was a very animal sound, the sound of—

The Daisha came plunging through the clouds of dust and smoke, her long paws spread out to catch them. As she caught them up into the sky, the rock upon which they'd taken refuge gave way to the avalanche. Then the ground was falling far beneath them and the wind whistled in their ears. Tellie had the brief revelation that she was flying, but after everything else that had happened in the last hours, that really didn't feel significant.

Beneath them, the earth rumbled, and all around them, the sky cracked with thunder. Then the sound of something rent in half, like a curtain torn in two, and then a burst of light and wind that pelted their skin with bitter sand.

And then...silence. A calm, peaceful silence, not fitting to their surroundings. The wind no longer howled, the lightning no longer flashed. When Tellie dared to open her eyes again she saw the clouds were thinning, vanishing away as smoke on the breeze.

The ground beneath them, where once Tertorem had been, was now nothing more than rubble. The only sign that it had existed were the flattened wood buildings of the human workers. Yet her stomach dropped even more when she saw that the mountains themselves were no longer present. Not the mountains she'd seen anyway; these were more ordinary sort of hills with steep spots and low valleys.

"Are you all right, children?" They heard Tryss's voice above them, and they could see her foot from where they hung beneath The Daisha's belly. Not only her foot, but also one of a man.

"Tryss!" they shrilled. "Tryss, is that you? Is Errance with you?"

"Yes, yes," The Daisha huffed. "I have you all, and it is quite strenuous, believe me. Don't struggle and let me find a place to land. I am hurt and very tired."

"There's the elf army," Tryss said, pointing.

"The…" Whatever Errance had been going to say faded on his lips. But even that one word had said quite enough in its fragile and wavering way.

Continuing to gripe, The Daisha circled down and with a few clumsy flaps, alighted on the ground on her back haunches, setting the children down in front of her carefully.

The moment Errance slid to earth, Tellie flung herself towards him, tears already streaming down her face. "I thought you were gone," she cried. "Gone forever! What happened—" And she would have hugged him, but she ground to a halt in both speech and speed. She did not stop because she remembered Errance's aversion to touch. No, she stopped for an entirely different reason, a reason that made her eyes wide as moons.

Her stunned silence drew the others to look in curious observation as well, and a similar expression dawned on their own faces.

Uncomfortable, Errance stepped back. "What. What is it?" he asked stiffly.

"Your brands," Tellie whispered. "Where are they?"

His eyes flew wide, and his hands fluttered over the bruised surface of his skin, searching under the remnant rags of his jacket, but no mark could be seen. No trace of the words inscribed across his heart. "I don't understand—" His fingers flew up to his face. "What about the *deltha* marks through my eye? The mark of the Red Three? Is it…?"

"It's gone!" Tellie cried, clapping her hands in amazement. "Oh, oh, whatever did happen to you?"

He continued to hold his fingers on his brow as if to make sure the mark didn't return. "I suppose…you could say I was…reborn."

"What?" Kelm wrinkled his nose. "That doesn't make any sense. Are you sure you're all right?"

But Tellie stared into Errance's eyes and she did not find the dark anger that always hunkered in that brilliant color, but instead a hopeful and kindling wonder. And as she guessed a little of what had happened, her heart began to soar.

It was surely a dream. Only Errance could not remember a dream where he felt so weightless and free and whole. The scars had always come and gone, but he'd been doomed to bear the shameful brands of his masters forever, only now forever had ended. One by one his first three masters had slashed their mark until the triad was complete and the Darkness had given him the painful truth of his soul not so long ago—and in one moment the light and love of the One had erased those claims away.

He closed his eyes, unable to bear the questioning looks of his friends, unable to begin to explain. He just wanted to be alone and think for a few moments, without any interruptions—

He was interrupted.

"Brights! Errance! Tryss, kids! Thank the One you made it out! That was quite the feat Miss Daisha performed, never seen anything like it. Do you know why there was an earthquake and most of Tertorem vanished? A bit shaking, you might say, haha."

Tryss had said the elf army had come, and he'd seen their glittering mass with the same surreal, doubtful vision he was seeing everything else by, but somehow he had not expected to first be reunited with that one certain elf. The redhead, the smuggler, the savior of his skin.

Errance turned and stared as Captain Coren picked his way towards them across the sharp rocks, still very much in his sailor garb and not looking a bit like a soldier of any kind. When he'd quite arrived, he stopped smiling and simply looked him over in a long and uncomfortable silence.

"What are you doing here?" Errance said at last, face wrinkling.

"Bird-watching."

The jest was weak at best, weaker still when said so flatly. Perhaps because even Coren did not much feel like avoiding the truth. Unbelievable but undeniable truth. They had come—after years and years and years of knowing they never would—his people had finally come.

"Why?" Errance whispered. Why now.

Coren looked him in the eye, sober, searching. "I sent for the elves in order to bring home a broken slave," he said slowly. "But I was wrong." He dropped to one knee, crossed an arm across his chest, and bowed. "I see only a king."

Amid the faint gasps of the others, Errance stepped back in retreat. His heart had gone thundering; he could feel the beat of it in his chest. "If you see a king," he said, voice scraping out from a raw throat, "then it is not me."

Glancing up with a glinting smile, Coren nodded. "I can accept that. Humility and self-awareness, that's good in a ruler." He shoved back up to his feet. "Well then, are you coming?"

"Coming?"

"Coming to see your people."

A small hand slipped into Errance's own. He had not realized till that touch that his hand had been shaking, and he sought to be still as he looked down into Tellie's face. Her blue eyes were very wet and very bright. "They love you, Errance," she said. "They love you so much, you know. I can't even imagine how they must feel to have you so close, but still so far away. If Casara's your aunt, that means Leoren is your uncle now. You have family in them, Errance. And family is precious."

"You have more family than that!" Coren said, whisking another bow. "Meet me, your cousin!"

Errance stared. He barely heard the exclamations of everyone else, only the echoes of those words ringing in his ears. "What."

"You heard me." The red-headed rogue looked very pleased, as if being cousins had been all his idea. "The elegant son of the demure Casara and the stately Leoren? You mean it wasn't obvious?"

"This has been a long day," Errance muttered, pressing a hand to his brow which had now gone incredibly light.

"A long night actually," Coren corrected. "But it's morning now. A new day. A new start. A fine time to return to your people." Softening, he held out a hand. "Come on, Errance. It's time."

For only a moment more, he hesitated. Then, ignoring Coren's hand, he walked forward three steps. Because he made it that far, he kept going. He walked and the others fell in line behind him in a strange and solemn procession.

Before them, no longer distant across the rocky ground, stood the elves. They stood in silent formation, the drapes of their tunics and cloaks wafting around their rigid bodies. All their opponents were fled or slain, and the only sign of the battle could be found in the blood and grime on their armor. At their head stood Lord Leoren.

Lord Leoren, who was pale and drawn as if he looked upon a ghost.

In a sense, he did.

When he was within ten paces, Errance stopped, the strength of his legs and will evaporating. He couldn't look upon those faces anymore, so familiar and yet so forgotten. He couldn't bear to see the faded colors so vivid or the crests of his kingdom so bright. He stared at the ground, hands clenched by his sides.

Shale crunched. The slight flicker of movement brought Errance's flinching gaze up ever so slightly, and he saw Leoren very near to him, the lord's head tilted to the side in an effort for a better look.

Their eyes met.

Not allowing another second to pass, the elven lord caught him into his arms and held him with all his strength against a heart beating with immeasurable joy.

Something within Errance broke, in the same way as it had when he'd been held by the One. And it was a good sort of breaking, even if it sent hot tears streaming down his cheeks and made his limbs so weak he only stood by the steadfastness of Leoren's embrace. It was somehow painful and relieving all at once, like a thorn plucked free from its hold. And the fears of the return journey, the shock of seeing the kingdom again—it was all retreating. Because deep inside, he knew.

He was already home.

38

oOo

*Z*izain was the sort of woman who hated to be left behind. Ever since that strange, pointy-eared man had saved her long ago, she'd become his shadow through the thick and the thin, but now he had left her behind. It was to keep her safe, he'd said. All fine and noble, to be sure, but who would keep him safe? How was she to know he'd return?

In the time that he'd been gone, she'd paced at the edge of the camp and glared up at the mountain wall barring her way. She'd flexed her fingers, dry and cracked from the sun, and thought how empty they were.

And when the mountains roared and faded into dust, leaving behind ordinary hills, they might as well have come down by her will for Zizain was a woman who had made up her mind.

With that mind, she was the first to stride through the valley into the desolate land of Tertorem. She hardly batted an eye at the forsaken landscape, only set her course for the glitter in the grey. And amid all the fair elves, she had eyes for only one, one with bright red hair and a matching red sash. In the corner of her eyes and mind, she noticed the children and Tryss and that dark, interesting elf, but even that did not deter her long.

She bounded straight up to Coren before he noticed her coming, grabbed him by the pointy ears, pulled his face down to hers, and kissed him full on the lips. "Coren, darling!" she cried. "Marry me, won't you?"

He gaped at her, eyes round. "Brights, Zi! I never asked because I thought you'd say no!"

"Ask me now," she said with a quick tug on his collar.

"Marry me?" he gasped.

"Aye!" She bounced up again to land another peck. "Aye, aye, Captain!"

The elven healers and tribal folk gathered upon Tertorem's ashes in a whir of excitement, their languages blurring together in wild colors, but the sound of joy exactly the same. Wives embraced husbands, fathers kissed their children, siblings laughed and danced.

Somewhere in the crush of the company's arrival, Tellie lost sight of Errance and she wandered through the crowd, Kelm close by her side. Poor Errance, she didn't suppose even redemption had prepared him for so much affection and crowding at once.

"It is quite remarkable," Kelm was saying, his voice vague in her ear. "I knew Tertorem was strange, but how does anything just disappear like that?"

Tellie didn't answer right away, thinking instead of the kiss Coren and Zizain had shared shortly before the healers had arrived. The couple had been in their own happy place, quite oblivious and uncaring to the shocked expressions of the surrounding faces, none more shocked than Coren's own father. With Errance and now this, Tellie was not surprised Leoren hadn't come to her yet, and she tried very hard not to feel so disappointed.

"Are you even listening, Tellie?" Kelm exclaimed.

She forced her gaze to him. "Hmm?"

"This!" He waved his arm around at the open sky. "How does it all just vanish?"

"Tertorem was part of the Unseen," Tellie said practically. "It is very clear that Errance has been saved by the One, and with such a humiliating defeat, the Darkness has fled away and drug his dark realm along with him. One day I am sure Ayeshune will defeat him altogether."

Kelm blinked at her. "Oh bother," he groaned. "And here I thought we were both normal."

"No one is ever quite normal," someone said.

It was a voice of violet, starlight, and mountain streams. A voice she'd treasured away in her heart and feared never hearing again.

Tellie flushed and spun to face Casara with clasped hands. "Oh! Oh, my lady. I—"

She was wrapped in Casara's gentle arms before she could say a thing more. After a moment's embrace, the woman stepped back and cupped her face in her hands, lifting it up to look into hers. Tellie was struck dizzy to see that there were tears shining in those beautiful eyes. "We thought we'd lost you forever," Casara cried. "Leoren and I blamed ourselves for your fate, and when we heard Coren had found you..."

"Oh!" she said again, hardly able to speak straight over the thrill shuddering through her body. "Well, it all worked out for the best, it seems. I did find your king after all!"

"So you did!" Casara laughed. "Coren told us the tale, though you will have to tell it in full!"

"You've seen Errance, haven't you?" she asked anxiously.

"I have." Her voice trembled. "When Rendar spoke of you finding an heir, I never dreamed it would be him...my lost nephew. Thank you, Tellie. Thank you for everything." And then she knelt and kissed the girl on the cheek, holding her close to her heart.

Melting, Tellie held onto her in return and would have liked to just rest that way for a while more, but she saw Leoren and Errance coming through the crowd. The lord's eyes lit up as he saw her and he hurried forward.

"You're safe, God be praised!" he cried.

"I am," she said, pulling out of Casara's arms in order to dip a quick curtsy. But even he pulled her into an embrace, never mind his lordly self. It was quite enough to threaten tears.

Before tears or anything else could commence, the crowd suddenly stirred and cried out in sudden fear and surprise. Snatches of exclamations rippled towards them, things like, "Who is that?" and "A spy!" and "To arms!"

Tellie clung to Leoren's arm, only to find herself stumbling after him as he speared through the crowd in pursuit of Errance who had gone off in search of the distress. When they came to the fringe of the gathering, the elves there all facing outward in defense, they found a single figure standing upon the stony ground.

He was so dusty and grey he could have blended in with the ashes. His bent and broken figure bespoke the presence of one who'd spent their entire life attempting to be overlooked. But everyone saw him now.

More than that, Tellie knew him. Her heart skipped a beat in joy at the sight of the older miner. She'd been certain he must have died in that bold onslaught against the guards, but here he stood, a bit bloodied and yet somehow stronger.

He looked upon Errance with clear and certain eyes, and slowly he straightened.

Errance stared back at him, brow furrowing. He raised a hand to halt Leoren from drawing his sword. "I know you," he said. But he bit his lip, apparently unable to come up with a name.

"I don't have a name that matters anymore," the old man said with a shrug. "And I never knew ye as anything but Lord. For that's what ye were to me, more than any of those masters of ours. I would have served ye then and I would serve ye now." Very stiffly and full of pain, he bent down to one knee. "I've heard tales of your kind," he said. "I don't know if ye would accept the service of such a pathetic creature as myself or even if ye would have any pity, but I pledge myself to ye."

The air softly stirred as Errance inhaled, his lips parted without any response. Then almost as carefully as the miner, he crouched down to face him. "We were all slaves," he said. "Not one of us better than the other. The One sent the Darkness fleeing today, not me."

"Aye." The miner nodded. "But ye were the one who opened our eyes to see the light and those who love ye reminded us of all the good that we'd lost. We remembered the name of Ayeshune and loved it."

"How many of you have survived?" Errance asked, looking past him to the broken rocks beyond where other miserable bodies peered out at the glittering company.

"The only death came from battle, not the breaking of the prison," the old man said. "Most have already fled. But they'll be lost in the shadows. We few want to remain in the light."

"Our healers will tend all of your injuries," Leoren told the man kindly, his posture easing from the initial rigid suspicion. "And on the return to our realm, we would gladly escort you all to your homes."

The old man bowed, but his hands were rubbing together anxiously. "Well, er, thank ye. Some of us might 'ave homes to return to or some sort of future to pick back up. But as for me and some of the lads, we have nothing left. Nothing but shattered memories and lost paths. Would ye...Lord, would ye let us come with ye to your kingdom and begin again there? We would repay ya however we could, whatever the price."

Leoren looked slightly perplexed at this, but the old miner had not been addressing him.

"Yes," Errance said, ignoring the intakes of breath all around him, both from the slaves and the elves. "There is no price, I know what you suffered. If you have nowhere to go, you are welcome to come with me."

Relief cast over the wretched man's face for the first time in an age, and years of suffering washed away from his features. He bowed again, so low that he almost tottered over, and then he turned and staggered back to the other watching and whispering slaves.

The stunned silence was broken by the ring of Coren's laugh. "Hail, our king," he said, doffing his hat to Errance. "I think I will quite enjoy serving under you! Now then, shall we off? This place is a bit grave, if you know what I mean."

oOo

The chema village was full that night, so full that the forest around it was filled with little camps and lanterns for a good circling mile. The fires were dying now, the scent of savory meat still in the smoke. The sun may have gone beyond the horizon but the shadows of the mountains were gone, and the atmosphere was hushed with contentment and peace.

In all her life, Tryss could not remember having trouble falling asleep in her cot surrounded by wheezing siblings and the lulling snores of her parents in the room below. Of course, she'd been weary to the bone back then after each day, but she was likewise weary tonight, so it couldn't be that. And she certainly couldn't claim to have become accustomed to quiet over her journey. No, something different was afoot. Shock, perhaps. Elation. But more than that. Uncertainty. Anxiety. Even disappointment.

The dark demesne outside their borders was gone now, thank the One. Meaning that her tribe would not have to move, better still. Yet she couldn't help but feel saddened that the adventure with her new friends had come to an end and they would likely go on in that adventure, while she remained behind, trying to retrace old steps.

The night felt too humid, too stifling. She frowned to find herself thinking so, but decided that a fresh wind might do a miracle to her spinning head. So creeping quietly down the stair, she headed for the tallest tree outside the village.

It had always been a favorite post of hers, this tree. Easily the highest of the surrounding jungle and vastly thick with all sorts of knobs and branches that made it ideal for climbing. She'd sought its refuge since she was five, though she knew she was not the only one to do so.

Tonight, however, she hadn't planned on meeting anyone already up at the top. As she gripped a final branch and pulled herself up to a seat above the tree canopy, she suddenly noticed the figure already there, leaning against another thick branch. She couldn't quite make out their face in the dark, but somehow she guessed their identity before they spoke.

"Don't fall," Errance said.

She exhaled, clutching the branch a little tighter, but then breathed a laugh. "I've been scampering in the treetops since I was a babe, don't worry about me.

You on the other hand—"

"I'm an earth elf."

"So climbing trees comes naturally?"

"Naturally."

Blinking, she looked away, for even though she could not see his face clearly, she could see the star-gleam in his eyes, and that was unnerving enough. Of all people to meet and of all places to do so…and at all times, when her heart and mind had just been arguing with each other.

A branch creaked under Errance's weight as he shifted to climb lower. "You don't—" Tryss blurted. "You don't have to leave. I only came up for some fresh air. I mean…you can go…if you wanted solitude. Actually, in that case I should go, I can always have this tree another time."

Solitude. There was a whole small army of elves under the eaves of the jungle tonight and did any of them know where Errance was?

He paused and then slowly lifted back up. "The fresh air and stars were also what I sought. And perhaps a little solitude, but only from—" He trailed off into an unintelligible murmur.

"Must have been quite a feat, if you snuck out."

"I have some skill at sneaking away, in case you hadn't noticed."

Well. That was certainly a joke. Or sarcasm, more accurately. But it was said with good-natured humor, none of the bite she'd first known.

Smiling, she settled onto her branch and leaned her arms against another in front. "I suppose it will be stifling at first. The attention, the adoration, the eager company. But they do love you, Errance, and family is a wonderful thing. I'm happy for you."

A slight scraping sound caught her ear. His fingers were nervously plucking at the bark. "It is difficult to accept something," he said, "that you do not fully understand. In the beginning, I thought I knew love, but I see now I only understand a few layers of it. What I witnessed…what has changed me…was the fullness of that love. But I do not know if my heart, my mind, or my soul is too small to take it all in, because the vision and grasp of it fades even now."

While he spoke, she had gone perfectly still. Not even a breath was disturbing her lips, for fear that she might somehow provide a reason for him to stop.

"My physical scars will fade," he said. "But I know the ones inside remain and will come back to haunt me. I'm not sure how I can do this...this...beginning again."

"You won't have to do it alone," she whispered. "We're with you."

He turned to her and looked long and thoughtfully. "I never thanked you."

"What?"

"I never thanked you for coming with the children and me. It was dangerous to leave your home and venture into a world you hardly know. I know I frightened you. I meant to. I'm sorry for that."

She swallowed and gave a nod, though it was so small as to be lost in the dark.

He glanced away again. "Are you still coming to Aselvia?"

"What?"

"Am I speaking too quietly or something?"

She blushed furiously before she glimpsed slight starlight on a smile. Daring to smile in return, she replied, "I suppose my people will stay here. Our village is in no danger anymore, and we are well-established."

"I suspected as much. But that's not what I asked. I was asking if you were coming to Aselvia."

She jolted, gripping the branch hard enough that it creaked. "Oh. Well. I...I will have to speak with the Ancient and my people, but I believe they would give their blessing. I certainly would...like to come and see your kingdom. I know it must be very beautiful. There might be others who would wish to visit as well, though I promise we would not impose..."

"Invite whoever you wish," he said carelessly. "Stay as long as you want."

He *would* just be so calm about that. Coolly speak of something that set her heart racing ten times faster than it ought to have done. She knew she couldn't hide the excitement pulsing through her blood if she stayed up much longer, so she managed a grateful murmur and began descent.

"Tryss?"

"Yes?" She paused for just a moment.

"Thank you."

39

oOo

The stars of the Unseen were as colorful as a garden, and Tellie thought they even smelled as sweet as flowers. She wandered through the aurora with complete ease and peace, not even bothering to know why she had come to this world amid the heavens or why she seemed to be alone. Ah, but she was not alone, as she knew by the golden pulse within her heart, one that she was becoming more aware and in awe of. She rather hoped that if she wandered these gardens long enough, she might find Him here as well.

A stroll through the stars was a welcome retreat from the energy of the last few days. The former slaves of Tertorem, though drawn to the light they had glimpsed, were not easy people to deal with, and helping many of them remember and reach home was no simple task.

In the end, it was quite the gathering that boarded the ships of Coren's contacts. Tellie was not surprised to discover herself susceptible to seasickness, but the crossing of the strait was pleasant enough as far as weather.

They'd had no choice but to dock at Dormandy, causing quite a bit of a stir among the people who were still curious as to why such a large assembly of elves had crossed in the first place.

There, of all things, they'd run into Kelm's former master. For a horrid moment, Tellie had thought that she was going to have to say good-bye. But the man had gone and taken a new apprentice, quite unable to account for Kelm's disappearance and having thought him a runaway. There was no room, rhyme, *or reason for the man to have two apprentices, so after Kelm explained what he could, he spoke of his decision to stay with the elves. The man had seemed a bit sorry, but understanding, even a tad envious as he glanced at the fine elven things.*

They'd skirted Shadowshade on the way to Aselvia, and Tellie wasn't sure if she felt nostalgia or fear from looking at it from afar. But it was past now, and the last thing she remembered before falling asleep in Casara's arms, lulled by the sway of the horse, was the dark ridges of mountains reaching up into the stars.

The stars through which she now walked.

And just as she hoped, she found someone else enjoying the celestial gardens. Not Ayeshune, but a welcome friend nevertheless, one tall and with long silver hair.

"Rendar!" she cried. "Oh Rendar, it has been such a time since we last talked! Did you see it all? Wasn't it just marvelous?"

"I saw," he said, and she noticed he was very faint here, almost sheer. His voice trembled like a leaf. "I saw and my prayers have been answered. There were days I came so close to losing faith that this hope would ever come true." Light circled in his hands, a thoughtful and melodic rhythm, almost as if it managed to keep him calm and controlled. "The road ahead will not be easy," he said. "He will need you now more than ever."

"We can do it. I'll only become more powerful in the Unseen, and you can teach me more!"

"I am afraid not," he said. "We have set out what we accomplished to do and now we must part ways."

"What!" she cried. "Are we never to meet again? Am I to never come back here?"

"That I cannot tell," he said, squeezing his hand shut and letting the light drift away in ribbons. "Ayeshune gave you the gift of Walking in the Unseen, so I suspect you shall come here again. Whether we'll meet here or not is doubtful, but do not despair, we shall meet again in the coming life."

The words gave her little joy. The blue of the stars bled into her soul, staining everything she saw. But his hand touched her cheek, sending a little warmth back in. "Now then, child, do not weep. Remember what you have learned here. Do not forget that you are still a warrior on the other side. Do not underestimate a little love and a faithful prayer."

She found her tears were not water, just little sparkles of vanishing light, and she wiped them from her face with a deep breath. "I will miss you."

"And I you. You have been a comfort and courage to me in these dark days. I am glad you can now rest at last in Aselvia."

"I can't wait to see it!"

His brows bunched in confusion, and then suddenly, he laughed. "Ah. That's right. You were asleep when they came in."

"What? What do you mean?"

"You were sleeping on Casara's horse when they arrived in the middle of the night. You were so exhausted, and it was too dark to see anything well, so they just tucked you in bed."

"I'm in Aselvia?" she squeaked.

"That's right. Wake up."

Her eyes flew open to the light of morning. The white ceiling and walls were awash with the golden glow, countering the delicate floral carvings in the stone. She blinked once, then twice, hardly daring to move her gaze more than a bit at a time. Soft blankets bundled on top of her, tucked in against a cool breeze. Her fingers brushed the silky fabric before gripping hold and throwing them back. She lunged from bed and spun in a circle, taking in everything with one heady rush.

Oh, there had never been such a beautiful room, so bright and clean and hung with colorful tapestries and flowers. There was a very tall and very shining mirror, and several intricately carved cabinets, and the marble floor was covered with an embroidered rug, and there was even a balcony to the outside. Was it her room? Was it really hers? Or perhaps, she quickly amended, it was just a temporary setting until another place could be prepared, but even if that place was in the attic she hardly cared because she was here.

She flung herself out the door onto the balcony, unable to bear a second longer from seeing just what 'here' was.

Aselvia spread out before her.

The mountains framed the horizon, every shade of blue and purple capped in grey or glistening white. From the mountain roots spread dark blankets of evergreen forest, and as the hills descended into valleys, the forests gave way to vibrant, rolling plains of green. Rivers trailed ribbons of blue through the green, pooling here into a lake, cascading into a waterfall of white over there. Bright white structures rose from the depths of the forests, peeking through the treetops, and those in the city below her little balcony reflected the sunrise in a shimmering glow.

Nothing in Dormandy, nothing in Denji, nothing even in her latest jaunt about the world compared to the craftsmanship of the city. Little wonder that anyone but elves would have had the patience to carve white stone into patterns of lace and leaves, every edge and curve a work of art. Spires and arches rose everywhere, perhaps purely for the beauty of it rather than any other purpose. Vines lavished the stone, climbing wherever they pleased.

She could have stared all morning. Just looked and looked and looked and slowly soaked it all in.

But there was a knock on her door. A light patter of knuckles against wood. "Tellie?" Casara called. "Are you awake?"

"Yes!" She leapt back into the room, swiping down her frazzled hair. "Come in!"

The woman swept in with a smile, taking a glance about. "Do you like it?"

"Like it? I love it!" But wait, did she mean the realm or just the room or both of them at once?

"Well, we shall make it more your own in the next few days," Casara said with a nod of satisfaction. "But I was able to borrow a few dresses from a friend that should fit you until we meet with a seamstress."

"You mean this room is really mine? Really?"

"Yes," Casara laughed. "Aselvia is your home now. Are you ready for the day or do you need some more time?"

"I'm perfectly awake," she said, gazing in awe at the dresses that Casara was spreading out on her bed. Or if she wasn't, then it was a delicious dream she'd happily stay in forever.

"Then I'll give you a few minutes. I'll be waiting out in the hall."

The moment the door clicked shut, Tellie sprang for the green dress like a wild thing. It was the hue of pale spring and just as soft as it looked. She hurried into it, feeling a bit sorry that she'd not yet taken a bath and would mar its peerless perfection. But even wearing it made her feel like something pure and radiant.

That is, until she took a look in the mirror. Oh dear. When, just when, had she gotten so skinny? There were shadows under her eyes and her cheeks were even a bit sunken. A closer inspection revealed that the smattering of freckles had exploded into a cloud. Over the journey, her hair had tangled and broken and altogether frizzed. Even when it did return to its normal curling state, she wasn't sure it would look decent. Curls didn't seem to be the fashion here. And the dress hem pooling on the floor reminded her that she was not exactly the tall and elegant type.

Folding her hands and sucking in her breath, she stepped out the door. Despite her best attempt, she could not quite look the woman in the face.

"Beautiful," Casara said and it sounded like she meant it.

Just a little more confident, Tellie hurried in the woman's swift footsteps down the arched halls, past epic murals and even more epic views of the landscape and city outside. "Where are we going?" she whispered. Now that she was here, she wasn't even sure how to start. Adjusting to this kind of life, well, it would take some getting used to.

"To breakfast with Leoren and I," she said, casting a smile over her shoulder. "We have something we'd like to discuss with you."

Not even daring to imagine what that might be, Tellie nodded and kept mute the rest of the walk. They passed through an indoor garden which opened up into a small dining room. Only one set of table and chairs was taken, laid out with steaming dishes of food and tea. Leoren stood beside it, adjusting the napkins with a critical eye.

"Good morning, Tellie," he said as the came in and pulled out a seat for her.

Tellie folded her hands in her lap, not even noticing the savory smell coming from the covered plate before her. She could only stare at Leoren and Casara as they sat down, giving each other a meaningful glance.

"Tellie," Leoren said with a deep breath. "Back at the inn, when we bought your freedom to take you back here, we were hoping…"

"We want to adopt you, Tellie. Have you as part of our family."

Tellie couldn't speak. She just looked, lips slowly parting.

"We realize you are quickly growing into a young lady," Leoren continued, "and no doubt feel much older after these recent events, but we could still be of great help and support as you continue to—"

"What does age have to do with it?" she burst out. "I've always wanted a family! Do you really mean it? Am I dreaming?"

"We mean it," Casara said, laughing. "When we lost you, you left us with your custody papers. Written word carries weight, so our next step will be to write up new papers that acknowledge you as part of our family in the eyes of elves and humans."

"Please," she gasped. As tears began to spill down her cheeks, she found Casara had come over, so she buried her face in the woman's sleeve. Somewhere behind her, she felt Leoren's arm circle her shoulders in a strong and secure embrace.

Dreams didn't come true very often, not like this. But sometimes they did. And it was those kinds of miracles that made the world so much brighter.

oOo

Kelm wandered down a long bridge, eyeing the tall pillars that supported the roof arching above him. The bridge spanned from tower to tower, and roofs of elegant buildings and clusters of trees spread out below him. He wondered how Tellie felt about the height, and then suspected she'd been too excited to notice. He'd barely seen a thing of her in the last few days, though that wasn't a surprise considering her delighted distraction. She had her family now, and what a family!

The words of Leoren from just the previous day drifted back to him. *"Do you wish for us to adopt you as well?"*

"Golly no!" Kelm had gasped. *"I don't want Tellie to think of me as a brother!"*

Leoren had smiled at this and moved on.

Sighing, the boy scuffed his shoe along the vibrant stones. Aselvia was a beautiful place, most beautiful place in the world probably, but he couldn't help but feel that he didn't belong in it. There didn't seem to be anything for him to do.

In the week since their arrival, Errance hadn't been seen after he'd entered his palace, though plenty of excited rumors about his activities spread amongst his adoring people. Tryss and the few accompanying chemas with her had been taken on an exploration in the forests. The Daisha was likewise off roaming the wilderness.

"Gloomy faces are out of place here," a voice said.

Startled, Kelm looked up into the smirking face of Coren, who stood in the shadows of one of the pillars, so casually near the edge that the boy's stomach gave a queasy twist.

"I almost don't recognize you," Kelm returned. "You look like an elf."

"Shocking, isn't it? Mother persuaded me to wear attire more appropriate to my surroundings," Coren explained, fingering his blue-bordered coat. "But I wouldn't get rid of my chin patch. I think it's glued on there permanently, anyway." He glanced back up, smiling. "So then, what's the frown for?"

Kelm shrugged. When Coren continued staring, he stammered, "Well, I guess I just feel sort of left out."

"Do you wish you'd stayed with the merchant?"

"My master was a good man," Kelm said with a shrug. "And I really, really like traveling the world. Whatever I do when I grow up must include that, I think. And I liked seeing the crafts he sold. But I couldn't leave my friends behind." Sadly, he looked at his feet.

"But now you feel your friends are leaving you behind," Coren perceived.

Jolting, the boy looked up with gaping mouth. "How'd you...?"

"Your thoughts are written all over your face." With a kind laugh, Coren threw an arm around the boy's shoulder. "Don't worry, Kelm, you just need to give them time to adjust. And you need to find something to occupy yourself."

"What do elven boys do all day? Crochet?" Kelm asked, wrinkling his nose.

Coren made a face. "If that was true, I'd have run away as a child. No, no, Aselvia is a wondrous place for youth. Our young elves mostly explore outdoors, building castles and fortresses; acting out histories and fantasies. They compete in horse-riding, falconry, archery, and dueling. They learn how to paint, carve, draw, sculpt, sew and weave. Reading is a favorite quiet-time, and they'll often try their own hand at writing books."

Kelm listened in growing interest and when Coren was finished, he swallowed hard. "Golly," he said. "That doesn't sound so bad."

"Indeed, it isn't. I doubt you'll be bored unless you wish to be."

"Then why'd you leave?" Kelm asked.

Coren considered. "I love Aselvia, but I'll admit that it isn't the home for everyone. I felt myself called elsewhere. And after my marriage with Zizain here," his smile widened at the thought, "I will return to Oolum."

"There?" Kelm frowned. "Not the most decent place in the world."

"Most of the world is indecent, I'm sure you'll come to learn. But it needs help." Coren looked thoughtful. "I know Errance needs time to recover, which is why I won't bring this up to him now, but I hope he will not forget everything he saw in the world. He could do great things one day, I know it." After a long moment of silence, Coren slapped Kelm on the shoulder and started on his way.

oOo

The chambers of the prince and the chambers of the king were on the same level of the palace and now both belonged to him. So Errance took them as his refuge and wandered from wing to wing, seeing no one except for the occasional visit of Leoren or Casara, but even they sensed his desire for solitude and so kept away. He did not sleep in either of the beds as the days passed, but sometimes he did drift off while sitting by one of the windows, staring out at the blue sky or bright stars.

It was all so familiar, yet strange. A world in which he had once lived, the memories distant reflections in a looking glass. He tended to keep away from his own chambers as best he could...it was too painfully obvious that no one had lived in them for a very long time, though the servants had not let it go to dust and decay. As a boy, he'd never spent much time there anyway, preferring his father's company. But his father no longer lived here...that was the keenest change in his absence, one hard to believe as he drifted about the rooms.

Everywhere, Rendar's presence lingered...from the books left out on a small table, to the smell of his clothes hung in the wardrobe. Too often Errance pulled out a robe just to bury his face in it. His father had never quite smelled like the evergreen of the earth elves. A scent as sharp and clear as crystal had clung to him instead.

On the second morning, he finally shrugged into one of those robes. They fit him better than his old clothes—which smelled a bit musty despite the elves' best efforts—or any of the new ones brought in by Casara. True, the hem dragged longer than was fashionable, so apparently he'd never grown as tall as his father, which was amazing considering all the stretching he'd gone through.

Some things in those rooms that he'd taken for granted in the old days now stared at him with a demanding need for more attention. There were two large portraits in the room, beautifully painted by the finest artist in the kingdom. One was of Rendar and his wife, the mother Errance had never met. Strange how he'd forgotten exactly what she'd looked like...perhaps because he had never met her in person. But looking at her again, he was startled all over at the similarity between mother and son.

The other portrait was of Rendar and him as a boy. Only now did he notice that the portrait had been painted in the exact same position as the first, leaving room for the Queen to be on his other side, though she was not there.

When the ghostly memories of the chambers closed in too bitterly, dropping him to the floor in grief, a nearer and clearer memory came to comfort him…that of enveloping, warm light and cool, cleansing tears…his father's hands steady and secure in their embrace.

That was not the only comfort…another ornament to draw his eye again and again was a long tapestry draping down the length of a wall. How many times had he looked at it without reading the elegant script sewn into the fabric? Oh, he'd known what it said…but that was not quite the same as *reading*.

"The Lord is my Redeemer, my Light, the Treasurer of my Soul. So then shall my enemies falter and fall," he murmured aloud as he read it over. His father's belief had always been so strong, so sure. A faith Errance had once kept in childlike innocence, and he was not quite certain when he'd lost it.

But he felt the change of it within him, the strange lightness where once had been a core of solid black. It left him feeling weightless and fragile, uncertain of taking a step for fear of blowing away.

It was the eighth morning since he came, he pondered, meandering into a plant-shaded and glass-paned sitting room. Breakfast waited there now, laid out fresh by some recent visitor. A bit perturbed someone had been through and out without his noticing, he inspected the tray cautiously, flipping back the pale blue cloth to see the warm rolls, wild strawberries, and the saucer of cream next to a cup of steaming tea. His stomach was still resistant to the whole concept of meals, but the tea he took, because if his stomach did not remember it, well, his mind did. The warm water brewed with fresh mint leaves plucked from the moist shores of a lake…the honey combed from a hive in a tree while herb-scented smoke calmed its little golden guardians…oh yes, he recalled it all. The layers he'd hidden all his memories beneath were not as hard as he'd believed, once wetted with the right water.

But recalling was not the same as returning, and the latter…he wasn't sure. The hand holding the cup trembled, threatening to spill the tea. He just wasn't—

Someone stood in the doorway.

He dropped the tea in favor for the butter knife, dull as it was. There was only one kind of being that could sneak up on him without a sound, only one—

Or…or another elf. Yes. Yes, light-footed elves, they might be able to approach without alarming. Also, Leoren was wearing slippers.

Leoren stared for a long moment at the shattered cup amongst the miniature lake of tea, and while he did so, Errance fumbled to return the knife to its proper place. "Yes, Lord Leoren?" he said.

When Leoren looked up, any surprise had wiped away from his features, leaving only the kind smile he'd first walked in with. "I was wondering how you felt this morning about coming out of here for a little while. We know you need time, but…we are missing you. We've missed you ever so long, and well, they are finding it hard to be patient."

"They?" He blinked, still trying to calm his racing pulse.

"Your people. The elves. Your new friends. All of us."

"I…" He bent over the breakfast tray, scrambling for some pretense of normality. Perceptions of people had never mattered before; let them think what they want, so long as he was safe. But it would have to be different now—it was different. They knew him, or at least the old version. And for their sakes he had to try to find it again. So he popped a strawberry into his mouth and pretended its tartness didn't startle and overwhelm his taste.

"So I was thinking," Leoren said, easing into a chair and helping himself to the strawberries, "that you might need a role to help you re-merge. You are the heir, already the king by right, and the people would feel more secure with the throne taken again—"

Errance choked on his last swallow. After a moment of hard coughing, he braced himself against the table and faced his uncle. "Leoren, I…I am no true king. Father appointed you as steward, and I thought you could continue as such until I find…my footing."

"Sometimes it's hard to get up without a helping hand," Leoren said gently. "Sometimes it's hard to move forward without motivation. Yes, I am a steward and I would be there to guide and teach you, but the crown is something you need to wear. Give yourself a chance and a responsibility. It will give you a path on which to walk. Trust me. You'll need one."

A breeze slipped through the only open window, stirring the curtains and ringing the chimes. Errance's gaze followed its invisible path through the room until everything had settled into calm again.

"I'll think on it," he said at last.

40

oOo

"Please come, Errance." Casara's eyes were misty, the same mournful color as a heather field in twilight. "I've been telling her you've come home, but I don't think she believes me."

"Will she recognize me?" His fingers clenched tight, hidden beneath the long sleeves of his robe. His grandmother…her mind had been a fragile thing even when he was young. Rendar had always called him a healing balm to her, coaxing her out of the webbed corners of her soul. But he feared what his appearance would do to her now. Send her into more shock? Trouble her with his change? Or worse—would she look at him and feel nothing at all? What if he had been lost to her memory?

"She will." She grabbed his sleeves, tugging his hands out of their hiding place. "You need to see one another."

He had no more excuses. He couldn't prolong it forever. So he let himself be led through the halls and up the stairs to an upper tier garden. The air was still cool with morning dew, the light twinkling through pale green leaves to paint a golden lattice upon the earth. In the corner of the garden, sitting at a table half covered in ivy, was a figure huddled in a cloak, staring into the pond at her feet where silver-blue fish glittered at the surface.

"Maava," Casara whispered, kneeling beside the woman and cupping her thin face. "It's Errance. I've brought him to see you."

She lifted her head, but she didn't look for him. Her expression remained unchanged, unseeing. Strange. It was true he felt many things in Aselvia had stayed still in in his absence, but the feeling wasn't so strong as it was now. She looked exactly as she had in his childhood. Frail with waxen skin and hair streaked with grey. Perhaps her expression a bit more empty than before.

He took the last few steps into her vision and took his place kneeling before her as Casara slipped to the side. Her thin hands were folded in her lap, and he felt the urge to take them in his as he used to. His nails bit into his own palms instead.

"It's me," he said, voice barely scrapping through his throat. Why was he starting to shake? She needed more than that, she needed his name, she needed some prompt, some trigger to remember—

Fingers touched his cheek. "There you are," his grandmother whispered. "There's my Errance."

His eyes widened as he looked up into her face. She was staring right at him. A gentle smile curved her lips. His chin trembled. "I—" But he could say no more than that. A loose tear slipped down to his jaw, but she caught it on her finger and brushed it away.

"I've been wondering when you would come see me," she said, voice still so soft it could have been carried away on the lightest breeze.

"I'm sorry," he choked. "I'm here now." Somehow her hand had guided his head to her lap like the old days, her other hand running down his hair. Everything had changed, and yet nothing had. Here, even if just for this moment, he was a boy again.

"You will be a good king."

He jerked upright. "What?" Startled, he looked to Casara and then back again. Did she mean in the future, a mere encouragement such as she used to speak to him, or was she more aware of what had taken place than he guessed?

But she did not seem ready to explain herself, only continued smiling at him in tired contentment.

After a few moments, he gathered her hands up in his and gave them a small squeeze. "I'll...I will try."

oOo

"Errance is getting crowned king!" Tellie chanted, dancing around Kelm in a circle.

"Like nobody knows," Kelm groaned.

"Tellie, hold still, the flowers are falling out of your hair. There, that's better," Casara said, reaching out and rearranging a bright starflower.

"You are such a mother," Kelm said, glancing at the woman with a teasing grin.

"Feeling left out?" Casara said with a raised eyebrow and smile. She reached out, catching the boy before he could run and straightened his collar. She cast a final look over both of them, nodded in approval, and led the way out the passage into the grand throne room.

Swallowing hard, Tellie folded her hands and followed after, trying her hardest to stay straight and exude elegance. Except elegance didn't exude, drat, it simply was—like an aura.

They stepped out onto the high dais overlooking the grand hall which was already filled with a colorful crowd, blending in a blur voices and laughter. Sheer banners and lush vinery hung from the white pillars and walls all the way down to the far end where the tall double doors were framed by live trees.

From this height, Tellie could see most of the gathering, and she was glad that many faces were already becoming familiar to her. There were those healers who had tended all the hurts of the prisoners. The priest who'd welcomed her so warmly. And there was the old miner, already looking not so old, bashfully holding conversation with a few friendly elves. Her wandering gaze caught on a scowl, and while she hardly could be the reason which had that auburn-haired elf scowling, she suddenly become aware that here on the dais, everyone else had just as good a view of her. Her silly, awkward self.

"Don't be daunted, you are beautiful," Tryss said softly from across the way.

There was something comforting about being complimented by someone who knew what it meant to be beautiful. Tryss, swathed in a pale blue dress with her hair unbound, surely had no reason to fear fitting in with the surrounding splendor.

"And what about me?" The Daisha asked primly from where she lay on the dais, her head arching above Tryss's shoulder. "Don't I look elegant?"

"Very," Tellie answered. She winced and placed a hand over her stomach.

"Don't get sick," Kelm told her, taking his place beside her. "It's not like this is your coronation."

"I'm having sympathy pain," Tellie snapped. "Augh, I hope he doesn't take much longer."

Coren chuckled, and she looked up to where he stood with Zizain on the second level of the dais opposite his mother. "You'll have to be patient," he said. "Leoren will do his best not to keep everyone waiting, but you know Errance will drag it out as long as he can."

"He should just get it over with," Tellie mumbled, shifting from one foot to the other. She fixed her gaze on the passageway in the wall opposite her at the bottom of the dais where Errance and Leoren would be appearing at any moment. She'd originally thought it would be more exciting and poetic if he walked down the entire hall through the crowd, but now she agreed that would be far too nerve-wracking.

A long silver note of a trumpet rang out, slowly joined by several more, till the great hall was silenced by the sound. The Aselvian guard filed out of the hall first and spread out at the bottom of the dais, their spears strung with banners. Then came Lord Leoren, radiant in white robes. He walked up the steps of the platform and stood before the throne, turning to face the multitude.

Every eye turned to the shadowed doorway, every breath held in baited anticipation. And Errance stepped out into the hall.

His long, fitted coat could have been swept from the fabric of a night sky, all midnight blue and glittering. A shining white cloak clasped to his shoulder, falling in drapes behind him and then catching again at his hip.

Without a glance behind him or to his right or left, he stepped forward and began the ascent of the stairs. No measure of practice or patience could have given one the grace and presence of one who belonged on those steps. One whose heritage and destiny waited before them.

And yet, as Errance drew near, Tellie saw the pallor of his face and the way his hands clenched, almost hidden by the length of his sleeves. Briefly, his hard gaze flickered to Tellie, and she smiled from ear to ear in an effort to ease the fear. It seemed to work, his shoulders relaxed a little anyway.

He reached the top of the stair, but instead of bowing on one knee before Leoren, he turned and faced the people.

For a tense, lingering moment, he simply stood there, and they waited in suspended silence. Then he cleared his throat and lifted his eyes to meet every gaze in the hall.

"I stand before you a stranger. Perhaps there were those who used to know me, and those whom I used to know. Perhaps the years since that time have passed more swiftly for you than they have for me. When I lived here, I did so in innocence but also in ignorance. I did not understand the history of this land's devastation or the power behind its rebirth. But now I know devastation, and I hope I will come to know the same redeeming grace that runs through your blood and the water of this earth. I see courage and strength that dares to defy the darkness of the world. One that has looked to me and found…worth." He closed his eyes. "I am afraid I am not what you deserve. But with the grace that has been offered me, perhaps I too can rise and become a leader like my father before me. Everything I have been given, I promise to give to you."

He turned and knelt before Lord Leoren.

At Casara's nod, Tellie hurried up to the top to join them. As she looked down at Errance, the elegant little speech she'd written up completely flew from her mind. "Rendar told me to give this to the next king of Aselvia," she said. "And I'm awfully glad it's you." She raised the moon medallion and slipped it over his head. And then, before she could stop herself, she ducked down and kissed him on the cheek.

Blushing bright red at the chuckles filling the hall, she hurried down to her place. Kelm crossed his eyes at her, and she pinched his arm. Quite possibly, she thought with a stab of regret, she'd gone over Errance's boundaries. But when she glanced up, she could see the elf trying to hide something that looked very much like an amused smirk.

Leoren turned and took the crown from Casara's hands. Its craft was like no other: three crescent moons arching like bridges over the back and top of the head, shooting stars sweeping back from the brow and temple. "Errance Celestrum, son of Rendar and Cerene Celestrum, heir to the throne of Aselvia, last of the Celestial blood on this Lower World, redeemed by the One…I now declare you king of Aselvia." He lifted the crown, the light reflecting off its silver surfaces with stunning brilliance, and set it down upon Errance's dark hair.

The assembly erupted into cheers of adoration and excitement. The air was filled with the choir of their voices, the silver ringing of bells, and the toss of flower petals. Tellie took Kelm's hand, swinging it back and forth, and ran across to hug Tryss and The Daisha, who flapped her wings and trumpeted to the rooftop.

The world was filled to the brim with full, happy hearts all joined together in celebration, and it was in those moments that heaven came so much closer.

And out over Aselvia the sun descended behind the mountains and the stars began to shine through the rosy veil.

It was late into the night, but the celebrations continued long after the feasting. Songs rose to the rooftops and ancient tales were told anew, mesmerizing all over again no matter if heard for the first or hundredth time.

When Errance slipped away from the sight of his people, he left in the company of his aunt and uncle, and few noticed their quiet exit. As they went deeper into the heart of the palace, the sounds of gaiety faded away into a calm serenity. Not even the whisper of turning leaves or the sparkle of water stirred the silence of those halls. Even footsteps were quiet and muted.

At last, the small company of the king halted at the end of the dark passage. There a door waited and every shadow receded under the gentle light haloing the door's surface.

"May you find comfort," Casara said, touching his arm in hesitant affection. "Your father and mother always found it a haven of rest and renewing."

"We will leave you to your solace," Leoren said at length when no response came. He took his wife's arm, and together they slipped away, leaving the new young king quite by himself.

Errance had come to this door many times throughout his childhood. Either just to gaze and wonder and dream, or to sit and wait and sulk until his father's return. He never saw his father use his inner light much, but the shimmering shield across the door was one example of its power. His father's light had not crafted like others of his kind, but was a tool of warfare, for defense, for attack, and for healing...and this shield only suffered those who carried the light within them to pass through.

He'd never been allowed to go in, his father gently telling him it would not be wise until he was older.

Standing there alone, he could hear the ghosts of long gone voices still echoing in the hall. *"This summer, when you come of age...would you like to come in with me to read it?"*

"I...don't know, Daava."

His father had stared at him, unable to believe what he'd heard. When he spoke again, there was no hiding the hurt. "Errance...I thought you were waiting for this."

"I'm sorry, I know...I was. But...I was hoping you might let me travel out into Orim as my gift for coming of age."

There was a long and sad silence.

"Oh...I see."

Errance released his breath in a shuddering swell. "I'm here now, Daava," he whispered. He reached out, grasped the handle, and opened the door.

He looked into a small haven of well-loved and well-worn comfort and beauty. A window high above let in a prism of light, resting on a couch covered in pillows with a blanket thrown over the side. A stand of burned candles stood beside it, and before it was a low table upon which rested a book, an empty glass, and a plate with a stale piece of bread.

Errance stared, entranced. His father's chambers had been well cleaned by servants before he'd ever arrived, so while memories of his father had still lingered, it was still so…organized. But this. This was left exactly as it had been. Lived in. Prayed in.

His feet made no sound on either the cold, marble floor or the soft, dusty carpet. He sank onto the couch and stared down at the book on the table. Or rather he stared at what was on top of it. An envelope. He slit it open with his finger and startled as two cold rings dropped into his hand. He lifted them into the shaft of moonlight for better inspection, and his heart clenched so hard it hurt.

The rings of his father and mother. One wide, elegant, and strong, the other delicate and immensely complex. His father had left them here for him instead of taking them beneath root and soil.

Holding them tight in one hand, he turned to the letter inside the envelope.

My dear son, I can only hope you read this someday. I know that will mean you are saved, in all ways. I wish I could have been there to share this moment with you, but I share this instead. Through my brightest and darkest days, I have come here. To think, to pray, even sleep. And the book you are about to read has always helped comfort and counsel me. Or rather not the book, but the person who writes from the other side. I have not told you of them before, for I did not think you would understand the separation. Perhaps I was wrong to wait. But I hope now that you will come to love them as I did, and find the same comfort and joy.

You are forever in my heart.

Errance read it over a few more times, and then he did what he'd been dreading for so many long years. He looked down at the book.

He looked upon the Moonscript.

To be sure, it was no ordinary book. It was made by the same unknown craft as the moon medallion, and he remembered something about his father saying the artisan had been one and the same. The cover was intricately woven of a substance not quite cloth, leather, or metal. The pages glowed faintly at the edges.

When he opened it, the pages appeared blank at first, but then they came to life under his eyes in a bright script that faded to blue ink. He fluttered through the pages to see how many were written in, and a sudden realization tilted his reality. The pages were infinite. He could turn as many pages as he liked and neither amount on either side seemed to change.

It was too much to consider, so he kept flipping the pages, noticing the exchanging handwriting. One was his father's, the other unknown. He wanted to read them all, but that could take…well, years, since his father had lived so long. But he most wished to see whatever had last been left, and so he came to the first blank page. He turned back to see the last letter written.

The hand belonged to the stranger. His heart stood still.

Errance, it began. *My beloved nephew…*

41

oOo

The sky above the land of Aselvia was filled with a splendor of stars, more magnificent here than from any view in all Orim. Perhaps the beauty of it came from a blessing of the celestials or perhaps the stars themselves understood the significance of this night.

Tellie wandered out onto an open and lonely terrace, glad for a cool wind that washed through her gown and across her skin. She was flushed from the dance and becoming a bit dizzy with exhaustion from staying up too late. Here in the open air, surrounded above and beyond by beauty, she began to understand how elves found their rest and sustaining endurance. This quiet under a sparkling night was a balm to the soul, a place where one could go alone and find—

Only she wasn't alone.

She started to back away so as not to interrupt, before recognizing the face in the candlelight that stretched out from the distant hall. "Oh," she said. "Do you mind if I stay?"

Errance shrugged. "I don't suppose I can refuse since you're officially my cousin now."

She eagerly sat beside him and nudged his shoulder. "Just like Coren."

"Which makes him your brother, I suppose," Errance said, tilting his head into his hand. "And I hear Zizain is to become family as well. Quite the odd bunch we're becoming."

"And then there's Tryss," Tellie said.

He pulled back rather sharply. "What about her?"

"Well, she's moving into the forest, so close by. I'm awfully glad she came along. She's very pretty. And very sweet."

He looked down at her, face blank in the shadows. "Cousin, ha," he said with a small smirk in his voice. "You're much more suited to the role of a scheming little sister."

With a nervous laugh and swing of her legs, she gripped the sides of the bench and managed, "Would you mind? If I was like your little sister? Not scheming? Well, not always scheming."

He did not answer at first, perhaps taken aback. "I don't suppose I would." He paused. "And anyway, it would be an honor to have a powerful Walker of the Unseen as a sister."

She muffled a small cry behind the hand she flung across her mouth. "Who told you that?"

"Mm, someone like my father and the Creator of worlds."

"You met them!" she cried, leaping to her feet. "I knew you must have met the One, but your father as well? Oh, Errance!"

"He spoke quite highly of you."

Heart hammering, she looked at the ground. "I never thought you'd know," she murmured. "About me, that is."

"I suppose I knew all along. Or rather had a vague impression that someone was fighting battles for me."

In a supreme effort to remain humble, she said, "Well, I'm sure it was mostly your father. I can still hardly believe I was chosen for that role."

"Says she whose days were known before they began, who faced Darkness alongside an elven king of old in an effort to rescue a soul lost to the shadows," he remarked dryly.

"You almost sound like a proper elf there," she parried, before wondering if that was an insensitive jest.

"Why, thank you," was his only reply. He said no more for the next several moments and in that quiet only a waterfall could be heard rushing down a wall and an undulating trill of a bird sweeping through the night.

"What I can't believe," he said, voice low as he began again, "is that I should be saved after all these years. I who had accepted Darkness even as I strove to fight him. How is it that even after all this time I could be saved and given the chance to read the Moonscript in freedom?"

Tellie gasped, whirling towards him in amazement. "You read the Moonscript?"

"Only the most recent entry." In the faint light, his eyes filled with tears. "It was a letter," he said. "A letter to me. From my uncle. An uncle I never knew I had. My father's brother."

"You never knew?" she whispered, eyes rounding. "Why not?"

"It was always painful for Daava to speak of the past. And he hesitated glorifying the celestial realm lest I try to seek it and endanger it in my reckless, foolish youth."

It made a little sense, in a painful way. She couldn't even imagine the feeling of discovering one had a hitherto unknown relative. "What was his name?"

"Erran."

"Oh," she breathed, clasping her hands together. "Oh, Errance. How wonderful...your namesake..."

His words were thick with tears. "He wrote to me with wisdom I am still trying to comprehend. And he thanked me, Tellie. Me, who bitterly had resented them as naïve and uncaring of my suffering, who had even blamed them as the cause! I am such a fool!" He buried his face into his hands, elbows braced against knees.

Tellie sat frozen, unsure of how much to comfort in the face of this unhidden emotion. A slight rustle of wings drew her attention to the balcony railing where the magpie landed and gave them a curious look. "Well," she said slowly. "I think we all have an inner fool. In the same way, I guess we all have a chance for forgiveness."

He took a deep, shuddering breath, nodded, and then straightened.

She could only let the silence reside another minute before she burst out, "But was it there?"

"Was what there?" He arched his eyebrow.

"In the Moonscript. The Darkness's sole goal was to read the Moonscript so he could find a way into the Higher World. Was he right? Is there a way?"

Errance's expression remained fixed in place, his brow still quirked. Then he closed his eyes and turned away. When he looked back, his face was gentle but reproving. "That," he said, "is only for me to know."

Oh. She blushed. Of course.

The magpie gave an unexpected cry and dove from the railing to Errance's shoulder. "What—" He drew back, his arm reaching out to cover Tellie, when a musical bugle filled the air.

Swooping up from the city below them, The Daisha spun into the sky, her wings sending a current of air that nearly knocked Errance and Tellie to the ground. Circling around, she swept to the terrace railing and hooked her front paws over it, her hind legs resting against the wall with a thump.

"Here's a happy meeting!" she said, grinning at their ruffled state. With a thrust of her wings, she slid over the railing and sat in the terrace with them.

"Tellie, there you are!" Kelm sat atop The Daisha's shoulders, looking very comfortable and pleased with his current position in life.

Brushing back her mussed hair, Tellie frowned at her friend indignantly. "Fine time to drop in," she said. "What are you doing here?"

Laughing, Kelm exchanged a mischievous glance with The Daisha. "Why, I'm here to rescue you, of course," he said. "Sweep you off to safety on my fine steed."

Tellie looked between their amused expressions and recognized where the conversation was headed. "Oh no, you don't," she said, backing away. "I am not riding The Daisha. You know I'm terrified of heights."

"Rubbish!" The Daisha sniffed. "Flying is a remarkable experience. I carried you once already. I promise it will be much more comfortable up on top."

"Aw, come on, Tellie," the boy begged. He scooted backwards. "Look, you can even sit in front of me, so you have something behind and in front of you."

She hesitated. If the ride was gentle and slow enough, perhaps...

Strong hands encircled her waist, lifting her from the ground, and set her upon The Daisha's back.

"She's all yours, Kelm," Errance said.

"Errance! You traitor!" she squealed, plastering herself to The Daisha's neck.

"It's awfully nice he came along," the elf king said, mimicking her earlier tease. "He's very handsome. And very sweet."

Ignoring Kelm's chortle, she pertly stuck her tongue out at the elf king. "Oh, fine." Taking a deep breath, she took a tight hold of her mount's fur. It *was* reassuring to feel Kelm's arms securing her waist. The sooner they flew, the sooner she'd forget about blushing. "If we start off slow—"

Her sentence was lost in a scream as The Daisha dove off the terrace. But that scream of terror melted into a laugh of delight as the creature swept up again into the sky.

The young king listened to the bell-like laughter of the children as he watched them dance above the mountains, the meadows, and the star-kissed streams. He watched as they rose into the vaults of the night, where the moon shone brighter than ever before.

And he smiled.

"So," Rendar said, sighing in contentment. "We have come to the end."

"The end?" said the One. "No. It is only the beginning."

ACKNOWLEDGEMENTS

It has been such a journey to this point, so many people along the way who have helped me stand where I am today. Firstly, my parents, who gave me the teaching and support I needed to turn from a bookish fangirl into an aspiring author. They encouraged me every step of the way. To my brother and cousins who always had to listen to my storytelling ventures and were so patient and kind! To my loving grandparents, who believed in me. All my family, you are the best.

To Anne Elisabeth who encouraged me to choose ONE writing project to complete and guided me with her experiences and the inspiration from her own wonderful books.

To my Alpha readers, my dear friends! Yes, those who read the drafts at various stages and helped me figure out what was working and what wasn't…Clara, Beka, Jill, Allison, Jacob, Hannah, and Bryn—

—Bryn, who took *such* an interest that she became my constant writing partner, bolstering me to develop the world, characters, and series in a way that stretched my mind beyond its previous limits.

Thank you to my editor, Jane Maree, whose endless enthusasiam for this story blessed me over and over!

And then all you lovely people who have been waiting for this story for over seven years….thank you for your patience, for your enduring interest, and now this story is here for you.

From the beginning, H. S. J. Williams has loved stories and all the forms they take. Whether with word, art, or costume, she has always been fascinated with the magic of imagination. She lives in a real fantastical kingdom, the beautiful Pacific Northwest, with her very own array of animal friends and royally loving family. Williams taught Fantasy Illustration at MSOA. She may also be a part-time elf.

FAIREST SON was her first venture into the publishing world, a novella to teach her the ropes.

She is also an artist and has long dreamed of illustrating her own books, a dream realized today. You can check out and follow William's art page over at hsjwilliams.wordpress.com

SIGN UP FOR H.S.J. WILLIAM'S NEWSLETTER
hsjwilliams.com

Follow her for writing updates and art at
Facebook: @hsjwilliams
Instagram: @hsjwilliams

THE ARTISTS

Cover Art by Salome Totladze
@morgana0anagrom

Map Art by Noverantale
@noverantale

Interior Illustrations by Hannah S.J. Williams
@hsjwilliams

Part I, II, II Art by Hannah Rogers
@inscape.studio

KINGS OF ASELVIA

COLLUSION

Currently in Development